FATROPOLIS

A NOVEL

TRACEY L. THOMPSON

PEARLSONG PRESS
NASHVILLE, TN

Pearlsong Press
P.O. Box 58065
Nashville, TN 37205
www.pearlsong.com
www.pearlsongpress.com

Book & cover design by Zelda Pudding.
Cover art by © WaD—Fotolia.com.
Photo of Phyllis Burns by Lana Stanimirovich.

Original trade paperback ISBN: 9781597190572
Ebook ISBN: 9781597190589

Library of Congress Cataloging-in-Publication Data

Thompson, Tracey L.
 Fatropolis : a novel / Tracey L. Thompson.
   p. cm.
ISBN 978-1-59719-057-2 (original trade pbk. : alk. paper)—ISBN 978-1-59719-058-9 (ebook) 1. Overweight persons—Fiction. 2. Self-realization in women—Fiction. I. Title.
PS3620.H697F38 2012
 813'.6—dc23
                                        2012023394

This book is dedicated to
the memory of my good friend and Lodge Sister
Phyllis Burns,
who, when I asked her if
she would be the first to read my manuscript
and tell me what she thought,
said,
"I'd be honored."

CONTENTS

PROLOGUE

THERE'S A FUNNY THING ABOUT FALLING. IT tends to wake a person up, and sometimes things are never the same after that. If Jenny hadn't been too busy trying to brace herself for the impact, this might have occurred to her. She lay there trying to compose herself enough to sit up, her back and rump sore.

The floor was carpeted. She sat up. She was sitting in a different fitting room. She got up slowly and straightened her clothes. Where was her bag? She felt uneasy that she had been separated from it. Where were the dresses she had tried on? She found the place on the wall where she had fallen through and pushed on it, but it was solid. She felt all around the space again with both hands. Where was she? What had happened to her? She wanted to get back to the dressing room where she had been.

Moving cautiously, she slowly opened the fitting room door. That's when she saw a sign she remembered. *Out Of Order.* She found herself in a very posh dressing room—large and decorated stylishly, its many fitting rooms particularly wide and spacious. Even the decorations on the walls were different. Large women were entering and leaving the individual fitting rooms with their chosen garments over their arms. She couldn't see her bag anywhere.

"What's going on here?" she asked aloud. "Where am I?"

A very large, well-dressed woman, with a few garments, smiled as she passed Jenny. She entered one of the fitting rooms.

"Ma'am?"

"Yes?" The woman opened the door.

"Uh—uh—" Jenny stammered. "Could I ask—where am I?"

7

"You're at Burley's," the woman said matter-of-factly, and started to close the door.

"Excuse me. What did you say?"

The woman peeked back out. "You're at Burley's Department Store. In the women's department, of course." The woman giggled and went back in, latching the door behind her.

Jenny left her fitting room. *Burley's? I didn't know they put in a new department store. I'll never find a dress here,* she thought. How odd to see such big women in an upscale department store. This thought reminded her that she could no longer shop for clothes in department stores.

A plump attendant approached Jenny. "Is there something I can help you find, ma'am?"

"No—no, I don't think so." She was amazed watching these large women going into the fitting rooms carrying garments of all kinds. A thin woman stood on a pedestal in front of a full length mirror, looking at her dress. Another attendant stood nearby, looking up at her, trying to be helpful.

"Does this make me look fat?" the thin woman asked hopefully.

"I'm sorry, hon, but no," the attendant replied, shaking her head sorrowfully.

The thin woman sighed and looked disappointed.

"We do have an *exciting* line of undergarments designed to pad your figure, though," the attendant added, smiling as if to give the thin woman some hope.

"Well—I do need a lot of padding. Don't you think?"

The attendant chuckled. "Well, now that you mention it, I was wondering if you ever eat."

The thin woman laughed too, but nervously.

I should have come here to buy my dress, Jenny said to herself. After staring at the women for a few moments, she remembered that she had left her bag in the other dressing room. *I gotta get my bag back,* she thought. *I gotta figure out where I am so I can get back to that store.*

But suddenly she had to use the facilities. She went to find the bathroom and entered a stall. It was huge, and it wasn't the stall for the handicapped. She had plenty of room—unlike so many public bathrooms she had visited in the past, with their narrow little stalls that were obviously made for thin people, with no room to spread out. There would be no need for contortionism in *this* stall. The toilet paper holder was even in a convenient location, and she didn't need to straddle the toilet just to open the door so she could get out. It was refreshing. It seemed like the designers of this bathroom had been mindful of large women.

She wandered slowly back into the dressing room and stopped to take a long drink from the drinking fountain. She went into the fitting room marked with the *Out Of Order* sign. Could she get back to the place she'd started from? The wall was still solid. The only exit from this dressing room was the door out to the store.

"Okay," she muttered. "This is just plain weird."

As she stood there in this fitting room, she looked at her reflection in the extra-wide mirror. Her mind drifted back to how the most difficult week of her life had begun with trying on dresses at a Manhattan department store . . .

CHAPTER 1
ENGAGEMENT RING
GLISTENING
IN THE
SUNLIGHT

JENNY STOOD THERE IN THE SKIN-TIGHT DRESS. It was obvious that the shapely salesgirl was trying not to laugh at her as Jenny asked, "Do you have this in a larger size?" She was determined that somehow she would be able to buy something here without having to skulk uptown to the "fat lady" store.

The salesgirl looked Jenny up and down with a slight snicker. "No, we don't," was her reply, "but you might want to go to Bountiful Britches. They have *huge* dresses that just might fit you." It appeared that Jenny's not being able to find a big enough dress had somehow brightened the salesgirl's day. She smirked, pursed her perfectly glossed lips, and sauntered away using her runway walk. Once the salesgirl was out of the dressing room, she burst out laughing without any effort to be quiet about it.

Defeated, Jenny walked back to her fitting room. She turned to her thin friend. "Well, what do *you* think, Katy—does it make me look fat?"

Katy searched for the right words. "Well—uh—"

"Don't answer that," Jenny interrupted. "I know it does."

"For what it's worth, *I* found a really nice dress," Katy said in a feeble attempt at consoling her.

"I'm really happy for you." As always, Jenny wished she were thin. "Why don't you just go on ahead? I'll see if I can go uptown and find a dress."

Katy looked hesitant. "Are you sure? I don't want to leave you in the lurch."

"No—I'm sure. Go on ahead." Jenny was almost ready to give up on finding a dress for her company's Annual Awards Event, which was coming up soon. It had been several pounds since the last time she'd gone out to buy new clothes. In fact, according to her bathroom scale, she had gained two since yesterday.

It dawned on her that she had arrived at the time she hoped to never see—the time when clothes from *normal* stores no longer fit. She gathered her things, and left the department store.

She was hungry. That was the problem. She wanted to be thin like the beautiful people, but her body betrayed her on a daily basis. She craved sweets and loved breads and cheeses. Ice cream and cookies made her feel warm all over and gave her a glow that made her feel loved. Mashed potatoes and gravy were old friends. As she took the subway back toward home, she daydreamed about a home-cooked meal with all the trimmings.

As she came up from the train and out onto the street, the smell of fresh baked bread and Italian meatballs wafted past. She decided to stop at the deli and get a sandwich. She enjoyed seeing all the different cheeses and deli meats, but meatball sandwiches were her favorite. She loved the way the mozzarella melted over the meatballs as the bread toasted. Her mouth was already watering.

The handsome man behind the counter seemed not to notice her. An older lady pushed in front of her in line, but she didn't say anything.

I should go on a diet again, she told herself. *I have no business eating anything ever again.*

All she could think about was a meatball sandwich.

Finally the man behind the counter looked at her. "What'll it be, lady?"

Jenny glanced at his wedding ring. "Uh—uh—I guess I'll have a turkey and swiss on rye, no mayo." She always ordered her food "to go," as she was too embarrassed to eat in front of anyone for fear of what people might think about such a fat woman enjoying her food. New Yorkers were particularly hard on fat people.

On the way to her apartment, a couple was walking ahead of her, holding hands. The sight made her feel resentful. When they stopped in front of their building, the sun hit the woman's wedding ring just right and a ray of light shone right into Jenny's eyes.

Oh God, all these happy couples. I could just gag, she thought as she continued walking. *Just let me get home. What's wrong with me? Why can't I find happiness? When am I going to find my Mister Right?*

At last she arrived at her building, a four story walk-up. By the time she had gone up the two flights of stairs and inside, she was in tears. As always, the first thing Jenny saw when she opened her door was a life-size poster of a thin woman in an exercise outfit that showed off her perfectly flat abs.

Jenny hung her bag on the handlebars of her exercise bike and sat down at her tiny kitchen table. "I can't believe I've gained back all the weight I lost two years ago—*again*," she cried out. She remembered the strict diet regimen she had been on—no carbs, no sugar, no bread. No taste. No fun.

Just then she heard a voice through the wall, "Maybe if ya was ta stop eatin' ice cream late at night."

"Mrs. Grabowski," Jenny shouted at her neighbor, "do you have a glass up to the wall again?"

Mrs. Grabowski, who seemed to be able to hear everything, did not respond.

Jenny sat there for a while, feeling that life was just not fair for some folks. Finally she pushed herself away from the table, went into the bathroom, took care of business, and weighed herself. She was a pound heavier than she had been that morning, and that was without shoes. She returned to the kitchen and ate her sandwich, but did not enjoy it, and decided to take a nap. She went into her bedroom and shooed her cat off the bed, then lay down, hugged a pillow, and pondered life. *Why can't God find it in his plan for me to be happy with someone?* At last she fell asleep.

When she woke up, it was late at night. She wasn't tired anymore, and knowing that she would be starting her diet tomorrow, she got up and got some ice cream. She turned the TV on as she went toward the couch, holding her bowl up to the wall as if offering a toast to her neighbor. A man on the History Channel was droning on about an archeological dig that had recently gone awry. After listening for a bit Jenny changed the channel, but every click on the remote showed either happy couples or commercials for luscious, delicious food.

Suddenly her cat jumped up on the couch next to her and eyed the ice cream. "They want you to eat, Patches," she said to the cat, "but God forbid you put on any weight."

Jenny's train of thought was derailed again by her neighbor. "Could ya please eat a little quieta? And toin the TV down. It's late."

"Sorry, Mrs. Grabowski!" Jenny hollered back, absently chewing her ice cream but still thinking about a meatball sandwich. "I am definitely starting my diet tomorrow," she declared under her breath as she turned the volume down on the TV.

She always felt hopeful and in control when she started a new diet—all she had to do was eat only what was allowed. She was optimistic that finally her rogue behavior around eating and weight would be bridled and restrained. She would finally be a "good girl." Whenever she was on a diet, she felt noble and worthy of love, for it would only be a matter of time until she was thinner, and more acceptable.

Another channel had late night news. Jenny usually didn't like the news, but it caught her attention. The anchor announced, "University students in the New York area were recently polled about obesity. Forty-nine percent said they would rather be stupid than fat." At this the news anchor chuckled. "Twenty-six percent said they would rather be lame than fat. Thirteen percent preferred to be blind than fat, and a whopping twelve percent said they would rather be dead than fat." The anchor looked into the camera and stated with a cheesy grin, "Wow, that's some heavy news, folks."

Jenny took another spoonful of her ice cream and changed the channel in protest. She caught the tail end of an infomercial for a new diet product that promised to burn away stubborn belly fat easily while a person slept. No dieting was necessary. One simply had to take the easy-to-swallow capsules before bed and within a few weeks there would be significant weight loss. That's what the announcer said. Jenny was hooked. She found a pen and wrote down the number, as she had for many other weight loss products, on the TV magazine. She hoped this one would actually deliver on its promise to make her like everyone else—thin and socially acceptable.

Then, yawning, she changed the channel again, found a movie already in progress, and made herself comfortable on the couch.

SHE WOKE UP THE NEXT MORNING in the same place, the TV still on. It was Sunday. She got up, used the bathroom, and weighed herself. It was, she knew, always best to weigh after going to the bathroom, but she couldn't understand why she was the same weight as yesterday. She stepped off the scale, then stepped back on, hoping for a lower reading. No luck. She wolfed down some cereal, showered, and then looked in her closet. The only dress she had left that even remotely fit was snug around the middle and made her feel uncomfortable, as if she were trying to show off her ample behind. Well, it would have to do for church.

She was planning to go uptown to Bountiful Britches after church. She had to run a little to catch the bus, which made her dress ride up. She struggled to pull the hem back down, hoping no one had seen her fat knees.

She always carried books in her bag, along with her wallet, a bottle of water, and a calorie counter booklet complete with a height-to-weight ratio chart. She was supposed to drink eight bottles of water a day to deter her appetite, but she could never force herself to drink more than three or four.

When she arrived at church, she slipped into the sanctuary and took her usual spot. It was quiet and peaceful. Candles had been lit at the altar and the saints were all in their places. Being in church always gave her goose bumps and made her want to cry. She felt that she was in the very presence of God.

She was lost in thought, pondering life's unfairness, when a small crowd of people opened the door and came in. Mrs. Shumaker, a friendly older lady who was busy helping to raise her grandchildren, was first of the crowd to dip her fingers in the holy water. Mrs. Shumaker had been one of the first parishioners to welcome Jenny to the church when she had first moved to New York.

Next to come in was Gloria Pringle, a young woman who had recently had a baby. It had been a terrible struggle to bring the child into the world. Every Sunday since the baby was a week old, Jenny was glad to see a steady improvement in Gloria's health. Gloria blessed herself and her baby and sat in the baby room.

Robert Van Brune, a single older man who was quite popular with the church's widows and a very active parishioner, next took his turn standing in line. He blessed himself and went to sit in his favorite pew, three rows from the front.

Following Robert was Lieutenant Leland, in uniform as always. As he entered the church he took off his head cover and carried it in one hand. Jenny had met the U.S. Air Force lieutenant at a church bazaar last fall when he was new to the church and being introduced around by Mrs. Balducci, a long-time member of the Ladies' Auxiliary. Mrs. Balducci had brought him over to Jenny and said, "Jenny Crandell, this is Lieutenant—uh—Leland," and smiled at him sweetly and nodded her head. At first Jenny's heart had almost stopped because he was so handsome, with thick reddish-brown hair and piercing green eyes. But then, as Mrs. Balducci led him to someone else, she had caught sight of his wedding ring. *All the cute ones are taken,* she had thought. Later that same week Jenny had heard that the lieutenant's wife didn't like to attend church, and that was why he was always alone. He always liked to sit with two elderly sisters who were accompanied by a chubby little girl. When she saw him walk up the aisle, he looked over at her. They waved at each other.

Just then the two elderly sisters with the little girl in tow came through the doors and waited in line. The chubby little girl was so cute with her red curly hair. Jenny figured that one of the sisters was her grandmother. The toddler was always pretty good during mass, but sometimes one of the women would have to take her to the baby room. They walked up the aisle and took a seat one row behind the lieutenant, who was kneeling silently.

A minute later a young couple with a baby walked in and sat down a few rows ahead of Jenny. The man's left arm was around his wife's back. His wedding ring glistened. Jenny looked down. Everywhere she went, even in church, she was reminded that she was alone. Then an old couple entered the church, the woman holding her husband's arm as she assisted him with walking. Over the next half hour, the church filled up nicely.

The mass was pleasant. Jenny sang all the hymns, knelt and prayed each time, and partook of communion. As much as Jenny enjoyed church and felt it gave meaning and purpose to her existence, she still felt empty without someone to share her life with. She saw her inability to find a mate as directly related to her large size, and she blamed herself for being weak and having no willpower.

After mass, she waited until everyone else had left and still sat there, looking at the altar, feeling hopeless and abandoned. At last she stood up, picked up her bag, and walked slowly toward the front of the church, staring at the statues of Jesus and the saints and feeling as though she were approaching a council of heavenly beings. She stepped into the front pew and slowly sank to her knees, hoping for some miraculous happening. Tears rolled down her cheeks and dripped onto her praying hands.

"God—tell me what I'm doing wrong," she whispered. "Why can't I be happy? Why can't I find a man who loves me? Why? Please show me what I need to do to be happy." She started sobbing. "Please, God, I'm begging you." The candles on the altar flickered softly as she prayed. "Why can't I be thin? Why do I have to struggle with my weight? Why am I so tempted by food? What am I supposed to learn from this? Please show me the way, Lord. *Show me.*" She sat back in the pew for a good long while in silence.

When she felt that her prayers were complete, she slowly rose to her feet, picked up her bag again, and walked out of the church. The sun shone down on her. She was not expecting such bright light. She squinted, then closed her eyes and smiled, letting the sun warm her face.

A couple crossed her path.

"I love you," the woman said to the man.

"I love you more," the man responded.

"No, I think I love you more."

"That's not possible. You can't love me more than I love you."

They giggled and kept walking.

Overhearing this ridiculous conversation, Jenny started to feel rage welling up. The woman's engagement ring glistened and flashed in the sunlight. Jenny turned away.

God is just taunting me now, she thought, glaring at the couple. She felt so overwhelmed with resentment that it would not have taken much to push her over the edge.

Instead of catching the train downtown, she took the bus back to her own neighborhood. All she wanted was a nap. Longing for the solitude of her apartment, she walked quickly past two good-looking men, hoping they wouldn't stare at her large behind, and acting as if she hadn't noticed them.

"Two six-packs," one man said to the other.

"Nah. Two six-packs wouldn't be enough for me to do *her.*"

Jenny didn't pay much attention, but as she arrived at her own building their conversation suddenly registered. She'd heard about this cruel game. But how in the world could perfect strangers judge her just by looking at her? She couldn't stop her tears.

That afternoon she was convinced that the only thing that could save her from spinsterhood was another torturous diet. The comments of the two men replayed in her mind over and over. She changed into her old bathrobe and called her friend Katy, but after she told Katy about the insult, she only felt worse. She couldn't look at herself in the mirror. She pushed her cat away. Soon she began to feel rage again. She marched to the kitchen, ripped open the refrigerator door, and began to throw away everything she deemed to be fattening. Crying again, she picked up the canister of sugar, tore it open, and poured the contents down the drain. She threw open cupboard doors and began throwing boxes and more boxes of cereals and dried goods on the floor. Some boxes broke open and scattered all over the kitchen. Her crying got louder. Soon she began gasping for breath.

"Jenny? Ah you okay?" Mrs. Grabowski was screeching through the wall again.

"I'm okay, Mrs. Grabowski!" Jenny screeched back. She wiped her runny nose on her sleeve and pushed the sweat-soaked hair out of her face. *I must look crazy,* she thought.

She bent down, sobbing more quietly now, and leaned back against a cupboard, letting herself slide down to the floor. She sat there in the scattered corn flakes, macaroni, and cookies and had a good cry. Eventually she crawled to a kitchen chair and pulled herself up, then stumbled to her bed. She flopped down, grabbing a pillow to hug, and finally began to calm down. She lay back and eventually allowed her cat to curl up at her feet.

Looking at the ceiling, she whispered, "Two six-packs," and began to cry again. By this time her rage had changed into hopelessness. She wondered if this was God's answer to her prayer—to be mocked. She lay there brooding until she fell asleep.

CHAPTER 2
THE CHANCE OF A LIFETIME

THE NEXT MORNING JENNY AWOKE VERY EARLY. She felt numb, and now she wanted to do something risky. She thought about going out and getting drunk or standing on a ledge until someone noticed she was there and asked her to come down. She wanted to go find those two men and beat the daylights out of them, or at least threaten them within an inch of their lives, or maybe scream at the top of her lungs and inform them that she didn't need them to take pity on her. She wanted to shout that she was a wonderful woman, fun to be with, and a lover any man would feel lucky to have. She wanted to say *something—anything*—that would make them suffer as much as they had made her suffer.

After further thought, however, she finally realized she was not thinking clearly and needed to do something for herself. She went in the bathroom and took her clothes off before weighing. She was elated to see that she had lost a pound since yesterday. She took a shower and washed the cornflakes out of her hair, which made her feel almost human again.

"You gonna clean that mess up?" Mrs. Grabowski called through the wall.

"Put the glass down, Mrs. Grabowski," Jenny shouted back. She might have stopped to ponder how her neighbor could possibly know about the mess she had made, but Mrs. Grabowski had, on other occasions, made stranger comments through the wall, leading Jenny to wonder if she could perhaps see through it as well. Jenny also thought that Mrs. Grabowski must not ever sleep. She had almost never failed to comment on whatever activity Jenny was doing at any given time.

Feeling somewhat more cheerful after her shower, she could not believe the disarray of dried foods on the floor. By the time she had cleaned up the mess it was past time for her to get going to work. The energy she exerted cleaning made her feel better still. Before dressing she weighed again, just to make sure she had read the scale correctly. She got dressed and decided that to save time she would buy something for breakfast uptown.

She slung her bag over her shoulder, petted her cat, and locked the door behind her, then hurried down the stairs and out to the street. She was instantly seized by fear of running into those two men again. "Two six-packs," she said under her breath.

A man who happened to be coming out of the building at the same time overheard her and gave her a funny look.

She decided not to be afraid, and when she came to the spot where the men had been sitting, muttered, "Two six-packs! Jackasses!"

During the subway ride uptown, she engaged in a fantasy confrontation with the men over and over. If she ever saw them again, she knew what she would say.

Jenny didn't care for riding the subway, although it saved her a lot of money that she didn't want to spend on cab fares. The seats were narrow and uncomfortable and she didn't like the nasty looks she got from other passengers when she happened to be taking up more than her allotted space.

She exited the train at her stop. She had to climb the stairs as fast as she could so she wouldn't get pushed by the throng of people trying to get to the street above. But she just didn't feel like moving quickly today, so she stood aside and let most of the crowd go past so she could take her time. Breathing a little heavier, she finally made it to the street and began the walk to the building where she worked, a few blocks away.

When the smell of fresh-brewed coffee caught her attention, her stomach growled in response. Knowing she shouldn't be having anything fattening, she stopped at a small bakery where, to save time, she bought a doughnut and some coffee. She poured some nondairy creamer and the contents of a few packets of sweetener into her coffee, shoved the doughnut into her bag, and merged back into the crowd on the sidewalk. She kept walking briskly to her destination, sipping the scalding coffee each time she had to slow down for the crowd of people to dissipate in front of her.

As she entered the lobby of her building she could hear the phones already ringing and the echoing voices of the receptionists. "Kronkin International. How may I direct your call?" Every day she challenged herself to walk up the stairs instead of taking the elevator. She gauged her energy, her mood, and how much time she had before work. She was in no mood to climb the stairs today. Thanks to yesterday, all bets and diets were off.

Jenny still felt like she had been violated, but she was feeling stronger every minute. In spite of the fact that she'd survived in New York City for eleven years, she was still sensitive to criticism and still was not accustomed to the callousness with which people interacted.

She walked into the records department, where a group of her co-workers were talking. They fell insultingly quiet when she entered the room. She knew Katy had told them what had happened with the two men. Everyone looked up at her with worried looks on their faces, then a couple of chubby records workers came over to her with knowing, pitying looks on their faces. "How are you doing, sweetie?" one of the girls asked.

The group accompanied her to her desk, staring at her as if she might explode.

"Uh, I'm fine, you guys. Really." She gave Katy a resentful glare, but her friend just shrugged as if she were not responsible for the others knowing what had happened.

"Let's just all get to work, shall we?" Jenny used her official, supervisory tone. It worked. The group dispersed.

Jenny loved working in records because she could hide there. She sat at her desk behind the high walls of her cubicle and looked forward to enjoying her doughnut and coffee in private. She flicked her computer on and sat back with a sigh. She loved the predictability of her job, and loved losing herself in the work of the day. But when the workday ended, she was always reminded how ordinary and boring her life was.

She took the doughnut out of her bag, where she always hid any food she brought into the office. She didn't like people seeing her loot as she came back after buying something to eat. She knew they would stare at her judgmentally and that they were always thinking *No wonder she's fat—look at what she eats.* She would always rearrange her trash, too, so people couldn't readily see the wrappers of what she had been eating.

Taking a bite of her doughnut, she looked at the bright colors of the flyer for the Annual Awards Event that someone had hung on her wall. This was the social event of the season at Kronkin International, a huge catered affair with champagne and little finger desserts. Everyone who was anyone in the company would be there, and the employees would be talking about it for at least the next two seasons. Some of her female co-workers—especially Katy and some from other departments—were particularly cruel about what people wore to the Event, and often talked about fashion blunders for weeks on end. Jenny's last diet had been initiated on the coattails of the Annual Awards Event two years earlier, a dinner that had left her sick from overeating poached salmon and mini-cheesecake bites. She had vowed never to eat again.

Today the office was all a-flutter with chatter about who was accompanying whom to the Event. Jenny always went solo, except for the fiasco three years ago when her date (who was much too young to be wearing a toupee) had ended up ditching her halfway through the evening. He had spent the rest of the evening dancing every song and then going home with some woman from accounting.

Above the conversations in the records room Jenny could overhear Katy bragging that she was going with her fiancé, and that he had already rented his tuxedo for the Event.

Still thinking about the two six-packs, Jenny wondered—for the first time since she had started at the company—if she should stay home. Nothing very good ever came to her from attending the Event, although every year she was filled to overflowing with hopes that she would find her Mister Right there. But every year her lonely ride home left her feeling empty. As of late, she was also feeling unappreciated. She had gotten a hard time from one of the executives some months back, when she had called a particularly costly error of his to the attention of the accounting department. She wasn't keen about having to put on a nice face for him at the Event.

Jenny could also overhear two of her thin subordinates talking about their latest workout at the gym. "I got on the scale today," a size-six woman named Linda was saying, "and I was *horrified* when I realized I haven't lost any weight for two weeks. According to the height and weight chart at the gym, if I want to be at my target weight, I need to lose twelve more pounds. Well, you know that made me work out even harder—"

"You know, I've gone up two sizes since I got married," the other thin woman chimed in.

"You're so lucky you got married. My boyfriend says I have to lose at least fifteen more pounds before we can even talk about marriage—he's so cute, but he's so macho—I know he just wants me to be healthy, though."

Jenny rolled her eyes. She couldn't stand how fat she was, but worse, she couldn't stand the insensitive prattle of thin women complaining about their weight when they had no idea what it was like to not fit into a booth at a restaurant, to not have enough room in a public bathroom stall, to sit through a company meeting in a chair with arms that dug into their thighs, or to work at fitting into the unforgiving seats in a movie theater. Jenny wanted to stand up and shout at these skinny women who never let a moment go by without mentioning how naughty or good they had been based on the food they put in their mouths. What's more, she couldn't stand to hear about Linda's chauvinistic jerk of a boyfriend.

Jenny had just ripped off a much-too-big bite from her doughnut when Linda stuck her head around the corner of the cubicle to ask a question. Nearly choking, Jenny turned so Linda couldn't see that she had food in her mouth. This was the worst thing that could happen while Jenny was eating—for someone to catch her in the act of enjoying something fattening. She spent a lot of time and energy trying to avoid scenes like this. She felt entirely different when she was on a diet. She would go out of her way to eat her tuna salad with fat-free dressing in front of people so she would get their supportive comments. But just let them catch her with some chocolate, and the judgmental glares would commence. Diet advice would not be far behind.

"I was wondering—" Linda sounded embarrassed to have interrupted her supervisor's breakfast.

"Yes?" Jenny coughed, spitting the bite of doughnut into a napkin. She turned around but wiped her mouth intermittently, afraid she still had traces of the doughnut on her face.

"When is the cutoff date for buying tickets to the Awards Event?"

Jenny cleared her throat. "You can buy tickets right up to the day of the Event. But remember, Linda, they really stick it to you if you buy your tickets at the door."

"Thanks, Jenny." She turned to leave, stopped short, and turned back toward Jenny. "Are you losing weight?"

"I—I—don't know."

"I think you are. You look thinner." Linda smiled approvingly. "Keep up the good work." She winked and headed back to her desk.

Jenny didn't know what to think. She knew she was fatter than ever because her clothes didn't fit, but she wanted to believe she had somehow lost some weight without even trying. Still deep in thought, she ripped another bite off her doughnut.

Kronkin International's Annual Awards Event was always held on a Tuesday night so the employees would not drink too much, or so it was rumored. Statistically, however, the day after the Event ranked at the top of the list for absenteeism. Other employees subscribed to the belief that the higher-ups held the event on a weeknight so they could save money on the rental of the ballroom where the Event was held. Still others believed that it was because those in charge did not want it to cut into their weekend social calendar.

The day went by unusually slowly. Jenny's thoughts kept revolving around two six-packs, plus the fact that she didn't have a dress or a date for the Event. She felt she didn't have much of a life, either. After work, on her way home, she didn't have one bit of desire to go uptown and look for a dress.

It's not until next Tuesday, so maybe I'll go this weekend, she told herself. Then she remembered that nearly a month ago she had asked for Friday off for just that purpose.

AS THE NEXT TWO DAYS WENT BY Jenny felt stronger, and the two-six-packs insult faded. She was feeling somewhat normal again—and despite her doughnut indulgence, she had lost two pounds. When quitting time came on Thursday afternoon she was ready for a few days off even though she had nothing special planned. Over the week she had mustered up some excitement around going uptown to Bountiful Britches to look for a dress. Her two-pound weight loss boosted her enthusiasm that much more.

During the bus ride she kept hoping she wasn't destined to repeat the scene at the department store. She hurried off the bus. *Bountiful Britches has got to have something that I can wear,* she told herself.

She walked quickly along the sidewalk, glancing at store windows lit up with bright colors and beautiful thin mannequins. When she passed a nutrition supplement and vitamin store the diet product she had seen on the infomercial was in the window, so she promised herself she would stop there on the way home. *God knows I need some kind of help to take this weight off.*

She finally caught sight of her destination. The dresses in the window were striking. She was filled with hope that she would find something nice to wear to the Awards Event, and felt she had finally put the events of the past week behind her.

As she entered the store the salesgirls were attentive and treated her as if she were a valued customer. To her surprise, there were a lot of people in the store. *Wow, this must be a popular place,* she said to herself. *I should have come here a long time ago.* Some shoppers had apparently not found anything to buy, as they were leaving the store empty-handed. There were even a few men in the store.

Within twenty minutes she was headed to the dressing room holding several nice choices to try on. She had decided to try the next size up. There were only a few fitting rooms, and one had a sign taped to the door that said *Out Of Order.* She wondered how a fitting room could be out of order, so she had to look. Just as she was about to take hold of the door handle the door opened from the inside and five fat teenagers came out, chatting excitedly and not noticing Jenny.

She always liked to use the fitting room furthest from the door to have more privacy. A loose strap on her shoe caught her attention, but she didn't want to fix it right now. She took a sip of water from a nearby drinking fountain and then entered the fitting room and latched the door.

It was an interesting room—quite large, but Jenny wondered how five fat girls had fit in it. Antique plaques were hung all around, and a large space on the wall had nothing at all. Above the blank space was a black-and-yellow sign that read *Step Down*. Jenny didn't think much of it and began looking around as she was dressing and undressing. One wall adornment was very old. It was a poster showing jolly, plump, scantily clad women. The caption read: *We can fatten you up. Fatroplis Publishing Co. 1921.*

Fatropolis? What does that mean? Why would anyone want to get fat?

Two other women had come and gone from the dressing room in the time it took Jenny to try on the dresses. Well, they had gone out, but Jenny had never heard them come in. They apparently changed fitting rooms as soon as they found that the other one was out of order, whatever that meant. She could see their feet walking out under the partition.

Alone now, Jenny left her fitting room to look at herself in the huge full-length mirror. She saw the reflection of a metal plaque on the wall behind her and turned to look at it more closely. *Festival Fatropolis, 1932.* These decorations were a mystery. Where had they come from? They looked like antiques, but what on Earth was Fatropolis? There was nothing she remembered from history about such a place.

Now that she had tried on the last dress, she put her own clothes back on, wanting to look for more dresses. Her attention returned to her loose shoe. She bent down to tighten the strap. That's when she lost her balance and began to fall against the blank spot on the wall. But when she put her hand out to catch herself, her hand went right through. Something pulled her in. Suddenly she found herself tumbling down onto a floor that was lower than the floor in the fitting room.

THIS PLACE WAS UNLIKE ANYTHING she had ever seen. A thin woman disappointed because a dress doesn't make her look fat? Big women actually finding clothes that fit in a department store?

It had to be a dream.

CHAPTER 3
FAT PEOPLE
IN SPORTING GOODS

JENNY DECIDED TO VENTURE OUT INTO THE STORE to see if she could figure out where she was. Maybe she could get out to the street and somehow get back to Bountiful Britches.

Walking onto the floor of the department store, she saw more fat women of all shapes and sizes than she had ever seen before in one place. They were looking through racks of dresses and pants and blouses with the frenzy of New York shoppers on the day after Thanksgiving. Jenny was astonished that some women were even bigger than she was.

This must be the best-kept secret in New York.

She walked to another section of the women's department, just to investigate for future reference. There were a few thinner women here milling around, looking at racks of clothes, but the section for thin women was much smaller and out of the way, almost hidden. It was obviously not a popular section, as it was darker and seemed to not be maintained very well. Soon she came to the wall of padded undergarments the attendant had referred to, designed to make stomachs, backsides, and almost any other body part look bigger—some even looked like bustles from the nineteenth century. Even though this section was for thinner women, there were pictures of fat women in the advertisements above the racks of clothes, as if the ads were aimed at only the fat women.

Jenny could not help but overhear one of the thin women talking to another. She didn't look directly at them so as not to be so obvious in her eavesdropping.

"These clothes never look as good on me as they do on the models in the pictures." The woman paused and then added proudly, "I just started a new plumping powder that's guaranteed to put twenty pounds on me in just a month. I'm really hopeful it will work this time."

"Don't count on it," her friend admonished. "I've been on every plumping plan known to man, and I just can't maintain it."

At this point Jenny could not help but look at them. When the two women glanced up and caught her, they abruptly stopped talking, looked at each other, and moved to another rack.

A picture of a fat foot in a wide shoe hung above the shoe department, which had a great variety of wide and extra-wide shoes—most of them flat or with modest heels. Jenny overheard a thin man talking to a sales attendant about specially ordering a pair of narrow shoes that would fit his thin feet. "We just don't sell enough narrow shoes to carry them all the time," the attendant told the man. He agreed to order the shoes.

A very fat woman came waddling over to the shoes, eyeballing them carefully and selecting a stylish boot. Jenny was surprised that such a big woman would even consider wearing boots, and even more surprised that the store would carry boots wide enough for such big calves. Jenny had given up on wearing boots years ago, as there were never any in the stores that would even come close to fitting. Minutes later the fat woman was seated and an attendant was zipping her large legs into a nice pair of shiny boots.

Jenny moved on to the jewelry department, where she was surprised at the display cases. Bracelets long enough to go all the way around her wrist. Necklaces that were long, comfortable, and didn't look like chokers. Rings made for fat fingers, with fine large stones in beautiful settings. There was a poster showing a fat bride, with a close-up of her lovely wedding ring perched atop her fat fingers. Squinting at this picture, Jenny was suddenly struck by how repulsed she was at the sight of the fat fingers—fingers that resembled hers.

Next she passed through the furniture department, where all the chairs and sofas were large and wide. There was an ad hanging above showing a fat couple sitting together on a new sofa enjoying a large bowl of popcorn. A chunky sales attendant in a tie stood nearby with a young fat couple who were deciding which living room set they wanted, trying out all the chairs. The woman was wearing a sleeveless blouse that left her fat upper arms exposed, which made Jenny uncomfortable. *Doesn't she have any sense of decency?*

"I like this green chair," the wife was saying. "I like the paisley pattern." As she brushed her hair back with her left hand, her wedding ring caught the light and sparkled brightly. That was all it took to make Jenny keep on moving to the next section of the store.

"Even in my dreams," she muttered, "God is taunting me."

All the merchandise in this store made especially for fat folks? It *had* to be a dream. She was a little offended by the pictures in all the ads around the store. *Why would they use pictures of such fat people? Don't they know what sells?*

In the kitchen department a plump teenaged girl walked past Jenny with a tall, thin young man, his two plump sisters trailing behind. The girl was wearing a pair of pants that hugged her hefty hips and a top that exposed her fat midriff. The girl's stomach bulged out over the top of her pants.

She's too fat to wear those pants. And look at that muffin top.

The girl was teasing the young man, all four of them laughing and having a good time. Just then the girl's mother intercepted them all. She had seen the girl flirting with the boy, and now she looked at the boy disapprovingly. Jenny thought it was sad that the mother disapproved of her daughter's flirting with a boy of color. As the mother took the girl off to the side, the young man and his sisters said their goodbyes and left.

Jenny moved behind a tall display of small kitchen appliances. The mother sounded angry. "Olivia Donna," she said, "I will lock you in a closet before you will date a thin boy like that! Do you hear me?"

The daughter rolled her eyes, but it was obvious to Jenny that she felt guilty and uncomfortable, as if she had been caught doing something wrong.

"Do you want to discuss this with your father?" the mother asked as they walked away, the mother still pulling the girl by her arm.

Wondering if she had heard this conversation correctly, Jenny crossed the aisle into the sporting goods section. Everything here also seemed to be larger than usual. Two large men were examining the skiing equipment.

Now that's something you don't see every day. Fat people in sporting goods. She chuckled, and the men looked up as she approached.

"Hello there," one of the men greeted her, nudging his friend to look her way. Both men looked her up and down appreciatively.

Jenny realized that they were talking to her. It had been a long time since a man had acknowledged her presence—in a good way. Her last date had been with her fickle toupee'd co-worker. Many sizes before that she had gone on a date, but the man had never called her again and she was unable to figure out why. She had become resigned to being invisible to the opposite sex and had all but given up on finding love. *Yes,* she had recently told herself, *I'll live out my lonely life as a spinster with a cat.*

"Uh—hi." Her voice came out as a squeak. She cleared her throat and turned away, but when she turned back around they were still looking at her. She finally found her voice. "Do you two really ski?" she asked, not believing that fat men could ski.

The first man thought for a bit, as if trying to find the right words. Clearing his throat, he said, "I was telling my friend here that he should have combed his hair before we came here—" his friend gave him an irritated look "—because you never know when you'll run into a beautiful woman." He extended his hand to shake Jenny's. "I'm Craig, and this is Larry. And yes, we ski. Do you?"

Jenny stared at them with suspicion, as if their interest in her was some kind of cruel joke. They were handsome. *A little too fat,* she thought, *but handsome.* "What is this?" she asked. "Do fat people get a discount today?"

"What do you mean?" Craig asked.

"Well—I don't mean to be insulting—but there are a lot of *big* people in this store."

"Yeah. There's a lot of us hearty-weight people in the world," he answered in a matter-of-fact voice.

"Hearty-weight? Don't you mean overweight?" she asked.

"No. I don't think so. Over *what* weight?"

"Overweight. As in fatter than you are supposed to be," she responded.

"How is a person supposed to be?" Craig inquired. He and Larry looked at each other, perplexed.

"Well, slim. Slender. Thin." She realized they were not comprehending what she was saying. *What planet are they from?*

At hearing the word "thin," the men looked at each other and laughed. "Thin?" Craig repeated. "Why would anyone want to be *thin?*"

Now it was Jenny who was not following the conversation. She was quite sure the men were playing some sort of prank, making fun of her for being fat. Her eyes began to water, and she turned and walked away. She could hear a commotion behind her, but she kept walking.

"Nice going, genius," Larry was saying to Craig in a loud whisper. "You offended her."

She walked even faster. Near the entrance of the store lines of fat people were checking out at the cash registers. More fat clerks and fat store attendants were busy there. Suddenly she gasped as she caught a glimpse of two fat mannequins in the front window. They were wearing the latest in super-sized fashions, which exposed way too much of their fat mannequin bodies. She looked around in disbelief.

She hurried out of the store and entered the stream of foot traffic on the busy city sidewalk. She walked for several moments before noticing that almost everyone around her was fat. She broke away from the crowd and began walking more slowly, looking in the store windows as she passed. She walked for a while, trying not to look at all the fat people.

The window of a nutrition supplement and vitamin store displayed a product promising the plumping of body mass. Hoping to get more information on the diet product she'd seen on TV, she decided to go in and look around.

A muscular, thinnish young man in an apron that was printed with *Trujillo's Nutrition Supplement & Vitamin Store* was standing behind the counter checking a customer out. When he heard the bell on the door, he hollered, "I'll be with you in a minute, ma'am. Feel free to look around."

"Thank you," Jenny replied. "I'm just browsing." She walked slowly up the first aisle and found herself in the weight-gain-product section.

The store clerk approached her. He was tall and gorgeous—according to Jenny's standards—with rock hard muscles, beautiful eyes, and wavy hair. Jenny thought it odd that with such a fantastic physique he was wearing a shirt with a high neck and long sleeves, as if he were hiding something. She guessed she had about ten years on him and outweighed him by about a hundred pounds.

"Hello," he said. "I'm Argus. Can I help you find anything, ma'am?"

Now she was feeling nervous. "Where's the diet section?" she asked. "I saw a product in the window of another nutrition store—and—uh—and I wanted to get some more information on it—"

"What's a 'diet?'" he asked.

Jenny giggled. This thin, gorgeous young man must be teasing her. She laughed out loud. Because of their age difference she knew he would never look at her *like that,* so she immediately felt comfortable with him.

"That's a good one, Argus," she said lightly. "*'What's a diet?'*" The young man stood looking at her with a serious face. "I know I shouldn't put my body through that again, but I've gained, like, two sizes since my last diet, and—" She looked for any sign of validation on his face.

He smiled. "That's great. You've increased two sizes. Were you woefully thin before you started? If you keep going, you might get as big as my aunt. She was really thin, but within a year she was able to gain enough so she started to look healthy. I've tried for years to gain, but I must have one of those weird unfortunate metabolisms that just burns stuff up the minute I eat. But even though I'm thin, my girlfriend says she's okay with me the way I am," he added proudly.

Her eyes got bigger as she asked, "What? Why would it be *great* that I've increased in size? Have you ever heard of a little thing called customer service?" By now she believed he was being just plain rude.

He took a step back. "I'm sorry, ma'am," he said. "Did I say something to upset you?"

"Please direct me to the diet products," she said. "Now. Before I leave and never come back to this store." *Why is he poking fun at me?*

"Ma'am, I'm sorry, but I don't know what you mean by 'diet product.' Could you explain what that is?"

Talking slowly, as if this young man did not speak ordinary English, she explained. "A reducing product. To help people lose weight." Resigning herself to the fact that he would be no help at all and that she would have to find the right section on her own, she began to walk away.

He followed her. "Why do you want to lose weight?" he asked.

"None of your business," she snapped, walking faster to get away from him.

But he matched her pace, as if he were accepting the challenge of trying to understand this customer and help her regardless of all obstacles. Just then, as she stopped and turned to face him, they were standing almost nose to nose. It was an awkward moment, but they both stood still, frozen. She glared up at him as if he were a pesky younger brother.

He was looking longingly into her eyes. "I think you look just great," he said.

They were so close to each other that the hair covering the lad's forehead fluffed slightly when she said, "Please leave me alone!" Dismissing his compliment, she took a step back and said, "I don't need any further assistance, *Argus*. I will find what I need for myself." She pointed emphatically at the cash register, and ordered him to "Go over there!"

The young clerk backed away. He turned and walked slowly, but unwillingly, back to the cash register, muttering to himself, "This is the first time in all the years I've worked here that I haven't been able to help a customer find exactly what they need. Customers are *usually* grateful for my help."

As he moped, Jenny continued to search the store, stalking up and down the aisles, looking at all the products. There seemed to be nothing but products that promised to enhance, enlarge, augment, plump up, supplement, add to, expand, enhance, increase, boost, or bump up one's size. Soon she was at the back of the store. Argus was standing behind the counter, wiping it down and munching on a cookie. Her head popped up from behind the shelf and she glared at him, all of her anger and confusion directed at him.

Chunks of cookie fell out of his mouth. "What?" he asked, brushing the crumbs off the front of his shirt and apron.

"There are *no* reducing products in this whole store?"

"Well—" he started, swallowing the last bite of cookie. It appeared he would try another approach, as if hoping he could still help her in some way.

"We only carry the products that the public demands here, and reducing is not something the folks around here want to do."

All she could do was shake her head. "I must have taken a wrong turn somewhere," she muttered. "Okay. Well, then, I need to get out of here." One of her eyelids was twitching. She was feeling fragile and lost. "I'll take my business somewhere else."

She began to move to the front of the store. Argus stepped into her path. "Are you sure I can't help you find something else?" he asked.

She scowled at him.

Startled, he stepped out of her way, as if he finally got it that she was less than happy. "Oh. Well, okay, then," he stammered. He raised one hand and gave her a weak wave. "Good luck with your gain—ing," he said, knowing that probably was not the right thing to say, "—er, I mean—I hope I see you aga—that is, I hope you find what you're looking for." He gave her a pathetic smile.

She brushed her hair back, took a deep breath, held her head high, adjusted her bosom, and exited the store, feeling proud but a tad unstable. What were these mind games being inflicted on her everywhere she turned? *What the hell is going on here?*

She stood still on the sidewalk and leaned against the store wall, looking around and nervously wringing her hands. Hardly knowing what to do, she took a step and reentered the flow of people walking down the street. But she felt repulsed by all the fat bodies around her.

She had never seen so much fat in her life. Fat women, in short skirts and dresses that revealed their fat thighs and fat upper arms, were walking along the street, their buttocks unabashedly wiggling to and fro. Fat couples were holding hands and kissing on the street. A fat old man was walking his fat dog. A fat old lady sat reading a book on a wider than usual bus bench. A fat policeman on a huge, fat horse was clip-clopping down the street.

She startled as a fat passerby accidentally brushed against her.

Fat people sat at large tables in large chairs in large windows in cafés along the street. Jenny stopped, trying to take it all in. She read the sign above the café: *Fatropolis Bar and Grille.*

The city began spinning around her. She felt herself beginning to slip away, but could not stop herself from fainting on the street.

CHAPTER 4
JENNY IS REUNITED WITH AN OLD DELICIOUS FRIEND

THE FIRST THING JENNY SAW WHEN SHE OPENED her eyes was the color green. The world was green and fuzzy. After blinking a few times, she felt herself become fully present in the room. But what room was she in? She could smell bread baking, and hearing her stomach growling told her that she hadn't eaten for hours. She blinked again. She was lying on a green velvet settee with a crocheted blanket over her legs. There was a half-open door across the room.

"Hello?" she called.

As if in reply a fat older woman came through the door carrying an ornate tea service, steam rising from the teapot. She had gray hair with the remainder of auburn in it. "How are ya feelin'?" the woman asked with an Irish accent as she set the tray down on the hand-crocheted tablecloth covering the little table near Jenny.

"Where am I?" Jenny looked at the woman. She couldn't help but notice how fat she was. "I'm Jenny. May I ask who you are? And what happened to me?"

"Well—dearie, ya fainted on the street just a few blocks from my bakery, and some of my boarders brought ya here to lie down fer awhile. The policeman told us that if none of us knew who ya were, he would have to take ya to the hospital, and then God knows what would've become of ya. And ya look like such a nice hearty girl. That would've been a shame. So I told him yer my kinfolk. I hope that was okay." The woman adjusted her spectacles. "Here," she added, pouring a cup of tea and handing it to her guest, "drink

31

some tea, dearie. I'm havin' my helper make ya a sandwich, I can hear yer stomach growlin.' Cream? Sugar?"

A big, tall man in a white apron tapped lightly on the open door and looked in.

"Come on in, Hank," the woman said.

"Here's the sandwich you asked for, Dotty," he said.

She took the sandwich from him and handed it to Jenny. "Please eat this, dearie. You'll be feelin' much better in no time."

Jenny was feeling very hungry and dove into the sandwich as Dotty and Hank stood by, watching her. The bread was fresh-baked and the lunchmeat was fresh and cold. It was just how she liked a turkey sandwich.

Jenny didn't know why, but she already trusted this old woman. "Thank you, ma'am," she said as she chewed. She looked up at Hank, then quickly looked down again. "And thank you, Hank," she added in a softer voice. She took another big bite.

"You're very welcome, miss," Hank replied. He smiled, and then turned to his employer. "Dotty, I'm going to get back to the front."

"Thank ya, dearie," she called after him.

As she ate, Jenny was beginning to have flashes of memory—being pulled into the mysterious fitting room wall, seeing the fat women in the store, the fat feet, the fat fingers, the fat mannequins. Where was she? What was going on? Why was everything and everyone fat?

"Child, what's the matter?" Dotty leaned down and brushed Jenny's hair back out of her eyes. "What's frightenin' ya?"

At this, Jenny began to cry. "I was trying on a dress at Bountiful Britches," she began, "for the Annual Awards Event. I was in the fitting room—and—and—well, I got pulled through a wall into another fitting room. It was in Burley's Department Store and all I could see was fat people and I came out onto the street, and then I went into a diet product store." She took a deep breath. "Except there were no diet products." She knew she must be sounding crazy, but she had to go on. "And there were more fat people. And fat dogs and fat horses and fat bus benches—and—and—and—" She had to talk fast or she would collapse into tears. "And that's all I remember." Another memory hit her between the eyes. "Oh, and I saw a sign that said *Fatropolis Bar and Grille.*" She paused again to catch her breath. "What is Fatropolis? Am I in Fatropolis?"

The woman sat down and took a deep breath. "Yes, child, that ya are." She paused to let Jenny absorb this news. "There's a handful of portals in the city. That's why I fibbed to the policeman and told him yer my kin. Ya didn't have anythin' with ya, so I figured ya must've come from the other place." She calmly refilled Jenny's cup.

"What—what do I do now?" She swallowed hard, nearly choking on her tea. "What do I do now? I need to get my bag. I don't even know where it is. I've got to get home. My job. People will wonder where I've gone."

"There's no such thing as coincidence," was Dotty's reply. "Child, ya ended up here fer a reason. Everyone who ends up here needs to be here." She leaned forward again and looked down at Jenny over her spectacles. "Let me guess. Ya hate yerself—ya spend everyday wishin' ya were someone else. Ya can't understand why the menfolk don't take a shine to ya." She stood up, nodded wisely, and walked over to the window. Standing with her back to Jenny, she went on. "And ya live alone, with yer cat. And ya wonder why God made ya the way ya are. Hearty-weight." She suddenly wheeled around and peered into Jenny's astonished eyes. "Am I hittin' the nail on the head, dearie?"

Jenny could only blink again. There was something about the way Dotty expressed herself that seemed familiar, although she knew they had never met. "Are you some sort of a psychic? Or a witch? How did you know all that about me?"

"No, child, I'm no psychic." Dotty came back, sat down again, and picked up her own cup of tea. "Anyone can read yer kind as easy as readin' a book. I could see the disregard ya had fer me when ya first saw how hefty I am. Oh, ya didn't mean any harm, but I could tell right away that ya hate us fatfolk. We sometimes hate the very thing we can't help bein' ourselves." She spooned some sugar into her cup. "And I knew right away ya were from that other place. That place is merciless towards us fatfolk. Why, even fatfolk themselves in that other place hate the fatfolk, so that makes them hate themselves with a hatred that only the worst kind of brainwashin' can conjure into a body." She sipped her tea again, swallowed quickly, and took a breath as if she forgot to say something. "And I know ya have a cat because ya got cat hair on ya." She reared back and cackled. "Witch!" she shouted through her laughter. "Land o' Goshen, child, ya make me laugh."

Jenny took another deep breath and exhaled in relief. "I didn't mean to insult you," she murmured, and looked down, brushing at the cat hair on the arm of her blouse. "And I do appreciate you taking care of me like this. I mean you are very sweet—Mrs.— uh, Ma'am—"

"Dorothy O'Flannigan is the name, child. Ya can call me Dotty, like everyone else. And I'm not a missus anymore. My mister, rest his soul, went to see St. Peter nearly ten years ago. Well, some straight-laced folk still call me Mrs. O'Flannigan, but I prefer just plain Dotty."

"Dotty." Jenny repeated the name. Then she asked, "How do you know so much about where I'm from?"

Dotty cleared her throat as if the question made her uncomfortable. "Just rumors I've heard over the years," was all she would say about the matter. "Child, we've got to figure out what we're to do with ya. Besides a bakery, I run a boardin' house, so ya can stay with me if ya like until ya get on yer feet. I'm assumin' you've got nowhere else to go?"

"I don't suppose I do. I don't know anyone here. Except you."

"I'm supposin' ya don't know many folks from where yer from, either. And what do ya suppose will become of yer cat?"

"Well, my neighbor, Mrs. Grabowski, and I have made an agreement to watch out for one another. She notices when I'm not home for awhile and checks on Patches. I suppose when I don't come back tonight she'll assume I went to Connecticut for the weekend. She'll just use the key I gave her to go over and feed the cat. But I don't know what will happen after that."

"Well, it's good that the cat will be looked after," Dotty said. She pushed herself out of the chair. "Let me show ya to yer room."

She motioned for Jenny to follow her. Just then a loud *beep* sounded, startling Jenny. "Don't let that startle ya," Dotty said. "The sun's just gone down. This house is old."

Jenny followed Dotty out of the small sitting room and into a parlor full of antique furniture. Old photographs hung on the walls along with beautiful works of art. These and the fine Persian carpets on the floor made the room warm and inviting. All the photographs and paintings were of fat people. There were even statuettes of fat women used as knickknacks around the room. A larger statue depicting a fat couple embracing was on the floor by one of the elaborately upholstered sofas. An antique picture of a young woman sat on the mantel over the fireplace with a candle burning beside it. The frame around the picture was exquisitely crafted with gold leaf. A small, square plate with what looked like a small bite of cheesecake on it sat in front of the picture.

Seeing Jenny looking at this makeshift altar, Dotty smiled. "Let me show ya around before I take ya to yer room," she said. A door off of the parlor led to the office for the bakery. "This is my office, where I do all my paperwork."

There was a strange glass box on the desk. What looked like a computer was encased in glass, with fine glass circuitry inside. There weren't many wires, but it certainly looked complicated. "Is that a computer?" she asked, pointing.

"Yes. It's old, but it still works fer what I need it fer. The boarders tease me because I don't have all the newfangled technologies, but I figure if it's not broke, why fix it?" Dotty looked over her spectacles at Jenny. "Do ya like baked goods, child?"

"Are you kidding? Just look at me."

"Now I can tell only certain things about ya by lookin' at ya," she said. "What do ya mean by sayin' that?"

Jenny had to stop and think for a moment. "Well, I guess I meant that you can tell how much I like baked goods if you look at how fat I am."

Dotty gave her a disapproving look and said, "Ya say 'fat' like it's a bad thing. There are plenty of women here that would give their eyeteeth to be so *fortunate.*" She looked Jenny up and down. "Besides, I think ya could stand to gain a few pounds."

Jenny gasped at the thought of gaining any more weight.

"So ya meant it as an insult on yer person? Ya know yer broadcastin' to everyone that ya hate yerself by attemptin' to put yerself down like that."

Dotty opened the door to the kitchen. Two big men were kneading dough on wide countertops. "Ya know Hank already," she said. Hank turned and nodded to Jenny. "And the other one is Charles—Charlie for short."

Charlie turned and nodded to Jenny. "Pleased to meet you, ma'am," he said before returning to his kneading. Neither Hank nor Charlie was wearing a ring, which made Jenny feel uncomfortable. She hated to see a wedding ring on a man's finger, but she didn't know how to act around single men, either. This made her feel especially hopeless. She knew she would never find someone to love.

She and Dotty made their way through the kitchen and went into the front of the store, where two more workers were helping customers. Seeing all the pastries behind the glass, Jenny felt like a child entering an amusement park. There was every kind of pastry imaginable. Raised, glazed, cake, and filled doughnuts. Huge cinnamon rolls brimming over with icing. Slices of cheesecakes of all different flavors. Coffee cakes. Muffins of every sort— blueberry, banana nut, chocolate chip, orange cranberry, and bran muffins with raisins. Chocolate chip cookies, oatmeal cookies, peanut butter cookies, and sugar cookies. Fresh baked baguettes, breadsticks, and rolls. There was even a refrigerator filled with beautifully decorated cakes for every occasion and a large assortment of fresh whole cheesecakes. Jenny's mouth started watering.

"Child, have somethin.' I can tell yer hankerin' fer a treat," Dotty said with an even thicker Irish brogue.

"Oh." Jenny looked again. "Well—it's just that I was going to start a diet soon. Pretty soon." She licked her lips. "Oh, all right. Maybe a small piece of cheesecake." She held her thumb and forefinger an inch apart. "Just a little bit."

"What kind'll I get ya?" Dotty went behind the counter and opened the display case.

"I like regular New York cheesecake the best."

"Just like me grandmother—she loved her cheesecake." Dotty handed a generous slice to Jenny with a fork. "May ya eat it in good health, dearie."

"I feel bad," Jenny said. "I have nothing to offer you. All my money's in my bag, and I left it—"

"Child, yer money's no good here. Ya can help yerself to the eats. Of course, once yer rested, ya can do some chores to help out the boarders. But we can hash that out later." Dotty opened the steel-door refrigerator and took out a bottle of milk. "Here's somethin' to help wash it down," she said as she poured a glass and handed it to Jenny.

Jenny took a bite of the cheesecake and closed her eyes, savoring the taste. It was the most delicious cheesecake she had ever tried. Its texture was creamy and smooth. As she swallowed, she remembered the first time she had tried cheesecake as a child and the certainty she felt that she had discovered a treasure of immeasurable proportions. "This is delicious." She took a drink of the cold milk.

"Does me heart good to see ya enjoyin' yerself." The old baker patted her guest on the back. She invited Jenny to sit down and finish her cheesecake and milk at one of the tables in the store while she visited with the customers, laughing and joking. When Jenny finally finished, Dotty said, "On to the rest of the house now."

She led Jenny to a door at the other end of the store that took them into a hallway that led back to the parlor. Jenny followed Dotty up a flight of stairs to a long hallway with many doors. Dotty stopped at one, took the key out of the lock and opened it. "This'll be yer room, child," she said, handing her the key.

Jenny followed her in. There was a single bed with a brass headboard, a nightstand with an antique glass lamp, and an old dresser with a television on it. *I think it's a television—I wonder why electronics are made with glass.* The television, too, had fine glass circuitry inside. "Is that a TV?" she asked.

"Yes it's a TV."

"I love to watch TV. Especially at night. Does it work?"

"Sure it works, but just be mindful of the other boarders around ya."

"Oh, of course. I won't have it too loud." Jenny thought of Mrs. Grabowski. She went through a door leading to a private bathroom. There were fresh towels, washcloths, and a kit with a toothbrush, toothpaste, and a comb and brush. There was also a small window with pretty yellow curtains. She looked down into a courtyard.

"That's the back o' the house," Dotty said. "Ya can sit out there if ya need some fresh air sometimes. Now, child, I'll leave ya alone to rest and get yer bearin's." She started to walk out, then opened the closet and seemed surprised and embarrassed to see clothes still hanging there. "The last girl that roomed here left in a hurry because she skipped out on the rent. Looks like she left some of her things in the closet. Ya can go through them and see if ya want anythin.' I don't imagine she'll be comin' back."

After Dotty left the room, Jenny sat down on the bed. She already missed her home. There were few surprises there, and even though she was miserable, she generally knew what to expect. A creature of habit, not fond of spontaneity and with little time in her life for the unplanned, she knew what her day-to-day routine was and she stuck to it without fail.

After several minutes she got up slowly and walked over to turn on the television. As the picture came on, it was very sharp. Fat dancers were in the middle of a routine on a dancing competition show. She was appalled. Back home she had only seen fat people dancing for laughs on television, but this was a serious competition. There were five of them—three women and two men—dancing in unison. She watched with her mouth gaping open. They turned and twisted, their bellies and backsides jiggling together.

Though she was repulsed by all the bouncing flesh, she couldn't look away. She was stunned. The dance ended and the show went to a commercial in which a fat woman advertised a popular cereal product and boasted that it had "more calories than ever." Next came a campy advertisement for Burley's Department Store, showing a bunch of young fat people dancing around in the latest seasonal fashions.

The next program was a game show that featured a fat host and two huge contestants. The cameras swept the audience. Nearly everyone was fat, and the studio seats were wide enough for fat people to sit comfortably. The studio audience waved, laughed, and made faces at the camera as it panned across them. Jenny remembered the times she had tried to go to the movies, only to be uncomfortable in seats that were obviously made for thin people. She also remembered the jokes she had made at her own expense about keeping a stick of butter in her purse to grease her sides so she could slide into the seats. She felt the sting of her own self deprecation and heard Dotty's words echoing in her head: *Yer broadcastin' to everyone that ya hate yerself by puttin' yerself down like that.*

Jenny sat on the edge of the bed watching the television for some time. The people looked just like her, with double chins and round bellies. But they seemed to not be afraid to wear clothes that showed their bodies or their bare skin. The female contestant's dress had no sleeves. Jenny tried to look at the woman's bulging upper arms and not feel disgusted. They looked soft and round, and moved with her gestures. Her upper arms seemed to express her excitement as clearly as her face and voice did. In fact, her whole body seemed to express what she was feeling. She could tell the woman was not ashamed to be alive, not ashamed to be taking up room, not interested in making herself smaller to please others.

The male contestant high-fived the woman when she got an answer right. The man had a large belly and a double chin, too, and looked handsome in his attractive suit. It occurred to Jenny that she felt different about the man being fat. She felt hardly any disgust or disdain for his substantial body.

The show went to commercial again, the camera swept the audience once more, and viewers saw a crowd that was a jiggling mass of flesh, excited and brazenly waving and screaming. Everyone in the commercials was fat—the men, the women, the children, the pets—and it didn't seem to matter if the commercials were for floor wax or pizza rolls. The subliminal message was always the same: *Use this and you'll be happy, popular, and hearty.*

The ads for weight-gain products seemed to be geared toward singles who wanted to find a mate. In one ad there was a not-so-fat guy (before using the product being advertised) miserable and alone, then they showed him after gaining a lot of weight with a fat woman on each arm, smiling flirtatiously at him. He looked at the camera with a sparkle in his eye and winked, confidently declaring, "Thank you Miracle Mass."

Jenny could only stare at the TV. She remembered seeing that product in the nutrition supplement and vitamin store.

She changed the channel and stopped at what looked like a reality show called *No Pain No Gain.* A very thin contestant was standing on a huge scale. He was dressed in an exercise outfit that accentuated his boniness; the outline of his ribs could be seen through the tight spandex. His family, most of them fat, stood to one side, waiting to see the readout. All of a sudden a number appeared. The contestant's knees buckled as he began to cry.

"You've gained eight pounds!" the host shouted. The family members cheered.

A slightly chunkier contestant stepped up to the scale. Her husband and daughter waited anxiously for the results of the weigh-in.

"You've gained *thirteen pounds!*" The host shouted even more excitedly. The contestant jumped up and down while hugging her hefty hubby.

Finally Jenny had to laugh. "If only the folks back in New York could see this," she said aloud, and shook her head.

Movement caught her eye at the threshold to her room. The shadow stopped and a card slid in under her door. Jenny walked over and picked it up.

You are cordially invited to join us for the Festival Fatropolis, Saturday at 9 o'clock a.m.

Dotty's Bakery will have a booth of baked goods. It would be appreciated if all the boarders would sign up for a half hour or hour to help with the bakery sales at the festival. All of you who help will get free entry. Before and after your allotted time, you will be able to have a lovely time at the festival.

This is not required. You can go on your own to the festival. The signup sheet is in the office.

Love & blessings to all,
Dotty

As she finished watching her reality show, Jenny decided to go downstairs to find the signup sheet. When she found it in the bakery office, there were already seven names on it. As she was signing, Charlie came in, apparently with the same intention. She stepped aside and tripped over one of the tiles in the office floor. Luckily Charlie caught her and set her back upright.

"I didn't even see that," she said.

"Yeah," he replied. "There's something wrong with it—it's not quite level with the rest, and I think it's loose. It's been like that for a long time. We've offered to fix it, but Dotty keeps putting it off."

She turned and was walking back upstairs when her eye caught the picture of the young woman, the burning candle, and the plate with the cheesecake. She made sure she was alone in the parlor and walked over to the picture to look more closely at it. The young woman was not very fat, just a little plump. She had smooth skin and beautiful eyes that twinkled with her smile, which was similar to Dotty's. Jenny knew this was an altar of some sort, but she couldn't understand the meaning of the cheesecake on the plate.

"That's Mona McBain, my grandmother, ya know."

Dotty's comment startled Jenny, causing her to exclaim, "Oh, Dotty. It's you." She put her hand on her chest and heaved a sigh. "She's very beautiful. But can I ask what the cheesecake is for?"

"Of course, child. Ya can ask me anythin'. I may not want to answer ya," she joked, "but ya can ask. Ya see child, my grandmother and grandfather were born of poor Irish immigrants. My grandfather was nice and hearty, but my grandmother was a wee bit more fragile. When the Great Depression hit, my grandfather was workin' as a baker in another city, but the owner of the bakery couldn't afford to pay him, so he lost his job. They had no money. They were hungry most of the time. My mother was just a wee lass, and they sacrificed a lot so she could eat. My poor grandmother, when she was so hungry, she could smell the cheesecakes bakin' at the bakery. She always told my grandfather that when they had money, she was goin' to have cheesecake every day." Tears welled up in Dotty's eyes, and her voice quivered as she told the story. "She wasn't able to survive the Depression, ya know. Many weren't. It was a horrible time fer everyone. Most of the people that died here in Fatropolis were the thinfolk. They had no reserves to withstand the hunger. When my grandmother died, my grandfather and mother were taken in by the kind old man that owned this bakery, and when the old man died, he left the bakery to my grandfather. Ever since then, my grandfather, then my mother, and now me, we always leave her a bit of cheesecake every day. Like she said she would have. God rest her soul."

"I'm so sorry she wasn't able to see the bakery." Jenny was now becoming teary herself. "What a sad story."

"Ever since the Depression, when so many thinfolk died off, it caused—I guess ya could say it caused folks to have a lower opinion of the thinfolk. Most of the folks left over were hearty and healthy, and over the years we've been wantin' to keep it that way. But occasionally we have a young'un that still takes after a thin ancestor. There's no stoppin' the genes when they have a mind to come out."

"I don't understand," Jenny said. "We had the Depression back home, in—in my world, too." She stopped, barely able to accept the fact that she was in another world. "And thin people are the most popular ones there. Everyone seems to hate fat people. Like you said, we even hate ourselves. Why is that? When did the brainwashing start? Where did it come from?"

Dotty yawned. "Child," she said, "I can't be goin' into all that tonight. It's gettin' late, and the saints know I need my beauty sleep." Chuckling at her little joke, she ushered Jenny back up the stairs.

Jenny went reluctantly, feeling as if she had been put off. *How could things be so different in these two worlds? And why does Dotty's accent seem to get thicker at times?*

Jenny felt like a child being sent to her room. Closing her door, she listened as Dotty walked to her own bedroom. Then she sat down on the edge of her bed and pondered the conversation. The strange events of the day had tired her out, so she decided to take a shower and go to bed.

For the last ten years Jenny had resigned herself to taking showers, as she could not easily fit into a standard bathtub. She had gotten used to showers, but she still missed soaking in a tub of water. Occasionally when she would go on a trip she would make sure she got a hotel room with a Jacuzzi tub so she could again indulge in a real bath. She knew her thin friends took bathtubs for granted. They always fit. Now, as she looked at the bathtub in Dotty's boarding house, she was pleasantly surprised to find that it was big enough to accommodate her large behind with room to spare.

As she began to draw her bath, she glanced at the towel rack. It was right where it needed to be, where she could reach it from the tub. An intercom speaker was built into the wall between the commode and the shower. On a shelf near the tub stood an old-fashioned yellow glass bottle filled with bath crystals. When she poured some into the bath, the water began to sparkle as if it were magical.

While the water was running she went back out into the bedroom and looked in the closet. Her eyes went straight to a soft, thick pink bathrobe that looked like it would fit her. She took it into the bathroom and hung it on a large hook on the wall. Then she undressed and stuck in a toe to test the water. The tub was easy to get into, and there were waterproof handles attached to the yellow and white tiles all around the tub to hang onto. She climbed into the tub, held onto two of the handles, and slowly lowered herself into the water.

The temperature was perfect and gave her tingles of pleasure all over her body. She hadn't felt the pleasure of a bath in over a year. She sank down into the water and allowed it to run long enough to cover her up to her neck. Steam rose up off of the surface and caressed her face. Her knees poked out of the water as she slid down even further to cover the back of her head. Jenny groaned with pleasure.

After a little while she sat up, giggled and began splashing the water with her feet. There was a lot of water in the tub, and she could move easily to and fro. Thanks to the bath crystals, everything was slippery. She turned on one side and suddenly her backside slipped on the bottom of the tub and she flipped over on her belly, causing her face to go under the water. Her head popped up quickly as she gasped for breath.

"Wow!" she exclaimed. Then she began to laugh out loud. She splashed and kicked her feet. She turned from her stomach to her back several more times. She soaked in the tub for over an hour, enjoying the rich softness of the water, then leisurely washed her hair and scrubbed herself all over. From time to time she sat up and replaced the cooling water with new warm water and lay back down, surrendering to the relaxing effects of the most luscious find in all of Fatropolis.

Finally, when her feet and hands had reached an acceptable level of prunification, she opened the drain and began to lift herself out of the tub using the many handles. She grabbed a towel and was surprised that it easily went around her entire body, leaving no cold gap in the front. This luxurious towel was much longer and wider than standard-sized towels, and it was also very thick. She wrapped it around and tucked the end in at the top, just as she had when she was thinner. Feeling pampered and relaxed, she rubbed her hair dry with another towel, then dried herself and put on the bathrobe.

Sauntering back into the bedroom, she decided to check and see what other clothes the prior tenant had left. She opened the closet again. This time she saw the shoes on the floor and the garments hanging from the rod. Her mouth fell open in surprise as she came upon a lovely dress in a flower print with sequins. The dress looked as if it had been made for her. She slipped it on. It hugged her figure in all the right places. She stood before the large mirror on the back of the closet door and stared at how beautiful she looked.

Apparently the former tenant was a snappy dresser and loved to match her clothes with accessories. Jenny could hardly believe the other woman had carelessly left such a lovely dress. There were even shoes that matched. Feeling like Cinderella, Jenny slipped into the shoes and looked at the other garments—two pairs of pants, three blouses, and another, simpler dress. The pants fit her, too, though they were a bit long; the tops were also a little long, but acceptable, and the other dress didn't fit perfectly, but would do. Her chest of drawers held some other things as well.

Trying on these clothes made her remember Bountiful Britches. That led to thoughts of her home and her cat. Would she ever get back home? Back to her real life? She began to think about her job and her friends. She had never been completely satisfied with her job, but it was a means to an end, and it did give her some sense of accomplishment, especially since she had been promoted to records supervisor. But with the recent developments at Kronkin International she had begun to doubt that she wanted to stay in that field. She had a good relationship with most of her co-workers there, especially Katy, and felt sad that if this visit went on much longer they might start to worry and wonder where she was.

Of late, Jenny had been wondering how her life had become so disappointing. When she was younger her dream had been to become a dancer, so she had moved to New York City to continue her dance classes. She'd had to give up on that dream, though, when she started to gain weight. So she settled into her average American life. Her next dream was to marry and eventually become a mother, but that, too, was fading away before her eyes. She had just passed her thirty-first birthday, and now her biological clock seemed to be ticking unbearably loudly.

She shook her dreams and memories out of her head and turned on the television again. The clock showed it was almost midnight. What a long day it had been.

She snuggled down into the bedding. The pillows behind her head were large and fluffy, the mattress overstuffed and comfy. Jenny settled in and looked up at the television screen to see a large evangelist in his sparkling jacket, praying for the audience. *I can't wait to see what's on the other channels,* she thought, looking over at the remote control on the nightstand. Beside it was a little statuette of a fat lady that looked old and was made of some sort of shiny, milky stone. Jenny picked up the extra-large transparent remote with its large buttons and flipped through the channels, stopping at a news report for the Festival Fatropolis.

"Festival Fever is spreading throughout the entire Fatropolitan area," the broadcaster was saying, "as Flint Mackelroy and his band are gearing up for their appearance at the Festival Fatropolis. Making this Festival Fever even more intense is the fact that comedian Dewey Henderson will be opening for Mackelroy's Band."

Jenny could hardly believe her ears. *Flint Mackelroy? Dewey Henderson? That can't be. They're from—from back home.* She was suddenly excited. *I've always wanted to see them in person. I'm going to get to see them on Saturday!*

But then she began to wonder why these entertainers would be in Fatropolis. *Of course. They're fat.* They must know about this world she had stumbled into. "Maybe other artists and entertainers come here, too," she said aloud. She wanted to ask Dotty if there were others who knew about Fatropolis and came here to entertain. It dawned on her that if entertainers came here, there must be a way to get home. And that meant maybe she could go home, too.

A commercial caught her attention. It was for a new movie starring Josie Hanover and Eddie Sandoval. These actors, too, belonged to the other world. They were both comedians, and they were both fat. Jenny had never seen them in a movie together before. She couldn't believe that they were starring. She had seen the occasional movie with a fat character, but never more than one at a time, and the fat actor was almost always the comic relief, not the lead role. But this movie with two fat stars looked like a romantic comedy.

After the commercials the local news came back, and the anchor began talking about a bus that had stalled in the middle of an intersection and had caused a huge traffic jam in Lower Fathattan. *Fathattan? Could this be their equivalent to Manhattan?*

Jenny was glued to the television. While even the news was interesting, the commercials were fascinating. She had never seen anything back home like she was seeing now. The only thing missing was a bowl of ice cream, but she felt embarrassed to go and try to get something to eat at such a late hour, so she turned out the light.

She began to get sleepy, but the light from the screen flickered and the shadowy figures danced on the walls for some time more until she drifted off to sleep.

CHAPTER 5
THE MAN ABOUT TOWN
AND THE BOARDERS

JENNY WAS DREAMING ABOUT BEING IN HER apartment and petting her cat. In her dream, the phone rang. When she answered it, the person calling said, "Breakfast will be served in the dining room in one half hour." *Well,* Jenny thought in her dream, *that's odd. Why would someone call me to announce breakfast?* Then the voice spoke again. "Breakfast will be served in the dining room in one half hour."

This time she opened her eyes. The voice was coming from a speaker on the wall. The little box looked exactly like the intercom speaker in the bathroom. She looked at the clock. It was only six-thirty in the morning. *Time to get up.* Perhaps today she would get some answers to her questions.

She went into the wonderful bathroom. After she had brushed her teeth and her hair, she felt that familiar feeling of dread come over her as she searched the entire bathroom for the scale that would tell her what kind of day she was going to have.

No scale anywhere in the bathroom. No scale with which to judge herself. She felt relieved, yet a little disappointed, as she always looked forward to the elation she felt if she happened to weigh less than the day before, even if only by one pound.

She was tired of her boring hairdo, but had no idea how to fix it. Giving her hair another swipe with the brush, she went back into the bedroom and tried on a couple of the outfits she had found in the close, deciding on a pair of pants with one of the blouses. Now she was dressy enough to participate in whatever the day had in store, but casual enough to help out with chores. She put on a pair of the abandoned socks in the chest of drawers, then a pair of athletic shoes—a bit too big, so she tightened the laces.

She walked cautiously out of her room, not wanting to wake anyone up, but as she came closer to the stairwell she began to hear voices and laughter down below. Along with the laughter heavenly smells wafted up from the kitchen. She walked down the stairs. There was no one in the parlor, so she carefully opened the door to the dining room. A few people were already sitting at the table waiting for breakfast. The table was big enough to accommodate at least twenty large people.

Not recognizing anyone, Jenny decided to go and find Dotty and see if she could help. She could hear commotion coming from the kitchen.

"Come on in, dearie," Dotty said the moment Jenny peeked in, as if she knew she was at the door. "I want ya meet some of the guys and gals." She pulled Jenny into the kitchen.

Jenny was embarrassed at the attention being called to her, but she was also attracted to the excitement in the air. Everyone was chatting enthusiastically, but stopped as soon as they noticed her.

"Ya know Hank Ogilvie and Charlie Guillaume," Dotty said, and when Jenny nodded at the two men, they returned her nod. "And this is Trixie and Dixie Kavanagh." Dotty pointed to the fattest twenty-something twins Jenny had ever seen. They smiled sweetly and held out their plump hands in greeting. A younger girl, who in Jenny's opinion was just a little on the chunky side, started toward her. "And this is Clara Donelly," Dotty said. Clara reached out to shake Jenny's hand.

Just then a man Jenny thought she recognized backed into the kitchen from the bakery with a tray full of pastries and muffins. As soon as he turned, she did recognize him. It was the young clerk from the nutrition supplement and vitamin store. Through the open door, Jenny got a glimpse of the bakery packed with customers.

"And this here's our friend, Argus Lippencott," Dotty said with pride. "He's our wonder man. Helps with everythin'."

"Dotty," he said as he set the tray on one of the huge kitchen countertops, "you know I prefer 'man about town.'" He grinned at Jenny and wiped his hand on his apron. "Milady." He winked and reached for her hand.

Jenny flushed with embarrassment as she remembered the scene she had made at the nutrition supplement and vitamin store. She looked down as she reached for his hand, and shook it less than enthusiastically.

Dotty sensed something right away. "The two of ya know each other, do ya?"

Clara was looking suspiciously at her. The girl turned to Argus with a jealous glare, then looked back at Jenny.

Dotty continued, "Everyone, this is Jenny—er—child, I don't believe I know yer surname."

"I'm Jenny Crandell," she said. "It's nice to meet you all."

Breakfast was due to be served in only ten minutes, so Jenny offered to help out in any way necessary. The food was carried into the dining room, where four other boarders waited. Soon the huge buffet table was heaped with breakfast goodies. Scrambled eggs. Thick ham steaks, a huge plate of bacon, and another platter overflowing with sausages. Platters stacked with pancakes and waffles. Another with orange slices, melon pieces, and grapes of nearly every kind. A basket of slices of different kinds of bread, all toasted to perfection. Jellies, jams, preserves, real butter, and pancake syrups of every flavor. A huge tray of pastries, muffins, and doughnuts. And finally the beverages—a large urn of piping hot coffee, plus pitchers of orange, cranberry, apple, and tomato juices.

The delicious smells of fresh brewed coffee and bacon made Jenny's stomach begin to growl. It had been a long time since last night's slice of cheesecake. She poured herself a cup of coffee. The plates, cups, and glasses were all nice and large. How often she had wanted a huge cup of coffee instead of those dinky cups that barely hold eight ounces. How often she had felt embarrassed at having to get up and refill her cup several times just to get satisfied.

She found the cream and just stood there, feeling ill at ease, holding the pitcher.

"Is there something I can help you find?" Trixie, one of the twins, asked as she doused her generously buttered waffles with thick maple syrup.

"Do you have any nondairy creamer? Or sugar substitute?"

"'Nondairy?' 'Creamer?' 'Sugar substitute?' What's that?"

"Uh—" She glanced over at Argus, remembering but not wanting to repeat the misunderstanding that had happened the afternoon before. "Ahhh—yes, sugar. Here it is," she said loud enough for him to hear. She spooned some into her coffee. "And the cream, yes, real cream." She poured some into her coffee.

She was so hungry, she wanted some of everything. Everyone was helping themselves, and they all seemed to be getting what they wanted, so she took the cue and decided to eat what she really wanted for the first time—at least in public, or since she'd started gaining weight.

Eating what she really wanted was a new concept for Jenny, as she usually only ate what she felt she deserved, based on what the scale read that morning or how she felt about herself. If she felt fat, she wouldn't allow herself to indulge in anything she deemed fattening or naughty.

Still, she felt as if everyone was watching what she chose. *If I take too many sweets, they'll think "no wonder she's fat."* But this was an automatic thought pattern; today she stopped it before it even got going. *No, they won't. Some of these people are even fatter than I am.*

She still felt self-conscious, however, and took only modest portions. She could decide later if she would eat more based on whether anyone else got up for seconds. Feeling shy, she sat down and began to eat.

After everyone in the room had finally moved through the line and sat down, Dotty seemed to remember that there were still some folks that had not been introduced. Jenny was lifting a forkful of pancakes to her mouth when Dotty caught her off guard. "Jenny Crandell."

Jenny choked on her pancakes.

Dotty continued, pointing at each person. "This is Lidia Orozco, Maddison Colby, Theodore Chiang, and Dwyre Kendall."

Jenny remembered seeing two of them working in the bakery the night before. She swallowed her mouthful of pancakes. "Pleased to meet you all," she sputtered. She looked up to see Argus staring at her from across the huge table. Her glance did not interrupt his gaze. He grinned at her, and then returned to his plate.

Jenny took another, slightly smaller bite of pancake. Now feeling a tad uncomfortable, she ate carefully, as if she were on display, trying not to spill anything or look too hungry or get anything on her face. This was how she usually ate in front of people, as if she knew she should not be eating at all. Every time she looked up, however, Argus was looking her way. Now she *really* felt uncomfortable, especially because Clara's glare had given her a strong hint that she was the girlfriend Argus had referred to yesterday at the nutrition supplement and vitamin store.

"So, Jenny," he finally inquired, "tell us, where have you been hiding yourself? I've never seen you around here before."

A hush fell over the room. Everyone looked at Jenny as if they were all wondering the same thing.

"She's my friend's daughter from out of state," Dotty said. "She's just visitin' fer awhile. So ya just stop bein' so nosey, Argus. Land sakes, son, a body might think you've never seen a pretty girl before."

As the room erupted with laughter Charlie nudged Argus, and Clara glared at Jenny over her coffee cup. Jenny blushed again. Everyone seemed to be enjoying their food, and the people who hadn't helped prepare the breakfast seemed especially appreciative.

"Don't worry. It'll be yer turn to cook soon enough," Dotty told the four who hadn't helped prepare breakfast.

Some of the boarders stood up and got seconds; they ate as much as they wanted. Argus, particularly, seemed to be eating a lot. Because he was on the thin side, it seemed to be expected of him to eat more than anyone else. Clara, too, who was encouraged to eat more so she could get bigger, accepted the others' comments good-naturedly.

Jenny, on the other hand, felt anxious about eating such rich food and tried to be conservative with the butter, the cream, and the syrups and jams. She would have liked to have more bacon, but she didn't want to appear wanton and insatiable. Even though she wasn't quite full, she decided not to eat any more and put her plate in the dirty dish bin before anyone else had finished. A few people looked her way and wondered in whispers what the problem was. "Have a little more, child?" Dotty asked her.

"No, I'm quite full," she lied, holding her stomach.

Three of the boarders who hadn't helped prepare the breakfast soon finished eating, excused themselves, and went into the bakery to relieve the clerks on duty so they could come in and eat breakfast.

Dotty caught them as they picked up plates from the buffet table. "Delia Levington, Alana Girdwood, and Ramsey Whittaker, meet Jenny Crandell."

"Nice to meet you all. It looked like you were pretty busy out there."

"A tour bus from Rotundicut came through this morning and nearly cleaned us out of glazed doughnuts," Delia replied. "Charlie and Hank had to make more."

Rotundicut. Could that be their version of Connecticut? Jenny wondered.

"Are ya sure ya don't want more to eat, child?" Dotty asked her. "Have some more coffee and one of my doughnuts. You'll be swearin' they're made with somethin' sinful." The old woman laughed.

"Okay. Maybe one," Jenny conceded. She poured herself more coffee, added cream and sugar, and took a doughnut from the ravaged pastry tray. As she sat back down, Argus was watching her again.

When breakfast was over, those who had not helped cook cleared away the food and took the dishes into the kitchen. The others sat chatting with Dotty about the Festival Fatropolis with eager anticipation.

"I can't wait to see Flint Mackelroy," Dixie said.

Trixie giggled. "I saw him five years ago at the Festival, and I think he's fattened up a little more this year. Oh, he is such a hearty hunk!" Some of the other women laughed in agreement.

Jenny had always thought Flint Mackelroy was a great singer, but she had never felt attracted to him. It seemed strange to her now that fat Flint could be considered a heartthrob.

"Well," Dotty said, "we've got a lot to do today to prepare fer the booth at the Festival." She looked at Hank and Charlie. "And we should get started now. The rest of ya, off to work with ya." She shooed them out of the dining room by waving her arms as if herding a flock of chickens out of the coop.

As everyone filed out Jenny lagged behind, not knowing what to do. Argus lagged as well. They arrived at the door at the same time and found themselves alone in the room. He picked up a napkin and gently wiped a speck of chocolate from Jenny's mouth. When he grinned at her, she felt a warm glow.

She blushed, embarrassed that she had obvious evidence of her indulgence on her face, and grabbed the napkin out of his hand. Turning away, she began scrubbing at her face. Suddenly she felt a hand on her shoulder.

"I didn't mean to embarrass you," he said. "I would appreciate someone wiping my face for me."

"Uh—I'm sorry I made such a scene yesterday at your store," she said. "I didn't realize—" She stopped. For some reason she didn't want him to know she was from the other place.

"No harm done," he said calmly. "I hope you found what you were looking for."

"Well—I guess you could say that." She looked away.

In just two days she already had conflicted feelings about him. She thought it was cute the way he stared at her. Impossible, but cute. Even though he seemed to be smitten with her, she felt fat and old around him. She couldn't imagine ever keeping company with such a young man—such a gorgeous man. If they ever got together, she would constantly feel self-conscious. Her flaws would stand out in contrast to his perfect physique. Besides, he already had a girlfriend. A much younger, much thinner girlfriend.

Suddenly that girlfriend came through the door. "Gus, what's going on?" Clara asked. "You gonna get going to work pretty soon?"

It was an awkward moment. Clara's question jolted Argus out of his trance, and he reluctantly left with her.

A few of the boarders stayed behind to help with the cleanup and start preparing for lunch. As Jenny soon found out, lunch during the week was not the feast they had to prepare on the weekends, as more than half the boarders had jobs elsewhere. Some worked at the bakery for their room and board, however, and were content to hang around the boarding house night and day. Trixie had a job in upper Fathattan, but her sister was one who liked to help Dotty in the bakery and would take on any role where help was needed.

After Argus and Clara had left together, Jenny entered the kitchen and caught Dotty alone for a moment. "Dotty, do you have a scale?" Jenny asked hopefully.

Dotty pointed across the kitchen—the only scale was one used for measuring flour and sugar for the bakery.

"No," Jenny said. "I mean a regular bathroom scale. One for me. So I can weigh myself."

"Why are ya wantin' to weigh yerself?" the baker asked. "Are ya about to be sold at auction?" With that, she gave a hearty laugh. Several of the boarders came into the kitchen to find out what the joke was. "Scales are fer measurin' ingredients fer the bakery, not people," Dotty added. "And if I catch ya sittin' on my bakery scale, I'm goin' to have a stern talk with ya."

Everyone laughed except Jenny.

JENNY FELT OUT OF PLACE. Everyone else was cleaning or running to help in the bakery. She didn't know what to do to help, and having just been scolded, didn't want to bother Dotty anymore. She took the opportunity to sneak back to her room and soak in the tub again. Jenny was in love with that bathtub. When she soaked in it she felt like a pampered princess.

She thought she had only been soaking for twenty minutes when she was startled by the knock at her door. She felt ashamed to be caught in the tub. "Just a minute," she called.

Apparently Dotty had not heard Jenny's reply from the bathroom, as she opened the door with her key and walked into the room, looking around. When she peered into the bathroom she found Jenny in the tub with her hair pinned up on top of her head.

"Land sakes, child. Yer in the bathtub? Fer the last hour you've had all of us runnin' around like a pack of hounds lookin' fer ya. Ya had me worryin' somethin' might've happened. I even sent someone out to the street."

"I'm sorry, Dotty, I must have dozed off. I'll get out. But I'm just in love with this tub," Jenny said, pulling the shower curtain. "You can come in now."

Dotty entered the bathroom slowly and sat down on the toilet lid. "I'm not sure I quite understand what ya mean."

"Do you have any idea how wonderful this tub is? Have you ever tried to bathe in a tub that's too small?"

"No, I can't say as I have," Dotty replied.

"That's what the tubs are like in my world," Jenny told her. "Like fat people don't deserve to soak in a tub, for crying out loud. We can't enjoy the movies at some theaters because the seats are too narrow, we can't sit in most restaurant booths because the table's too close, and we can't wipe ourselves clean in those tiny little public bathroom stalls. And then when we go home, we can't even soak in the bathtub. It's criminal."

"I didn't know that," Dotty said in a quiet voice. "I love to soak in a hot tub myself. I think I'd be a little daft if I couldn't indulge in a good soak now and again."

"Exactly," Jenny said to the shower curtain as she batted at a few bubbles. "Do you know," she said a moment later, "it's been over a year since I soaked like this? Well, before last night, that is."

"Child, that's a shame." Dotty stood up and walked out of the bathroom. "Soak in there as long as ya want to. We'll make do till ya get done."

Jenny heard the door to her room close and lock as Dotty left. Despite having permission to loiter in the bath, she finished fairly quickly, dressed, and went back downstairs.

She felt a little awkward going back into the kitchen with her hair still wet around the edges. She thought everyone would be busy working and she could just slip back in without anyone noticing. But it was not at all like that. Everyone was on some sort of break, all of them standing around the kitchen talking, and a few eating. As Jenny cracked the door and peeked in, she got a cheer.

"Welcome back," Dotty shouted. "Here's our Lady of Leisure."

Everyone laughed again. Those eating held up their doughnuts and muffins to toast her.

Blushing, Jenny came in. So much for her dramatic soliloquy about how tough it was to live in her world and not be able to take baths.

"Grab yerself a little somethin' from the bakery, if ya like," Dotty said, "and then get to work peelin' those boiled potatoes fer the potato salad."

Jenny went into the bakery and asked Alana for a glazed twist. Walking back into the kitchen, she thought, *well, that's two doughnuts within a few hours—I wonder how many calories that is.* She was still hungry from not eating enough at breakfast, so she finished the whole thing.

Dixie was slicing lunch meats and arranging the slices on a platter along with cheeses of almost every kind. They had meal preparations down to a science, Jenny was learning. Everyone worked well together. There were never any disagreements.

Dixie turned to her. "That new movie with Josie Hanover and Eddie Sandoval is coming out tonight. It looks like it'll be really good. A bunch of us are going to see it. Wanna come with us, Jenny?"

Dotty, who was across the kitchen, looked over at Jenny and nodded that she should go.

"Why, uh—sure, Dixie. I saw the preview on TV last night. I think it'll be a good one. I'd love to go. Thanks for the invite." She looked back for Dotty's approval, but when Dotty nodded Jenny was instantly filled with a sense of dread. In the past eight years, since she had put on the majority of her weight, she had resigned herself to waiting until movies came out on video so she could watch them comfortably at home. That way she didn't have to worry about whether she would fit in the theater seat. *Well,* she thought, *it might not be that way here in Fatropolis.*

Jenny peeled all the potatoes, her mouth watering as she thought of potato salad. Bread was baking, making the kitchen very warm, and soon she started to sweat. The smell of the bread was heavenly.

The loaves came out of the oven and were set on large racks to cool. Dotty separated some of the loaves to be sliced for lunch, and within minutes Dixie was arranging lettuce leaves, slices of onions, tomatoes, and pickles on a large plate. Dotty handed Jenny a huge bowl of hard-boiled eggs to peel and chop, which were added to the potatoes along with mayonnaise, a little mustard, and some chopped dill pickle and celery. Dotty came by from time to time and doused the mixture with herbs, salt, and pepper. Jenny was really working up a sweat now, stirring the big bowl with a huge spoon.

"Now for my secret ingredient." Dotty signaled for her workers to turn their backs, but Jenny glanced over just as she sprinkled pickle juice over the bowl. Dotty stirred the juice in and tasted the salad. She picked up a spoon from a small bucket of clean spoons nearby and offered a heaping spoonful to Jenny. "Taste it, child."

Jenny accepted the sample and leaned back against the countertop. This was positively the best potato salad she had ever had the pleasure of eating. She couldn't wait for lunch. Even after eating her second doughnut, she was already hungry again.

Dotty ran the cooled bread through a big slicer and stacked the slices on another plate. As the food was carried into the dining room, she called everyone to come in.

Lidia and Maddison had been outside watering plants, pulling weeds, and hosing down walkways. Because Theodore had been working in the bakery, Dotty spelled him so he could come in and eat. He was allowed to be first in the buffet line. Next Dotty called to Charlie and Hank to cart in the huge urn of iced tea that had been steeping for most of the morning. Also on the cart were a big bowl of ice and two pairs of tongs. Dotty had thought of everything. There was ham, turkey, and roast beef on the platter that Dixie had arranged, along with bowls of mayonnaise and mustard for the sandwiches. The cheese platter was beautiful, with all the yellow and orange slices arranged to please the eye before pleasing the palate.

But Jenny still felt self-conscious, aware that everyone knew that while they were working she had been soaking in the bathtub, so she stayed back in the line. Everyone already knew she was fat, but she didn't want them to think she was lazy, too, which was an assumption often made of fat people in her world. When it was her turn she made herself a sandwich, slathering mayonnaise on the fresh-baked bread and piling on roast beef, cheese, tomatoes, and lettuce. After grabbing a few pickle slices she scooped a helping of potato salad, then helped herself to a glass of iced tea with lots of ice and sugar. Cold and sweet, just how she liked it.

She sat down next to Dixie and enjoyed every mouthful of lunch. She also enjoyed watching the others eat.

Compared to Dixie, she felt thin. Theodore, too, was quite large, and Jenny caught herself staring at him, as it was not often she had seen a fat Asian. He was also quite popular with the ladies. Maddison and Lidia were talking about the movie they were going to see that night. The ads promised it to be "the best romantic comedy of the season." When Theodore finished eating and went back out to the bakery, Dotty came in and made herself a plate of food.

The room changed the minute Dotty entered. Festive conversation erupted as her presence enlivened everyone.

"Are you going to go to the movies with us tonight?" Hank asked Dotty.

"No, child. I've got some chores to do to get ready fer the festival. Go and enjoy yer time off, all of ya. I'll be workin' ya plenty tomorrow." As her boarders groaned, Dotty chuckled goodnaturedly. "And I hope yer all goin' out fer dinner tonight, as I won't be cookin,'" she added.

"Yes, we can eat out," Dixie replied.

But that made Jenny uncomfortable. Her bag was back in the other world. She realized she had no money to pay for a movie ticket, much less a restaurant dinner.

After lunch, while the boarders were still sitting around the table, Dotty left the room. Jenny slipped out and followed her to the sitting room. Dotty sat down in an easy chair and took out a piece she was crocheting.

"Dotty," Jenny began in a soft voice, "could I just hang around here tonight? I left my bag in the other place, and I don't feel comfortable—"

"Now that we're alone," Dotty interrupted, "here, take this." She handed Jenny some money. "Take this, child, and get yerself somethin' to eat and go see that movie tonight with the rest of them. And keep the change so ya got somethin' in yer pocket."

Jenny looked at the money. The bill was orange and yellow with a huge face on it. "Dotty, who is this?" she asked.

"Why, that's President Fergus Abernathy, the twenty-ninth President of the United States of America."

"But—but, I live in the United States." Jenny shook her head. "How can *this* be the United States, too? There's no Fatropolis in the United States I live in."

"Fatropolis is another name for the city of New York, *our* City of New York."

When Jenny blinked in incomprehension, Dotty continued. "I'm certainly no expert, child, but our history differs from yers. I'm not sure at what point our worlds diverged, but at some point—well, our histories went in different ways. It might've been sometime before the Great War. No one is sure. My grandfather knew a lot about such things, but when he went to meet his maker, all that knowledge died with him. My mother once said she thought he was keepin' a journal, but after his death she wasn't able to find it."

"Does everyone in this world know about my world? About the portals?"

"A lot of the folks in this world know about yer world. But not all of us. It seems that there are more folks around here that know because the largest concentration of portals to yer world are in Fatropolis. There may be a few in other parts of the world."

"Have you ever gone through the portal?"

"Heavens, no, child. Us older folks think the younger folks are foolish to criss-cross between the worlds. No one knows what caused the portals to open in the first place, and no one knows how long they might be stayin' open." The old woman's expression turned very serious. "When a person criss-crosses to the other world, they might be stuck there fer the rest of their days. What's more, in rare cases, a person goin' from this world into the other world can have some sort of strange reaction that makes 'em look mad. Their constitution is too sensitive for them to travel between the worlds. Why, I've heard that the only thing that can save 'em is to come back as soon as they can."

Jenny blinked again. Would she ever get home? "Speaking of criss-crossing, I noticed that the entertainers playing at the Festival Fatropolis are from my world—"

"Oh, no, child, ya got it all wrong," Dotty interrupted again. "Backwards, in fact. Those fat entertainers may make appearances in yer world, but they were born and raised in this world. That's why they demand so much money in yer world. They never know if they'll go over there and get stuck. The hearty comedians take advantage of the fact that people in yer world think the hearty folk are so funny. They know how to work the brainwashin' to their own advantage."

Jenny was astounded. The fat entertainers were from this world? Her mind started to whirl with possibilities, which led to more questions. "About the brainwashing—"

"What about it?" Dotty's crocheting picked up speed as she looked down at her work.

"What happened to make it start?"

Ignoring the question, Dotty merely said, "As a matter of fact, dearie, here, take another thirty." She took another bill out of her apron pocket and handed it to Jenny. "Get yerself a purse or a handbag while yer out, so ya don't look so conspicuous."

"Dotty, that's very generous of you. Thank you. I'm not feeling quite right about taking your money, but—thank you." Unspoken was another question. *Why didn't Dotty want to talk about the brainwashing?*

"Don't ya be feelin' bad about takin' my money, child. I have plenty, and—and no—grand—babies to spend it on." Dotty began counting stitches and fiddling with her yarn.

"Do you have any children?" Jenny asked.

"Yes, child. God blessed me and Mr. O'Flannigan with a son. But he's no longer with us." As tears welled up in her eyes, Dotty turned her head. "Get goin' now," she said in a voice that was too loud. "Shoo! Off with ya."

Jenny knew she had struck a nerve. She hurried back to the dining room and burst through the door, which startled the boarders still sitting around the table. She sat down by Dixie and took a deep breath. Within seconds the others got up and started to clean up the lunch dishes. Jenny also stood up and picked up a bowl and some flatware, trying to look busy. Everyone soon cleared out of the dining room, leaving Dixie and Jenny alone.

"What happened?" Dixie asked.

"I—I think I upset Dotty."

"How?"

"Oh, I asked her if she had any children."

"Oops!"

"Then she told me that her son had died."

"No," Dixie replied. "He isn't dead."

"But she said he's no longer with us."

"What she meant," Dixie said in a quiet voice, "is that he's no longer *here.* He's no longer *here in Fatropolis.*"

Jenny's jaw dropped. "Where did he go?"

Dixie peeked out of the dining room door to make sure Dotty was not within earshot, and whispered, "He crossed through a portal." She continued cleaning crumbs off the table. "I can't say as I blame him, though. Aunt Dotty was always after him trying to fatten him up and—"

"Dotty is your aunt?"

"Yes. Her husband and my mother were brother and sister. Anyway, she just couldn't accept that he couldn't get any heartier. Her whole side of the family was just *nuts* about wanting everyone to be hearty. I guess that's what happens when you have a family member die of being thin like Dotty's grandmother did. Poor soul."

Jenny began wiping the dining room table with an abandoned napkin. "Has Dotty ever heard from her son?"

"And how would that happen?" Dixie replied. "You know as well as I do that there's no mail service that goes between the worlds." Dixie was quiet for a minute. "I suspect he likes it there and he settled in and stayed. God knows. As thin as he was—he probably found a woman over there who would give him the time of day. Poor guy. I used to feel sorry for him, he was so gangly and tall." Remembering her cousin, Dixie smiled fondly. "One of our friends that criss-crosses all the time told us he thought he saw my cousin with a woman, but that was—oh, three or four years ago now."

"How many years has it been since he left?"

"Well, I think he's been gone about ten years. He hung in there until he was about twenty-five, I think, and when he couldn't get any girls to take him seriously, well, he just gave up. Like I said, I don't blame him. I wouldn't live in a place either that kept giving me messages that I'm not okay, if I had the choice."

Jenny was too stunned to say anything, thinking of her own circumstances.

"Well, Aunt Dotty just found a note from him one day. It said he was leaving and probably wouldn't be back. He had to make a life for himself somewhere. Fatropolis was not the place for him." Dixie wiped away a tear. "Aunt Dotty has always blamed herself. And then Uncle Nevan died less than a year later, and she really blamed herself after that. That's probably why she got upset." She paused again. "Gosh, my cousin must be in his mid-thirties by now." She shook her head and stood up. "Well, enough about that."

The two girls took the last of the dishes into the kitchen. Jenny followed behind Dixie, hoping Dotty wouldn't notice her. But Dotty was busy talking to Charlie about the booth they had planned for the Festival.

"You sure you won't change your mind and go with us tonight, Aunt Dotty?" Dixie asked.

"I don't mean to sound testy," the baker replied, "but I've got a lot of things to do to prepare fer the Festival."

Charlie gave Dotty a suspicious look, but he didn't say anything.

CHAPTER 6
FAT PEOPLE IN
THEATER SEATS

BY LATE AFTERNOON THE WORKING BOARDERS BE-
gan arriving home. They all disappeared to their rooms to get
ready for their night out.

Jenny, too, escaped to her room after Dotty had dismissed everyone from
their kitchen duties. While soaking in the tub she thought about how sad it
was that Dotty had lost everyone in her family. Thinking about Dotty and
her dilemma almost rendered her unable to enjoy her long soak. Her dread
about going out seemed to have dissipated, but now she couldn't figure out
if it was actual excitement about going out or just relief that she didn't have
to stay at the boarding house alone with Dotty. She still had many questions
about Fatropolis, the portals, and this world she was enjoying.

Suddenly a voice came over the intercom announcing that the excursion
to dinner and a movie would be leaving in a half hour. Jenny had to hurry.
She hopped out of the tub, dressed in a hurry, being careful to remember the
money Dotty had given her for the evening, and practically ran down the
stairs to meet the others.

A crowd was slowly growing in the parlor as one by one all the boarders
appeared. Argus seemed particularly eager to go out on the town with all the
ladies. Everyone was assigned a group to stick with, which made Jenny feel
more comfortable about going. She was particularly interested in knowing
the group she would be in, as she was uneasy about not knowing her way
around or how she would get back or even communicate with someone if
she got lost. She had discussed the plans with the others and knew that they

would all go on the subway. She was an old hand at the New York subway system, but didn't know what to expect from the trains in *this* New York.

Finally the crowd set off to the nearest subway stop. As they left, Jenny picked up one of Dotty's business cards. Just having the card in her pocket made her feel more secure. She tripped over the uneven tile in the office floor again, but this time caught herself.

Once outside the boarders filed along the sidewalk, trying to stay together, the men walking ahead and talking about their day and what they were going to eat at the restaurant. The women walked slower, also chatting as they went along. Trixie and Dixie were engaged in a spirited discussion about Flint Mackelroy and how he compared in heartiness to an actor named Slade Barringer. Jenny liked Slade Barringer, too, and thought him an accomplished actor, but heard Trixie say she was attracted to his "sexy physique." Although Jenny was starting to get used to the different way men and women gauged sex appeal in Fatropolis, she kept quiet and listened to the conversations around her. She knew if she cut loose with *her* idea of sexy, the other girls would stare at her in disbelief.

The sights reminded Jenny of her familiar New York City, except that there were fat people everywhere, coming out of and going into every building—walking, sitting, pushing strollers, walking dogs, driving, doing everything that people do in their lives. A fat woman sat on a bus bench burping her baby while her big and tall husband wrangled their husky little boy.

Before they had even walked a couple of blocks Argus looked back at Jenny two or three times and smiled. She tried not to look at him, but his gaze was hard to ignore. While she didn't want to lead him on, she thought the attention from such a good-looking young man was fun to entertain. Clara seemed very quiet tonight. Jenny could tell she had low self-esteem.

Trixie was the leader of the women, and Charlie and Hank were definitely the strong leaders of the group, imparting a no-nonsense presence that set Jenny at ease. The boarders were starting to grow on her. She sensed they were a good bunch of people.

They soon reached the station, and all descended to the subway on the escalator. As they approached the turnstiles Jenny stuck her prune-skinned hand into her pocket to get her money out, but Charlie saw her and said, "Put that back, I've got it."

"Thanks." Jenny put her money back.

The group boarded the uptown train and found seats, though not all together. Jenny found herself sitting next to a fat old man with a beard. The seats in this subway car were nice and large, and there were plenty of handles and bars to hang on to. There was also a scrolling announcement board above their heads that showed what the next stop was.

The doors closed and the train lurched forward. It seemed to take the train a long time to build up momentum, and it moved much slower than the trains in her New York. The train went up and out, and soon they were on elevated rails above the city streets.

Jenny carefully kept her eye on the others, still afraid of getting lost. "What stop are we getting off at?" she asked Trixie, who was sitting across from her. The train was turning left.

"Port Copious near the Hudson River," Trixie answered. "They have a wonderful seafood restaurant where you can see the water. It's called The Stout Trout. The whole place is done in a pirate theme—the men are so handsome, with their eye patches and all—it's wonderful. You'll love it."

Jenny turned to study the diagram on the wall of the car, which showed all the stops on their route. There were only three more stops before their destination. Compared to her New York, it seemed to take twice as long for them to get half as far.

The train went back underground. They finally reached Port Copious, at which point the boarders got off the train. At this station she was delighted to find another functioning escalator, next to the stairs. A fat old lady with a cane was hobbling over to board the escalator. They all got on, going up behind her, and Charlie asked, "Are you happy about something, Jenny?"

"Do you have escalators at *every subway stop* here?"

"Yeah," he replied nonchalantly.

"And they all *work?*"

"Yeah." He looked at her, puzzled.

Jenny giggled with delight. "Well, isn't that something." She thought about home, where only some of the stations had escalators and everyone was used to taking the stairs.

Moments later the old lady arrived at the top and was having trouble getting her bearings being on solid ground again. She stumbled a little. Hank hurried up the remainder of the escalator steps to help her. Jenny was surprised at his willingness to help a stranger.

They walked along for several blocks. There were a lot of people on the sidewalks, but not as many as in the heart of the city. She was starting to feel hungry and beginning to wonder when they would get to the restaurant. Everyone in the group was now talking about food.

"I didn't realize it was so far to walk," Hank finally admitted. "Maybe we should have taken cabs."

"Just wait," Trixie said. "You'll be able to see the water as soon as we turn that corner up there."

She was right, but it was already getting dark. There were lights on the boats, but little detail was visible. The restaurant was about a hundred yards farther along.

When they arrived at the restaurant about ten minutes early for their reservation, the place was already crowded with hungry patrons. It was a typical fish house—all wood, ropes, and nets, decorated in a nautical theme. A huge, scruffy bearded man wearing a bright bandana greeted them near the door. He looked very convincing as a pirate, with a big knife stuck in the waistband of his pants.

Jenny peered into the main part of the restaurant. Big, bosomy barmaids in wench dresses were delivering huge mugs of ale to the customers. The smell of seafood wafted through the air. The group sat down in the large waiting area until their table was ready. Jenny always felt sorry for the poor lobsters in the tank awaiting their doom.

When they were called, the host apologized for not having a table large enough to accommodate all of them. Would two booths, side by side, be satisfactory?

The idea of a restaurant booth immediately filled Jenny with dread. She hardly ever fit one. She knew how to scope out a booth on the spot and figure out if she would fit before she actually tried to get in it. She had learned to do this fast as she put on her weight, to avoid embarrassing stares from onlookers as she attempted to squeeze into a booth only to have to push herself out again and ask for other arrangements. There had been a few times she had just forced herself into the booth so as not to make a scene, but then had to sit through an excruciating meal feeling that the table was cutting her in two. Sometimes, if the table was not fastened to the floor, she could make the booth easier to bear by asking whomever she was dining with if they wouldn't mind pulling the table a little more toward them. That was what she had done on her date with the young man who had never called back. Was that, she often wondered, why he hadn't called again?

But in this restaurant her friends seemed happy with booths. They followed the host through what seemed like a maze to the other side of the main dining room. As they arrived at their tables, Jenny was pleasantly surprised that there was enough room. All the tables around the perimeter of the restaurant were suspended from the ceiling and attached to a track, allowing the staff to pull the tables away from the booth seats so the pudgy patrons could get comfortable. Once seated, the tables were positioned to stay a comfortable distance from diners' bellies. The suspension cables were anchored to the middle of the tables so they were out of the way.

As everyone chose a seat Argus was obvious in his attempts to manipulate the seating arrangements so he could sit next to Jenny, but she sat down next to Dixie, her best friend so far. Trixie pushed Argus out of the way and sat on the other side of Jenny, telling him to go somewhere else. It seemed as though Trixie did not like the thin man.

Once everyone was comfortably seated, waiters came and adjusted the tables. The men ended up sitting together in one booth, the women in the other. Jenny felt awkward having to sit at the same table as Clara.

Next the curvy, plump serving wench arrived, bosoms burgeoning over the top of her peasant blouse. The men in the party seemed delighted with her. She brought menus and took their drink orders. Soon she appeared again with a huge tray of beverages and baskets of bread, pieces of which could be ripped off the loaves and dipped into dishes of soft butter. As everyone began drinking their beverages and eating the bread, they opened their menus. Jenny loved seafood and was quite hungry by now.

After taking everyone's order, the serving wench was off to the kitchen and her other tables. Hank had told her he wanted his lobster tail extra large and slipped her a bill, which she hastily stuffed in her cleavage. She was very pretty, very round, and very loud. Men all over the restaurant flirted with her, as they did with all the female servers. A rotund male server dressed as a rough-looking pirate strolled over to the ladies' table and started to make comments about how lovely they were. Trixie took the lead in flirtatious banter with the supposed ruffian, who gave the table his undivided attention as the meal progressed. He was adept at gauging when they were in need of refills of both drinks and bread, and he also helped deliver their meals.

Jenny had ordered a thick steak, tender and seasoned to perfection, along with six huge grilled shrimp. She also had a bulging baked potato and steamed vegetables. She loved a good baked potato, oozing with butter and sour cream. Upon receiving her plate she respectfully waited until everyone had theirs and had begun eating, then dug in enthusiastically.

As the boarders were enjoying their food, a scream rang out. Everyone looked up, forks halfway to their mouths, to see one of the serving wenches hurrying through the restaurant. "It's a fight! It's a fight!" she screamed. She pointed at a door through which tumbled two angry pirates.

"Arrrgh," one growled at the other, "I don't know what in blue blazes you thinks you be doin' with me woman, you lily-livered scallywag!"

After some struggling, the first pirate got his hands around the other's throat. "I'm gonna choke the livin' daylights outta ye!"

The two pirates scuffled for several minutes, both shouting threats. Fists flew, and one pirate actually threw the other into a room divider, which broke into pieces. This angered the tossed pirate, and he drew his sword. The first pirate accepted the challenge to a duel and they scrambled around the dining area, thrusting and dodging, even involving some of the patrons in their skirmish.

Oh, Jenny thought, *it's their show.*

Everyone enjoyed both feast and pirate show, and before their meal was over Trixie had the phone number of their waiter.

Trixie and Dixie, although identical twins, were quite different. Trixie loved to flirt and was quite proficient at it, whereas Dixie was more subdued but quietly confident. On many occasions Dixie shook her head at her sister's antics.

Jenny was not allowed to pay for any part of her meal, which made her feel privileged, but also beholden. She was not told who exactly paid for her meal, but she suspected it was one of the men. When the group got up from their tables a few of the boarders, including Trixie, had not finished their plates. They were full, happy, and satisfied, ready for their movie now, and while the servers seemed sorry to see them leave they appeared to be gratified, knowing they had flirted up some good tips.

Jenny and her friends found their way out of the restaurant, murmuring compliments about the wonderful service, the good food, and the madcap pirate show. When Dixie announced that they didn't have much time to get to the theater, her friends immediately protested that they didn't want to walk any faster.

"I don't know about you all," Charlie said, "but I'm taking a cab."

As heads nodded, Charlie and Hank flagged down three cabs and all of the boarders piled in.

In the confusion and shuffle, Argus managed to finagle a spot in the same car as Jenny. Six people could fit comfortably in each cab. Once they were settled, only four of them were in this one. Jenny discovered she was facing Argus, who had apparently ditched Clara. It seemed obvious that he was trying to ignore the girl.

It bothered Jenny that Clara had been very quiet all evening. If not for her own inadvertent arrival in this world, Jenny thought, Clara and Argus would still be a happy couple. Jenny was starting to get annoyed both with Argus's cold attitude toward Clara and his corny attempts to pursue her with his smiles, winks, and longing glances. But she felt confused about him, as she did when any man paid attention to her. She still looked at him as she would a younger brother. *Should I be grateful,* she wondered, *and just go with it, even if I know he's too young and too gorgeous? God knows how long it will be until another man takes pity on me and shows me some affection.*

She pondered all of this over and over, trying to ignore Argus's stares, until they arrived at the theater. She especially didn't want to contemplate entangling herself with a man who was spoken for—she wouldn't like someone doing that to her. That's why the situation made her so uncomfortable.

As soon as everyone reached the theater they were already talking about popcorn and candy. Jenny joined the line near Trixie and Dixie, who were now actively arguing about Slade Barringer. Was he better as an action hero or serious leading man? What everyone else in the group was chattering about, however, was the Festival Fatropolis—what to wear, what booths would be there, Flint Mackelroy and Dewey Henderson, what kind and how much food would be there, and whether the weather would hold up. When someone mentioned Dotty and her plans for getting everything ready for the Festival, someone else chimed in, expressing guilt over leaving her alone tonight with so much to do.

Charlie spoke up. "Dotty would not have appreciated company tonight. Every year Dotty hires that same temporary crew to come in for the day so all of us can help out at the Festival and enjoy ourselves. All the extra dough and batter has already been made, and the crew was due there to take over shortly after we left. The real reason Dotty wanted to make sure we were all out for the evening is because every year since her mother died, the night before the Festival she goes to church and prays for a successful year in her business ventures."

Charlie looked like he knew he shouldn't be sharing all of this about his boss. "She also prays that this will finally be the year she sees her son again. It's kind of a ritual for her. She told me that the Festival Fatropolis always marks a new year for her business and gives her new hope of finally finding out what happened to him."

Jenny felt relieved to hear this, as she, too, felt guilty about leaving Dotty alone.

Jenny had always had an over-developed sense of obligation and duty. She didn't know where it came from, but she sometimes felt that she didn't just have it, she suffered from it as if it were a disease. When Charlie spoke up, therefore, she finally felt she could enjoy the evening. For now she could put all her questions about Fatropolis, the portals, and the brainwashing on a shelf and have a good time at the movie.

Knowing she was going to see a movie she had been looking forward to, that there was a huge bathtub waiting for her, and that tomorrow she would get to see Flint Mackelroy and Dewey Henderson in person all filled her with so much excitement she felt almost giddy.

She finally had a chance to use the money Dotty had given her. She paid for her own ticket at the box office. Everyone who wanted some bought popcorn, soft drinks, and candy.

Finding an empty row of seats so everyone could sit together was pretty much impossible. There were three theaters in the Cineplex showing the same movie, and all three were already filling up. Jenny wanted to stick with the twins, but they had already found a spot and were settling in. She was amazed at how much leg room there was between the rows of seats here. People could pass in front of others freely without having to turn sideways.

Everyone else seemed to have found good seats, and Jenny was beginning to wonder where she could sit when someone waved at her. Her eyes went to Argus, who was sitting with Clara. There was an empty seat next to them. Jenny tried not to make eye contact, but he stood up, came to her and took her arm, insisting that she come along as the theater was filling up fast. His extra seat might be the only seat left.

Jenny looked at Clara and smiled, trying to gauge whether her presence would be welcomed. As Clara returned a half-hearted smile, Jenny reluctantly sat down. Clara was between her and Argus.

"Thanks for letting me join you and Argus," Jenny said to her. She had been expecting the usual big squeeze, but these seats were wide and deep, with arm rests that could be pulled up and out of the way. Fat people were able to sit and enjoy the show without struggling or feeling uncomfortable.

"Don't mention it," Clara muttered flatly.

Jenny could tell that Argus had wanted to be in the middle, but he didn't push the issue. He settled in and made small talk with Clara. Jenny didn't feel too hungry, but smelling the butter and hearing everyone start crunching popcorn as the movie started made her want some. As the opening trailers began, Clara politely offered some of her popcorn to Jenny. She took a handful, said thanks, and sipped on her soda.

As Jenny watched this movie in a fat world, she was amazed to see the culture depicted. Nearly everyone in the film was fat—the leading players, all the character actors, all the extras. There was a mixture of ethnicities, but they had one thing in common—they all were fat. Jenny kept expecting something funny to happen to the fat leading man, for him to slip and land on his behind or for something to fall on him, but nothing comical happened.

Eddie Sandoval gave a moving performance, revealing a side of him she had not seen in his movies in her world. He played a much-too-straight-laced university science professor who was married to a woman (the only thin actress in the movie) who was making his life miserable. Having been brought up in a very strict and religious family, he was henpecked and unable to break away from her for fear of what his mother would think. His character was very funny because of the limitations he put on himself. He seemed not to want to be happy, and because he had no control over his marriage or any other part of his nonprofessional life, he ruled his classes with an iron fist, much to the misery of his students and other faculty at the university.

Josie Hanover turned in another amazing performance. She played the college dean who insisted that Eddie's character change his curriculum to keep up with the changes in his scientific field. He refused to do so, and so the two went to war. The action between them as they clashed helped them see that they were more alike than different. His encounters with Josie also sparked something in his character that would not be extinguished. Soon Eddie realized how miserable his wife made him. Then he figured out how attracted he was to the dean. Eventually, of course, the two leading characters got together. Eddie's character came to several realizations about himself that suddenly reminded Jenny of her own life. The funniest part of the story was when Eddie finally got up the nerve to tell his evil, thin wife he was leaving her. His mother didn't take it well either, but Eddie didn't care. He pressed on and claimed the lady he loved.

Jenny cried at several points in the story and laughed more often. It amazed her that the comedy arose from the characters' interactions with each other, not because they were fat and acting silly as comic relief to the central action of the movie. The actors' performances made Jenny realize how fat actors were constantly used in her world to portray stupidity, laziness, and gluttony.

There was also a love scene between the lead characters, which Jenny could not believe. While the scene was staged tastefully, there were a lot of bare bellies, backs, and thrashing legs in view. Jenny was somewhat taken aback, though this didn't seem to faze anyone else. At several points in the movie, feeling that she just didn't belong here, Jenny began to feel homesick, but at other points, she looked away from the screen at all the fat moviegoers and felt a sense of belonging. One minute she loathed the abundant flesh of her own body and of all the bodies around her, but in the next instant she felt only relief that there were others like her leading happy, productive lives.

The movie opened Jenny's eyes. She left the theater feeling weird and ill at ease, yet happy—and even more smitten with Eddie Sandoval.

When the boarders met up again in the lobby to plan their trip home, Argus announced that he and Clara were taking their own cab back to the boarding house, and that they'd see everyone tomorrow. Clara looked happier than she had all night. Jenny decided to stick with the twins, as it was well after ten o'clock and she didn't want to get lost in this confusing version of New York City.

The gang finally rounded up two cabs and rode six and six to the subway station. They had to wait for a while to catch the next train back to their neighborhood, but they spent the time talking about the movie and how much they had enjoyed it.

The whole evening had been one new experience after another for Jenny. She didn't know how to feel about the movie, but she was glad Argus and Clara were having some alone time together. As the train approached the neighborhood of the boarding house she felt herself longing for another nice warm bath in her wonderful tub. The train ride going home did not seem as long, and it was nearly half past eleven when they arrived back at Dotty's.

As everyone expressed their appreciation for the wonderful evening, Jenny added her thanks to whomever it was that bought her dinner, then headed upstairs to her room. She locked the door and went into the bathroom to prepare her bath. It was a little warm, so she pushed up on the window in her bathroom, opening it a few inches, then undressed and lowered herself into the tub.

With a grin she asked herself if she was starting to get addicted to her baths, but told herself to enjoy them while her time in Fatropolis lasted. She was just settling into the water and thinking how splendid it was when she heard a woman crying in the courtyard below.

Jenny nearly jumped out of the tub. She wrapped a towel around herself, turning off the light so as not to be so obvious in her eavesdropping, and went to the window. She peered down into the courtyard. Two figures were sitting side by side on one of the benches, one crying with her head on the other's shoulder. Jenny recognized Trixie and Clara. The twin had her arm around Clara as she was sobbing into her shoulder.

"I can't believe he dumped me," Clara was saying through her tears. "I just knew he'd leave me for someone heartier. What am I going to do?" She buried her face in Trixie's large bosom.

Jenny could not believe how clearly she could hear their voices.

"You're going to be fine," Trixie said. "You'll find someone else. You two were obviously not meant for each other."

"*Obviously?* What do you mean, obviously?"

"Well, I didn't want to say anything before," Trixie said in a matter-of-fact voice, "but Argus is too thin for you."

Jenny could not believe her ears.

Clara looked at Trixie. "I don't know—I was sorta willing to overlook that."

"Clara, think about it." Trixie turned to face her and gently put her hands on her shoulders. "You're barely plump enough to be considered hearty yourself—" She was interrupted by Clara's defensive gasp "—and then you marry him and start losing, then before you know it you get pregnant and have no reserves for the child, and then he becomes a laughingstock of the community because he can't keep you hearty enough. And what about the children? What if they take after *him?* Do you want a bunch of little beanpoles running around?" Ignoring Clara's defensive protests, she plowed right on. "Then someday you have to console your children because no one wants to marry them because they're too skinny. Or maybe you start a whole new line of thin folks who have to move to the other place to find any happiness. Even if *one* of your kids turned out to be thin and had to move to the other place, you know that would devastate you. Right? Wouldn't it? Do you want that, Clara? Huh?"

Clara was silent for several moments. "I know, I know," she finally admitted. "You sound just like my parents. But you don't have to be so hard on him. He can't help it that he's thin." She gulped, then began crying again. "But you *can* be hard on him for dumping me."

"Oh, puh-leeze," Trixie replied. "He could beef up if he really wanted to. I don't understand why you're so upset—it's not like he's some handsome, hearty hunk who dumped you. Hah! You just let Jenny have at him. Let her worry about whether he'll survive into old age with that bag of bones he calls a physique." She gave her friend's shoulders a sympathetic shake. "Try to get ahold of yourself now, Clara. This is for the best. It really is. Give yourself a couple of weeks and you won't even know he exists."

They stood up. Trixie hugged Clara and then affectionately brushed her hair away from her face. "You just gain a few pounds," she suggested, "and you'll have all the hearty young men in town eating out of your hand." There was another hug, and the two women went inside.

Jenny stood there in her towel, flabbergasted. She could not believe the conversation she just overheard. Even with everything she had already seen in Fatropolis, it amazed her. Objecting to a man because he was thin? She could only shake her head. What's more, she could not believe Argus had broken up with Clara during their ride home. She shook her head again. It seemed as though it would be understood by one and all that Jenny would be his next girlfriend. She could only assume Argus must have said something to Clara about her. She started to feel angry. She felt sorry for Clara, as she, too—on too many occasions—had been the one on the same end of such a breakup— well, in high school.

She pushed down on the window to close it, smacked the light back on, tromped back to the tub, threw her towel down, and plopped back into the water. "Yuck! It's cold." She turned the hot water faucet on and lay back, pondering the conversation and planning what she would say to Argus when she saw him again.

TRACEY L. THOMPSON

AFTER HER LONG SOAK Jenny lay in bed, still pondering her evening and trying to watch *The Heavy Harvey Show* to relax. All the events of the evening were spinning around in her head. She was looking forward to the Festival Fatropolis, but dreaded having to face Trixie, Clara, and Argus in the morning. Then she remembered that Dotty was upset with her, too, which brought additional unease to the pit of her stomach.

Sometime after two in the morning the thought occurred to her that no one knew she had overheard the conversation between Trixie and Clara. That was a relief. She didn't have to dread anything. She could just pretend not to know about the breakup and let them tell her. Yes, that would work.

The show had changed on the television—the same evangelist as the night before was praying before his rotund flock of parishioners. Jenny left that channel on and fell asleep. It had been a very long day.

CHAPTER 7
ACTUARIAL TABLES
FOR TWO

JENNY WAS STILL DREAMING ABOUT A FAT PIRATE with a huge parrot perched on his shoulder when the call to breakfast sounded from the intercom and woke her up. She didn't know what to expect if she saw Clara or Trixie, or especially Argus, but she knew there would be no time for drama or lollygagging today. She dressed in one of the pants outfits she'd found in the closet, slipped her shoes on, combed her hair, brushed her teeth, went downstairs and walked straight into the kitchen, resolving not to let anything that had happened last night bother her today.

Dotty seemed to be in a pretty good mood, so Jenny asked her what needed to be done to help with breakfast.

"Today's omelet day," Dotty told her. "Ya can help with the omelets."

Jenny made a three-egg omelet for each boarder, and could not believe the heap of eggshells that resulted. She piled the omelets in a warming pan and took them to the dining room just in time for everyone to start serving themselves. The omelets disappeared quickly, and everyone gave Jenny rave reviews. She ate her own omelet, plus bacon, toast, and coffee, and then indulged in another one of Dotty's doughnuts. She was feeling more comfortable with life in Fatropolis now, and she was also feeling less self-conscious, though she had no idea how the situation with Argus would play out. As she ate she decided to relax and let it go until she had to deal with it.

The dining room was abuzz with excited chatter about the Festival and Flint Mackelroy. As breakfast ended the food and dishes were cleared away and everyone seemed to be hustling faster than usual.

Dotty assigned each boarder one of the many tasks on her list. Trays of pastries, doughnuts, muffins, cookies, and brownies, along with crates and boxes of refrigerated beverages, were taken to the delivery truck bound for the Festival. When Dotty asked Jenny to ride with her and a few of the other women, Jenny felt a little uncomfortable to see that Trixie would be riding with Dotty, too.

Dotty owned a huge passenger van that was usually driven by Hank. The seats were roomy and comfortable, and unlike seatbelts back at home these seatbelts easily went around everyone, even the twins, and the buckles were longer and easier to hook the belts into. There was also more legroom in this van than any other vehicle she had ever been in. The make and model of the van were not familiar to Jenny. It was a Chrysalis Vast Van—very luxurious, with leather seats, tinted windows, and the capacity to carry ten large passengers. Jenny could hardly believe how comfortable it was, how the seats seemed to be made just for people of her size, or bigger. She couldn't hide her enthusiasm. The others in the van looked at one another, puzzled, surprised at Jenny's reaction.

"Stop yer carryin' on, child," Dotty finally said. "Everyone's seen a Vast Van before." She seemed not to want the other boarders to know that Jenny was from the other place.

"I—I—usually ride the bus or the train," Jenny murmured. She wondered if Dotty was still upset about what had happened the previous afternoon.

The boarders who did not ride in Dotty's van traveled to the Festival in their own cars or rode the bus and met Dotty and company there. The ride took about fifteen minutes. They passed the Fat Cat Amphitheater, a restaurant named Los Gorditos Redondos, and a host of clothing boutiques, shoe stores, hot food takeout places, pizza parlors, and hobby shops, as well as grocery stores, gas stations, and at least one weight-gain center. Jenny gazed out the windows, then would catch someone staring at her and would clear her throat and look down. But within a few moments she'd be taking in the sights of this new world again. It was taking her some time to become accustomed to seeing all the fat people out on the streets going about their lives.

Jenny felt as if she were arriving at the royal palace of Fatropolis when they arrived at the Festival grounds, which occupied the same space as Central Park in her New York City. Huge shiny gates guarded the entrance to this wonderland where Jenny would soon see one of her favorite singers and his band, up close and in person. Service vehicles and delivery trucks were waved in one after the other. A short distance inside the gates all the vehicles were herded aside as a huge black limousine passed.

"That must be Flint Mackelroy!" Trixie squealed. "Oh, what I wouldn't give to be sitting right there beside him." As she swooned, her sister and friends giggled.

Once inside the gates the van drove slowly for another ten minutes or so. Jenny could feel excitement welling up in her stomach. There were booths with flags, awnings, tents, and drapes of every color as far as the eye could see. Each booth was decorated in a unique and appealing way. Hundreds of fat people were milling around, preparing for the opening. Jenny felt as if she had gone back in time, as some of the booths looked Celtic, others were Greek or Roman, some Oriental, and others looked like movie sets.

Dotty's crew worked tirelessly to get the bakery's booth ready for the influx of shoppers, setting up glass cases for the baked goods and tables for the bags of bread. It was like the bakery away from the bakery. They had even brought in a solar-powered glass cash register—which according to the boarders had already been outdated years ago—and a refrigerator for the milk, juices, and soft drinks. Gold drapes lined the inside of the awning that covered the booth, and transparent, silky curtains blew to and fro in the breeze, appealing to the romantic side of passersby and inviting them to come in and soothe their cravings for sweet baked goods and refreshing beverages. Small bistro tables with large comfortable chairs sat outside the booth, inviting Festival goers to sit and rest their feet.

Jenny looked at the other booths around them. Vendors were still hauling in every sort of goods imaginable—clothing and costumes, jewelry, furniture, area rugs, gadgets, appliances, pottery, wood carvings, paintings, books, collectibles, beauty products, games and toys, bedding, and an endless array of food and drink. Jenny saw a few scantily clad fat women who were similarly dressed in bright colors, their garments made of gorgeous silky material, their shoes hanging over their shoulders—it was obvious they were performers. These women were hurrying along as if they were late. Other performers also crossed in front of the bakery booth, including fat men in satin sequin-studded suits, chubby children clickety clacking by in tap shoes, exotic dark-haired beauties with veils covering their bulging midriffs, and a huge clown with a fat dog wearing a cute little hat.

When the bakery booth was completely set up the crew disbanded, telling Dotty they would be back for their appointed shifts. Soon Dotty and Jenny were alone in the booth.

"Child," Dotty began, "I'm sorry about snappin' at ya that way in the van, but ya gotta be careful who ya let onto that yer from the other place. Not everyone will welcome ya with open arms like I have."

"Why? Are some people afraid of the other place?"

"I don't know if I'd go so far as to say they're *afraid,* so much as they don't want the prejudice against the hearty folk of yer world to be rubbin' off on any of the folks in ours. Like I said before, we're fat and happy and we aim to keep it that way." Dotty loved to laugh at her own comments.

"Dotty, I'm sorry I upset you yesterday afternoon."

"Don't think anythin' of it, child. Sometimes I can be oversensitive in my old age."

"Well, I didn't mean to talk about such a sensitive subject. Next time, just tell me to hush." Jenny paused. "And by the way, thank you again for the money you gave me yesterday." She hoped she was back in Dotty's good graces. "I had a wonderful time last night with the others."

"I had a nice evenin' myself," Dotty replied. There was a slight smile on her face.

"I still have a lot of questions about this place," Jenny said after a moment. She was feeling more comfortable around fat people, but she still wanted to know where on Earth she was. "I really would like to know more about the prejudice and the brainwashing you were talking about—if you have any time. Could we sit down and talk about it sometime?" Jenny felt she didn't have anything to lose by simply asking.

"Well," Dotty turned away to spread a tablecloth on one of the tables, "do ya know how the prejudice against the fat folk started in yer world?"

"Uhh, well, I'm embarrassed to say it, but no." Jenny picked up a tablecloth and spread it on the next table.

"Ya mean ya don't know anythin' about the insurance company in yer world that put out the actuarial tables in the 1940s?"

"Actuarial tables? What's that?"

"Ya know. The mortality tables? That include ratio tables that measure a body's height compared to weight?" Dotty spoke carefully, as if she thought Jenny was slow to understand what everybody knew.

Jenny looked confused. "But I thought it was the doctors who put out the height-to-weight-ratio tables," she said.

"No, child. It was an insurance company."

"But why would an insurance company want to get into the business of telling people what they should weigh?"

Instead of answering this question, Dotty said, "After a while, the doctors just adopted the insurance company's height-to-weight-ratio tables as law." Her voice was rising. "And that's where it all began."

"How do you know all this, Dotty? If you're from here?"

"There's a lot to the story, child." Dotty looked at her watch. "We haven't the time right now, and this isn't the place to be talkin' about it. Maybe we can sit down tomorrow and discuss it. When we're not so busy."

Even though she had gotten a little bit of the puzzle, Jenny still felt put off. She still didn't understand what that point in the history of her world could possibly have to do with Dotty's world. A sense of determination swept over her. She would not let it rest until she heard the whole story.

EXCITEMENT WAS BUILDING INSIDE and outside the huge gates as eleven o'clock approached. As soon as the gates swung open, people poured in. Jenny had signed up to staff the bakery booth at one o'clock, but she didn't feel quite comfortable leaving Dotty alone. At the same time, however, she was determined to see all the wonderful booths at the Festival. Well, there were two helpers here now, and people were starting to come and buy the baked goods.

Jenny headed for the first booth that caught her eye. Not far from the bakery was what appeared to be an Egyptian throne room with huge statues of Isis and Nefertiti. Beautiful wide necklaces, headbands, bracelets and anklets were on display. All the jewelry was much too expensive, so she merely thanked the vendor and walked on.

It almost felt good to be by herself and take in the sights. She passed booth after booth, gawking at everything she saw. She passed one filled with paintings of wooded areas, lakes, and beaches, then paintings of women, too, all of them wearing almost nothing or nude. They looked like the old-fashioned paintings of fat women in her world, draped with silk scarves and lying gracefully on grassy beds. There were angels in other paintings and goddesses in still others. Every feminine figure was round-bodied, smooth-skinned, and lovely.

Next, Jenny passed a vendor selling statues, the most popular ones showing plump women and fat couples embracing or kissing. Jenny stopped and stared, then kept going. She wanted to buy something, but didn't know what she wanted yet.

Soon she stopped again, captivated by gorgeous, sequined garments hanging from a rack. Little sparkling pouches were displayed on a nearby table. This booth was ripe with rich colors, which Jenny had always loved. There were garments of every shape and size. Feathers, sequins, and shiny stones were delicately sewn on dresses, capes, pants, scarves, and veils.

As she examined the clothing she could hear festive music and the delighted exclamations of other visitors to the Festival. The clamor of the crowd not far away made Jenny want to see what was going on over there. She picked up one of the little pouches and asked the merchant for the price, quickly paid the man, and set out to find the crowd.

She passed several more booths and was distracted at every turn by the goods on display and for sale. She finally found the crowd and went to the back of the people who had gathered in front of the stage. She stood there, mouth gaping open, eyes wide, staring at the male dance troupe that was clogging—fat men with no shirts, bellies bouncing to the rhythm of the Irish music.

At first she started to snicker, as she remembered a television show with a fat clogger she had seen years ago. But this crowd applauded with serious enthusiasm at the end of each number. Several minutes later the men were joined by hefty handmaidens who clogged alongside them. After watching a while, Jenny's disapproval of fat people dancing began to fade and she began to see how talented they were, how they carried off their difficult dance moves and routines. Suddenly she saw them as dancers—not *fat* dancers, just dancers. She applauded loudly and stuck her fingers in her mouth and sounded off a loud whistle.

People around her laughed, and one teenager said, "I wish I could do that."

She grinned and stood there for a long time, watching the dancers. As the songs changed, different dancers took the stage—fat jazz dancers, fat contemporary dancers, and fat hip-hop dancers. At one point Jenny was moved to tears by the dancing. She loved how synchronized their moves were.

Caught in the spell of the dancing, Jenny looked around at the crowd. It was like a sea of fat people—large, ample bodies, bare flesh showing here and there. She looked down at her own fat body. *I belong here! I'm like everyone else.*

Everyone was different in their own way, but they were all similar, too. All human. People with jobs and lives and mates and kids and problems. *Just like me.* Suddenly, and for a fleeting moment, Jenny felt perfectly comfortable in her own skin. *I never thought I could ever feel like I fit in,* she thought, overwhelmed with a sense of sadness, wishing every fat person from her world could experience this world.

As if awakening to the moment, Jenny realized that a long time had passed and started looking frantically for a clock. There were none in sight. She turned to someone nearby and asked for the time. To her great surprise it was nearly one o'clock. She had to get back to the bakery booth.

She started to pass through the crowd back the way she had come, but where was the booth? She'd somehow lost her sense of direction. She tried to figure out which way to go and moved against the crowd, pushing and shoving through the many people who had moved in behind her to see the dancers. It was hard to get past them, and now she began to feel panicked, thinking she could never make it back to the bakery booth in time for her shift.

So many people. So many fat strangers. She couldn't believe how many people were bigger than she was. She passed a huge man who must have stood six feet five inches tall and weighed over four hundred pounds. He was like a wall. The man's wife stood about six feet three inches tall and was not only very heavy, but very pregnant, too. Jenny felt dwarfed in their presence. The couple looked down at her, taking in her puzzled expression, then looked at each other and shrugged.

She finally broke free and began to walk very fast, as if she would turn into a pumpkin if she didn't make it back to the booth in time. It was important to her not to let Dotty down. The baker had already done so much for her in her short stay. But she didn't recognize any of the booths she was passing as she hurried past row after row. She stopped several people along the way, asking if they could direct her to the bakery booth.

"Excuse me, sir," she said, now out of breath, to a fat older man who looked friendly, "do you know where a bakery booth is? I've got to get back there."

He shook his head. "I don't know, girl. A body would think you'd never been to the Festival grounds before." He pointed over his shoulder. "Just go to the road you came in by." Shaking his head, he walked away.

It had to be after one o'clock by now. She began to feel afraid, as she had when she was a child and had gotten lost at the county fair. When her parents had finally found her she was nearly hysterical. They had comforted her by buying her a vanilla ice cream cone. Ever since that day every time she got upset she had to have something to eat, especially something sweet, to make her feel like all would soon be well. She tried to calm down. After all, she wasn't a child anymore. All was not lost.

But she still had no idea where she was. *I'm lost. I'm heading in the wrong direction.* She turned completely around and bolted in the opposite direction. She didn't see Argus walking toward her and ran smack into his chest.

"Whoa, there," he exclaimed. "Jenny? Are you okay?" There was something about the way he said "Jenny" that was both kind and comforting.

"I just got lost," she said, trying to wipe the sweat off her forehead and brush her hair out of her face. "I'm trying to find my way back to Dotty's booth. It's my shift. I'm late."

"Did you forget what color section the booth was in?" he asked.

"Color? Section?" She realized she didn't have a clue about color sections. "Uhhh, yeah, I forgot." Looking up, she could see the signs with colored squares on them. She felt self-conscious again and took several deep breaths to calm herself. She didn't want him to know she was from the other place. "Okay. I'll be okay now. Thanks, Argus."

He put a hand on her arm. "You want me to just take you back to the booth?"

"Yeah. That might be faster. I'm kinda turned around. I've never been good at directions," she fibbed. Actually Jenny prided herself on practically being able to find her way around New York blindfolded, no matter where she was. But that was in her New York City.

They weren't far from Dotty's booth. Argus cut straight across in a direction Jenny hadn't even considered and in a few minutes they arrived. Clara, who was working the booth with Dotty, watched them suspiciously as they approached.

Jenny couldn't help but notice Clara looking at her rival's midsection and realized that she'd often done the same thing, looking jealously at thin women. Clara didn't have any reason to be jealous, as Jenny considered Argus more like a little brother and thought it cute that he seemed to have a crush on her. She wanted to tell Clara to just bide her time, that he would come around, but something inside her felt good. Someone was jealous of her. A handsome young hunk seemed to really be smitten with her. Besides, no one had said anything about their breakup. She wondered if this situation would ever happen to her again, and decided not to worry about Clara.

"Dotty," she called out, "I'm sorry I'm late. I kinda got lost—good thing I ran into Argus."

Argus laughed. "Well, now that I have delivered the fair maiden back to you, I'll be off. There are some bulging beauties dancing right now." As he glanced at Clara, his expression went flat. Clara turned completely away from him, but no one missed the look of disdain on her face.

"What's goin' on with ya two lovebirds?" Dotty asked.

"We broke up last night," Argus muttered under his breath, looking guilty.

"Broke up?" Dotty asked.

Clara took her apron off, threw it down on the counter and stormed out of the booth. Dotty gave Argus a disapproving look. "What in the name of Glory Be Good is goin' on with the both of ya?"

He wasn't ready to have this scene happen so soon, and looked from Dotty to Jenny. "Uhh—er—I—I don't know what to say. I just don't feel anything for Clara any more—"

"So ya broke the girl's heart, did ya?"

He took a step back. "Would you rather I just stayed with her forever? When I'm not in love with her?"

"Well, no—I suppose not," Dotty admitted slowly. She shook her head. "Son, if ya don't feel it, ya don't feel it. But this just comes as such a shock. I hope she's gonna be okay." She looked for Clara, but the young woman was nowhere in sight. "Well," she finally said, her voice quieter, "Gus, ya go get yourself somethin' to eat. Jenny's here now. She'll help me."

With a sad nod Argus walked off into the crowd, alone.

Dotty grabbed up an apron and gave it to Jenny, who hastily put it on. "Give the folks what they want out of the case," she said, "and I'll collect their money." A long line had formed while they were changing shifts.

The steady stream of pastry seekers never ended, and Jenny worked nonstop for the whole hour. At two o'clock two other boarders, Lidia and Dwyer, showed up to take their shift. They slipped into aprons and stepped up to relieve Dotty and Jenny.

"I never dreamed there would be this many people here at the Festival," Jenny commented as she and Dotty stepped out from behind the counter to take their aprons off. Dotty got herself a bottle of iced tea and offered one to Jenny. They took their tea and went to sit down outside the booth at one of the bistro tables.

"People come to this Festival from all over the world," Dotty said proudly, her accent thicker than ever. "Every year I make as much in the one day of the Festival as I do in a whole week of business at me bakery. That's why I keep doin' it, year after year. Plus it's a family tradition. Me grandfather set up the first bakery booth at the Festival back in 1931. The people count on it. I own the best bakery in all of Fatropolis. Why, I imagine that if I don't show up to the Festival one year, I'll have folks beatin' me door down to see if I'm still alive and breathin.'" She giggled and checked the pins in her hair. "I imagine the only way I'll miss a year is when I go to meet me maker at the Pearly Gates."

"Dotty, don't talk like that."

"Well, child, do ya think I'm goin' to live forever?"

Jenny didn't like talking about death. The topic made her feel very uncomfortable and sad. She didn't want to think about Dotty dying when she had just met her and already felt so close to her.

"So how did ya do?" Dotty asked. "Did you find anything or anyone interestin'?"

Jenny held up the little pouch. "I bought this."

"That's very pretty."

Dotty and Jenny had finished their beverages but were still sitting enjoying their rest. Just then Trixie came waddling up to them. She was loaded down with several bags packed full of things she had bought at the Festival.

"Look at ya, child," Dotty exclaimed, "loaded for bear, like ya been buying things from every booth here."

"That's probably about the size of it," Trixie laughed. "Can I put these bags in the van?"

"Of course ya can," Dotty said. The van was parked close to the bakery booth, so she pulled her keys out of her pocket, clicked on the electronic gadget that unlocked the van's doors, and handed the keys to Trixie. "I never get tired of doin' that," Dotty said, giggling.

Trixie quickly put her bags in the van and relocked it, coming back over to return the keys to Dotty.

"Ya must be famished." Dotty got up and walked behind the counter, reached into the bakery case and pulled out an apple fritter. She went back over to the table and pushed the pastry into Trixie's hand.

"Thank you, Aunt Dotty," Trixie said around her first mouthful of fritter.

Dotty sat back down and gestured toward Jenny. "Trixie, would ya take this child to see some sights and, fer cryin' out in the night, get her somethin' to eat? I can't bear to hear her stomach growlin' anymore. I'm just too tired to do it. Maybe later I'll send Hank out to get me a hot dog or somethin', but ya two young'uns get goin'. Off with ya now."

Jenny felt uncomfortable being sent off with Trixie. On the other hand, she loved being around the twins because they were so big, which made her feel smaller and more attractive. She didn't like it that this bolstered her self-confidence, but she had to acknowledge the truth of the matter.

Trixie motioned to Jenny to follow her, and the two walked off together. "Why do you look worried?" she asked a moment later.

"Oh, I'm just worried about Dotty," Jenny said, avoiding the subject of Argus and Clara. "She looks tired."

"Aunt Dotty is fine," Trixie replied. "She's a very hard worker. Sometimes she just doesn't know when to slow down."

Jenny was surprised that Trixie didn't seem to be mad at her.

Trixie led Jenny to an outdoor restaurant organized around a trailer flying an Italian flag. The aroma of the food there was positively heavenly.

"This is Papa Panson's Pizza. It's the best food place in the entire Festival," Trixie said. "They have the most delicious meatball sandwiches you've ever wrapped your lips around."

The two young women stepped up to the window, where a handsome, generously proportioned black man—who would have made a linebacker feel puny—stuck his head out and asked them what they wanted to eat.

Trixie put on her best coquettish look. "Hiya, Jimmy."

"My little plump dumplin'," he responded. "What are you doing here?"

"This is my friend, Jenny," she said, pointing at Jenny but still staring longingly into the man's dark eyes.

He didn't take his eyes off of Trixie, either. "What do you wanna eat, Trix?"

Jenny felt slightly offended. After all, she was thinner and thus more attractive than Trixie. As Trixie ordered two meatball sandwiches and two soft drinks, Jenny interjected, "Make mine a diet—er—I mean a cola—regular, sugary cola, p-please."

The two took a table close to the side of the trailer. The table was small, just large enough to hold their sandwiches, but the chairs were large and comfortable. After a few minutes the man delivered their sandwiches and drinks. Up close he was even bigger and more intimidating, and Jenny couldn't help but stare.

But Trixie mustered up all her feminine wiles. "Thanks, Jimmy," she whispered.

Jimmy kissed her lightly on the cheek and whispered something in her ear that made her giggle. Then he glanced at Jenny, muttered "nice to meet you," and disappeared back into the trailer.

Jenny was hungry and not shy about digging into her sandwich. The combination of the meatballs, sauce, melted mozzarella and toasted fresh-baked roll was positively delicious. She closed her eyes and relished the taste. When she opened her eyes again, Trixie was staring at her.

"You okay?" she asked.

Jenny grinned. "Sorry. It's just been a long time since I've had such a wonderful sandwich."

Trixie grinned back. "Oh, I go to Papa Panson's all the time. Their pizzas are delicious, too." She was pulling on a long string of mozzarella cheese that didn't seem to want to detach from her sandwich. Finally the string of cheese snapped and splattered marinara sauce on her face. She giggled again, but was in no hurry to wipe her face.

Jenny looked around to see if anyone was looking. She always meticulously wiped her mouth after every bite she took, not wanting to leave any trace of the sauce on her face.

"So—how long are you visiting for?" Trixie sounded like she was trying to find something to talk about.

She caught Jenny with her mouth full. Jenny coughed, chewed more rapidly, swallowed hard, and then said, "I'm not exactly sure. I like it here real well, but I may have to be getting back—" Before she finished the sentence, she remembered that she had to be careful not to slip and say something stupid.

Jenny pulled on a long string of mozzarella in her sandwich. The cheese was thick and stubborn, and as she struggled with it people at nearby tables watched her battling with the cheese. It finally snapped and curled around Jenny's nose, flicking sauce in several directions, even into her hair. As the onlookers started to laugh, Jenny wiped her face. She realized that their laughter was not meant to poke fun at her, but probably at how stubborn the cheese seemed to be. Jenny had to laugh herself.

Just then Trixie squealed with delight. "Flint Mackelroy will be coming on soon. Oh, my gosh, I can't wait! And Dewey Henderson—he's one of my favorite comedians. He's pretty cute, too, for an older guy. All these hearty hunks—oh, I don't know if I can contain myself." Suddenly she changed the subject, which seemed unintentional. "So, Jenny, this isn't your *first* visit to Fatropolis, is it?"

"Well—uh, yeah." Jenny was still wiping sauce out of her hair. "Have you ever had the chance to travel much?" Jenny probed to see if Trixie would guess what she didn't want to come out and ask.

"Yeah. When I was little, my father used to take the whole family on his business trips. It was fun."

"Have you ever been—uh, out of the country?" Jenny inched closer to the subject of where she was from.

Trixie finally caught on. "Oh. You mean through the portal?" She shook her head. "Our dad strictly forbid it, so Dixie and I went through once when we were in high school, but we got scared and came right back."

"Dixie and I were talking yesterday about your cousin going through the portal," Jenny said, but Trixie gave her a disapproving look, as if to say the subject was off limits.

They finished their sandwiches in silence and Trixie slurped the last few drops of her cola. Still silent, they rose, threw away their trash, and started to walk on. Jenny was still carrying her drink. Trixie recognized other people as they walked along and smiled, waving at one lady she knew. After a minute or two she took Jenny by the arm and pulled her close.

"You already knew about the portals, didn't you?" she whispered. "I mean, you didn't just hear it from my sister for the first time yesterday, did you?" She looked worried.

Jenny swallowed hard. "No. Sure, I already knew—yeah—I knew."

"'Cause I would feel mighty bad if I knew she had told somebody—" She suddenly looked up at Jenny with a look of sheer astonishment on her face. "Wait! You're *from* the other place, aren't you?"

Jenny gasped. How had Trixie guessed? "Uh—um—uh—"

"I knew it!" Trixie grabbed Jenny's arm and shook her enthusiastically, looking at her with awe, as if she were a movie star. She pulled Jenny over to a bench and pushed her down on it. "You have got to tell me what it's like," she said. "You are the first person I've ever talked to that's *from* there! Oh my gosh! That explains EVERYTHING. You looking for sugar sub—stitute— sub—" She didn't seem to know the word.

"Substitute." Jenny lowered her voice, too, looking around to make sure no one had overheard. "Please don't tell anyone. Dotty told me I shouldn't let on to people that I'm from the other place. She said they might not like it."

Trixie sat down beside her and nodded. "Yeah, she's right. There's lots of old-fashioned folks who still think our heartiness could be threatened by the other world. So I guess it's good that you don't tell everyone. But you can tell me. Please, please, tell me what it's like. Say—wait a minute. How did you know about the portal? Is the word out in your world that our world exists? Oh, please tell me that they don't know about us."

Jenny was surprised by Trixie's concern, but she was also beginning to understand why the hearty folk in this world would not want people from her world to know about Fatropolis. "I fell through the portal by accident," she replied. "I can hardly believe it myself, but I did."

Now Trixie looked both relieved and puzzled by Jenny's reply. "How could you fall through a portal *by accident?* No, no—don't tell me yet. First I want to know what it's like over there. What's it like in your world?"

Jenny wasn't sure what to say. "Well," she began, "for a fat person, or a heartyweight person, it's rough."

"Rough?" Trixie repeated. "What do you mean?"

Jenny thought carefully about what to say. "Well, for starters, the word 'fat' is a bad word there. It's very insulting to be called fat, even if you *are* fat." Suddenly realizing that she had been dying to tell someone about how it was in the place she called home, she went on, letting her anger and frustration come through her voice. "It's very tough, you know, especially for a fat woman— yes, it's excruciating at times. People stare and sometimes even laugh at you. Men ignore you. You have to really search for clothes that fit, and they're more expensive than 'normal' clothes. And you don't fit in. Not just socially, not just around thin people, but physically. You don't fit easily into bathroom stalls, booths at restaurants, or a lot of theater seats. Car seats are too small, and seatbelts don't go all the way around you, except for the most expensive luxury cars. Some airlines in my world make fat people pay for two seats because their seats are so small. If you want to fly in a normal-sized seat, you can pay double or triple the price for what they call a first-class seat, but what working-class person can afford that? And it's not just in public. I can't even fit in my own bathtub. And when you go to the doctor, you may be there for the same ailment as thin people, but because you're fat you get told that you would be *fine* if you would just *lose some weight*. You know what? My brother-in-law actually asked me why I had 'let myself get so fat.'" Running out of breath and with tears in her eyes, she took a drink of her cola. "Trust me. It's rough. And some of that's true for fat men, too. Well, it seems more acceptable, though, for men to be fat. But women can't be fat. They just can't be. Fat women can't ever eat and enjoy what they're eating, unless it's a salad."

Trixie was hanging on every word. "That sounds just terrible," she murmured. "Terrible."

Jenny wasn't finished. "And—and I think it just stinks that I have to enter another frickin' *dimension* before a gorgeous man like Argus will even look at me—oh, God." She realized what she had let slip and blushed. "I mean—"

"You think *Argus* is *gorgeous?*" Trixie scoffed. "Oh, my word, girlfriend, do we have some work to do on you." She grinned. "It's obvious that he's smitten with you, but I had no idea the feeling was mutual."

"But—but—you have to realize that he's *the ideal* of what men are supposed to be in my world."

Trixie started to laugh, but stopped herself. "Oh, dear heavens. That is really sad. He's so *scrawny.* And he doesn't act right. You know?"

Jenny knew. "That's what low self-esteem will get you," she replied. "He doesn't have any confidence in himself because the women here don't like the way he looks. I know exactly how that feels." She could feel the tears coming again.

Realizing that Jenny had recognized something important about herself, Trixie allowed her the moment. "You know, I wondered why you seemed backward and shy, even though you're so hearty and beautiful." She paused and gently patted Jenny on the shoulder. "It all makes sense to me now."

"Do you—do you really think I'm—I'm—*beautiful?*"

Trixie giggled. "Well, yes. But not more beautiful than me and my sister."

Jenny had to laugh, but she got the feeling there was a lot of truth to what Trixie was saying.

The twin went on. "But yeah, I think you're a beautiful woman who could have her pick of men. But you gotta start believing it. My gosh, look at me—" Jenny assumed that Trixie would start talking about her struggle with weight, but no. "I have this scar on my chin," she continued, leaning closer to Jenny to show her the scar. "But," she sat up straight, "do I let it ruin my confidence in myself? No. I'm telling you—men love me." A self-confident, flirty grin swept over Trixie's face.

Jenny could see why men found her attractive. Her self-confidence was beautiful. Although Jenny was astonished by Trixie's self-confidence, seeing that she was the fattest woman she had ever had the pleasure to meet, she also wished she could feel that way about herself. Feeling as though she had made a new friend, she decided to come clean about eavesdropping. "I overheard you and Clara talking in the courtyard last night. I was—"

"—in the bathtub." They said the words in unison and started to laugh together. Trixie pointed at Jenny as if she had her pegged, and Jenny nodded.

"I heard her crying and looked out the window," she said. "She was saying Argus had broken up with her. I also heard you telling her that she should let me have him." She paused as Trixie gave her a penetrating look. "Well, I think it's cute that he has a crush on me," she admitted, "but I think of him just as a little brother, no more—"

She was interrupted by a nudge from Trixie. While they were talking Argus had come up behind them. He seemed to have heard every word of their conversation about him, and had a horrible, crushed look on his face.

"I'm sorry you feel that way, Miss," he said, smiling awkwardly, tears in his eyes. "I'll get out of your hair now." He walked away.

"Oh, my gosh." Jenny didn't know how to respond. "I didn't mean for him to overhear—"

"Oh, he'll get over it," Trixie said, dismissing it with a wave of her hand. "Just like Clara will get over it. They're not right for each other. He's not the man for *you*, either, and you know it. Why waste time pretending he is?"

CHAPTER 8
HE WAS BARELY RECOGNIZABLE WITHOUT HIS HAIR

IT WAS LATE AFTERNOON, AND THE SUN WAS BEGINning to sink in the sky. Jenny felt relieved that someone finally knew she was from the other world. She didn't like keeping secrets, although she could if she had to. Nevertheless, she felt glad she had told Trixie. She was also relieved she'd admitted to overhearing last night's conversation between Trixie and Clara. Now she wondered if she could safely ask Trixie some questions.

"Can I ask you about something that's puzzling me?"

"Sure. I guess."

"Dotty told me that the people in my world are brainwashed against fat folks," Jenny began. "Then she told me about the actuarial tables. Do you know about them? What about them? So an insurance company came out with the tables, not doctors—so what? What does that have to do with *this* world? Do you have any idea what the big deal is?"

Trixie thought for a moment. "Well, I know it was a young man from Fatropolis who was the brains behind the tables."

Jenny sucked in her breath so loudly that several passersby looked at her. "What? Who?"

"They say it was a young thin man who was jilted by a hearty girl," Trixie said. "Well, actually, it was her father who wouldn't allow them to marry. So the thin young man swore he'd get back at the heartyweights for ruining his chance at love. He disappeared right after that. It was rumored that he crossed into your world and got a job with an insurance company." She stopped for a dramatic pause. "And within a year or so, the tables appeared."

"Okay, I understand a little bit more now. But what happened next?"

"No one ever heard from him again. He never came back."

"I think I understand. So far. But I'm still confused about something. Why does it make Dotty so uncomfortable to talk about it?"

Trixie shrugged her shoulders. "I've never tried to talk to her about it. It must make her uncomfortable for some reason, but I don't know what it could be." And with that, she dismissed the subject.

The two young women sat and talked about the Festival for several minutes, then got up and started visiting nearby booths. Trixie wanted to show Jenny some of her favorite booths and some of her favorite things. They also ate ice cream cones and cotton candy.

Jenny was eating what she wanted to eat. She was starting to feel a lot more comfortable around eating. It had never really mattered what she ate, she realized, as her weight always fluctuated by only two or three pounds.

As they shopped she also met some of Trixie and Dixie's friends. They visited, laughed and joked, shopped, and had a grand time.

Just as the sun was setting Jenny went to check out a small stand to see what they had to offer. They had metal signs that looked like the one she'd seen in the dressing room at Bountiful Britches. The signs were embellished and stamped with information about this year's Festival Fatropolis. Jenny gasped. "How much are these?"

"These are free, ma'am," the lady sitting at the stand replied. "They're just a souvenir of the Festival."

Trixie gave the sign a disdainful look. "Oh, gosh, what would you want one of those for?" she asked.

"I want a souvenir," Jenny said. She turned back to the lady. "Can I have one, please?"

The lady wrapped one in paper and gave it to her. Trixie offered to carry it in one of the many bags of loot she had again collected along the way.

A little while later Jenny, Trixie and some of their friends were sitting at a cluster of tables in another restaurant booth eating giant pretzels when Trixie realized the concert would be starting soon. "I don't want to miss Dewey Henderson," she said as she stood up. "We should probably move towards the concert stage." She gestured to Jenny and the rest to come with her.

As Jenny got up she was feeling a little stiff from walking all day, and found herself longing for a good hot soak in her bathtub. She followed Trixie and the other young women to the huge concert stage. They arrived just in time to get a good spot. A crowd of people had already gathered in front, and hundreds more were pushing forward from every walkway and street on the

Festival grounds, in anticipation for the show to begin.

Excitement was thick in the air. Jenny had butterflies in her stomach. The wait was excruciating. It was almost completely dark. Just when Jenny thought she couldn't wait another minute, the voice of the master of ceremonies loudly announced the show would start soon.

What seemed like an eternity passed. Finally the lights came on and the emcee came out. The crowd went wild with applause, screaming and whistling. He worked the crowd, getting them ready for the show. As the audience was beginning to quiet down he shouted, "Ladies and gentlemen— it is my distinct pleasure to present—the one, the only—Dewey Henderson!"

The horde of adoring fans erupted again as the comedian took the stage. Like everyone else, Trixie and Jenny were beside themselves, screaming as loud as they could. Jenny whistled loudly, making Trixie laugh every time.

It took several minutes for the crowd to calm down so he could speak. Dewey bowed and finally held up one large hand. "My God, people," he said, "you'd think you'd never seen a comedian before." He laughed, and his crowd laughed with him. "I've been touring a lot, and I've got to say it's GREAT to be back in Fatropolis." Here the crowd went wild again, whistling and cheering. With that he went into his act, which lasted about forty-five minutes and kept the crowd roaring with laughter.

Jenny was surprised that Dewey's stand-up routine didn't have anything to do with being fat, as it did when he was on TV in her world. Here he was just a funny man who talked about funny stuff.

Dewey's act ended way too soon for his fans, but he finally walked off the stage as the emcee walked on again. The crowd knew this could mean only one thing—Flint Mackelroy and his band were about to play.

The lights went down, fog started to billow out from the stage, and mist came down from above. Spotlights of different colors began to search the audience. The anticipation in the air could be felt by everyone.

The stage was still dark as the music began. It was one of Jenny's favorite songs. She had to keep telling herself she wouldn't faint. Suddenly a spotlight lit up the stage, revealing Flint Mackelroy with a banjo. He was dressed in a shimmering periwinkle suit, wearing his customary sunglasses and signature pompadour.

Jenny was confused. *I didn't know he played the banjo.* She listened for a few seconds. *That certainly makes the song sound different.*

"I LOVE YOU, FLINT!" Trixie screamed above the crowd, and when she began to cry, so did Jenny. As Flint began singing, his two biggest fans hugged each other and began sobbing uncontrollably.

The music picked up pace and more lights came on, finally revealing the whole band. In addition to performing his solo numbers and instrumental riffs, occasionally Flint would bust out and dance in sync with his backup singers and dancers. Fat acrobats and other fleshy contortionists in colorful outfits were suspended above the crowd from wires and tethers.

The show lasted an hour and a half. Jenny had been to a lot of concerts in her day, but she had never seen such a spectacle and had never been so thoroughly entertained. She and Trixie laughed and screamed and cried the whole time. When the concert ended they were hoarse, and exhausted both physically and emotionally.

This had been one of the best days of Jenny's life. She had seen her favorite entertainers and felt she and Trixie had embarked on a new friendship.

After the concert attendees at the Festival began to go home, as the concert had been the main attraction. It was now well after ten o'clock, but the Festival Fatropolis did not officially end until midnight.

Jenny and Trixie were filled to overflowing with admiration for Flint Mackelroy and Dewey Henderson. They recited some of Dewey's best lines and giggled over and over. Then they looked adoringly into each other's eyes and sang lines from Flint's songs and burst into laughter. They were slowly making their way back to Dotty's booth when Trixie was struck by the need to use the bathroom. Jenny told her she would wait in a nearby booth that sold clothing.

She paid little attention to the huge man rifling through a rack of men's clothing as she started to look through one of the women's racks. There were garments of every size, dresses and gowns that would fit her with room to spare. Soon, however, she began to notice out of the corner of her eye that the man kept looking at her, though when she turned to look at him he quickly turned away. They played hide and seek for several minutes until she finally caught him. When she asked, he had to admit he had been staring at her. So there they were, standing there, a rack of men's jackets between them, looking at each other. Then it hit her. She was standing face to face with Flint himself.

But he didn't seem to be the Flint she adored. He didn't have the pompadour now, just thinning hair drenched with sweat. He wasn't dressed fancy, either. Instead of his shimmering suit he had on a plain shirt, jeans, and sneakers.

"Uh, uh, uh—" All she could do was stammer.

"I'm sorry, miss," he said. "I know I was staring, but do you know what a delectable delight you are? You're so lovely and round. I got a glimpse of you while I was singing."

"Uh, uh, uh." *Why can't I get any words out?* She finally got hold of herself and asked, "What are you doing out here? People will mob you."

He gave her an aw-shucks grin. "They don't recognize me without my hair. I like to shop at the Festival. They have clothes in my size here."

"Can I just say that I think you are the best—" She was feeling dizzy. She didn't realize it, but Trixie had come in and was standing next to her.

"—and can I say," he replied, "I think you are so beautiful." He was not looking at Trixie.

"What?" Trixie demanded, evidently not realizing the stranger was the famous Flint Mackelroy. Jenny and Flint were standing there, staring into each other's eyes. "Jenny! You can't just let *any old sweaty guy* talk to you like that."

Trixie grabbed Jenny by the arm, but she was as stiff as a mannequin, Trixie looked the man up and down, frowning at him, then up and down again. Finally she stopped at his face. She froze. She opened her mouth and let out a scream that resounded through the entire area.

At Trixie's scream Flint lunged forward, grabbed Jenny's hand, kissed it, and fled the booth. Trixie stood there, still screaming. Jenny was paralyzed, her hand still up in the air in the same position as when Flint had kissed it, a silly frozen grin on her face.

Trixie's scream attracted attention from people passing by who came running over to help.

"WE JUST SAW FLINT MACKELROY!"

The would-be rescuers rolled their eyes and walked away.

Trixie, who was used to being the one who attracted male attention, was not sure she quite approved of Jenny's getting any attention, or so it seemed. Especially the attention of Flint Mackelroy.

Jenny finally got it. "I just got hit on by Flint Mackelroy!"

Now both women were screaming and bouncing up and down. It took awhile before they were able to calm down enough to resume their trek back to the bakery booth, where Dotty and the others enjoyed Trixie's story about the concert and seeing Flint.

BY ABOUT ELEVEN THE CROWDS had dwindled and the merchants were starting to take down their booths and pack away their goods and wares, so Dotty also decided to pack it in. She looked even more tired. Everyone helped break down the booth and carry the empty trays to the bakery truck, and then the whole gang piled into the van. The boarders who had come to the Festival on public transportation returned to the boarding house in the bakery truck.

Trixie and Jenny laughed and teased each other the whole ride home, getting Dotty and the others chuckling as Trixie finally accepted Jenny's luck in getting such a compliment from Flint. Still she teased her unmercifully about it, calling her "Mrs. Mackelroy," then "Mrs. Flinty," and then just plain "Mack."

Jenny enjoyed every bit of the affectionate teasing, especially when the boarders joined in. Jenny teased Trixie plenty, too, about referring to Flint Mackelroy as "any old sweaty guy," which made the others—and eventually Trixie—roar with laughter.

She had never had such a wonderful thing happen to her, and never had such a wonderful day. When they arrived back at Dotty's and unloaded the truck, she thanked everyone and asked Trixie for her souvenir. After they all said their goodnights and all the doors closed almost in unison, she could not get into the bathroom to draw her bath fast enough. She quickly tucked her souvenir in the chest of drawers and left her clothes strewn in a trail that led into the bathroom. She was sore and sunburned and her feet hurt, but she wouldn't trade one precious moment of her day for anything that had ever happened to her back home.

As she soaked in the tub, it dawned on her that she didn't hate herself anymore. She looked down at her fat body and saw the soft curves of her femininity. For probably the first time in her life, she felt comfortable looking at herself. She washed herself lovingly, and propped one leg up on the wall and gazed at it admiringly. She scrubbed her hair and lay back in the water, closing her eyes as the steam rose off the water.

After her bath, still wrapped in a towel, she opened the closet door, turned on the light, and looked at herself in the full-length mirror. That was something she had never wanted to do in the past, and would only do to see if her slip was showing or something like that. But tonight she *wanted* to see her body.

She made sure the door was locked and she had complete privacy, then let the towel droop a bit. She stood there gazing at her reflection, her wet hair touching her soft, round shoulders. She turned to give her back a good long look, then turned around again, facing herself. She parted the towel to reveal one of her meaty thighs. It looked soft, round and thick. She finally got up enough nerve to let the towel fall slowly to the floor.

It was as though she was seeing her body for the first time. In the light of the closet, she looked like one of the paintings she had seen for sale at the Festival. She had always found it impossible to accept herself as heavy as she had gotten, but tonight was a good start toward self-acceptance. She stood there for a long, long time, turning to see different parts of her nude body, looking at the curves that made her uniquely feminine. She could see why Flint had found her so attractive. She felt glimmers of love for herself starting to grow.

She realized she had let the culture of her world influence her to hate herself and her body, and began to cry. But her tears turned into tears of joy, and she began to feel a sense of gratitude that she had stumbled into Fatropolis.

CHAPTER 9
THE SKINNY ABOUT NEARLY EVERYTHING

JENNY AWOKE AT ABOUT HALF PAST SIX IN THE morning. Unable to go back to sleep, she got up and because it was Sunday put on the less fancy dress. After brushing her teeth and combing her hair, she decided she looked presentable enough. She was early for breakfast and wondered what was on the menu for Sunday mornings. Her stomach was already growling. She quietly crept downstairs. There was no one around. She found Dotty in the office, going over some financial paperwork. Her computer was glowing with a soft light. As Dotty tapped lightly on the interactive screen with the fingers of her right hand, columns of numbers appeared and changed with each tap. There was also a strange keyboard that resembled a court reporter's machine. It, too, was made of glass and had more than a dozen keys on it. Dotty touched the keys from time to time with her left hand, and words appeared on the screen.

"Good morning, Dotty," Jenny said. "How'd you like me to help toward breakfast?"

Dotty looked up. "Breakfast isn't a big to-do on Sundays, child. Everyone just fends fer themselves. It's been that way fer years. I was just plannin' to leave fer church."

"I usually go to church on Sundays," Jenny said. "Do you mind if I tag along?"

Dotty got up from her desk. "No, I don't mind. Sure, ya can come." She gave Jenny's back a happy pat. "Yer the only one who's ever asked to come along. Let's go, then." She picked up her purse, and they set off for morning mass. "So ya go to church every Sunday, do ya?" Dotty asked.

"Yes, I do. I wouldn't miss it," Jenny told her proudly. "I think it helps get my head straight for the coming week."

Dotty looked impressed. "I knew I liked ya fer a reason."

The church was only a few blocks from the bakery—about a fifteen-minute walk—so they arrived early. The sanctuary was quiet and nearly empty. They blessed themselves with the holy water and walked down the center aisle.

The statues were very different. Jenny wanted to walk right up to them and stare, but Dotty was leading the way. She entered Dotty's pew of choice and knelt down, but instead of praying looked at the statues.

At the front stood a hefty Madonna holding a chubby child. Above the altar a hearty Christ hung from the cross. The saints all around the church were all round.

Jenny was accustomed to seeing different representations of Jesus—baby Jesus, long-haired Jesus, short-haired Jesus, bearded Jesus, clean-shaven Jesus, and Jesuses of different ethnicities. But she had never seen a fat Jesus. These statues seemed almost irreverent, almost insulting to the heavenly beings they represented.

Except for the holy figures, everything else was almost the same as church back home.

Fat people were starting to file in now, and the church was filling up fast. Dotty prayed for several minutes, weeping at times.

The mass began with the procession into the church led by a stout priest and his chubby attendants, all of them walking up the wide center aisle and carrying a cross bearing an even more corpulent Christ. As they took their places around the altar, both clergy and the laity who had anything to do with the service were hefty and hearty.

She wasn't sure what she had expected, but she was taken aback by how familiar, yet how different, church was in Fatropolis.

As she let the familiar words roll over her, she pondered how she felt about the difference in the statues. She could accept nearly everything else in Fatropolis, but not fat saints. She ranted and raved about it in her head as she went through the motions of the service, but she couldn't get into it. After a while, however, she started to really examine why she was having such a hard time with the fat statues.

Over the course of the mass she realized that she had always felt that God, Jesus, and the saints were judging her harshly for her weight, just as she had always judged herself. Further, she had come to feel that it was because of their harsh judgment that she could not find a mate. But it was difficult for her to continue along this line of thought when Christ, Mary, and the saints were all as hefty as she was.

She had always wondered why people of different ethnicities had representations of Christ and the saints with their skin color or eyes or hair, and now she realized that it was comforting to see them looking like her. Fat. Finally she began to relax and feel another new sense of belonging.

At the same time, while sitting there in Dotty's church she also realized how much she missed her former life—her church, her apartment, her cat, her work, even her nosey neighbor. She was enjoying herself here in Fatropolis, but she also longed for the comfort and predictability of home. She couldn't imagine staying here much longer. Even with all the wonderful things that had happened, she knew she couldn't stay.

She wondered how it would happen—how she would return home. She trusted that she would be able to go home.

AFTER THE SERVICE Dotty invited Jenny to breakfast. They ate at a diner up the block from the church. After they put in their food order they sat at the spacious table, enjoying their coffee and talking. Jenny was glad to finally have some alone time with Dotty where there were no distractions.

"I sure had a great time yesterday at the Festival," Jenny commented, hoping to get a good conversation going. "That Trixie is such a character. She's so confident, and the men just love her. Which is something you don't find in my world."

"What don't ya find in yer world?" Dotty asked.

Jenny laughed. "A fat woman who has confidence in herself and can get men. It just doesn't happen."

"Haven't ya ever met a fat woman in yer world that had the backbone to talk to men?" Dotty asked, sipping her coffee loudly.

"Well, yeah." Jenny thought about it for a minute. "Yes, I knew a fat girl when I was in high school. She could talk to anybody, and she was never without a date."

"And have ya ever met a man in yer world who likes his women on the hefty side?"

"Dotty, what are you getting at?"

"Well, those folks are probably from this world," Dotty said. "Or direct descendants of us hearty folk."

That's interesting. Jenny had never thought of this, and she filed it away for future consideration. But what she wanted to do now was to get Dotty to answer some of the questions that were still plaguing her. "Speaking of people from this world going to my world," she said, "Trixie was telling me that the brains behind the actuarial tables you told me about were from this world. Is that true?"

Dotty's tone was casual. "Yes, child. I'm afraid it is."

"Do you know who he was? What's the story?"

"Well—they say that when the young girl's father found out about the two of them, he ran the boy off with a pistol."

Jenny gasped. "Oh, no!"

"The boy ran away, but he yelled back at the old man, 'I'll get ya hearty bastards, if it's the last thing I do.' That was because that girl probably wasn't the only one the boy had lost on account of his bein' thin."

"How sad."

"Not many of the folks knew about the portals at that time, and God only knows how he found out about them," Dotty continued. "In fact, he may've been the first one to criss-cross into yer world. Who knows? But—well, as the story goes, he landed a good job with an insurance company in yer New York City, and it was after that that the tables came out." Dotty took a long minute to drink some more of her coffee. "The tables made it look like folks with higher weights were more of a risk to insure. Then eventually those tables became a way to regulate the people in yer society. That was the beginnin' of the prejudice against the heartyweights that's so pervasive now in yer world."

The waitress walked over with their breakfast plates and set them in front of the women.

"But how do you suppose he thought he was getting back at the heartyweights in *this* world by causing prejudice in *my* world?" Jenny asked as she salted her potatoes.

"Ya know, child, I don't rightly know. I guess he just figured if he could wreak havoc on *any* hearty folks, he'd be satisfied. And I have to say he's gotten back at a lot of the heartyweights in *this* world." She paused to take a bite of her toast.

A new idea occurred to Jenny. "It sounds to me like he was trying to ensure that only his kind would be popular in my world."

"I think you might have somethin' there." Dotty took a deep breath and exhaled. "All I know is I don't like talkin' about this."

Jenny knew that was all she would be getting out of Dotty for now. They finished their breakfast almost in silence. Dotty paid the check and they walked back to the boarding house, where Jenny thanked her for allowing her to go to church with her and for breakfast. Then she walked up to her room and turned on the television. There was an old movie from the 1940s on. It was filled with fat actors. Jenny was still easily taken by surprise with the things she saw in this world.

It was mid-morning and Jenny was tired, so she lay down on the bed. She wasn't sure how long she had been asleep when she was awakened by people walking down the hall. Looking at the clock, she decided to have a soak in the glorious bathtub. She pinned up her hair and slathered her face with the blue facial cream she had found in the cabinet and lay back in the water to reflect on her conversation with Dotty. She also thought about the fat statues, fat Flint, the concert, the movie, and the fat pirates in the restaurant.

Suddenly Dotty's voice came over the intercom. "Child? Are ya comin' down to help with lunch?"

Jenny sat bolt upright in the tub, splashing water everywhere. She could hear Dotty laugh.

"Yer in the tub again? Land o' Goshen, child, yer goin' to end up lookin' like an old prune." Now others in the kitchen were laughing, too, and Trixie got on the intercom.

"Whatcha doin' up there, Mack? You need us to send someone up there to help you?" Peals of laughter came now through the intercom.

Jenny rolled her eyes, smiling. "Nope," she retorted. "I wouldn't want to get anyone involved in anything they couldn't handle."

Now the laughter in the kitchen turned to reproachful comments directed at the men. She could hear Charlie and Hank chuckling, too, and she decided that since she had an audience, she'd go with it. "Dotty," she said with a British accent, "could you tell the masseur that I'm ready for my massage?"

Roars of laughter made the intercom speaker vibrate, and Jenny laughed, too.

The next voice was Dotty's. "I'm turnin' off the speaker now, child. We'll be waitin' fer ya down here. Ya gotta cut up the vegetables fer the pasta salad." The speaker went off with a loud click.

She finished her bath, wondering how many more of these luscious watery retreats she would be able to enjoy in Fatropolis, then dressed and went downstairs to help. The lunch crew was working diligently to get the meal on the table. All the other boarders were already waiting in the dining room, looking forward to a wonderful Sunday lunch. Dotty had prepared a huge vat of cold chicken salad with small golden raisins, celery, chopped sweet pickles, diced onions, and walnuts. It looked wonderful. Jenny added chopped vegetables to the pasta salad, then one of the boarders added the oil and vinegar dressing and some spices and stirred. There was also a huge tray of breads and cheeses. Everything was finally delivered to the dining room, where a line of hungry boarders formed, plates at the ready. Jenny, one of the last in line, put food on her plate, got her sweet tea, and sat down to eat and enjoy visiting.

Argus made himself scarce after getting his plate. *Maybe he's uncomfortable with the way things turned out for him,* she thought. Sometimes boarders took their plates out to the courtyard, as there were tables there, so Jenny assumed he was outside. Dotty also sat down and enjoyed her lunch with her boarders. When the meal was finished and everyone was sitting around making small talk, she disappeared for a few minutes, then reappeared in the dining room with a bucket of vanilla ice cream and some fresh strawberries. The boarders lined up again to indulge in the treat.

After the ice cream the cleanup crew began to remove empty dishes from the table, and Dotty walked out to the courtyard to sit for a spell. Jenny followed her, as did some of the others. Argus was nowhere to be seen. The courtyard was nice, with flowers and potted plants of all kinds, plus a few shade trees to sit under. There were benches all around, so plenty of people could enjoy themselves there. Several of them sat in the courtyard for half an hour, and then one by one went on to other activities. But Dotty seemed to be enjoying her time outside, sitting under the shade tree and breathing deeply.

There was a warm afternoon breeze, and Jenny, too, was enjoying the sunshine and the sweet smell of the roses. After the others had all gone in, Dotty looked at Jenny with an expression of regret, and motioned for her to come closer. Jenny went over and sat next to Dotty in the shade. They sat there in the quiet for a few minutes.

Dotty finally broke the silence, "I'm sorry I keep puttin' ya off every time ya ask me a question about the brainwashin' and whatnot."

By now, Jenny had a feeling that her time in Fatropolis was short. She knew she had to be at work tomorrow morning, but she had no idea how she would accomplish what seemed like an impossible feat. How on Earth would she get back to her own world? "Dotty," she said carefully, "I just don't understand why you're so concerned with what happens in the other world. Why do you care so much? People here don't discriminate against the hearty folk, so what's the big deal?"

Dotty's brow wrinkled. "Ya just don't fully understand the consequences that one selfish act can have on folks from that point in time forward," she said.

It was obvious to Jenny that something was weighing heavily on the old baker's mind.

Dotty got up, crossed the courtyard, and sank slowly down onto another bench. Jenny followed her. "Oh, Dotty. I want to understand, *but you won't tell me what you mean!*" She was nearly shouting.

"Child, I don't want ya to hate me."

Seeing the old woman beginning to cry, Jenny sat down and tried to speak more calmly. "Well—"She gave up and said, "I don't think you're ready to tell me, Dotty." She got up and started for the door to the parlor. "When you're ready," she added, "I'll be waiting to hear about why you care so much about what happens over there—"

"Dontcha get it, child?" Dotty called after her. "The man that was the brains behind the actuarial tables was my *father!*" She buried her face in her hands.

Jenny froze. *So that's the secret Dotty's been trying to keep covered up all this time.* She slowly turned and walked back to the bench where Dotty was sobbing. Sitting down beside her, she gently put one hand on Dotty's back.

After awhile, Dotty stopped crying. She sniffled a few times, then looked up. She seemed surprised to see Jenny sitting beside her. She wiped her face with her hanky and cleared her throat. "Two weeks after my father disappeared into yer world, they found out that my mother was expectin.' It was me she was expectin.' But by then it was too late. No one found out about the portals until much later. Everyone thought my grandfather was a brute of a man for running my father off, and Grandfather went to his grave regrettin' the mistake he'd made. As I grew up momma just didn't seem to have any spark of life in her. She never laughed, she never had any fun, she just worked all the time. I guess she figured that was her penance for carryin' on before she was wed."

"Dotty, I—I—don't know what to say." It was hurting her terribly to see Dotty so upset. She tried to say something comforting. "But—what your father and grandfather did? Well, it wasn't *your* fault."

"No. But I'm the sole heir to the problems that my grandfather and father inflicted upon yer world." She began sobbing again. "A whole world full of hearty folk bein' persecuted day and night just fer breathin'! It's an awful burden to bear. And don't ya see? I ran my own son off, just like my grandfather did to my father. My own flesh and blood. He couldn't stand me naggin' him day in and day out about heartyin' himself up. So he left, too. Takin' with him the possibility of givin' me a grandbaby to love and spoil." She buried her face in her hands again. "And I'm not so sure that's not what caused my beloved Nevan to lose so much of his reserves and die of a broken heart."

Jenny sat silently, taking in what Dotty had said.

"So there ya have it, child. If it weren't for my kinfolk, ya wouldn't be thinkin' so poorly of yerself. And the hearty folk in yer world wouldn't be so miserable."

Jenny gave this some more thought. "But Dotty," she said, "that can be changed. Why, I already feel better about myself. Every minute I spend in

Fatropolis I feel better. I mean, it's in *my attitude*. What matters is how I *feel* about myself. Each one of us hearty folks that live in my world are just going to have to stand up for ourselves. We have to stop believing the brainwashing that we're second class citizens because we're fat. We have to stop accepting that without question."

Jenny's voice was rising. She stood up. "I'm not going to take it anymore," she proclaimed. "I'm going to eat what I want, when I want. I'm going to wear clothes I feel comfortable in. I'm going to pursue any man I feel is worthy of my company." She took a deep breath. "I'm Large and in Charge. And I'm not going to let any doctor tell me that I'd be fine if I'd just lose some weight. And I'm not going to let anyone say to me, 'It's a shame, you have such a pretty face.' And I'm not going to let men judge me by how many six-packs they'd have to drink before they could sleep with me. And—and I'm not going to let some thin, starving waif of a salesgirl laugh at me. NOT EVER AGAIN!"

Jenny's dramatic soliloquy was interrupted by applause coming from above, along with exclamations of agreement and praise. Blushing, she looked up to see Trixie and Dixie hanging over the balcony railing and clapping. They all started laughing, even Dotty.

Jenny was soon enveloped in a hug, and Dotty patted her vigorously on the back. "Now that's what I like to hear," the old woman said. "A strong, confident woman who knows what she wants." She ran her hands affectionately down Jenny's arms and took her hands. They stood together in the courtyard, hand in hand, as the twins on the balcony continued to cheer and applaud Jenny's new-found inner strength. Jenny wondered how much of the conversation they had overheard.

Dotty cast her gaze at Trixie and Dixie. "Don't the two of ya have preparations to make fer supper?" she asked. "Off with ya now." The twins grumbled but went back inside, leaving Dotty and Jenny alone again.

"I think I need to be getting back to my old life," Jenny said.

"I think yer right, dearie. Ya know, I think the reason why ya found yerself here is resolvin' itself."

"I'm still scared, though," Jenny confessed. "It's scary to think that the limitations I've been living with were put there by society, but kept there—*by me.*"

Dotty smiled. "Ya can make your own little Fatropolis in yer world," she said, "where no one can make ya feel bad about yerself again. Hatred is somethin' ya have to buy into. It doesn't just come natural. Only the Lord knows why a lot of the folks in yer world feel uncomfortable bein' around us hearty-folk. Deep down inside, they must think we overshadow them, and make them feel small. That's where the prejudice comes from—not wantin' people, especially us women-folk, to take up too much room in the world, to be too big. But look at ya! Yer young and round and beautiful, and yer bound to be doin' great things. Maybe yer destined to reverse some of the damage my father did in yer world."

Jenny nodded. "Who knows? All I can do is start with myself. I'm glad I learned all this *now* instead of spending another pathetic year in the place where I was, *where I was miserable.*"

"I knew they'd done a number on ya the minute I met ya," Dotty replied.

"Dotty, I couldn't have learned all this if it hadn't been for you." As she spoke, her chin quivered and her eyes became teary.

"Oh, 'tweren't nothin,' child. You know what they say? 'When the student is ready, the teacher will come.' Except this time, the teacher found the student unconscious on the street." She touched Jenny's cheek, then gently patted her on the back. "Stop yer carryin' on now, child."

Jenny gave her friend a serious, careful look. "You've got to stop beating yourself up about the brainwashing in my world," she said. "And you've got to stop beating yourself up about your son. Isn't there some way you can contact him? You've got to know someone who criss-crosses—maybe you could—"

"No, child. I'm gettin' on in years now."

Jenny realized it would be an impossible task to find Dotty's son. He could be anywhere in the world by now.

"And I'm too old to be riskin' my neck by criss-crossin' and the like, I made my bed, now I've got to lay in it."

Jenny sighed. "A big part of me doesn't want to go back," she admitted. "I'm so comfortable here. I feel like I belong. But another part of me wants to go back and prove that I can live in that world and be happy."

Dotty shook her head. "You've got to go back. That's yer home. Yer life."

"Yes. I know. How do I get back, though?"

"I'll talk to Trixie. She has connections with the criss-crossin' folk. She can find someone to take ya back to the other place."

"I really should be getting back tonight," she said at last. "Dotty, I have to be at work in the morning."

"Well, enough talk about criss-crossin.' I'll talk to her about it. Now let's go help get supper on the table."

ABOUT AN HOUR LATER when Jenny was in the kitchen peeling potatoes, she watched Dotty take Trixie aside and talk to her quietly. Trixie gave Jenny a serious look, then nodded and left the kitchen. Dotty gave Jenny a thumbs up and winked at her.

Once the potatoes were on to boil, Dotty crossed the kitchen to where Jenny was standing beside Dixie, who was making a green salad. "Dixie," she said, "would ya please mind the potatoes? Jenny and me, we have some business to attend to." She touched Jenny's elbow. "Come with me."

Jenny followed her up the stairs and down the long hallway. Dotty unlocked the door to her room and motioned her to come in. "Sit down, child. I have somethin' fer ya."

Jenny sat on the end of the bed and looked at the lovely antique chest of drawers, on top of which were at least a dozen framed pictures of Dotty's family, her mother, her grandfather, and her husband. A wedding photo of a young Dotty and her husband stood in the center, with a half-burned candle in a nice holder in front of it. There was also a photo of a young man wearing a graduation cap and gown.

Jenny thought for a moment the graduate looked familiar, but then dismissed the notion. "Dotty," she asked, "is this your son?"

She could hear Dotty rummaging around in her closet. "What was that, child?" Dotty reappeared holding a small empty suitcase. "Oh—yes, that would be my only son, when he graduated from high school." Her eyes began to water.

"He's very handsome," Jenny said, trying to distract her.

Dotty wiped her eyes. "Here, child. You'll be needin' somethin' to carry yer things in—when ya go."

Standing up, Jenny accepted the suitcase. "Thank you, Dotty," she said, and gave the old woman a hug.

"Don't ya worry about fixin' supper," Dotty said. "You just get yer things in order, in case they come fer ya."

Jenny thought for a minute. "Dotty, can I have the little statue of the fat lady that's in my room? As a souvenir?"

"Ya can have anything ya can fit into that bag, child." The old woman grinned. "Too bad ya can't fit the bathtub in there." She hooted with laughter. "I've never seen the beat of it in all my born days—" her voice trailed off as she walked back down the stairs.

CHAPTER 10
THE PIZZA MAN DELIVERS

JENNY WAS ALL PACKED AND READY TO GO HOME. The suitcase Dotty had given her was exactly big enough to hold the clothes and shoes she wanted to take back, plus the little statue and her souvenir of the Festival.

When the call to supper rang out she went down to the dining room to find the boarders standing around and looking gloomy. Dotty had obviously told them she was leaving.

They dined on salad, pot roast, mashed potatoes with gravy, green vegetables, and fresh dinner rolls from the bakery. The richness of the menu made Jenny think about how much she was going to miss the wonderful meals here.

Half way through dinner Jimmy, the huge man from the pizza trailer at the Festival, stuck his head through the door and caught Trixie's eye. Trixie motioned for him to come in and serve himself. He ate with enthusiasm, and even went back for a second helping.

Dotty turned to Jenny with a conspicuous look on her face that made Trixie have an exasperated one on hers. "Child," she said, "this lad is goin' to take ya to the airport. It's time fer ya to go get yer things."

As Jenny walked slowly up the stairs she had mixed feelings about leaving. As much as she wanted to go home, she recognized that she had never been somewhere so wonderful and perplexing in all her life. She had never had so many pleasing yet painful experiences. She remembered how scary it had been in the department store when she had first seen nothing but fat people, and the painful experience of realizing how much she'd hated to look at fat people, including herself. The embarrassment of the scene she'd made in Argus's store came into her mind. Then she remembered how chagrined she felt having to see him again in the kitchen. And she pondered the confusion of watching TV here for the first time and seeing all the advertisements, realizing that the fat entertainers appeared here as well, and later learning that they were actually from here.

Jenny made sure she hadn't left anything—which, she told herself with a smile, was ridiculous considering she hadn't come with anything. She walked into the bathroom to take one last look at the wonderfully large bathtub. "I'm sure going to miss you," she told the tub. As she stood in the doorway looking at the room for the last time, tears began rolling down her cheeks. She remembered falling into her bed exhausted from her outing with the others and her day at the Festival. She flashed on being able to look at her nude body in the mirror and not feel disgusted.

But she was resolute about going back to her world. She had some scores to settle with her life, and now she knew she didn't really belong in Fatropolis. She was hoping she would return to find her life still intact.

That's ridiculous, she thought. *What could possibly be different after just one long weekend?*

As she turned to leave the room Dotty's colorful business card caught her eye. She stuck it in her pocket, just to keep as a souvenir.

She descended the stairs suitcase in hand, and this time found the boarders in the parlor. Some of them seemed puzzled to see Jenny looking so sad. Well," said Dixie, "it's not like you can't come back and visit."

As the other boarders nodded, Trixie nudged her sister, then stepped forward and gave Jenny a warm hug. Jenny realized how good it feels to be hugged by someone so large. "You come back and see us when you can, Mack," Trixie whispered.

Jenny was hoping to say goodbye to Argus, but he wasn't present. She guessed he wasn't over the embarrassment of her rejection. As she hugged Dotty she whispered, "Have you heard anything from Argus?"

"No, child. Not a word."

Jenny made her way down the line of well-wishers and came face to face with Jimmy, Trixie's criss-crosser friend, who was most likely paid to see Jenny safely through the portal. Jimmy was still picking his teeth after the wonderful meal. He gave her a knowing look and gestured that they should get going.

The room fell silent. *What can I say?* Jenny asked herself. "Bye, everyone. Thanks for making my stay so enjoyable." It hardly seemed adequate.

Jimmy led her to a large black car and opened the back door. The horde of people followed them out to the street and watched as Jenny finally disappeared into the back of the car and Jimmy hopped into the passenger seat next to the driver.

The driver was a man Jenny had never met. He and Jimmy were unpleasantly silent. As the car pulled away Jenny turned and discovered a nervous-looking man sitting beside her. He had a little meat on his bones, but was not very big.

"Uh, is this your first time going?" the man asked her.

"Yes, you might say that," she answered shortly, looking out the window to avoid more questions.

"I don't know why I'm so nervous," he said, quivering slightly. "I just don't know what to expect. I've heard stories about the prejudice. Some people from here can be pretty harsh about the idea of criss-crossing. I sure hope we can get through the portal without anyone seeing us."

Jimmy turned around and gave the man a stern look that seemed to make him even more nervous.

"I don't think you have anything to worry about over there," Jenny told him reassuringly. "You're not very fat."

The man looked at Jenny; it was obvious he was insulted by her comment.

The car turned the corner and drove for all of two minutes. When the driver suddenly stopped Jimmy got out and opened the back door, ordering Jenny and the man out quickly. Puzzled, they obeyed him. Jenny had no sooner grabbed her suitcase and closed the door when the car sped away. She gave Jimmy a concerned look.

"What?" Jimmy said. "He's late for his tap class." Then he grinned and led them down the street to Burley's department store, where Jenny had gotten her first look at Fatropolis.

She had a peculiar feeling as they entered the store, as if someone were following her. But she only saw shoppers walking around inside. Jimmy also looked around suspiciously, and Jenny suddenly knew he was enjoying this clandestine operation way too much. He ducked into a deserted section of the store and motioned to them both to follow. A moment later he took off his jacket and handed it to Jenny, then his baseball cap. "Here, put these on," he said, adding, "and tuck your hair up in the cap."

"Why?" Jenny asked.

"The portal you came through was in the women's dressing room. Right?" he said. "Do you know where the portal is that will take you back? The one in the women's dressing room?"

"No, I guess not."

"I rest my case, your honor. Do you think I'd know where the portal is in the woman's dressing room? And what's more, do you think I could dress up like a woman? Be careful how you answer that." He grinned at her. "I'm sorry to break it to you, but we have to go through the men's dressing room and then the men's bathroom."

"What?" she asked, going pale.

"The portal we're going through is in the men's bathroom." He seemed to really enjoy breaking that bit of news to her.

"Oh." She tucked her hair up in the cap, trying not to think too much about it.

"And try to act more like a man."

Shaking her head in disbelief, Jenny slipped into the huge jacket and started snorting as if she were trying to hack up some phlegm. Both of the men eyed her skeptically. Then she adjusted her crotch, looking ridiculous in Jimmy's jacket.

Half insulted, half amused, the men shook their heads and then started down a tiled walkway separating the sporting goods department from kitchen appliances. Jenny tried to stay behind the men and kept her head down, looking at her suitcase.

An older lady suddenly tried to stop them. "Why, Jimmy Littleton," she gushed. "I haven't seen you in years. How's your mother? How's your grandmother? Gosh, I haven't seen you since you were just a tyke. That was— what?—back in 19—"

"Oh God," the nervous man swore under his breath.

"Nice to see you again, Mrs. Cranfield." Jimmy stepped in front of the nervous man, pushed him aside and then behind him. "Uh—my friend here is awfully sick. We've got to make it to the bathroom."

The nervous man obligingly acted as if he were about to throw up, and the old woman stepped aside. "Say hello to Helen and Grace for me," she said as they rushed away.

Again, Jenny got the feeling that someone was following them, but saw no one she knew.

Minutes later they stopped outside the men's dressing room. Jimmy and the nervous man walked right in, but Jenny hesitated at the door. A moment later Jimmy came back and gently pushed Jenny to go in. The dressing room seemed to be unoccupied. Just like the women's dressing room, there were many individual fitting rooms. They had almost made it to the door of the bathroom when a man walked out of his fitting room right in front of Jenny wearing a pair of stiff new pants but no shirt. His hairy man breasts were resting on top of his big belly. Jenny turned away from him and ran right into Jimmy's belly, then turned again and almost ran into the bare-bellied man.

They danced back and forth, trying to get out of each other's way several times.

Jenny finally made it around him and hurried toward the bathroom door. Now she felt *really* hesitant about going in. She had never before dared to think of entering a men's bathroom.

Just as Jimmy put his hand out to open the door, a man came out. "Hey, Brickman! What's shakin,' man?"

Jimmy was unable to avoid shaking hands with him.

"Did you get a chance to go to the Festival?" the man asked. "Talk about your bulgin' babes—"

"Oh, God." The nervous man moaned again, rolling his eyes. He was trembling noticeably now. Jimmy steadied him, then turned to his friend. "Uh, Donovan," he said, "I'm kinda busy right now."

"Oh, you mean you got some important *paperwork* to do?" The man let out a slimy chortle. "You three all gotta go at once, huh? What were you all eatin'? Blazin' hot nachos or somethin'?" He caught sight of Jenny, who was trying to hide behind Jimmy. "Hey, you look familiar. Is that Jepsin?" He struggled to look around the huge pizza man, who was trying to hide Jenny while also clutching the nervous man's arm.

Jenny began phlegm-snorting again, then coughed in a deep voice. The nervous man swayed as if he were going to faint.

"He's not feelin' too good, man," Jimmy said. "You gotta excuse us." He wrestled with the two and pushed them into the bathroom.

Donovan's enthusiasm changed into understanding. "I totally getcha, bro," he said sympathetically. "Hey. Catchya 'round." He finally walked away.

By now Jimmy was visibly annoyed as they stumbled over one another into the bathroom. "Man, this is the last time I try and help two at a time."

"Brickman? How'd you get that name?" she asked Jimmy under her breath.

"It's a long story, a long and complicated one," he said, pushing her further into the bathroom.

To Jenny's horror there were three men using the urinals along the wall. She could actually see—them. A man came out of the first stall zipping his fly and fiddling with his belt buckle. She lost her head and tried to bolt for the door, but Jimmy grabbed her and pointed her in the other direction. She awkwardly lifted her hand to cover her eyes.

Jimmy pushed her hand down. "Stop it!" he said loudly. "Man, you gotta work on your fear of public bathrooms."

It was all she could do to continue walking. They got past the urinals, Jenny looking steadily straight ahead. She was so focused on not seeing anything that she nearly bumped into the stall with the *Out of Order* notice taped to it. *It's just like in the dressing room at Bountiful Britches,* she thought.

Jimmy took them to the farthest corner of the bathroom, where there was no one around. They slipped into the supply closet. Jimmy pulled them both close and muttered, "Okay, the portal is right outside this door. We are going to go one at a time. I'm going first so I'll be there waiting for you. Jenny, you go next—"

At this the nervous man started to hyperventilate. "I don't know if I can do this. I can't take the pressure!"

"Calm down, man!" Jimmy told him. "There's nothing to be afraid of. We just don't want to call any attention to ourselves, like all that gasping you're doing right now." He peered out through the ventilation slats in the door. "Shhhh—breathe—calm down." Jimmy looked again at the nervous man and asked, "Are you sure you still wanna go?"

"Yes, I'm sure. I'll be okay," he said less than convincingly.

The nervous man was making Jenny nervous, too. She made a decision. "Just take him with you, Jimmy," she said. "I'll come right after you. I'm not going to have him here fainting on me."

Jimmy looked at Jenny over the man's shoulder and nodded. He moved closer to her so the nervous man couldn't hear and whispered, "Okay. We're gonna go. You look through the crack in the door here and watch where we go through the wall." He made sure she was watching. "I'll try to get him through without anyone noticing."

He practically dragged the nervous man, who was still groaning, out of the closet, then cautiously looked back toward the stalls. Jenny scooted up close to the door and looked out between the slats. She watched Jimmy feel along the wall, and then saw where his hand suddenly disappeared. He pulled the man against him and they both disappeared through the wall.

Jenny waited for several minutes, still unable to shake the feeling that someone was watching her. She was thinking about how she could sneak out of the dark closet when she noticed a glow was coming from her suitcase. She knelt down and popped the latches. As she opened it her face was struck by a soft blue light. The little statue of the fat lady lying among her new clothes was glowing.

What on Earth? But she didn't have time to give this any thought. She had to get through the portal *right now.* She closed the suitcase lid and fastened the latches.

She stuck her head out of the closet, made sure she wasn't being watched, then stepped out and felt the wall in the same place. It collapsed under her touch and pulled her in.

Unlike her first experience with a portal, she managed to stay on her feet when she landed on the other side. As soon as she got her bearings she saw Jimmy and the nervous man, who had finally fainted while going through the portal. Although Jimmy looked disgusted, Jenny couldn't help but laugh.

"Oh, you really think this is funny, do you?" He nodded his head. "You are one messed up lady." But he couldn't resist cracking a smile, and they shared a good but quiet laugh.

Now they were in another men's bathroom, all packed into one stall. Her suitcase was still glowing. She hoped Jimmy wouldn't notice, but he was busy with their unconscious friend, whom he picked up like a rag doll and carried effortlessly out of the stall. Luckily the bathroom was deserted. Jenny followed Jimmy out and looked back to see another *Out of Order* sign taped to the door.

Within moments they were standing in the main hallway of Bountiful Britches. *I've come home!* She took off Jimmy's cap and coat and handed them back to him, then slithered as fast as she could into the women's dressing room to see if her bag was still there. She was disappointed, though not surprised, to see that it was gone. When she came back out and asked Jimmy if he needed anything before she took off, he smiled, shook her hand, and wished her luck.

"See you around Brickster—I—I mean Brickmeister—uhhh, what was it again? Brickenheimer?" Jenny said, poking fun at him.

"It's Brickman, and that's Mr. Brickman to you." He grinned again.

The nervous man had come to by now and was more nervous than ever to be in Jenny's world. The man was obviously going to need some more coaching before Jimmy could leave him and return home to Fatropolis.

On her way out of the store Jenny stopped at the customer service desk to inquire about her lost bag. When the clerk asked her to describe it in detail she obliged, and the girl pulled it out from under the counter and handed it to her. The bag she had been worried about for the past three days was finally back in her possession. Stepping away, she set the suitcase down and rifled through the bag, taking out her wallet and reviewing its contents. She was surprised to find everything still there, even her money.

While she had her wallet open, she remembered Dotty's business card and stuck it in one of the slots. She also pulled one item out of her bag and tucked it in her pocket as she left the store, still toting her suitcase. As she passed a trashcan on the street she dropped the item into the trash. As she walked briskly away, her calorie counter booklet complete with height-to-weight ratio charts lay atop the pile of rubbish in the can.

The sun had set, and as the sky began to rain on New York City Jenny felt renewed, stronger, and more confident than she ever had before. Walking down the street, she came to the nutrition supplement and vitamin store she had passed before her adventure began. She had no interest in any of the diet products the store carried and displayed in the window, so she continued on to the bus stop.

Back in her own neighborhood, she stopped at a flower stand and bought a bouquet. She finally arrived at her building and climbed up the stairs to her apartment. She struggled a little as she was carrying her bag, her suitcase, and the flowers. She unlocked her door and went in. *I'm home! I'm really home.* Patches greeted her in the usual way, glancing up from her place by the window where she did all of her serious lounging.

The next sound Jenny heard was a familiar voice calling through the wall. "Jenny Crandell? Is that you?"

Still holding the flowers, Jenny returned to the hall and tapped lightly on Mrs. Grabowski's door.

"Who's there?" came from inside the apartment.

"It's me, Mrs. Grabowski—Jenny." She heard the loud clacks of the many deadbolts her neighbor was unlocking. The door came open a crack, the chain still in place, as her elderly neighbor peeked out to make sure it really was Jenny. Satisfied, she closed the door again and took off the chain.

"Where in the name o' creation have you been?" Mrs. Grabowski asked. "You know a cat can't survive on just well wishes." As Jenny handed the bouquet to her, Mrs. Grabowski's face softened, and then she looked at Jenny with surprise. "Fa me?" she asked.

"Yes," Jenny said. "I know I didn't let you know that I was leaving, and I really appreciate you taking care of Patches for me. I really am glad we have you to look out for us. Thank you."

The old woman took the flowers from Jenny's hands. "Oh, she's no problem," she said. "In fact, I kinda enjoy it when ya go away so I can come ova and see her. I get lonely, ya know," she admitted.

"Well—thank you again, Mrs. Grabowski. You're a sweetheart for taking such good care of Patches and me."

"Anytime ya need me, just let me know." Mrs. Grabowski retreated into her apartment and locked all the locks again.

Back in her apartment, Jenny locked her own locks and sat down on her sofa. At last she had some time to really think about how lucky she was to have stumbled into Fatropolis. Within minutes she was up again, tearing the "ideal woman" poster off the wall and ripping it up.

This had the cat very interested. They next went into the bedroom, where Jenny unpacked her suitcase and put away the dresses she had brought home. The flowered dress with the sparkly sequins was hung outside the closet to be ready for the Annual Awards Event, just two days away. She opened the little suitcase again and took out the statuette, which by now had stopped glowing. She set it in a prominent place on a little table in her bedroom. While the cat was investigating it, she carefully selected a space on her bedroom wall and hung the metal souvenir from the Festival.

She prepared for bed, shoved her scale in a bathroom cabinet, turned out her lights, and lay down in the dark. Suddenly it hit her—God had answered her fervent prayer. She made a mental note to light a special candle at church on Sunday.

Lying in her own bed again, she was tired but still felt rejuvenated from all she had seen and done in Fatropolis.

Patches came up and nuzzled her hand, asking to be petted. "Come on, kitty," Jenny whispered, cradling her in her arms. She yawned, closed her eyes, and with visions of Flint Mackelroy dancing in her head, drifted off to sleep.

CHAPTER 11
REVENGE OF THE FAT LADY

JENNY WOKE WITH A START TO THE RINGING OF her alarm clock. She had slept unusually hard and felt sluggish. Wondering if her weekend in Fatropolis had been a dream, she started to question it, but then caught sight of her beautiful dress. She smiled, got out of bed, and stumbled into the shower. She didn't even think about weighing herself.

Feeling like a new woman, she couldn't wait to get to work. She didn't dread riding the subway, either—she sat down and didn't even care if people didn't like how much of the next seat her large behind was taking up. To her surprise she didn't notice anyone looking at her crossways. She walked up the stairs from the subway at her own pace, and when someone pushed her she pushed back. She was resolute that she wasn't going to let anyone pick on her ever again.

Unlike just a few days ago, she didn't feel a bit guilty about stopping for a doughnut on her way to work. When the person behind the counter got confused and tried to take the order of a person who shouldn't have been next, Jenny spoke up and informed him she was next. When she arrived at Kronkin International she entered the records room with her coffee in one hand and her doughnut in the other. She didn't care what people thought about her eating a doughnut. Laying her bag, coffee, and doughnut on her desk, she walked over to the usual morning coffee klatch.

Katy was the first to spot her. "Where were you all weekend?" she asked. "I tried calling you, but you didn't answer." Katy looked her up and down. "You look different. Did you do something new with your hair?"

"Nope."

"Did you go out with somebody new?"

"Nope. Well, not yet, anyway."

"Well, what is it then? Where did you go? What's so different about you? And why are you *glowing?*" Katy's voice was getting louder and attracting the attention of the whole records department.

"I took a trip, that's all, and it was *out of this world,*" Jenny replied calmly. "I feel refreshed. Is that a crime or something?"

By this time a crowd of records workers had gathered around to see the new Jenny.

She looked at them. "Oh, for heaven's sake. I took a trip. Now I feel renewed and ready to work." She spoke in her supervisor voice. "Let's all get to work, shall we?" She shooed everyone away, then returned to her desk to find a pile of new reports.

But Katy, who seemed to think Jenny was deliberately keeping something from her, followed her. "Well," she said, "wherever you went, it sure has made a difference in you." Then she turned and walked back to her desk, as if admitting defeat for not getting the entire story out of Jenny.

Jenny knew Katy had used her for years as a way to make herself feel better about her own life. After all, Jenny was fat and Katy was thin. Jenny had been promoted to supervisor of the records department, but Katy was engaged. Jenny knew Katy didn't intend to be mean, but she always seemed to feel a little better about her life if Jenny was miserable. This morning it was obvious that Jenny's glow was making Katy feel uncomfortable. Perhaps she could sense that a new chapter in Jenny's life was starting and her reign as winner in their game of self-esteem might soon be called into question.

Still elated from the events of the weekend, Jenny booted up her computer. She felt someone watching her. She whirled around and spotted one of her subordinates, a young man, staring at her over the wall of her cubicle. His head disappeared the minute she turned.

She had to laugh. "It's not polite to stare, Justin."

"I—I—I—" he stammered.

Jenny heard some stern whispering. One of the other workers was reprimanding him.

The day seemed to pass uneventfully after that, even as the office buzzed with gossip about tomorrow's Annual Awards Event. Jenny couldn't wait for her co-workers to see her in her new dress—especially Katy. She had always cared what Katy thought about her, but now she found herself caring less. She was starting to see another side to Katy—a side she didn't like.

ON TUESDAY QUITTING TIME came mercifully early, at midday, and all the employees at Kronkin International hurried away to their hair appointments and makeovers. The workers' pay was not docked as long as they could staple their ticket stub to their timesheets the following pay period.

For the first time in eight years Katy was unable to fix Jenny's hair for the Event. After visiting with Mrs. Grabowski, Jenny had learned she had been a "hair dressah" for "thoity years," and then her neighbor had said, "I'd be glad to come ova and fix ya hair up real nice." Jenny donned her sparkly dress. With her hair done up fancy, she felt and looked like a plump princess. The shoes that went with the dress were perfect, and she also had a smart dress jacket that she saved for such occasions.

"Wait a minute," Mrs. Grabowski said as she hurried out the door and into her own apartment. Jenny could hear rustling coming from next door, then, a few minutes later, Mrs. Grabowski reappeared and handed Jenny a little handbag that nearly matched the dress and shoes. "Soes ya can carry a hanky and some mad money."

Jenny caught a cab uptown to the swanky Manhattan hotel where the Event was always held. In the past Jenny had always felt self-conscious to be arriving alone, but not this time. Tonight she looked more terrific than anyone else. Walking into the ballroom, she realized how much she was starting to like herself and enjoy her own company.

She picked a table, laid her bag down, took her fancy jacket off and draped it on her chair. A friend of Jenny's from accounting came over and raved about her hair and dress, sitting down next to her and making small talk as if she did not want it to be obvious that she, too, was alone. Just then the toupee'd man from three years ago passed the table with his girlfriend. The woman smacked him on the arm with her handbag when he wouldn't stop staring at Jenny.

Looking around, she also saw Linda coming back from the ladies' room. Jenny was hoping to get a glimpse of her Neanderthal beau, but he was nowhere to be seen.

Next she spotted Katy and her fiancé entering. Katy had a knack for doing her hair up just so, but Jenny was underwhelmed by her dress. Jenny was surprised Katy would commit such a fashion faux pas when she was one of the women who would go on and on so cruelly about other people's evening wear choices. Her fiancé was handsome enough in his tuxedo, but what man wasn't? They selected a table and sat down.

Twenty minutes later the ballroom was filled with employees milling about and chatting. The company had obviously grown in the past year, as there were a lot of people Jenny didn't recognize.

Promptly at five-thirty servers appeared and began serving dinner. The first course was a mixed green salad with cherry tomatoes, cucumbers, julienned carrots and a balsamic vinaigrette. The main entrée was chicken canzano, garlic- and herb-roasted fingerling potatoes, and brown-butter-sautéed asparagus. Dinner was not quite over when the awards ceremony started. The people at Jenny's table were supervisors from other departments, and chatted quietly as awards for the top executives were presented.

Sometime later Jenny was sipping champagne between intermittent bouts of applause when a familiar face across the room caught her eye. A man five tables away was trying to make eye contact with her. She gasped as Argus Lippencott stood up, said a few words to the woman he was with, and started to walk toward her. He was wearing a tuxedo and looked more handsome than ever.

Jenny couldn't imagine why he'd be here. She started to fidget with her champagne glass and her handbag as she realized that he was coming straight over to talk to her. Hoping she didn't have anything stuck in her teeth, she stood up as he approached the table.

"Jenny," he said cheerfully with a big smile. He reached out and shook her hand. "How are you?"

The Board of Directors was now standing for their round of applause.

"Argus," she said, becoming aware that the people at her table were staring at them, "would you like to join us?"

"That would be nice, thanks," he said, as everyone shifted their chairs to accommodate him. He sat down next to Jenny. A server came over and filled his empty glass with iced tea.

"And now, as our awards ceremony comes to a close," the announcer was saying, "we'd like to present a *special* award. An honor that hasn't been awarded to anyone in seven years. The Kronkin International Lion Heart Award."

Jenny was very uncomfortable seeing Argus again here.

The announcer continued, "This employee saved the company hundreds of thousands of dollars when she called an error to the attention of another supervisor in the accounting department a few months ago. It took a lot of courage for this person to come forward. This employee is none other than Jenny Crandell. Ladies and gentlemen, please join me in honoring Jenny Crandell. Jenny, please come forward and accept your award and our thanks."

As the crowd exploded with applause, Jenny, not knowing if she had actually heard her name, looked at Argus, who was applauding her as well. As she began to stand up Argus also stood up and held out his hand. She reluctantly took his arm. He smiled at her and led her to the stage.

As soon as the other employees saw Argus accompanying Jenny, a rustling and chattering erupted. As Jenny stepped up on the stage and accepted her award, the company's chief financial officer shook her hand, which began a standing ovation that to Jenny, lasted far too long. She didn't see the executive who had gotten her in trouble. She flushed, fidgeted with the award, looked out at the crowd, back at Argus, to the CFO, and back to the award. She felt awkward having attention drawn to her, but in that moment it felt good to be celebrated for something she had done out of honesty and integrity.

As the applause died down she moved in close to the microphone and said, "Thank you." Then she moved toward Argus and took his arm again. They walked back to the table. As soon as they sat down again, she took a big gulp of her champagne.

Finally recovering from her moment of fame, she turned to him. "Thank you for accompanying me. That was quite a shock. I might not have been able to make it all the way up there without holding on."

"Congratulations, Jenny," he said with a smile. "Anytime you need an arm to hold on to, you let me know."

"So what brought you here?"

"My cousin Amanda. She works in human resources. She couldn't get a date, so I said I'd come with her. As it turns out, she has plenty of friends at her table and I started feeling like a third wheel. When I saw you, I just had to come over and say hello."

"So now you get it," she whispered. "I'm from *here.*"

"I kinda had my suspicions about that when you came into the store looking for something to help you reduce," he admitted.

Just then the dance floor was opened and an orchestra began to play. Attendees began getting up to dance.

"I don't want to take you away from your cousin," Jenny said.

"She's going to dance with one of the guys in HR." Argus had already spotted Amanda moving to the dance floor, which was filling up fast. He stood up and extended one hand. "May I have this dance, milady?"

She didn't know how to react. "Argus," she began, "I—I'm sorry about what happened at the festival. I didn't mean to hurt you, or embarrass you—I really do like you as a friend—"

He leaned in close to her. "I was the one who was out of line," he murmured. "I've always been too pushy with beautiful women."

Katy and her fiancé were approaching the table. Overhearing what Argus was saying to Jenny, Katy gave them both a sour look. "Well, Jenny," she said, "aren't you going to introduce us?" Katy was sure this was the man Jenny had been trying to hide from her.

Jenny looked back at Katy. "Argus Lippencott," she said flatly, "this is Katy. And her fiancé, Josh."

Argus shook their hands, then promptly went back to staring into Jenny's eyes, obviously dismissing the intruders.

"You wanted to dance?" Jenny asked. She stood up, took Argus's arm, and let him lead her to the dance floor.

Katy just stood there with her mouth open. What had happened to her insecure fat friend?

Jenny winked at Argus. "Thanks for playing along."

"No problem. For you—anything."

As they danced, Jenny still felt embarrassed. She still felt Argus was young enough to be her little brother. In fact, her little brother was probably older than Argus. She couldn't shake that feeling, and she could feel everyone staring. *I wonder if they're thinking that he's too gorgeous to be with a fat lady like me.* After a few minutes, however, she decided to just enjoy the evening.

They danced several dances together, drank champagne, and indulged in the elaborate desserts, then danced some more. Linda and her boyfriend danced by, but he had his back turned to Jenny, so she couldn't see what he looked like.

Argus seemed to be enjoying his evening with Jenny. He looked her in the eyes as they danced and said, "I feel like I want to savor every minute I have with you. Jenny, I know we might never be anything more than just friends, but I have to tell you that I'm going to be really sad when this evening has to end."

Jenny blushed and wished that Argus wouldn't say things that would make her feelings of confusion about him return. All she could say was, "I'm going to be sad to see this evening end too, Argus."

They took a break and sat for a while chatting about how lovely the orchestra was playing.

The last dance was announced and the couple went back out to the dance floor. They were dancing and making small talk when Linda's boyfriend suddenly caught Jenny's eye. He was staring at her. She instantly felt fear. For a moment she couldn't remember where she had seen him. Then she recognized his face. He was one of the men who had made the "two six-packs" remark.

She gasped. Hearing her, Argus looked threateningly at the man. Then Linda looked at both of them, confusion and concern on her face.

Jenny happened to be a little on the tipsy side by now, and she had spent too much time fantasizing about what she would do if she ever got a chance to confront either of those men. She stopped dancing and got right up in his face. "How many six-packs will you have to drink before you can sleep with *her?*" she demanded in a loud voice, pointing at Linda.

Linda gasped. "What are you talking about, Jenny? How dare you ask him that?"

Jenny turned to her. "That's what your boyfriend does in his spare time." Her words were slurred. "He judges women on the street by how many six-packs he'd have to drink before he could sleep with them."

Linda blinked and looked at her partner. "Really?"

Everyone else was still dancing. They hadn't noticed the conversation yet.

Linda's boyfriend tried to gloss over his rudeness with an endearing look. "Baby, I don't know what this *fat cow* is talking about."

Hearing "fat cow," Jenny automatically lunged at him.

Now people noticed. The dancing stopped, although the music continued to play. Argus grabbed her from behind, then took her by the arms and led her aside. She kept struggling to break free and hurt this rude man, but Argus kept a firm hold on her. Then he turned to face the rude man. At the same time Linda stormed off the dance floor and out of the ballroom. Ignoring her, the man lunged back at Jenny, but Argus let loose of her and grabbed him, applying great pressure to certain points on his hands. The man struggled, but it appeared Argus's iron grip was unrelenting. He had to succumb to the pain, and within seconds the man dropped to his knees, whimpering.

Argus got down in the man's face. "Maybe it's time you start learning a little respect for the ladies. Huh?"

The man tried to pull away. "Let go! I won't ever do it again."

But he couldn't get away from Argus.

"I promise. Let go!" He obviously didn't want the crowd that had now gathered around them to witness his further humiliation.

Argus looked up at Jenny. "What will it take for you to let me turn him loose?" he asked.

Jenny thought for a few seconds as the man continued to whimper. "Two apologies," she finally said. "One for each rude comment."

Argus looked back at the man. "Well? You heard the lady."

The man glared at her, which made Argus apply more pressure to the points on his hands. He gave up. "I'm sorry. Now let go!"

Argus did not let go. "You heard the lady. You insulted her twice—"

"Okay, okay—I'm sorry," he finally muttered. "Twice."

As soon as Argus let go of his hands, the man fell over. The crowd moved back.

Jenny stepped forward and looked down at him. "Have a good evening, jackass!" she said. She turned to walk away, then doubled back. Leaning over him again, she said, "I can't even tell you how much beer I'd have to drink to sleep with the likes of you."

Finally satisfied, she took Argus's arm and they walked away. Argus looked over his shoulder and made sure the man understood he'd been defeated.

The man got up slowly, rubbing his hands. "Show's over," he announced, brushing himself off. The crowd began to disperse.

Jenny had no wish to stay any longer. She picked up her award, her handbag, and her jacket and asked Argus to take her out to a cab.

"Thanks for sticking up for me in there."

He looked at her and gently brushed her cheek with his fingers. "Well—I wouldn't want to tangle with you," he said, as they both started to laugh. "You looked like you were going to tear him to shreds."

"Did you study some sort of jujitsu or something?" she asked. "That was awesome, bringing that jackass to his knees like you did."

"I'm sorry, but I'm not allowed to talk about my special training."

Thinking he was serious Jenny's expression went flat, but when he burst out laughing, she began to laugh too. With a wink he flexed his fingers and said, "My hands are a secret weapon."

He paused, as if savoring the last few moments with her. "I had a lot of fun tonight, Jenny. Thanks for the good time. The evening turned out to be a lot more fun than I ever imagined it would be." When he hugged Jenny, however, the moment became awkward. Not wanting it to end, he leaned in and kissed her gently and respectfully on the cheek.

"I have to go now," she said. "I have to work tomorrow. It's almost ten thirty—and I'll turn into a pumpkin and rip out of this dress like that green monster guy if I don't get home soon."

He chuckled, enjoying her sense of humor, but looked at her puzzled. "Green monster guy?"

"Yeah, you know—the Incredible Hulk."

He still looked puzzled and shook his head. "Never heard of him. Sorry."

"It's okay. Never mind," she said, feeling less flushed now. "How long you gonna be in town?"

"I'm heading back tonight."

"Oh. Well—give my best to Dotty and the gang. And tell Trixie I made it back okay."

He turned away, then turned back again. "Jenny—there's something I've got to come clean about."

"Oh, yeah?"

"Yeah." He was looking sheepish. "I followed you through the portal. I just wanted to make sure you got here safely."

"So that's why I kept feeling like someone was following me. Thanks for telling me. I thought I had finally lost it," she said with a smile, pushing him on the arm.

He smiled. "It's true about me coming as my cousin's date," he said. "It's just that that wasn't the original reason I came here. Once I got here, she asked me to come with her, so I kind of fibbed about that."

"Argus, thank you for telling me. I hope you make it home safely." She got into the back of the cab and Argus closed the door. She rolled the window down to say goodbye.

"I don't know," he said with a laugh. "I may just pop in on you from time to time. This place is starting to grow on me."

The cab started to pull into the traffic. "Look me up if you do," she shouted out the window.

ALONG WITH APPROXIMATELY thirty percent of Kronkin International's employees, Jenny called in sick the next day, but not because she was hung over or otherwise ill. The night before had been another one of the most amazing nights of her life. She had a great feeling of accomplishment as she stared at her award. She felt a little bad about Argus, but she couldn't shake the feeling that he was just not the man of her dreams. He was too young and too perfect, and she felt her flaws were magnified when she was with him.

When she returned to work on Thursday she basked in her newfound celebrity in the records department. She took her award and gave it a place of significance on her desk.

Katy was barely speaking to her now. Everyone in records was hearing a lot less from Katy.

JENNY WAS ALSO EAGER to get back to her church. Although she felt like she hadn't been there in ages, it had only been two weeks. On Sunday she woke up, showered, and put on one of the simpler dresses from Fatropolis, along with matching shoes. Picking up her bag, she gave her cat a pet on the way out of her apartment. It was a beautiful morning. She could smell the aroma of fresh bagels in the neighborhood.

She rode the bus to church and stepped off with a spring in her step, stopping short when she saw a crowd and an ambulance with its lights flashing. She walked closer and stopped near a parked car. A man was lying in the street. Jenny couldn't see his face at first, as the paramedics were tending to him, but when one of them moved she finally got a glimpse. It was the nervous man with whom she'd come through the portal.

The paramedics were taking good care of him, and a police officer soon arrived and began ordering the crowd to disperse. *Poor guy—his nerves probably got the best of him again. Good thing he's in the hands of New York's finest,* she thought as she continued walking.

She entered the church and blessed herself, then went to the front, lit her special candle, and entered her favorite pew. She saw the lieutenant—*what was his name? Oh, yes, Leland.* He was coming in and waved at her again as he went by.

She enjoyed the mass more than usual as she thanked God for her visit to Fatropolis, for meeting Dotty and the rest of the wonderful people at the boarding house, for the splendid baths, and for the enlightening conversations she'd enjoyed while there. She especially gave thanks for all the extraordinary lessons in self-love she'd received. Then she said a special prayer for Argus and thanked God for the comfortable companionship he gave her. She prayed he would find the love he so longed for. She also said a prayer for the nervous man.

When the mass ended she filed out of the church and into the crowd outside. All traces of the ambulance and the nervous man were gone, to her relief. After a minute she saw Lieutenant Leland standing alone on the other side of the crowd. When he smiled at her and waved at her to come over, she asked herself *what could he possibly want?* She walked over to him, noticing how handsome he looked in his uniform and head cover.

As she approached him, Robert Van Brune walked by and stuck his hand out. "Good to see you again, Lieutenant O'Flannigan." They shook hands firmly, and the lieutenant looked back at Jenny.

The picture she had seen in Dotty's room of the young man in the cap and gown flashed in her mind. Jenny's face went white, and then red, and then white again. Was this—? Could he be—? *Dotty's son?*

She stood speechless for what seemed an eternity. He stood looking at her, a puzzled expression on his face.

"I thought your *last* name was Leland," she finally said.

"No. My name's Leland O'Flannigan." He extended his hand. "It's nice to meet you again," he said with a smile.

Just then an excited little voice came from the crowd. "Daddy!" The chubby little red-headed girl came running over, and Leland hoisted her up against his chest with his left arm. He wasn't wearing a wedding ring. "Ms. Crandell," he said, "this is my daughter, Dot."

The two older ladies who usually cared for the toddler during mass passed by. "We'll see ya, son," one of them said, kissing him on the cheek and then kissing the little girl.

"Bye, mom," he returned.

The two old ladies walked over to the bus stop arm in arm, clutching their pocket books.

Jenny looked up at Leland. *Wait—maybe that's his mother.* She looked at the little girl, who had the same eyes as Dotty.

"Say hello to the pretty lady, Dot," Leland told the little girl.

"Hi."

"She's a little shy," her father explained.

"Nice to meet you, Dot. My name is Jenny." She couldn't contain her curiosity any longer. "I've been seeing those two ladies taking care of her. Is one of them your mother?"

"Oh, no. Adele, the one that called me son just now, is Dot's grandma."

As Jenny still looked confused, he added, "She's my late wife's mother. She still calls me 'son.' The other lady is her sister. They like to attend church and help with Dot. It's extra time they get to spend with her." Like Jenny, he couldn't hide the fact that he was nervous. "And it gives me a break. Lets me pay better attention to the mass."

"I'm sorry, I didn't know you were a widower," she said, reaching for the right words.

He nodded. "Actually, it's been two years now. I just now stopped wearing my wedding ring." He paused and looked down at his naked ring finger. "I'm ready to move on now." He looked up at Jenny with a sparkle in his eye and smiled warmly.

"I—I don't know what to say."

"What's the matter?"

"I can't believe I just assumed your last name was Leland." Jenny was happy she could cover her astonishment.

"Dot and I always go grab a bite to eat after church. Would you join us?"

"I was just going to grab a kosher hotdog and a knish on my way home, but—I suppose I could." *That's going to mean eating in front of him, and he's so handsome.* She refused to let it stop her, though, and walked off with them, finally satisfying her curiosity of what had become of Dotty's son.

CHAPTER 12
BABY STEPS ON THE
JOURNEY TO SELF-LOVE

LELAND HAD GREAT TASTE IN EATERIES. HE INVITed Jenny to a nice café, where they sat outside and enjoyed fresh lemonade and cold sandwiches. It seemed surreal to be sitting here in her New York City eating lunch with Dotty's son and granddaughter. *If Dotty only knew that she has a granddaughter,* Jenny thought, *she'd be so proud that the little girl takes after the hearty family members.* Her curly red hair glistened in the sunlight. She was well behaved and liked to eat.

Leland talked a little about himself and his career in the military, but said nothing about where he was from. When he asked Jenny about her family, she took out her wallet to show him some pictures. Something in her wallet caught his eye. "What's that?" he asked. "It looks familiar." It was the business card from Dotty's bakery.

What can I say? "Uh—well—"

"May I?" He reached over and pulled the card out of her wallet. "I was wondering—if you were from—over there."

"Actually—"

"I can't believe that in ten years she hasn't changed her business cards. But she'd just say, 'if it's not broke, why fix it?'" he said, mimicking his mother's accent.

"She cracks me up with that accent of hers—that seems to come and go."

"I don't even know why she still has an accent. She only spent, like, seven years in Ireland, right after she and my dad were married. Technically she shouldn't even have an accent, but grandma said she came back talking like she was born there. I used to get the feeling she thought it was good for business or something."

"Oh, okay—now I understand why her accent seems to get thicker when customers are around," Jenny chuckled.

"So how is my mother?" Leland sat back and heaved a sigh.

She decided to give him an honest and straightforward answer. "She misses you. She's miserable not knowing if you're dead or alive. And I'm sure she would be thrilled to know about Dot."

"I'm just not ready for that. She put me through a lot, and—" he hesitated—"she wouldn't be happy to see me so—so trim. It's difficult when someone—when your own family can't accept you for who you are."

"Well, she might be different now. *Things* might be different now." Jenny sensed she needed to back off, but said, "All I know is that she's pretty lonely. That's easy to see."

"I doubt that. She always managed to have a lot of people around." Leland looked lost in thought. "As long as you're doing what she wants you to do, you're welcome. Anyway—" He shook his head as if releasing old thoughts. "I won't bore you with all that. So what made you come over here?"

"Actually," Jenny went back to what she had tried to say before, "I'm from New York. *This* New York." She lowered her voice and looked around to make sure no one was listening. "I fell through," she said. "I ended up over there when I fell through the wall in the dressing room of a dress store uptown."

"Bountiful Britches," he said matter-of-factly. "There are a couple more portals here in New York besides that one. What do you mean you fell through?"

"I—I literally fell through the wall. One minute I was fixing a strap on my shoe, the next I lost my balance and *bam!* I went through the wall and fell into the other place."

"How did you like it? I haven't been back since I left ten years ago."

"I thought it was wonderful. For a fat person from here, it's like Utopia. *Fatopia,* actually." She giggled at her own witticism. "You know what I liked best? The big bathtub in your mother's boarding house." She could tell by the look on Leland's face that he didn't understand. "You know. Because it's hard for fat people to fit into the regular bathtubs here."

"I didn't know that. Fitting in—that must be hard for you."

Jenny smiled. "I had so many baths while I was there, your mother thought I was going to end up like a prune." She paused, then decided to just ask. "Not to change the subject, but what was it that made you come here?"

It was obvious he was thinking about what he would say. "I just couldn't take it anymore—the constant nagging to eat more, the women looking down their noses at me. A friend of mine told me he was going to come over here and join the military. I was so unhappy, I decided to come with him. So I just left my mom a note and left with him. Then my buddy wasn't accepted—he was too fat—so I guess he just went back. I got in, though, and I've been in ever since. It's been good for me." He took a drink of his lemonade, "God, that's so sweet," he said, pursing his lips and squinting.

"I met your cousins, too," Jenny said. "Trixie and Dixie?" She thought that topic would give them something less painful to talk about.

"Yeah, good ol' Trixie. She was the one who introduced me to this girl I was seeing before I left—the one who told me I had to try harder to put on some weight. That was it for me. It was like my mother all over again. I wanted to join the military, I guess, just to show everyone that I could *be something*. I didn't have to just sit around hoping someday I would be fat enough to be acceptable. I had to live my life the way I was. We all have to play the hand we're dealt."

"I agree." As the waitress passed by, Jenny asked for a dessert menu. "Are you going to order dessert?" she asked him.

"Nah. I'm pretty full."

Jenny ordered her dessert, a slice of her favorite New York cheesecake. While they waited for the waitress to return she asked him about what Trixie had been like as a little girl. Jenny smiled at how cute Dot looked as she used the spoon to shovel food into her mouth.

Leland replied that Trixie had been bossy and full of herself, but pretty sweet. Although the twins were identical, their personalities were nothing alike. He commented about how shy and sweet Dixie had been. Because he didn't have any siblings, he had looked at the twins like little sisters. When they were Dot's age, he told her, he had played with them, chasing them around the boarding house, which had always made his mother angry.

Conjuring up these old family memories made Leland laugh, but he became noticeably sad when he mentioned a fishing trip he had taken with his dad and Uncle Roland, the twins' dad. He admitted to having heard about his father's death from a friend who criss-crossed.

At that point Dot had to go potty, so Leland took her to the bathroom. About the time they returned and settled back into their seats, Jenny's cheesecake was delivered to the table. She felt a little awkward eating it in front of Leland, but she decided it was good practice in exercising her newly adopted attitude toward food and eating in front of people. If she was craving it, she was going to have it. "I just love cheesecake," she said as she took the first bite. "Your mom's bakery makes the best cheesecake I've ever tasted."

He managed to smile. "Yeah. Sometimes I get a craving for the doughnuts from back home. They're so good."

"You don't have to tell me!" Jenny exclaimed. "I couldn't believe how good they are, like nothing I've ever tasted here. In fact, all of your mom's bakery goods are delectable. Where did she learn to make all those things?"

"Well, my great-grandfather was a baker's assistant when he was young. He was a good man. I heard he dabbled a little in art collecting, too."

"Really? What kind of art?"

"He loved to collect little trinkets he found interesting. I don't know if my mom still has them, but when I was still living at home she had all different kinds of little lady statuettes he had collected, supposedly from all over the world."

"Wow, that's interesting." Dot was staring at the cheesecake. "Can I give her some?"

"Well—I guess so. I don't give her a lot of sweets. I suppose a bite or two won't hurt her, though."

Jenny cut up some of the cheesecake and put it on Dot's little plate. Dot promptly scooped up a bite, balanced it on her spoon and carefully maneuvered the spoon into her mouth.

Leland smiled and looked at his daughter. "What do we say?" he prompted her.

"Thank you," she said around the mouthful.

"She's so beautiful," Jenny said. "Your mother would be so proud of her. She'd love to spoil her."

The two girls finished their cheesecake and Leland paid the check. They stood together in front of the restaurant making small talk. Eventually they exchanged phone numbers. Dot was getting fussy by this time, and Leland explained that she hadn't had her usual noontime nap. Seeing the bus from her neighborhood line approaching, Jenny thought it would be a good time to say goodbye. They hugged each other, and Leland said he would call her.

Riding home, Jenny felt elated. She wished she could call someone from Fatropolis to tell them about her lunch with Dotty's son. She knew she'd probably end up going back to Fatropolis to visit, but she wasn't sure how it would come about.

LELAND DIDN'T CALL JENNY as she hoped he would. Two weeks had gone by since their lunch together. The next time she saw him at church, he waved but did not speak. He was gone the next two weeks. She began to wonder if she had said something to offend him, then thought, *That's ridiculous. It probably has nothing to do with me.*

Jenny was busy with her new life. Somewhere along the way she realized that she had struggled with overeating in the past. She remembered times when she had eaten until she was sick, or put away whole packages of cookies and sweets in one sitting, or in just a few hours. Although her eating was different now, she still was uneasy around certain foods and felt she couldn't trust herself to be in control. She also feared that if she swore off diets she would eventually be incapacitated by her weight.

She did some searching on the Internet and found a group of women of all different sizes who met in New York City. They were like-minded, tired of dieting, tired of harsh societal judgments. They wanted to accept and love themselves as they were. Jenny started to attend weekly meetings of this group and found the support she got from the women and the information she learned in the group extremely helpful in keeping her on track with how she wanted to live her life now.

She wasn't out to lose weight. Instead she wanted to learn to accept herself as she was. She also wanted to learn how to live in a world of food without being afraid all the time. She was becoming more and more comfortable about food choices, and basically ate what she wanted when she got hungry and strove to stop eating when she felt full. *What a novel concept,* she thought— *eating what I want when I get hungry and stopping when I get full.*

AFTER ONE LONG DAY Jenny felt particularly tired and frustrated. She hadn't attended her support group in a couple of weeks, and was feeling negativity growing inside. She'd given up on waiting for Leland to call and was valiantly trying not to slip back into feeling sorry for herself. When she got home from work that day she took a nap and woke up about midnight. She decided to watch television and indulge in a bowl of chocolate chip ice cream.

She flipped the channel to get away from a boring seventies crime drama and stopped at a movie where a knight was kissing the hand of a fair maiden. "Milady," said the knight. Not wanting to be reminded of Argus, she promptly changed the channel.

The next channel had a loud advertisement for a protein powder. "Are you woefully thin?" the infomercial announcer was asking. "Just drink six servings of this each day and you'll have a healthy physique in no time."

Jenny couldn't believe her ears. At first she thought hearing the knight say "milady" was a coincidence, but this second reminder made her think twice—about Argus. Since she was feeling depressed about Leland's lack of interest, she was probably settling for the next best thing.

She tried to categorize her memories of Argus's kindness as desperation and disregard them, but she felt lonely for him. *What is he up to?* She found an old movie she wanted to see on another channel, and sat back. She covered her legs with a small throw, and in no time she was hooked. About ten minutes into the movie, however, the leading man looked at his leading lady and said, "Clara, I don't think we should see each other anymore."

That was all it took for Jenny to hit the off button and toss the remote onto her coffee table. She sat there in the dark, the only illumination in the room coming from the streetlights below, the only noise the gentle pitter patter of rain against the window. *Maybe God is trying to tell me something.* Dismissing the movie scene as mere coincidence, she got up and retreated to her bedroom. She wasn't sleepy, but when she looked at the clock and saw that she only had four hours until she had to get up to get ready for work, she forced herself to go to bed. She lay there hugging a pillow, staring at the ceiling. *What's happened to the confident, self-loving girl,* she wondered, *who returned from Fatropolis with resolve to love and accept herself?* A minute later she admitted what she knew—*I'm starting to feel worthless without a man in my life, again.*

She lay there thinking about all the wonders she'd enjoyed in Fatropolis, and began to smile. She imagined bathing in her glorious big bathtub, eating those delicious meals at the boarding house, having fun at the pirate restaurant with its ridiculous, over-dramatic pirate fight. Then in her imagination she was back at the theater, watching the movie starring Eddie Sandoval and Josie Hanover. She revisited the Festival Fatropolis and remembered laughing hysterically with Trixie at Dewey Henderson and crying with Trixie over Flint Mackelroy. When she thought how she'd been teased unmercifully by Trixie and the boarders, she remembered how good it felt to feel like she was part of a group of friends. She also recalled how confident she had felt in Fatropolis.

She rolled over and hugged the pillow closer. She missed her support group, and realized she needed to keep going each week to reinforce her new habits. *It's a good thing I recognized my defeating thoughts,* she told herself. And then just as she was starting to relax and feel sleepy, Argus popped into her mind.

His eyes were so blue and he exuded such an unconditional acceptance of her that tears welled up in her eyes. How she missed that acceptance. Then she remembered how he had looked when he'd overheard her rejecting comments at the Festival. *This is ridiculous. Pull yourself together, girl. You know he's not right for you.*

JENNY, WARM AND COZY in her bed, was dreaming she was back at the boarding house. Standing in the kitchen, Leland moved in for a kiss—from Clara. Just then Trixie walked in with a pregnant belly. The timer in the dream bakery kitchen began to ring. She tried to turn it off but it kept ringing, and ringing.

She woke up. Her alarm had gone off with disregard to her not getting enough sleep. She still felt groggy. *Wow, what a strange dream that was,* she thought, sitting on the edge of her bed. *It seemed so real.*

The next evening Jenny went straight from work to her support group. Usually she loved it, but sometimes she dreaded going, as the discussions often brought up feelings she didn't like to deal with. Some of the women had experienced horrible things as children that had made them turn to food for love and comfort. To hear these wonderful women talk about their childhood experiences made Jenny feel sad. She'd had a few bad experiences in her own childhood, but she didn't see much of a connection between feeling misunderstood by her parents and her love of eating. At the same time, she couldn't deny that some foods made her feel like she was wrapped up in a warm blanket of love. *I guess that's why they call it comfort food,* she thought. She was delighted that no one in the group ever talked about how to lose weight, their struggles with losing weight, or recipes for low calorie foods. None of that.

Jenny talked about how hard it was for her to wait until she got hungry to eat, and how hard it was to stop eating once she got full. That night the things she talked about resonated with all the women, and a lively discussion ensued. Jenny left feeling a new resolve. She didn't need any man to make her feel better about her life. She had to love herself before she could ever really love anyone else.

AFTER A MONTH of not being at church Leland finally returned, but he wasn't wearing his uniform. After church he apologized to Jenny for not calling, and explained that he had been in the process of getting out of the military, which had been a bigger ordeal than was expected. When she asked him why he was getting out, he explained that he felt it was best for Dot. The two years since his wife's death had been very hard for them, even though he hadn't been sent overseas. He wanted his daughter to have a normal life, so he'd secured a position at Kronkin International, as a new manager of the Business Development Department.

Sitting on a bench outside the church, they had a nice long conversation about what Jenny did for a living, and Leland seemed pleased that they would be working at the same company. Then he asked Jenny out on their first real date. He would secure a babysitter and they'd go out to dinner and the theater.

She tried to look at Leland's interest with a carefree nonchalance, but it was difficult. After all, she surmised, he would be the perfect man—a few years older, handsome and conditioned to be attracted to large women. He attended church regularly and even came with a mother-in-law she could get along with. Yes, he was a perfect match.

KNOWING THE DATE was only a few days away, Jenny went uptown and found a nice summer dress for the occasion. She had also, since her trip back through the portal, started wearing light makeup again.

The night of the date finally arrived, and Jenny burst through her door from work and scrambled around the apartment getting ready.

"Ah you okay, Jenny?" Mrs. Grabowski was apparently listening to all the noisy running around. "What's goin' on ovah there?"

"I'm going on a real date," Jenny called back, sucking her cheeks in and applying some rouge.

"Don't forget your hanky, then," her neighbor advised. "You want me ta fix ya hair?"

"No. I think I got it, but thanks!"

"If I hear ya come back with a fella, I promise I won't use the glass."

"Thanks, Mrs. Grabowski!" Jenny snickered to herself, knowing that if she ever had a man over they would have to tiptoe and use hand signals in order for her neighbor not to hear.

When Leland knocked at the door she opened it and found him dressed impeccably in a fetching dark suit. He had an orchid in a little box for her. She invited him in.

"May I?" he asked, setting the box on the table and taking the orchid out. He gently pinned the flower to the shoulder of her new dress. They were still standing very close, and Leland was looking into Jenny's eyes. He reached up and caressed her face, then moved in for a tender kiss. Their lips barely touched.

Jenny opened her eyes and blushed. "That was nice," she said.

"What was nice?" Mrs. Grabowski asked.

Leland looked at the wall in disbelief.

"Leland O'Flannigan," Jenny finally said in a loud voice, "meet my neighbor, Mrs. Grabowski." Then she took him by the hand and led him out into the hall and over to her neighbor's door.

The loud clacks echoed in the hallway as Mrs. Grabowski unlocked her locks. The old woman looked out the door under the chain, then closed it to undo the chain. She opened the door. "He's so handsome!" she exclaimed.

"Mrs. Grabowski, this is my date, Leland."

Leland reached out and shook her hand. "Nice to meet you, ma'am."

"Call me Gladys," she said with a coy smile.

Jenny looked from one to the other, then asked, "Well? Shall we get going?"

"You kids have fun now. It was nice ta meetcha, Leland." Mrs. Grabowski closed her door and locked all the locks again.

Jenny went into her own apartment and got her handbag and wrap and locked her door, too. They walked down the stairs to the cab he had waiting. Leland was a perfect gentleman. He opened the door and slid in after her.

They ate at an upscale restaurant that had linen tablecloths and matching napkins. Jenny ordered seared wild salmon with a lemon beurre blanc over a bed of herbed rice pilaf and an assortment of perfectly steamed vegetables. Leland ordered the same. They also shared a nine-year-old bottle of Pinot Grigio. Jenny, who didn't drink much, became flushed after just one glass, which made her feel good, like all was well. When the strolling violinist came by Leland slipped him a tip and he stood at their table and played for several minutes. The soft music was very enjoyable, and Jenny felt privileged to finally be on a date with Dotty's son.

The waiter came to the table just as they finished eating and asked if they would like to hear the dessert selections for the night. Jenny ordered the crème brulée, but again, Leland chose not to indulge in dessert.

She always loved a little something sweet after dinner. It just made the meal seem complete. Leland had more wine while Jenny ate her dessert, which was smooth, creamy, and delicious. She felt full after eating only half, so she pushed the dish off to the side. Eventually Leland finished the bottle, but didn't seem to be affected by the wine.

They took another cab to the theater and saw a wonderful play. They enjoyed each other's company, and Leland talked about what it was like to grow up in Fatropolis versus life in the military.

As their evening together was winding to its end and they were riding back to Jenny's building, he took hold of her hand. "I had a wonderful time tonight," he said.

"I did, too," she replied.

"I know this sounds old-fashioned—" He struggled to get the words out— "but would you do me the honor—uh, I mean, could we—just—um—"

Jenny was looking at him, her eyes wide, her mouth slightly open. What was he trying to ask her?

"Could we date—I mean, exclusively?" he finally said.

"Uh, sure," she said, all too quickly.

"Oh, God—thank God that's over," he said as he sighed and started to laugh. They both laughed, but Jenny still felt a little tension.

Leland saw her inside her door and kissed her goodnight. It had been a long time since she had really been kissed, and this kiss lasted for several minutes. Leland was gentle but strong, and she could already feel herself falling for him. He ran his forefinger down her cheek and gently chucked her under the chin. "I'll call you tomorrow," he said as he started down the stairs.

Jenny felt giddy and lightheaded. *This is it,* she thought. *I've finally found the man of my dreams.* She twirled around and danced into her bedroom to get ready for bed, feeling like Cinderella after the ball. She had met the prince and had dined with him.

She went back into her living room and lay down on the couch, thinking she'd watch a little television before turning in. When Patches jumped up with her, she grabbed the cat and held her up in the air, causing her to fluff up into a ball of fur. "And he wants to date me *exclusively,*" she giggled.

Mrs. Grabowski couldn't let that go without adding her two cents. "He wants to date you exclusively, huh? Things must be pretty serious."

"I hope so, Mrs. Grabowski!" Jenny couldn't stop smiling.

As PROMISED, Leland called her the very next day. They saw quite a lot of each other during the next few weeks. Jenny was head over heels in love. They went out on the town every weekend, and they'd even begun sitting together at church, after which they had a standing date for lunch. Jenny was also enjoying getting to know Dot.

By now they were feeling comfortable with each other, and Jenny felt she could talk to him about nearly anything. Leland had finally told her that his wife had died of a heart condition no one knew she had. He added that he was relieved when Dot's doctor said her tests for the same condition proved negative.

Yes, things were moving along smoothly, and Jenny was so busy with Leland that she had almost forgotten about Fatropolis. She had settled back into her job and enjoyed her support group. She was feeling more self-confidence than she'd ever felt before.

Sometimes when they were out together they ran into the members of Kronkin's management and occasionally one of the executives. When this happened, Leland always introduced Jenny as his girlfriend, which made her proud.

One evening a few nights after their fourth official date they were walking up to a restaurant hand in hand when they ran into the executive who had tried to get Jenny in trouble earlier that year. Leland greeted him and introduced Jenny as his girlfriend.

The executive gazed at her judgmentally and then looked back at Leland. He shook Leland's hand vigorously, then leaned in close and whispered, "I get it—fat girls try harder, huh?"

Jenny was perturbed that Leland seemed slightly amused, and the executive's tacky chortle revealed his assumption that Jenny could not possibly have overheard what he'd said.

She had to say something. She couldn't let another chance go by to educate an insensitive, callous man. She had only a few seconds to work up the nerve to contest his rude remark, and she could feel the window for responding back slipping away. Knowing she might never again have the chance, she forced herself to say something. "I heard what you said. What did you mean by that?" she asked him, her voice perhaps a tad too loud.

The executive looked flustered.

"What size is *your* girlfriend? Or do you even have a girlfriend? Is that why you're out alone tonight?"

Leland looked at Jenny, all amusement gone from his face, then turned back to the executive. "Uhhh, what she means is—uh—well, you know, maybe we should talk about this later." The executive walked away in a huff, leaving Leland looking at Jenny as if asking her why she would embarrass him like that.

Jenny could not believe that the man she loved had just allowed someone to insult her. "Thanks for throwing me under the bus," she said sarcastically.

"What do you mean? He was just joking," he said impatiently. "Surely you're used to a little good-natured fat joke now and then."

"You're defending him? And for your information, *mister,* I will *never* condone jokes that undermine my self-esteem!"

"Oh my God, Jenny—*he was just teasing!*"

"Then why did he whisper it to you?"

"I don't know." Leland took a step back. "Let's just try and let it go and enjoy our evening, shall we?"

Without another word Jenny stepped down into the street and raised her arm to hail a cab. One pulled up right away. As she was getting in she heard the disbelief in Leland's voice.

"Jenny, come on!" he called. As the cab was pulling away she heard his final plea. "Don't let stupid stuff like that bother you!"

She left him standing there on the street.

How could he defend that poor excuse for a man? How could he? And how could he condone fat jokes? As she rode home visions of Argus flashed into her mind. Argus at the Annual Awards Event, Argus standing over the man who had insulted her, Argus making him apologize. A tear rolled down her cheek. *People are so heartless. That man doesn't know me.* Although she was beginning to feel sorry for herself as she had in the days before her visit to Fatropolis, she also smiled. She had stood up to this man. She'd fired an insult back at him, and in a sophisticated way, too, instead of just swearing at him. She wasn't even very angry at him anymore. She wasn't angry with herself. But she was very angry at Leland. *What a coward! I can't believe he just stood there and didn't defend me. Argus would have torn that guy apart.*

THE NEXT DAY, and for several days after that, Jenny found flowers on her desk. Every day the card that came with the flowers said something like *Jenny, I hope you can find it in your heart to forgive me. I will never let something like that ever happen again. I love you, please call me.*

She avoided his calls, so he left apologetic messages on her answering machine at home.

What should I do? This was the first time Leland had said he loved her. She wanted to believe he was sincere, but she had a history of giving people who hurt her chance after chance to prove themselves. She saw that as a good Christian characteristic, but was tired of being hurt.

Finally after the fifth day in a row of flowers with pitiful cards, she caved in and picked up the phone. He pled with her to forgive him and let him back into her good graces. Her resolve to not be hurt again flew out the window as she agreed to give him another chance.

That Friday night he took her out to eat at his favorite steak house, which was renowned for its choice cuts of meat and barbecued ribs. Jenny enjoyed her steak, corn on the cob, and coleslaw, and Leland had a rack of ribs and corn. They laughed at how greasy and delicious everything was. When the waitress came by to refill their drinks and asked if they would like to see the dessert menu, Jenny opened her mouth to say yes. But without even looking at her Leland said that they would not be having dessert.

Jenny felt uncomfortable, but she couldn't find the words to protest. She was still in the early stages of her new eating habits and felt she was being denied the chance to exercise her preference. She knew she should speak up. She struggled to speak up, but all she could hear were her mother's words. *Don't make waves, Jenny.*

Suddenly she felt like the little Jenny who had disagreed with her father and was not allowed to voice her opinion because it was disrespectful. *You're not a little girl anymore,* she argued with herself. But even though Leland could see she was upset, she was still unable to say anything. When he asked her what was wrong, she replied only that she was tired and wanted to go home.

Visibly uncomfortable, Leland seemed unsure about why she was cutting their evening so short again. Jenny was angry, but too scared to risk their relationship for her piddling needs and wants about food. After all, she told herself, no one was perfect.

He saw her to her door. She turned and unlocked the door, while he waited expecting a kiss. She turned back to him and, without looking in his eyes, gave him a mechanical peck. "Good night," she muttered.

"What's wrong, Jenny?"

"I'm just really tired," she lied.

"Okay. Well, I'll call you tomorrow."

Jenny was speechless. He really didn't seem to have a clue as to what was bothering her. She also felt confused. She didn't want to risk what she saw as a good thing. This man had sent her flowers every day for five days. He had told her he loved her. And now she was starting to feel unsure of herself again. Why couldn't she feel confident around him? Why had she just clammed up instead of speaking her truth about what she wanted in regard to food?

They said their goodnights and he walked down the stairs. She retreated back inside her apartment and silently began to cry, just as she had done as a little girl after shutting herself in the privacy of her room. She sat at her dining table and sobbed as quietly as she could so t her neighbor wouldn't hear. Eventually she calmed down, went into the bathroom and washed her face. Then she got herself a package of cookies and a bowl of ice cream.

She sat on the couch, turned on the television, and ate her cookies one after the other between bites of ice cream, almost without thinking. As her discomfort dissipated and she became interested in what she was watching the old, familiar, warm and fuzzy feeling came over her. As she absently poked another cookie into her mouth, it finally dawned on her. The connection was clear. Memories of her childhood flashed through her mind.

As a child she had always kept a hidden stash of cookies in her room. Whenever she felt frustrated or angry, instead of lashing out and expressing her feelings, she had hidden in her room and devoured cookies—or better yet, she had snuck into the kitchen late at night for some ice cream. Her clandestine eating had always made her feel better. It was the only way she knew how to deal with her overbearing father and passive mother.

It wasn't until her early adulthood that this behavior had started to catch up with her as extra weight.

In that moment Jenny realized that she had a problem. *I'm one of those—those compulsive eaters, like I saw on television. Oh my God! That's what the ladies in the group were talking about. I understand now!*

She finally understood why she felt afraid of certain foods, why she couldn't diet. Food meant love to her. She felt that certain foods held magical qualities that could dispel anger, resentment, rejection, and boredom. Food was the faithful friend that loved her unconditionally, that never made her uncomfortable, that was always there for her, and that always understood her with no explanations. To deprive herself of these foods was to deprive herself of love and understanding.

It was as if a light had come on, Jenny could see so clearly. She also realized that she was overly full, and put the ice cream and the cookies away. Then she applied a principle she'd learned in the support group—she didn't beat herself up about eating through her feelings. She was thankful that she had finally seen the connection between her behavior around food now and how she had used food to deal with stress as a child.

God, thank you for this insight that has taken me a few steps farther on my journey to self-love.

Before she went to bed she vowed that she would let these uncomfortable events with Leland go, but if another incident of the same nature happened, she would have to speak her truth.

CHAPTER 13
CONNECTING THE DOTS

SUMMER WAS DRAWING TO A CLOSE, AND FALL— Jenny's favorite season—was inching closer with every day. She loved the way the trees changed colors. The cool nip on the evening air was always comforting.

Her life was pretty fulfilled nowadays. She finally had a boyfriend, work was going well, and she enjoyed church and her support group immensely.

She had, for the most part, let go of the unpleasant incidents with Leland. With her hurt feelings mended things were pretty much back to normal, except that she still felt a little self-conscious eating in front of him. She just couldn't shake the feeling that he was monitoring what she ate. She couldn't be positive that was the case, but she surmised as much. She also couldn't bring herself to talk to him about it. Although she knew that wasn't exactly healthy for their relationship, she was content for now to take a wait-and-see attitude.

Another thing that had changed was her ability to order dessert while out with Leland. She just couldn't bring herself to do it, which made her feel awkward and resentful, especially when she had a hankering for something sweet. She'd always wait until she got home, but never seemed to have what she was craving on hand, which sometimes made her overeat whatever sweets she did have. Telling herself these feelings were *her* hang-ups, she put off dealing with them.

One Sunday after church, when they were together as usual for lunch, Leland looked up and said, "Jenny, there's something I'd like to talk to you about."

"Okay." She had no idea what to expect.

"I've been thinking a lot about going back to see my mother."

"Really?"

"I don't like the idea of going back alone, though. What would you think about going with me?"

"I'd love to go. I have quite a bit of vacation leave saved up. When did you want to go? For how long?" As she thought about it, she seemed to be more excited than he was.

"Well," he said slowly, "we could figure out how long we'd stay later, but I'd like to go soon."

"How soon?"

"Well, as soon as possible. Next weekend? Would that be too soon?"

"I'll see what I can do," she replied. "What changed your mind about going—over there?"

"I think I'm ready now. And I'm lonely for my family. Besides, Dot's grandma is older and can't do much with her anymore. I don't want to wait until my own mom is too old to play with her. I want Dot to know that she has family."

"That's good. I know your mom will be so pleased." She felt excited thinking about seeing everyone again—but suddenly Argus flashed in her mind as one of the people she looked forward to seeing. Pushing him out of her mind, she focused on enjoying her lunch with her boyfriend and Dot. She was helping more and more with Dot, as the toddler was more comfortable around her now.

She put in for two weeks of vacation the very next day, and when she told Leland, he was pleased.

THE DAYS LEADING UP to their vacation went by slowly. Jenny occasionally invited Leland over for dinner. He'd usually get a sitter so they could enjoy each other's company. Tonight they were on the couch, watching TV and occasionally kissing. Jenny was sitting upright and Leland was lying with his head resting on her round, soft thigh. He suddenly propped himself up on one elbow and touched Jenny lightly on her big, round belly. She gave him a surprised look.

"You know," he said, "if you ever want me to show you how to do proper sit-ups, just let me know." He put his head back down on her thigh.

Jenny didn't know how to react. It was as if all her hopes and dreams for their relationship had just died, right in that moment.

"Uhh." *Say something, Jenny. You have to tell him how uncomfortable that made you feel. Say something. Now!* But she couldn't bring herself to say anything to him. She felt paralyzed, just as she had when she was a little girl. Finally she forced something out. "Uhh, Leland, do you realize what you just implied by that last comment?"

He looked at her blankly. "That if you ever want to learn how to do effective sit-ups, I'll help you?"

She knew he wasn't understanding the message behind his words—the message she was hearing. "Well," she said, "suppose you had a big nose, and I said, 'If you ever want the name of a good plastic surgeon, let me know.' What would I be saying?"

"But I don't have a big nose."

"Okay. Let's try this another way." She'd have to take a more direct approach. "Does my stomach bother you?"

"Well—uhh—no, I—well, uhh—no. I just thought that if you ever wanted to, you know, take the initiative and do something about your weight—" Seeing the reaction on her face, he stopped.

Under the pretext of getting the remote, she bent forward, forcing him off her lap. She wanted to yell at him and throw him out. *It's nine thirty,* she told herself. *He knows I go to bed at ten o'clock. He'll have to leave soon.*

Without a word she changed the channel and they started watching a documentary on the History Channel she had seen part of some months earlier. She remembered that it had looked very interesting. An archaeologist was reporting on a dig that had started after finding ancient scrolls somewhere in the Middle East. The scrolls were about artifacts that had been created during a secret gathering of important women from all the major cultures of the known world at the time. The scrolls had been dated between 3200 and 2000 B.C. The scientist being interviewed admitted that the dates were an estimate based on the scrolls. He showed drawings from the scrolls that identified the artifacts as having been carved by artisans according to the specifications of the women at the gathering. The scrolls also suggested a general region where these artifacts had been buried to protect the power they were supposedly imbued with. Top archaeologists and experts assumed they had calculated a possible location correctly, and had been expecting to find the greatest discovery since King Tut's Tomb. They were sadly disappointed, however, when their dig resulted in unearthing nothing more than a cavern full of broken pottery. The scientists considered the whole expedition to be a complete failure. They had no idea where the missing artifacts could be or what had happened to them.

Jenny turned to Leland. "This is where I came in the last time I saw this."

As the archaeologist showed the drawings of the artifacts, Jenny sat bolt upright. "Oh, my gosh!" She had totally forgotten about Leland's insensitive comments. "Look at that. Isn't that funny? That looks just like the little goddess statue I brought back from Fatropolis." She walked into her bedroom and brought the little statue for him to see.

He took it in his hands, looking at it carefully. "Yeah, I remember this," he said. "Wouldn't that be funny, you and me sitting here holding an artifact that is four or five thousand years old? And holding hidden secrets to the universe?" They both started to laugh as he handed it back to her.

"Maybe it's worth millions of dollas," Mrs. Grabowski called through the wall.

"Mrs. Grabowski," Jenny shouted back at the wall, "you said if I had a fella over, you wouldn't use the glass!"

"Glass? What glass? You two talk loud enough for everyone to heah," came the muffled response.

"Okay, Gladys, we'll try and keep it down," Leland assured her.

Getting back to the subject at hand, Jenny whispered, "Yeah. You're right, it's probably nothing. But you know what?" She motioned for Leland to follow her to her bedroom, where she turned to him and held up the statuette. "This thing glowed when I was coming back through the portal."

"What?"

Jenny still spoke very quietly. "Yeah. I was hiding in a storage closet in the men's bathroom waiting for my turn to go through the portal, and I saw this blue glow coming from my suitcase. I opened it. It was this little goddess. She was glowing."

"I don't believe you." With a grin he took the statuette and pulled Jenny into her closet. "Let's just see if it glows." He pulled the door shut and held the little goddess in the darkness in front of her face. "See? It's not glowing."

All of a sudden he grabbed her around the waist. She was still annoyed by his comments this evening, so she struggled to get free.

Then he whispered in her ear, "Finally! We're alone. Where Gladys can't hear us." And he kissed her.

She gave in to the moment. As they kissed in the dark, however, she found herself fantasizing that it was Argus she was kissing.

Then she felt Leland's hand move slowly down her back and stop below her waist. His hand on her behind reminded her that things had gotten sexy with Leland only once. On their fourth date they had agreed to forego the movie and get a hotel room. There wasn't one inch of her nude curves he hadn't explored that night. He had whispered that he loved her body as he nibbled on her earlobe and kissed her neck. He seemed to have especially enjoyed touching her belly—the same belly he was now trying to convince her to reduce. And he couldn't get enough as he had spooned her backside. How did he now want her to change the behind he was caressing?

She squirmed and wriggled out of his arms and opened the door to the closet. Leland's attempt at being affectionate again made her uncomfortable. She was especially uncomfortable that it was Argus in her imagination.

"It's getting late, Leland," she told him, feigning disappointment.

"I know." He set the little goddess back on the table. "My mom gave this to you, huh?"

"No, I stole it," she said sarcastically. "Of course she gave it to me."

She led him back to the living room, gave him a peck goodnight, and opened the door. Leland left.

Their vacation was only two days away. Despite feeling disappointed with Leland, Jenny wanted so much to go back through the portal. Even more, she wanted to see Dotty's reaction when she saw her son and grandbaby. She also couldn't wait to indulge in her glorious baths again. She locked her door and plopped back on the couch, deciding to catch the local news before bed. The anchor was just introducing a reporter on a street in Manhattan.

"A man was subdued by police due to his outbursts and odd behavior during rush hour traffic," the reporter said. "Commuters in cars had called 911, reporting that the man seemed to be *trying to get hit* by oncoming traffic. They said he was dancing around cars in the middle of the street here, and then he tried to evade police on foot. Here's what those motorists were seeing. This is an amateur video taken earlier."

As Jenny watched, she was astonished. *That looks like the nervous man who came through the portal when I did.* He looked absolutely crazy. He was laughing maniacally, and then barking and growling.

The reporter continued, "It took four policemen ten minutes to get him into the squad car. The man, whose identity is being withheld, was taken to St. Jacob's Hospital for evaluation. Back to you in the studio, Trina."

"Wow, that guy turned out to be wacko. I hope he'll get some help at the hospital," Jenny said under her breath. She turned off the TV and went to bed. *Please God, let someone help that man that came through the portal with me.*

AFTER TWO SEEMINGLY ENDLESS DAYS, their getaway finally arrived. They had agreed to meet at six o'clock at Bountiful Britches, since Jenny was familiar with that portal. They would go through and meet in the department store in Fatropolis, then make the trek to Dotty's Bakery. Jenny had her bag packed and ready to go. She had decided to take the small suitcase so as not to be so conspicuous carrying a large one. She had also made arrangements with Mrs. Grabowski to take care of Patches for possibly two weeks, which her neighbor was thrilled to do.

The evenings were beginning to get chilly, so Jenny put on her light coat, assuming the weather would be the same in Fatropolis. After all, it was New York, too. She went over the final instructions with her neighbor, got her things, locked her door, and set off to catch a cab to the dress shop.

As the cab approached Bountiful Britches she saw Leland and Dot standing in front, waiting for her. Dot was wearing a jumper and a warm hat that covered her ears. *She looks so cute with her rosy cheeks,* Jenny thought. Leland had his and Dot's clothes in a shoulder bag. They went over the plan again.

Jenny had tucked the little goddess in her coat pocket. Would it glow near the portal again?

They walked into the store and saw a few people milling around. When they came to the hall outside the dressing rooms and bathrooms, they kissed quickly and went their separate ways, Dot going with her father and Jenny entering the women's dressing room. There was no one else around. Going into the furthest fitting room from the door, she felt around the wall and found the spot she had fallen through. She looked down. Sure enough, there was a light blue glow coming from her coat. She reached in and pulled the little goddess out. *It must glow when it gets close to the portals.*

Then she stepped through the wall, being careful to step down as she entered the fitting room at Burley's Department Store. As she entered the little room for a second time, she recalled the confusion and fear she'd felt when she first came through. She was glad that this time she knew exactly what was happening and exactly where she was going.

She found Leland and Dot between women's and men's clothing. When she got up close to Leland, she discreetly showed him the little goddess and said in a soft voice, "It glowed again when it got close to the portal."

Leland gave her a skeptical look.

"Do you want to take it back in there?" she asked. "Do you need to see for yourself? I'm telling you, it glows when it gets near the portal. Here." She handed it to him. "Go and see. I'll watch Dot. We'll wait right here."

He reluctantly took the little statuette and put it in his pocket, then walked back into the men's dressing room. A few minutes later he came back out. There was no color in his face.

Jenny gave a triumphant smile. "See?"

"Yeah, I saw all right." When he handed it back to her it seemed as if he didn't want anything to do with it.

Fat people were walking and shopping in every department of the store as the three of them walked toward the front entrance. Jenny could tell that

Leland was already starting to feel uncomfortable.

"What's the matter?" she asked him.

"Culture shock," he said, looking at all the plump people around him. Everyone stared at Jenny as if she were matched with someone who was substandard, but then they smiled at Dot, apparently relieved that at least the child took after Jenny.

They moved quickly through the store and then walked along the sidewalk for awhile. When they passed the nutrition supplement and vitamin store, Jenny looked through the big plate glass window and caught Argus's eye. She immediately got butterflies. She waved. He was sweeping, and when he saw her he stopped and just stared, a big smile spreading over his face. Then he caught a glimpse of who she was with, and his expression went flat.

Leland hadn't even seen Argus—he was walking down the sidewalk as if he were on a mission. Soon Jenny saw the sign for the Fatropolis Bar & Grille and remembered that was where she'd fainted. They walked for a while, but she didn't remember the bakery being so far away from the department store.

At last she saw the bakery sign in the distance. How would Dotty react to seeing her son and realizing she had a grandbaby? It seemed to take forever to cover those last few blocks.

Leland, carrying his daughter, entered the bakery first and held the door open for Jenny. She had never seen him look so ill at ease. Though she felt a bit worried, she touched his arm reassuringly.

Clara Donnelly was working behind the counter. She gave Leland a big smile. "How can I help you, sir? And what a gorgeous little girl you have there." Jenny had never seen Clara with such a twinkle in her eye. Then Clara looked behind Leland and saw Jenny. The big, flirtatious smile disappeared. "Oh, hi, Jenny. How've you been?"

"I'm fine, Clara. How are you?" The moment was incredibly awkward. "Is Dotty available?"

"I'll go get her," Clara said.

There was no one else in the bakery. Clara disappeared into the kitchen, and a few moments later Dotty came through the doors with Clara trailing behind. Dotty and Leland just stood there, one behind the counter, one in front. They gazed at each other, unable to speak, tears streaming down Dotty's cheeks.

Finally she walked around the counter and reached for her son. He, too, was crying now. They hugged, and Dotty began to sob into her son's chest. "Oh, I've been prayin' for this moment fer ten long years!" Her voice was muffled in his coat. "And who is this precious little girl?" she asked, wiping her face with her apron.

"Mom," Leland's voice was quivering, "this is your granddaughter. Her name is Dot."

As Dotty reached for Dot, however, the little girl buried her face in her father's shoulder.

"She's shy," he said softly. "Mom, you've got to give her time to warm up—"

"I've never seen a more precious, hearty little girl."

Just then Jenny caught Dotty's eye. She was teary, too, and when Dotty went over to hug her they both burst into tears, laughing and crying at the same time.

Dotty soon returned her attention to her granddaughter. "I bet you'd like a doughnut," she said. She walked back to the display case to get a cream-filled doughnut.

"Mom—she doesn't—" Leland paused, then smiled. "Well, I guess one doughnut won't hurt her."

Dotty brought it around to the little girl, who looked up at her father for approval. He took it and handed it to her, and she took a bite.

"Mmmm," she said, "that's good, Daddy."

They all laughed.

Clara was still staring at Leland. Now, finding the right moment, she extended her hand to him. "I'm Clara Donnelly, one of the boarders. It's nice to meet you, sir," she said as politely yet flirtatiously as she could.

"It's nice to meet you, too," he replied. "Please call me Leland."

Jenny thought it funny that Clara seemed to be playing up to him so boldly, and right in front of her, too, but she let it go.

By now Dotty was holding a plate of doughnuts and had already asked Hank, who had come into the bakery sometime during the hugging, to put on a pot of tea for their guests. She invited her family into the parlor, leaving Clara to work in the bakery. "Take off yer coats and stay awhile," she said.

As they were hanging their coats on the coat rack Hank came through the office door with the tea set. Charlie was close behind. This led to a commotion of hugs and handshakes. Dotty poured their tea, then asked Leland what Dot liked to drink. At his reply Charlie ran to get a glass of milk. They all sat down and began trying to catch up on ten years of separation. The portrait of Dotty's grandmother watched the reunion from her spot on the mantel, around the customary offering of cheesecake.

"Saints be praised!" Dotty said. "Me only son has finally come home!" She leaned forward to hug and kiss him again.

Leland laughed. "This is Daddy's mommy," he said to Dot. "She's your grandma. Can you say 'grandma'?"

Dotty looked at her, eyes full of hope.

"Not grandma! Not grandma!" The little girl buried her face again in her daddy's shoulder.

He tried to help her understand who this new person was. "She's not Mommy's mommy," he said. "She's Daddy's mommy." He looked at his mother. "She'll come around. We just have to give her time."

Blinking back tears, Dotty managed a nod. "I understand, son. She doesn't know me from Adam." She looked down sadly, wanting to change the subject. "How long are ya kids plannin' on stayin'?" she asked. Then she turned to Jenny. "How did ya get him to come?"

Jenny gave her a broad smile. "Well, he and I have been going to the same church for over a year, but I didn't know he was your son. Isn't that wild?"

"Land o' Goshen! The two of ya already knew each other before ya came here?"

"Well, sort of. And now, well, we've been kind of—dating," Jenny said, but with very little enthusiasm in her voice.

"Dating? But what about the child's mother?"

Leland cleared his throat. "Mom, she passed away over two years ago."

Dotty gasped, crossed herself, and covered her mouth. "God rest her soul."

"I'll explain it all to you later," he added. "I don't like to talk about it in front of Dot."

"Of course. Of course."

At this point Trixie and Dixie came downstairs. "What's all the commotion?" Trixie asked, and then seeing who was in the parlor, she ran down the last three steps. "Leland!" she squealed as she hugged her cousin. "Mack!" She squealed again.

Dixie came in right behind her sister, but greeted them more calmly. Pretty soon all the boarders were coming down to see what was happening. Not all the boarders remembered Leland, but those who did were glad to see him again and greeted him enthusiastically. The excitement in the parlor was palpable.

After several minutes, while everyone was talking at the top of their voices, Argus came in, and Jenny learned that he and Leland knew each other—although she couldn't imagine how, as she guessed that Argus was about fifteen years younger. Trixie just had to hear all about Leland's marriage, and while Leland was talking she asked to hold Dot, but the little girl refused, still afraid of all the strangers.

When Leland explained to the group that he and Jenny already knew each other from church and that they had recently started seeing each other, Trixie squealed again. Argus's expression became serious, however, as he looked over at Jenny. She, too, felt very uncomfortable, thinking about the times she'd missed Argus and even fantasized about kissing him.

Everyone seemed to be talking all at once, except Jenny, who was quiet in all the commotion. This was the most she had ever heard Leland talk. They were all laughing at family stories, remembering the old days.

Argus inched his way over to Jenny. "How have you been?"

"Fine, thanks."

"So, you and Leland, huh?" he asked, as if admitting defeat. "Well, you two make a handsome couple. I—I'm happy for the both of you."

"Thank you," she said awkwardly, thinking he would probably be happier if he knew the truth about the current status of her and Leland's relationship. "How have *you* been?" she finally asked.

"Well, an opportunity to buy the store has just fallen into my lap, so I'm working towards that."

"Wow, that's great," she said. "Congratulations."

"And I've decided to have a little procedure done," he said.

"Oh, really? What's wrong?"

"It's nothing, really. Just a little minor surgery. Excuse me. I shouldn't have mentioned it." And with that Argus shook Leland's hand once more and left the room.

Jenny wondered what he was talking about. She didn't know he had any medical conditions. Leland had moved across the room by now and was talking with Charlie and Hank, who were school acquaintances of his. They were all talking about old times. Dot had somehow fallen asleep in spite of all the noise. Leland laid her down on one of the sofas.

Trixie came over and hugged Jenny again, then took her by the arm and led her out into the courtyard, where they sat on a bench. "Well you're looking heartier than ever! Yep, you look a little rounder than you did when you left. You look terrific!" Trixie said with a big smile on her face. But her enthusiasm waned when she saw the semi-horrified look on Jenny's face. "What? You'd think I just insulted you or something."

"Well, where I come from, that would be the very definition of an insult." Jenny had to smile. "We actually use the same greeting, but we say, 'Have you lost weight? You look *great!*' But what I don't like about that is it implies that I didn't look great before, which in itself is kind of an insult."

Then Trixie asked how it came about that she and Leland had found each other, so Jenny told her friend the whole story. "And how have *you* been?" she asked Trixie.

"Jimmy and I are dating now."

"Oh, that's a big surprise," Jenny said sarcastically, grinning at her.

Trixie just giggled.

"Hey," Jenny changed the subject. "Argus told me he's getting some sort of procedure done. Do you know——?"

Trixie nodded. "He's finally decided to do something about his health. He's getting the GAS procedure."

Jenny looked confused. "What? What's that?"

"A doctor from France came up with this surgery to make people hearty. It's called Gastric Augmentation Surgery. Coupled with medicines to slow down the metabolism, a person can be healthier and heartier in less than a year. I think it's great that he's finally decided to get some help and be healthier." Trixie's voice was matter-of-fact.

"But aren't there risks?" Jenny asked.

"Well, sure there are. Sometimes people lose all the weight they gained within three to five years. Some people have ended up thinner than they started out, and some people have a lot of complications. I've heard that some people have even died from it. I think the risks are worth it, though."

"I don't understand. How can they do a surgery that would make you *gain* weight?"

"They go in and make a pouch out of a piece of your intestine and add it to your stomach so it will hold more. Then, like I said before, they put you on medications to slow your metabolism. That causes you to gain a lot of weight really fast. A lot of people say they experience a lot of vomiting, gas, and constipation, though." Trixie made a face. "That wouldn't be any fun. Thank God I'm naturally hearty. I'd hate to have to go through all that to be as big as I am. But I think I'd consider it if I was unhealthy like Argus and couldn't gain any weight."

"That certainly doesn't sound like *a little minor surgery.*" The surgery sounded ridiculous to Jenny, but suddenly she thought about her side of the portal. People in her world went in for weight *loss* surgery all the time—lap bands, gastric bypass, liposuction, butt and tummy tucks. Not to mention plastic surgery—boob jobs, nose jobs, face lifts, cheek bone enhancement, and Botox. All to make them more socially acceptable. *How sad that Argus is so down on himself that he has to get surgery to feel more acceptable.*

She had to change the subject. "So you and Jimmy, huh?"

"Yeah." Trixie actually blushed.

"Is he *the* one?" Jenny asked. "The one you're going to give up all other men for?"

"Maybe," Trixie said. "He's the only one I've even considered giving up all my—*contacts* for."

"Well, good for you," Jenny said resolutely. She didn't mean to change the subject again, but she had to ask. "So how is Argus? How's he been?"

"You've still got a thing for him, don't you?"

Jenny blushed, and gasped defensively. *Am I that transparent?* "Well—I—I—"

"Oh, God," Trixie burst out, "why don't you just break up with my cousin and marry Argus if you're still so hung up on him?"

"I wish it were that easy. Trixie, I'm really confused. And if you say *one word* to anyone, I'll—"

Trixie giggled again. "Whoa—it's me you're talking to. You know I can keep a secret. Did I tell anyone when you said you liked him before? No, I did not. Calm down."

"I'm afraid Leland has let the brainwashing get to him," Jenny told her. "He condones fat jokes, and he offered to teach me how to do proper sit-ups."

"Fat jokes? I don't even want to know. But sit-ups? What's that?"

"An exercise in my world to help you slim your stomach down. Make it flat."

"Well, exercise in itself is good for a body—helps you stay flexible," Trixie grinned mischievously, "but he wants you to flatten your stomach?" She sounded offended.

"Well—that's what his offer would imply," Jenny explained. "And he doesn't seem to like it when I order dessert, and he hardly lets Dot eat any sweets—"

At this Trixie gasped. "Not let a little girl eat sweets?" she said, shaking her head. "Oh, my gosh, he's going to do the same thing to his kid that Aunt Dotty did to him." She looked through the French doors. Leland was still talking and laughing with his old friends and relatives. "What a shame," she added. Leland was so busy talking to the others that he didn't notice Trixie's stare.

"Please don't say anything to him," Jenny said. "Don't let on that you know."

"If he does it in front of me, you can bet I'm going to say something." She turned and patted Jenny on the knee. "Don't worry. I won't say anything about what you said. Your secret is safe with me. But I can't just sit idly by and watch him do that to a little girl."

Jenny suddenly regretted saying anything. She had an inkling the news would get back to Dotty, and she wasn't sure that was a good idea. *That might make all kinds of waves,* she thought. Then she had another thought. *But maybe making waves isn't always bad.*

As Leland's reunion went on in the parlor, Jenny and Trixie had a great gab session in the courtyard. Trixie caught Jenny up on all the boarding house gossip, including the fact that Jimmy had moved in shortly after Jenny had gone home. Jenny expressed surprise to hear that Jimmy was such a willing helper around the house and in the kitchen. They were chuckling about the Pizza Man when Dixie came out to join them. Now they started reminiscing about the Festival, and Jenny got some more teasing about Flint Mackelroy.

"Gosh, Jenny," Trixie finally said, "you've been here how long?" She looked at her watch. "And haven't excused yourself to go take a bath?" At that all three of them started howling with laughter.

"You're right. Talking to you two made me forget. Where's Dotty? I gotta find out where I'm rooming so I can go soak. I haven't been able to have a good soak since I left."

The twins stopped laughing. "What do you mean?" Dixie asked.

"I don't fit in my bathtub at home."

Thinking Jenny was joking, Dixie looked at Trixie and laughed, then looked back at Jenny and saw that she was serious. Dixie looked back at her sister, as if she could help her understand.

"Jenny told me when we got acquainted at the Festival that she didn't fit in the bathtub in her world," Trixie told her sister. "Isn't that sad?"

Jenny nodded. "That's why I was always in the tub when I was here. Because when I go home, I can only take showers. A standard bathtub in my world is not big enough for someone my size."

"Oh, my gosh!" said Dixie.

"And tell her what you said about the bathroom stalls," Trixie said. "And the restaurant booths. And the theater seats. How you don't fit in them, either."

"That's true," she told her friends. "I don't fit well in too many places in my world."

"Then why in the world do you want to live there?" Dixie asked.

"Well, I was raised there. It's my home."

Trixie seemed to be deep in thought. After a moment, she looked up. "So that must be why the brainwashing works so well over there," she said. "You actually have proof, everywhere you go, that you're too big. You don't fit in a lot of places, so naturally you think you need to get smaller." She looked as if she were beginning to understand. "No wonder people over there are so crazy about being thin. If they aren't, they don't *fit* in." Trixie seemed to think she had made a grand play on words and chuckled. "Get it? Don't *fit* in?" But neither Dixie nor Jenny was laughing. "Well, I thought it was funny," she finally said.

Jenny stared at her with a deadpan look on her face. "Oh, you're just hilarious, Trixie. Like a rubber crutch."

The twins looked at her with serious faces. They looked at each other, then got the joke and burst into laughter again.

"You're right, though," Jenny admitted. "I never thought of it that way, but you're right. I see proof everywhere I go that I'm too big, and I just don't fit."

Just then Leland peeked out the door and waved at Jenny to come inside. Jenny walked in to hear Dotty saying, "Let me show ya to yer rooms."

Leland picked up his daughter, Jenny picked up their bags, and they followed Dotty up the stairs. Dotty gave Jenny the key to the same room she'd occupied during her previous stay, then took Leland to a double room across the hall where there was more room for Dot.

As happy as she was to see her friends, Jenny was glad to be alone at last. She locked herself in, ripped her clothes off as fast as she could, and started to draw a nice warm bath. Lying happily in the tub, she began to think about Leland and Argus. She felt more confused about the two men than ever, and struggled as she argued with herself about what she had told Trixie about Leland not wanting her to order dessert.

Leland hasn't really kept me from ordering dessert, she told herself.

Yes, but I haven't tried to order dessert since that last time at the steakhouse.

Oh yeah? That's right. I haven't wanted to make waves.

But maybe he was just trying to be helpful with the sit-up comment?

She sat up and smacked the water, splashing the bath mat. *Now I know darned good and well that he's uncomfortable with my size.*

But the mischievous side of her had a comeback. *Well, it will work itself out soon enough. Breakfast should be pretty interesting. There will be tons of food, doughnuts and sweets galore. That ought to push him right over the edge.*

Even as she felt herself wanting to laugh, Jenny had an uneasy feeling the time was coming when she might have to end her relationship with Leland. She was resolute in her decision to not let another comment of his about her size or what she ate go without a reply. *Don't worry,* she told herself. *It'll all work out like it's supposed to.*

An hour later she was still soaking in the tub. She had examined everything she was worried about from every angle. Then she heard a knock at her door and Leland's voice.

"I'm in the tub!" she shouted.

"Oh, okay. I'll try back later!" his muffled voice said through the door.

She wished he would just let her have her time to herself. This was weird, being here with him. It was no longer her Fatropolis. Now she had to share it. What's more, it was Leland's Fatropolis, and had been long before it was ever hers. *Admit it,* she told herself. *You're just a little jealous that he had the advantage of growing up here.* But he had ended up with self esteem issues just like she did, even though they'd grown up in different worlds.

She was finally ready to get out of the tub. She found herself walking quietly, not wanting Leland to hear her. *This is ridiculous. I can just tell him I'm too tired and want to lounge by myself.* She put her robe on and turned the bed down, then turned her TV on, keeping the volume low. Sure enough, just as she got herself comfortable he knocked at the door again. She rolled her eyes.

"Yes?"

"You out yet?" he asked.

She got up and went over to the door and opened it. He looked like he was ready to cuddle.

"Hey, Leland, I'm kind of tired from all the excitement. I just want to be alone tonight."

"Oh? Are you all right?"

"Sure, I'm fine. Just thinking a lot."

"Tell me about it," he said. "Talk about memories coming up. Jeez."

There was a long pause. "Well, goodnight," she finally said.

"Goodnight."

She started to close the door, but he stopped her.

"What?" she asked.

"Can I at least have a goodnight kiss?" He sounded a little insulted.

"Oh. Sure." She leaned forward and gave him a little kiss.

"Wow, can you spare it?" She had never heard him sound so sarcastic.

"Good night, Leland." She closed the door and locked it.

He stood at her door for a few moments, then she heard his door close loudly.

Being in Fatropolis again gave her self-confidence a big boost. Being around the hearty folk was exactly what she needed to get her head on straight. She knew her relationship with Leland was probably ending, but she decided not to judge things just yet.

As she watched TV—Fatropolis's equivalent to *Nick at Night*, with its campy sitcoms from the sixties—she realized how much she had missed seeing all the fat people in the ads and on the shows.

"I could get used to this," she mumbled, yawning. She fell asleep somewhere between *Dizzy Donna* and *The Kent Drexel Show.*

CHAPTER 14
LELAND GOES TOO FAR, TWICE

THE BREAKFAST ANNOUNCEMENT WOKE JENNY out of a sound sleep. She had dreamt all night, but couldn't remember a single dream. She got up and dragged herself into the bathroom to get ready for the day.

She set out from her room down the hallway. Leland's room was quiet, and she wondered if they were still asleep. Downstairs she heard talking coming from the kitchen, and when she peeked in Leland was helping with breakfast, making the omelets. Dot was nowhere to be seen. Jenny then looked in the dining room. Dot was sitting on her grandmother's lap eating a berry pastry and a piece of sausage. Dotty's face was aglow with the loveliest smile. She looked up at Jenny and winked.

"What can I do to help with breakfast?" Jenny asked.

"Child, you'll have to ask someone in the kitchen. I'm busy here with my grandbaby."

Jenny went back into the kitchen. Although Leland didn't speak to her, he nodded as she walked in. Dixie put her to work peeling fruit. She had oranges, melons, and pineapple to prepare for the tray. She arranged the pieces of fruit and carried the tray into the dining room. The boarders were starting to gather, all commenting on the adorable little girl.

Food was carted in, tray after tray, and set on the buffet table. Jenny orchestrated things so Leland was several people ahead of her in the line of boarders. When it was her turn she took a plate and helped herself to coffee with cream and sugar. Leland took modest portions and then looked around at the others. They were all looking at him as well, no doubt wondering why he wasn't hungry or if he didn't like the looks of the food. Trixie arranged two plates of food, one for herself and the other for Dotty, then delivered a huge cup of coffee with cream and sugar to Dotty.

When Jenny arrived at the food she refused to worry if Leland would approve and took as much as she wanted. Though Leland had no sweets on his plate, Jenny picked up a doughnut to go with her omelet, a generous helping of crisp bacon, hash browns, a little bit of fruit, and toast with butter and boysenberry jam. She carried her plate to where he was seated and sat down next to him. He didn't even look at her plate, which made her glad. His coffee was black.

Dotty looked at his nearly empty plate and black coffee. "Land sakes, son, you aren't eatin' enough to keep a bird alive."

The room fell silent.

Leland sighed. "Mom, I'm out of the military now, but I could be recalled at any time in the next three years. I have to stay within the weight standards for my height. I can't very well pile on a bunch of weight. That would just make it harder for me if I did get called back."

No one said a word. The only sound in the room was the quiet clanking of the silverware against the china plates.

"So, Leland, tell us about your career in the military," Dixie said, hoping to ease the tension.

"Well, I served for ten years in the U.S. Air Force. I got a degree while I was in and was promoted to second lieutenant. I also got to travel a lot. I met Dot's mother when I was stationed in Europe." He paused to take a small bite of his omelet.

As Leland continued to speak about his career Argus came in quietly, took a plate, served himself, and sat down. Leland stopped speaking. Argus looked around, puzzled, as everyone was still eating quietly.

"Well, son," Dotty said, "we're all glad you came back. We've missed you."

Several people chimed in that they were glad, too, and conversations began to erupt around the room. Everyone seemed more at ease now, and breakfast proceeded as usual. Jenny looked up to see that she was across the table again from Argus. He was staring at her. Leland glared across the table at Argus, who then paid close attention to his plate. Jenny went on eating, trying not to pay attention to either of them. Although some of the boarders got up for seconds, when Leland finished his plate he stood up and took it to the dirty dish bin.

Then he looked at his mother. "Are you okay with Dot? That tile in the office is still not fixed. I'm going to check it out."

"I'm fine watchin' my grandbaby," Dotty replied.

Leland left the dining room. A few minutes later Jenny finished eating and figured she'd see if she could help with the tile. As she walked through the office Leland and Charlie had to get up and move out of her way so she could pass. Then they crouched back down, looking at the tile to see what exactly the problem was.

Jenny decided she'd help with dishes instead. She hurried to rinse the dishes so she could go back in the office and watch the men.

"I suppose it won't help just to put grout around the edges," Leland told Charlie.

"Well, I'm no expert," Charlie said, "but I suppose we better pull the tile up first and clean under it and see why it's not level with the others. Then we'll have to put some adhesive underneath so it won't come loose again."

Jenny thought it was cute to see the two men working together. Charlie left for a bit and brought back some tools. They squatted down and tried different tools to try to pry the big tile up from the floor. But the tile didn't cooperate. It refused to budge.

Dotty poked her head in the door. "The two of ya are blockin' the entrance to the office," she said. "I can't get in. And I don't want ya two makin' a big mess in here. We still have a business to run."

"We're not making a mess, Mom," Leland told her, still trying to pry the tile up. "Wouldn't you know it—this thing is uneven and loose for decades, and I try and fix it and this is the thanks I get. Then to make matters worse, the darned thing doesn't want to be fixed." He groaned as he tried to force the tile from its space.

"I'll have ya know," Dotty added from outside the door, holding on to Dot, who was also peeking in, "that tile was uneven and a little loose from the time my grandfather put in the new floor. And that was when I was in high school."

"Why didn't I notice this as much when I was younger?" Leland asked her.

"It wasn't as bad as it is now. And—I'm sorry, son, but ya weren't a very observant boy." Chuckling erupted.

Just then the big tile finally came loose and Leland was able to pry it up. The floor underneath didn't look like the usual cement slab. What Leland was looking at was old plywood, and it was very dirty. By now, there were seven or eight people in Dotty's office, all of them looking at the space where the tile had been.

Charlie said, "Oh, I've seen this before. This must be an underlayment." The plywood was cut to the size of the tile. When Charlie tapped on it, it sounded like it was hollow underneath.

Leland tapped on it, too, to make sure. Then he carefully poked at it. The underlayment was loose. He pried the plywood up. There was a hole under it about a foot deep and as big as the tile. In the hole was an old metal box.

Dotty was still looking in from the doorway. "What in the name of Glory B. Good can that be?" she asked.

Leland carefully pulled the box out of the hole. He had to work at it, as the hole and the box were very nearly the same size. He finally got it out and stood up. As everyone moved out of the way and Dotty came into the office, he set the box down on her desk.

"Look, Mom, the box is locked."

Dotty handed Dot to her father, then pulled her large ring of keys out of her apron pocket and looked at them. "I've got keys on here that are so old, I don't even know what they go to," she said. "I just love old keys. I think they're so pretty." She sorted through the old keys one after another and held them up to the lock, trying to guess if they would fit. "Let's try this one," she said, her eyes wide with excitement. She tried the key in the lock, but it wouldn't budge. She looked at some more keys, then handed the ring to Leland.

"Don't you have any other keys we could try, Mom?" he asked.

"Well, let me go look in my room," she said, starting for the stairs.

They waited, chatting about what could possibly be in the old box. After several minutes she returned, holding a smaller ring filled with even more old keys.

"This ring might have the key," she said, handing it to Leland and taking Dot back. "I've always thought these were old steamer trunk keys."

Leland tested several keys he thought would work, but without success. He stuck another key in the old lock. It seemed to fit, but the lock still wouldn't give up. He turned it, jiggled it, turned it the other way, and jiggled it again. At last the lock clicked open.

Everyone gasped and sighed, "Ohhhh." They all stared at the box for several moments.

"Well, Mom, are you gonna see what's inside?" He stood aside to let his mother be the first to open it.

But she hesitated. "I'm kinda scared to open it," she admitted. "My grandfather always thought I was bein' disrespectful when I messed with his things. Why would he have wanted to hide somethin' in the floor?"

"I don't know. But we'll never find out if you don't open it."

Everyone in the room was leaning forward, eager to see the contents of the old box. "Open it," several of the boarders urged.

Dotty handed Dot back to Leland, moved closer to the old box, and reached a shaking hand out to touch it. After another moment's hesitation she opened the box. The old hinges creaked.

Inside was an old photograph in a frame with broken glass. As Dotty picked up the photo a tear rolled down her cheek. "This is grandma, and momma when she was a baby. This must've been his favorite picture of them." She laid the photo gently on the desk and looked in the box again. There was something bigger in it. It was a big book with a dusty leather cover. "This is my grandfather's journal," she said as she pulled the big book out of the box. She clutched the book to her chest and started to cry. "There's a lot of information in here about our family. Information about a lot of things," she said, glancing over at Jenny.

Leland looked into the box again. "There's one more thing," he said.

"What is it son?"

"Look for yourself."

Dotty reached into the box and pulled out a small wrapped bundle. It, too, was very dusty. When she blew the dust off everyone turned away, coughing and groaning. "Sorry about that," she said. The bundle was wrapped in soft leather and tied with sinew. She looked from the bundle to her son's face. "Should I open it?" she asked.

"Why not?"

Dotty's hands were trembling. "I can't," she whispered. "Here, son. You open it. My hands just won't work fast enough."

Handing Dot back to his mother, Leland took the bundle and examined it carefully, looking for a place to start unwrapping. Slowly Leland began unwinding the sinew, then began to peel away the leather. Everyone was standing around Leland and Dotty with their mouths and eyes open wide, as if they were expecting something to jump out of the bundle.

Inside he found a little statue made of petrified wood, about the size of his hand. It was a very fat lady.

Jenny may have been the only one who saw the shocked look on Dotty's face.

"Where on earth did Granddad get this?" he asked in a hushed voice. "Maybe he talks about it in his journal. I can't wait to read it. Surely Granddad knew what it was and wrote down where he got it."

Jenny and Leland looked at each other. They both knew they were looking at another one of the little statuettes that were missing from the archaeological dig.

"Show's over, everyone," Dotty said loudly, taking the little goddess from Leland, hurriedly wrapping it back up in the leather and looking somewhat uncomfortable. Everyone groaned and started shuffling out of the office.

Leland seemed glad to relinquish the fat little goddess, and looked down at the floor again. "Now to get this dad-blamed tile fixed," he said. "Mom, you want that hole filled in, don't you?"

"Of course I do. What would I want a hole in the floor fer?"

"Okay. Just checking. I'm going to run to the hardware store and get the materials to repair it."

"Charlie," Dotty directed, "give Leland some cash so he can get what he needs."

Charlie was looking down at the hole and thinking. "You know," he said, "if we get a thinner piece of plywood, it won't be uneven anymore."

"Good thinking, Charlie," Leland said and patted him on the back.

By now everyone but Jenny had cleared out of the office and gone back to what they were doing. Dotty, with Dot hanging off her hip, took the things they had found, including the metal box, and went up to her room.

It wasn't long before Leland and Charlie were back with the supplies and tools they needed to fill the hole and reset the tile. Jenny was in the kitchen by then, but she came back to the office and watched them scooping the readymade cement out of the bucket and into the hole. When they had finished filling the hole they put a *Caution Wet Floor* sign beside it so no one would walk on it. They had to let the cement dry for at least a day before the tile could be repositioned.

Trixie came out of the bakery and into the office with Jimmy, who caught sight of Leland and shouted, "String Bean!" He paused for a moment. "And Jenny?"

"Brickman!" Leland yelled back.

They shook hands and Jimmy pulled Leland into a hug, picking him up off the floor, which made Jenny and Trixie laugh.

"How the heck have you been, man?" Jimmy asked, looking down at the wet floor sign and stepping to one side.

"I've been great. Here, meet my little girl—" He looked around for Dot. "Well, I don't quite know where she is right now. She's here somewhere with my mom."

Trixie looked from one man to the other. "You two are friends?"

"Heck, yeah," Leland said. "We met in kindergarten. We were best friends all through school. In fact Jimmy's the one who suggested we go join the military together in the other world."

Dotty and Dot arrived back in the office just in time to hear this. The baker looked at Jimmy. "So yer the one who put the notion in my boy's head to go off to the other world and join their military, huh?"

Jimmy cringed, and Leland hung his head. Both men knew how Dotty could get when she got riled up.

But she smiled. "Then, Jimmy, I guess I have ya to thank for my precious grandbaby I'm holdin' here." Dot laid her head on her grandmother's shoulder. Dotty took the little girl into the kitchen.

Leland turned back to Trixie, "Don't you remember? My friend, the black kid with the big feet and the *huge head?* He's the one I always called Brickman."

Trixie gasped. "Oh, my gosh, that was *you?*" She started to laugh, pointing at Jimmy, apparently remembering how huge and awkward he had been as an adolescent.

"Isn't that something," Jimmy said. "I remember you. You were that bratty little girl that used to spy on us all the time. You tattled to Dotty about every move we made. But for some mysterious reason you can't remember me? I'm insulted."

"So you two are dating?" Leland asked.

Trixie laughed and nodded. "We sure are. So tell me, I understand how Jimmy came up with the name 'String Bean' for you," she said, ignoring Leland's glare, "but where in the world did you get 'Brickman' for this one?" She pointed at Jimmy, who started to laugh. When he opened his mouth to speak, he was interrupted by Leland.

"No, I got this one," Leland said. He turned to Trixie. "Jimmy's favorite ice cream flavor is butter brickle, so I used to call him 'Brickle.' One day he says, 'Man you're gonna ruin my chances with the girls calling me that. Why can't you just call me 'Brick,' or something manly like that?' So then I said, 'Hey, what about 'Brickman'?' So I started calling him that, and it just stuck."

Overhearing this, Jenny had to say something. She looked at Jimmy. "'A long and complicated story'?" she asked.

"What?" Jimmy looked innocently at Jenny.

"The night Jimmy took me back, a friend of his saw us in the department store. He called Jimmy 'Brickman.' I asked Jimmy how he got that name, and he said 'It's a long story, a long and complicated one.'"

Trixie laughed. "'A long and complicated story,'" she repeated. Then she turned to Jimmy. "Leland and Jenny are dating now." When Jimmy looked confused, she pulled him closer and whispered, "Dot's mother died a couple of years ago."

"Oh—I'm sorry, man."

Just then Dotty poked her head in the door. "All of ya ought to go out to dinner or somethin' tonight and have some fun. I'll be glad to watch my grandbaby."

"That sounds great!" Trixie exclaimed.

Everyone was in agreement about going out on the town, and when Leland asked Jimmy if he'd go with him to get his currency changed, Jimmy agreed to go. They decided to go after lunch.

Jenny wanted to see the journal and find out how Dotty's grandfather had gotten the goddess statuettes. *Why does the one I have glow?* she wondered. *And why was the one in the box tied up in leather?*

After lunch, while Dotty was busy with Dot and Leland had gone uptown with Jimmy and Trixie, Jenny went up to her room to have a soak in her tub. She was looking forward to going out that evening with Leland, Jimmy, and Trixie. Leland seemed to be in a better mood since he had found the box and seen Jimmy again.

Jenny enjoyed being reunited with her own old friend the bathtub. She enjoyed the hot bath even more now, as the weather was colder than it had been on her first visit. After her bath she napped for awhile and was awakened by Leland knocking at her door. She got up and opened it.

"Hey, sleepyhead," he said.

"What time is it?" she asked.

"We want to leave for dinner in about half an hour."

"Okay. I'll get ready." She yawned and started to close her door.

"Hey, wait." He pushed the door open and stepped inside. "Don't you think we should have a talk with my mom about that little statuette that was with the box? That it's being looked for by archaeologists in our world?"

"Yeah, I suppose. But don't you think it might worry her?"

"Well, she's going to find out when she reads the journal, anyway," he reasoned.

"Okay. As soon as we get back tonight, if she's still up, we can do it then."

He started to leave, but turned back toward her. He hugged and kissed her and said, "I'm glad to be here with you."

"I'm glad to be here, too."

Leland left Jenny to get dressed and went back downstairs, not even noticing that she hadn't said, "with you, too."

Jenny curled her hair, put a little makeup on, and dressed in a nice outfit. When she walked down the stairs she found Leland and Jimmy in the parlor, immersed in a discussion about their high school days. Just as she entered the room Jimmy turned to Leland. "Remember what the football players used to chant about her and her padded butt?"

They laughed and started chanting in unison. "Two, four, six, eight, Gloria's butt is really fake!" Then they both started laughing and high-fived each other.

Trixie, who was sitting nearby, looked over at Jenny with disgust on her face, half smiling and rolling her eyes.

Leland let Dotty know they were leaving, and they went out to catch a cab. When they were all seated in the cab with room to spare, Leland seemed surprised. "Wow," he said, "I didn't realize how roomy the cabs are here. I didn't travel around by cab much back when I lived here."

When they arrived at the ferry terminal, Leland paid the cab driver. They took the Stouten Island Ferry across the Hudson River to dine at a restaurant with a stunning view of the Fathattan skyline.

The food was delicious. Jenny had steak, a huge lobster tail, and a baked potato with all the fixings. Leland had grilled fish with rice and vegetables and Jimmy also had the steak and lobster, but Trixie just ordered soup and salad. After several beers Leland and Jimmy were getting louder and louder, still talking about the good old days and laughing and joking about pranks they'd played on their teachers. It got so bad that Jenny felt as though she were on a date with Trixie, as she was the only one Jenny was talking to. As the meal wore on, Jenny and Trixie were both growing quite tired of their dates' rude disregard for them.

Trixie hadn't indulged her usually hearty appetite. She didn't look good—she was a little pale and was sweating a lot.

"Are you okay?" Jenny asked.

"I'm just not feeling very well right now."

After the plates were hauled away, Trixie and Jenny began perusing the dessert booklet that always stayed at the table. They decided on the carrot cake, although Trixie said she wasn't sure she could eat any. The waitress brought them a cake that was smaller than a regular cake, but still big enough for each of them to have a generous slice. Jenny began to cut into the cake, but Leland refused his piece. Jimmy accepted his and dug right in. Trixie, still not looking good, excused herself and headed toward the restroom. Jimmy followed her. They were gone for awhile.

As Jenny finished her last bite and reached for the knife to get another sliver, Leland looked at her. "You don't need any more cake," he said.

She looked right back at him and picked up the knife. "Sure I do."

He took the knife out of her hand. "You know, life would be a lot easier for you in our world if you would lose some weight."

Just then Trixie and Jimmy came back to the table. Trixie looked even paler than before.

"Excuse me, Leland." Jenny said, "I will be the judge of when I've had enough dessert." Absolutely hating him at that moment, she took the knife back.

Trixie and Jimmy just stared, not sure what they just walked in on. "Are you harassing her about the carrot cake?" Trixie asked Leland.

Jimmy touched her arm. "Let it go, Trix—"

"No, I'm not going to let it go." She pushed his hand away.

Jenny served herself a second piece of carrot cake and began eating it.

Leland looked at her, then at Trixie. "Come on, Trixie. Mind your own business."

At this Jimmy's head snapped around. "Now Leland, I love you, man, but don't talk to my lady that way."

Leland's eyes were a little glassy and he was slurring his words slightly. "All right, Brickman. You don't need to get all bent out of shape." Then he turned to his cousin. "I'm sorry, Trixie." But the expression on his face was anything but apologetic.

Jenny finished her cake. She was proud of herself for standing up to him. She tried to tell herself that he normally wouldn't have acted that way if he hadn't been drinking, but then she remembered what her grandmother had told her: "A drunk speaks a sober mind."

She knew from his previous comments and actions that her weight bothered him. There was no denying it anymore. Right now she wanted to leave and never see him again.

The return ferry ride, as well as the cab ride back to the boarding house, were less than enjoyable. Jenny stared out the window and avoided making eye contact with Leland, who was in the seat facing her. It was obvious that she was sore with him, as she eventually started talking to everyone except him. By the time they got back to the boarding house he had sobered up a bit. They entered through the bakery. Trixie and Jimmy thanked Leland for springing for dinner, and then they apparently decided to go elsewhere.

After Trixie and Jimmy headed for the kitchen, Leland opened the door leading to the parlor. The room was dark. "That's odd," he said to Jenny. "It's not even nine yet."

They walked into the parlor. The light clicked on and a crowd of people yelled "SURPRISE!"

Dotty was standing across the room with Dot on her hip. "Welcome home, son!" Dot was dressed in a lovely new frilly dress, her curly red hair decorated with ribbons.

The crowd rushed at Leland, shaking his hand and patting him on the back. Old ladies came to hug him. His face was red with embarrassment. Jenny just moved out of the way so everyone could get at him. Trixie and Jimmy were standing near the back of the crowd. Argus was there also, trying to make small talk with one of the boarders.

After most of the greetings had calmed down an old man shouted, "Leland, tell us about your world travels!"

Dotty took this as her cue and spoke up loudly enough for everyone to hear. "After Leland left here to travel the world like his grandfather, he worked fer the government fer a while."

Hearing this, Jenny surmised that Dotty had told people various stories to cover the fact that Leland had gone through the portal. Leland caught on and played along, telling some tall tales about his adventures. The crowd listened to him talk for quite a while.

As he told his stories Trixie was waving Jenny over from across the room. She and Jimmy were standing next to a huge man in a three-piece suit. He had a big round woman on his arm. Trixie resembled them. *That must be Trixie's parents,* she thought. Trying to get across the room was difficult, but she finally made it.

"Mom and Daddy, this is my friend, Jenny," Trixie said proudly.

"Roland Kavanagh," the large man said. "Nice to meet you, Jenny." He shook Jenny's hand enthusiastically with his huge, strong hand. Jimmy was a little taller than Mr. Kavanagh, but he looked almost thin in comparison.

Trixie's mother greeted her next. "Call me Murielle," she said as they shook hands.

Mr. Kavanagh looked at Trixie. "What's the matter, sweetie? You're looking pale."

"Oh, it's nothing, Daddy. I'm okay. Just feeling a little under the weather."

Jimmy, who already knew Trixie's parents, seemed to get along well with them, and they seemed to like him.

After a few minutes of polite conversation Jenny could hear the bathtub calling to her. She was already wishing she could escape the festivities and have a good soak, so she excused herself, shook hands again, and began the long journey back to the other side of the room. She was inching her way back over to the staircase, but found herself closer to where Leland was standing, by the fireplace. He saw her there and pulled her in close.

"Friends, family," he said in a loud voice, "I'd like you to meet my girlfriend, Jenny." The crowd of people then rushed forward, shaking Jenny's hand and patting her on the back. "May I have your attention, please!" Leland yelled over the crowd and motioned for them to quiet down. "I can't think of a better time to do this than right now." He reached into his jacket pocket. A hush fell over the room.

All Jenny could do was blink. *What the heck does he mean? What's going on?*

Leland pulled a little black box out of his pocket. He slowly lowered himself to one knee in front of her and opened the box. Inside it was an engagement ring with a huge diamond that glistened in the firelight. He looked up at her with a sheepish look on his face. "Jenny Crandell," he asked, "will you marry me?"

Time froze in that instant. Jenny heard a buzzing sound, but nothing else. All the people seemed frozen where they stood. The room was hot. She was perspiring.

Not knowing what to do or say, she looked across the crowd. Trixie, worried and pale, was staring at her, and then she caught a glimpse of Argus. His mouth had dropped open. Everything seemed to be moving in slow motion. Jenny blinked. She could hear her eyes closing and opening.

"I—I—" What could she say? "Uhh, um, I'm not feeling well." She was barely able to get words out.

She wiped the sweat from her cheek with one trembling hand. This feeling was familiar to her. She knew what would happen next.

The room started spinning around her. She fainted, right there in front of everyone.

CHAPTER 15
JENNY'S BELLYFUL AND TRIXIE'S FULL BELLY

JENNY WOKE UP ON THE SAME GREEN VELVET settee that she'd found herself on when she'd fainted the first time she came to Fatropolis. Although she remembered a little of what had happened, she felt relieved that instead of answering Leland's proposal she had fainted. She knew she couldn't marry him—not with the way he'd treated her. She knew her weight bothered him. She knew she couldn't live her life trying to be something that someone else wanted her to be. She had finally come to accept herself with all her bumps, bulges and faults, and she wasn't about to turn back the clock on her self-esteem. Feeling obliged to change herself to please a man or society was something she could not allow herself to do, not ever again.

Trixie came into the sitting room carrying the tea service and looking very worried.

Jenny, who still felt weak and light-headed, managed to sit up. "Oh, my God," she said. "Not again. How embarrassing. I suppose my little scene put the kibosh on the party?"

Trixie closed the door and poured a cup of tea for each of them. "Don't you worry about any of that right now." She pushed a cup of tea into Jenny's hands. "Here, drink your tea."

Jenny laughed quietly as she blew into her tea. "I had no idea I was such a ninny. That's twice now I've fainted. I never thought I was the kind of woman who would take to fainting." She batted her eyes and said, "I guess it's just because of my delicate frame and constitution." Both women laughed.

"Well," Trixie said, "that was a pretty dirty trick he pulled on you, proposing in front of all those people after acting like he did. I wanted to go over there and clobber him. I tell you, Jenny, my cousin has changed. A lot. He used to be the sweetest guy, but now he's a real jerk. I don't know what's gotten into him."

"Did you see that huge rock he bought?" Jenny asked. "My God, that diamond was huge. I just hope he can get his money back. Oh—I didn't say yes, did I?" She was laughing, but there was a serious edge to her voice. "Please, tell me I didn't say yes."

Trixie laughed too. "No. You just stammered around and then *boom!* You hit the floor. It was pretty funny, if you ask me. Leland was actually embarrassed that you fainted. What a jerk. Instead of being concerned for you, he just stood there like an idiot." She sipped her tea. "Argus is the one who pushed through the crowd to see if you were all right. That's when Leland started to act like he cared."

"Was Dotty mad?" As soon as the question came out of her mouth Jenny realized that she cared more about how Dotty reacted than Leland. She couldn't bear the thought of Dotty being upset with her.

"No. She was just concerned for you. She was also upset that Leland tried to upstage her welcome home party. She started planning that party from the minute you two got here."

Jenny started to get up. "I've got to apologize to Dotty—"

"You just sit back and relax. Dotty and everyone else are already in bed. It's after midnight. You were out for a long time."

Jenny looked worried. "Isn't that dangerous, when a person is out for a long period of time?" She looked at Trixie for reassurance.

"Don't worry, you're in good hands. We get medical training in grade school here. You didn't hit your head, and your pulse, blood pressure, and pupils were fine, so we just let you rest. Argus sat here for about an hour, but he didn't know how you would feel seeing him first thing when you woke up. I told him I'd look after you. I don't like to admit it when I'm wrong, Mack, but I think he really does love you."

Tears welled up in Jenny's eyes. "I can't believe how blind I was about Leland—and Argus, too. I totally betrayed what I knew inside, and I went down the wrong path. I just need some time to get my head straight." She paused for another sip of tea. "But I think I love him, too."

Peppermint tea always made her feel like everything was right with the world. "Would it be all right if I went up to bed now?"

Trixie opened the door and looked out, as if looking to see if anyone was lurking in the hall. Then she closed it again and came back to sit on the other end of the settee. "Mack," she said, her voice suddenly very serious, "I need to talk to you about something."

Jenny sat up straighter to give Trixie some room. "What is it?"

"Brace yourself." She paused dramatically. "I think I might be pregnant."

As Jenny gasped and put her hand up to her mouth, Trixie shushed her and looked at the door.

"Oh, my God. Are you sure?"

"Well, I'm pretty late, and I'm *never* late. And I'm nauseated. Tonight in the restaurant I had to go throw up, the smell of that lobster just made me so sick," Trixie said with a disgusted look on her face. "I don't know how it could have happened, either."

Jenny had to grin. "Well—I never thought I'd have to have *the talk* with you. So much for medical training in grade school." Jenny continued as if she were starting a speech, "You see when a man and a woman love each other—"

"Smarty pants! You crack me up." They both had a good laugh at that, which seemed to lighten the seriousness of the moment. "I know *how* it happened. I just don't understand, because I consider myself to be pretty careful."

"Does Jimmy know?" Jenny asked.

"Of course he knows, and he's happy about it. Well, he's gonna be happy about it—until my dad finds out. I'm actually afraid of what my dad will do."

"Why? Is your dad mean or something?" Jenny asked. "He sure looks like a nice man."

"Daddy? No, me and Dixie are just his pride and joy, and he still thinks of us like we're his little girls, even though we're twenty-six. Did you know that our family is one of the wealthiest families in Fatropolis?"

"No, I didn't know that. I'm not from here, remember?"

Trixie nodded. "Yeah. Well, my dad is not going to like the scandal of me getting pregnant out of wedlock."

"Why don't you and Jimmy just elope?"

"And deprive my dad of the pride and pleasure of walking his little girl down the aisle? Which he's been looking forward to since we were born?" Trixie looked worried and was wringing her hands. "Oh God—what am I going to do?"

Jenny pondered this for a moment. "Just tell him," she suggested, "and let him decide. If he doesn't want the scandal, he'll send you away to get married. Or forge your marriage license or something. If your family is that rich, I'm sure he has the power to do something like that. And if he doesn't care, you can just plan a wedding and get married the old-fashioned way. That's what I would do. He's going to find out sooner or later," she added, glancing at

Trixie's belly.

Trixie's expression softened. "I think you may have something there. I've been so worried I haven't thought it through like that. My dad is a reasonable man. And he loves Jimmy—the fact that he's hearty, he comes from a decent family, and he just got promoted to head chef at Papa Panson's Pizza. Yeah, that sounds like a good idea, Mack. Thanks. I'm glad I talked to you about it."

Trixie walked up the stairs with Jenny and made sure she got in safely. No one was stirring, so Jenny locked her door, kicked off her shoes, stripped down, and went in to draw a bath. She sat down on the lid of the toilet, waiting for the tub to fill, and began to cry. She felt as if her heart would break. *Why does Leland think he has the right to tell me how I should be?*

She thought about this for awhile. *I guess I gave him the idea,* she finally admitted to herself. *By not standing up for myself. Not telling him to stop when he first started it.* She remembered the wise words of her grandmother: "People only act how you let them."

At last she stopped crying. "I have to stop feeling sorry for myself, too," she told herself out loud.

All that was left was the breakup to go through, and then it would be done.

AS USUAL SHE SOAKED for a long time. After her bath she put her robe on and lay in her bed, watching television and wondering what tomorrow would bring. How would her breakup with Leland play out? She wanted to be past it. She felt like she should be anxious, but she wasn't. She knew she didn't want to be with him anymore. Then she started to wonder if Dotty would be mad at her, and worried about how their breakup would affect Dot. Although Leland hadn't allowed them to bond much, she figured Dot might already see her as a mother figure—another mother figure who would abandon her.

When she started paying attention to the television again, she was almost halfway through an old movie about a fat debutante and her many beaus. The last time she glanced at the clock it was after two in the morning. It took a long time for her to finally go to sleep.

When she woke at seven-thirty, the boarding house was quiet. *Oh, that's right,* she thought, *it's Sunday morning.* She lay there for a while, thinking. She knew Dotty was probably at church already, and she hoped Leland had gone with her. She thought about going to church, but she had no desire to get up or leave the safety of her room, so she whispered a prayer that God would help her get through the day and that everything would work out for the best for everyone concerned. She was still sleepy, the bed was cozy and warm, and she eventually fell back to sleep.

It was after nine when she woke again and decided to get up. She washed and got dressed, then walked out into the hall with butterflies in her stomach, not sure of what would be waiting for her downstairs. As she descended she could hear talking in the dining room. She peeked in. Trixie, Dixie, Argus, Leland, Clara, and Charlie were all sitting around the dining room table. Clara was sitting right next to Leland, totally enthralled by his every word.

Jenny went in and walked over to the buffet table.

"There's my little sleepyhead," Leland exclaimed.

Clara glared at Jenny, who didn't even acknowledge any of them. Remembering that Dotty's boarders always had to fend for themselves on Sunday morning, she found only a tray of pastries and an urn of coffee on the buffet table.

"Don't mind me," she finally said. "I'm just in desperate need of some coffee." She poured a cup, doctored it to her liking, then plopped a chocolate glazed doughnut on a napkin and walked over to the table and sat down across from Leland.

She didn't really want to talk to anyone about anything. The conversation had died down the minute she walked in the room, which annoyed her. "Carry on, everyone. Seriously."

"Anyway, like I said—" Trixie went on with what she'd been saying before Jenny came in.

Jenny didn't pay attention to their conversation. She was enjoying her doughnut and coffee and thinking about important things. *I can't stand it when someone acts like an ass and then pretends nothing happened.* She was in no mood for explanations or stories or excuses this morning. She just wanted to be done with Leland and his control issues. She was actually looking forward to getting it over with.

Argus glanced over at Jenny, concern evident on his face, but she didn't look up from her coffee. At the same time Leland was prattling on about his time in the military and his travels to Europe. The conversation finally broke up as Trixie said she was going to clean the kitchen. The others got up and started to help clear the table.

Clara reluctantly stood up, too, and turned to Leland. "I'd really like to hear more," she gushed before she picked up his dishes and carried them into the kitchen.

Argus, Leland, and Jenny were the only ones left in the dining room. Leland looked at Argus. "Argus, would you excuse us? Jenny and I need to talk."

Jenny continued to calmly sip her coffee.

"Sure," Argus finally said, trying to gauge Jenny's reaction. He looked uncomfortable, but left the room.

Leland and Jenny were alone, but Jenny continued to ignore him. After some uncomfortable silence, Leland said, "I can tell you're upset. I just wanted to apologize for last night."

She finally looked at him. "Which part?"

"Well—well, I guess all of it."

"What, specifically? You getting drunk and insulting me at the restaurant? You springing your little proposal on me in front of fifty strangers, after insulting me? Or you being embarrassed that I fainted and not even caring enough to see if I was all right?"

"Where did you get that idea? Who told you that?"

She shook her head. "I don't even know why I asked you that, Leland. I'm done. I'm tired of you monitoring what I eat and suggesting I exercise. I can tell you don't approve of how heavy I am. Well, that's too bad, mister! And let me tell you something else—you are doing the same thing to Dot that you say your mom did to you. Good luck with that, by the way." She didn't care that her voice was getting louder with each sentence.

"So this is all about me not wanting you to eat a second piece of carrot cake? Nobody needs a *second helping* of dessert."

"No," she said. "This isn't about dessert. It's about you thinking you have the right to tell me what I should be doing with my life. I am perfectly capable of deciding when I'm full. And everything else about what I want. Leland, you were trying to *control* me. If I just let this stuff go, pretty soon you'll be telling me what I can wear. How I can have my hair. What kinds of things I can say. Nope, I'm done!"

He leaned toward her and reached across the table for her hand. "Can't you see how much I love you? Can't you accept my apology? I'm just trying to make your life a little easier in our world, you know." When she didn't react, he went on. "I know you're uncomfortable being so heavy. You could be so beautiful if you would just lose some weight."

She sighed and got up to refresh her coffee. "It's difficult when someone can't accept you for who you are," she began. "We all have to play the hand we're dealt—I remember someone telling me that not too long ago. But I guess that was just a *bunch of hooey.* Just like all your pillow talk when we slept together. What a load of *crap!* People like you are the ones that make us fat people feel uncomfortable about being heavy. But you know what? We allow you to make us feel like that. I'm not ever going to let someone treat me like you have. Not ever again. So thank you, Leland. Thank you for helping me to see what I *don't want* in a man."

He pushed himself away from the table and stood up, obviously angry. "Well," he snapped back, "good luck finding someone to put up with you and all your hangups!"

The minute the words left his lips Argus burst through the door. "Don't talk to her like that!"

Leland looked at him. "She doesn't need any help from you, *Squirt!*"

"Squirt?" Argus started to laugh. "Say something mean to her again, and I'll show you how much of a squirt I am!"

"Oh, you're a tough guy, are ya?" Leland grabbed Argus by the front of his shirt and the two men began strong-arming each other.

"Oh, my God, stop it! I can't believe you two." Jenny stuck her head out the door to call for help.

Dotty came through the dining room door. "They told me ya two were fightin' in here," she said, "but I didn't believe it. I guess I was wrong." Dotty's voice was loud and stern. "Break it up—*break it up!* I won't have men barroom brawlin' in here like a couple of animals! Stop it!"

She got in between the two, still struggling, and forced them apart. Both men were breathing hard. Each one took a step back.

"Now calm down," Dotty demanded. "Go sit down!"

Hearing Dotty yelling, Trixie, Dixie, and Charlie had come into the room. They stood quietly by the door, listening to what was happening.

Leland turned to face his mother. "Jenny and I were just discussing things," he said. "And boy wonder over here thought he had to come in and tell me what I could say to my own girlfriend."

"No, Dotty," Jenny said before he could say anything else. "That's wrong. Leland and I won't be seeing each other anymore. He can't accept the fact that I'm so heavy. He wants to tell me what I should eat, and he thinks I should exercise to slim down. *And* he thinks he's going to save Dot from becoming fat, too." She spoke quickly, scared that Dotty would be mad.

"I was just trying to help her," Leland said. "She'd be so much more comfortable in our world if she would just lose some weight." He turned to Jenny. "Why do you have to be so stubborn?"

At that Argus dove at him again. "I told you to stop talking to her that way!"

Trixie, Dixie, and Charlie stepped forward and pushed Argus to the other end of the room, where he couldn't get near Leland.

"And what I let my daughter eat and not eat is no one else's business," Leland added. He obviously couldn't let it go.

That's when Dotty began to cry, which took everyone in the room by surprise.

"This is all my fault," Dotty wailed. "If I wasn't so hard on ya when ya were young, ya wouldn't be so biased against the fat folk." She took out her hankie and wiped her eyes. "I guess you take after yer grandfather. Can't we just sit down like reasonable folks and talk about this?"

At this point Clara walked in holding Dot, who was obviously hungry and crying. Dotty took her and went over and got a pastry, which she ripped into little pieces for the little girl. Clara moved to the back of the room as if she was glad to have had an excuse to come in and see what was going on.

Leland looked at his mother. "I don't want her to have a bunch of sweets," he said. "Can't you see she's already chubby?"

Everyone in the room gasped and turned to stare at him.

"So yer gonna put her through the same thing that I put ya through, huh?" Jenny had never seen Dotty so angry her voice cracked. "She can't help being chubby, *boy!* Ya know she comes from a long line of hearty folk."

Jenny didn't see any point in staying any longer. This was a family affair. "I'm going to go up and pack," she said. "Dotty, thank you for your hospitality again, but I need to be getting home."

"Yer not goin' anywhere, child! Please just go out into the courtyard, or into the kitchen. I'll be in to talk to ya in a few minutes. Trixie, take Jenny somewhere while I try to talk some sense into this lad."

Trixie accompanied Jenny out to the courtyard, where they sat down on a bench.

"God, that was an ugly scene," Jenny said.

"Yeah," Trixie agreed, "but it had to be done. No one blames you for what's going on. Hey, why don't you stay awhile and enjoy yourself? You're on vacation, you know."

Jenny thought it over. "Well, if Dotty says I should stay, then I'll stay, but I won't feel comfortable staying while Leland is here. I can't imagine him allowing me to feel comfortable."

"Speaking of feeling comfortable, you think you've got problems? I took a pregnancy test this morning and it was positive. Jimmy and I are meeting with my parents this afternoon."

"Oh, gosh. Well, good luck," Jenny replied. "I'd tell you to trade places with me, but I don't think that would make a good impression on your dad. 'Nice to see you again, Mr. Kavanagh. By the way, your daughter has a bun in the oven, and she doesn't know how it happened.'" She shook her head. "No, I don't think that would be good."

"Besides a bun," Trixie said, chuckling, "I have some potatoes in the oven, too. I need to go check them." She went back into the boarding house.

Alone now, Jenny sat down under a shade tree. She felt relieved that she'd succeeded in standing her ground with Leland. She realized the situation had become a lot more serious than it would have if she'd spoken up and voiced her displeasure when he'd first made the remarks, instead of waiting this long. She also realized how much she'd been beating herself up for not saying something to him earlier.

In her mind she saw a large old-fashioned balance scale. On one side of the scale was the discomfort she felt at Leland for the things he'd said. On the other side was her anger toward herself for not saying anything to him in the moment—for not standing up for herself. The anger she felt toward herself was much heavier than her anger toward Leland for being insensitive.

Then and there Jenny made up her mind to always try her best to take care of things like that in the moment, or at least as soon as she could bring herself to.

She felt so grateful for this lesson that she began to cry. Peeking out the French doors of the parlor, Argus saw her crying and called, "Jenny? Are you okay?"

"Yeah, I'm okay," she replied. She wiped her tears away. "I'm just thinking," she added.

He came out. "Do you mind if I sit down with you?"

"No, I don't mind. Are they still arguing in there?"

"No, they're done arguing. But now Dotty is lecturing him pretty good. It's kinda funny."

"Thanks for sticking up for me in there," she said. "I keep having to say that to you, don't I?"

They both started to laugh.

"No problem, milady," he said, then his look turned serious. "You know, I really hope you stay for a while. We could—we could all do stuff."

"I just don't want Dotty to be mad at me. I'll stay if she wants me to."

"Dotty's not going to be mad at you," he said. "I think she likes you more than she does her own son. You know I've heard they never got along that great."

They sat together under the tree, talking, reminiscing about the Annual Awards Event, and laughing. Finally Dotty came out and asked Argus to leave her and Jenny alone. He went back inside.

Jenny felt uncomfortable, as if she had somehow failed Dotty. But then she thought, *that's ridiculous.* "I'm sorry about all this," she said.

"Don't be silly, child. The saints know how difficult the men in my family are to get along with. He's no exception. I know ya did yer best to be his lady. I'm not blamin' ya fer any of it. So stop yer carryin' on now. You can stay here as long as ya like. Don't be rushin' off when ya got time fer a vacation."

"Thank you, Dotty. That means a lot to me."

"Jenny, I'm goin' to be leavin' for a few days, Leland has invited me to go to his apartment in the other place, to see where he lives. So I can visit my grandbaby when I can. Charlie and Hank are goin' to take care of the bakery. I'll be wantin' ya to stay and help out a little here and there, if ya can."

"My gosh, Dotty! You're going to go through the portal? Someday you'll have to come and visit me, too."

"Now don't be talkin' too much about the portals. I don't need to be thinkin' too much on it, or I might change my mind. We'll be leavin' this evenin.' So ya stay as long as ya like," Dotty said reassuringly.

Jenny hugged the old baker. "Thank you. I'm sure sorry about the way things worked out."

"I know, child, but it can't be helped. Now I've got to get back in and start packin.' This will be the first time I've left the bakery since my Nevan died." An excited look came over Dotty's face. "I'm goin' in to get packed now. Why don't ya go in and see if ya can help 'em with lunch?" She stood up and turned to go inside.

"Could I ask a favor, Dotty?" Jenny asked, stopping her.

"Sure, child."

"Since you'll be busy with Leland and Dot, would you mind if I read your grandfather's journal? That little statuette that you gave me glows whenever it gets near a portal. I just wanted to see if he mentions it."

"I'll leave it in yer room before I go," Dotty replied. "But don't ya be lettin' anyone else look at it. I don't need to be remindin' ya that not everyone here knows about the portals. Maybe ya can tell me about what ya read when I get back."

Jenny walked into the parlor with Dotty and the two went their separate ways, Dotty to her room to pack and Jenny to help with lunch. When Jenny walked into the kitchen Leland was nowhere in sight, and Clara was gone as well. Trixie, Dixie, Charlie, Hank, and Argus were getting lunch together, the twins working on condiments for sandwiches, Charlie and Hank slicing bread, and Argus chopping celery and sweet pickles for the tuna salad. Baked potatoes were already cooling on racks; they would be used for twice-baked potatoes for dinner. When Jenny asked what she could do to help, Trixie pointed at a huge bowl of cold macaroni. "Can you make a macaroni salad?"

"Sure, I'll try." Jenny mixed relish and chopped celery, mayonnaise, mustard, salt, pepper, and spices into the macaroni and stirred.

A little later, when the time came for them to haul all the food to the dining room she led the way with her big bowl of macaroni salad. And there sat Leland. Clara was massaging his shoulders, and his eyes were closed. It looked to Jenny like he was enjoying himself. She was a little surprised, but she tried her best not to show it.

When Leland opened his eyes and saw Jenny looking at him, he pushed Clara's hands away.

"Well," said Jenny, "I'm glad to see you've moved on, but if you'll excuse us, it's lunchtime."

As Trixie and Argus entered the dining room behind Jenny carrying their share of the spread, Clara walked out of the room in a huff. Trixie looked at Leland, rolled her eyes, and followed Clara out, the expression on her face suggesting that Clara was in for a talking-to. All the other boarders soon came in to eat lunch, but Leland didn't stay. He made himself and Dot a plate and went upstairs. Dotty also came down and got herself a plate, then went right back to her packing.

Jenny sat in the dining room with Argus, the twins, and some of the others. She enjoyed her lunch and even had seconds. It was nice not to have someone monitoring what she ate anymore. The tuna sandwiches were delicious, and everyone approved of her first attempt at macaroni salad.

When the boarders had finished and resumed their other activities, Jenny and Argus were left alone at the table. He was finishing his second plate, and Jenny was still working on a large glass of sweet tea.

She thought she ought to talk some sense into Argus. "Hey, can I talk to you about your plans for surgery?"

"Sure. You can talk to me about anything."

"Well, I know that you want to go in for weight gain surgery," she said.

"Yeah? What about it?"

"Have you *really* thought it through?"

"I know it sounds crazy," he said, "but I'm tired of going through life being unhealthy like this and having women just pass me by like moldy bread." He looked down at his plate. "It's easy for you heartyweights who can just gain weight whenever you want. And besides, my doctor recommended me for the surgery, and it's covered under my medical insurance."

"I know how you feel, Argus, I've struggled for a long time in my world, thinking that I'm unhealthy and that I had to change myself to fit in with the *thin-is-in* culture there. It wasn't until I came here that I realized that feeling acceptable and accepted is really in my own head, and that I have to accept myself. I haven't lost any weight since I left here, but I've gained confidence in myself, and people are noticing. Self confidence is what's attractive, no matter what size a person is."

Jenny could tell Argus was thinking about what she was saying. She really hoped her words would make an impression on him.

"I never heard that before," he said. "But you know, the idea that I can go in and get surgery and just be done with being thin—that really appeals to me."

"I've known people in my world who have gotten weight-*loss* surgery—"

"Weight-loss surgery?"

"Yes. Most fat people where I come from, especially fat women, feel compelled to *lose* weight." She paused to give the notion time to sink in. "Anyway, they go into surgery thinking it will be the answer to all their problems, a quick fix. And it just isn't. Sometimes they get a whole new set of problems. I've heard all kinds of horror stories about the side effects—about people looking at them differently because they're surgically altered. There have even been people who have died due to complications from the surgery. It's like rolling the dice with your life. You might become Mr. Big Stuff, but there's also a chance you could die. Or you might end up somewhere miserably in between. How would you feel if you went through all that just to end up thinner than you are now?"

Argus's eyes got wider, "Don't even say that. God, I don't know what I'd do if I ended up thinner. I'd *really* feel like a failure then." He looked down at his plate again as if all his hopes for a solution had been dashed to pieces.

She looked seriously at him. "Hey, Argus, look at me." He looked into her eyes, "Please don't do it. Don't get the surgery. You can find other ways to fatten up if you really want to—Heck, if you want to fatten up, just go on a diet. That's what made me fat. Just yo-yo diet for about eight years and you'll be fatter than ever!"

"What's yo-yo dieting?" Argus asked with a glimmer of hope in his eyes.

"I'm not serious, Argus—I wouldn't recommend yo-yo or *any* kind of dieting, for that matter, to *anyone*. So-called experts in my world devised different diets over the past century to help us hearty folks whip our thick bodies into thin submission. Diets are big fads in my world. But some of the diet fads have come with pretty hefty price tags in the overall health-side-effects department. It's just not good for a body to eat nothing but protein, or to cut fat completely out. You basically deprive yourself of entire groups of food. Of course you lose weight while you're dieting, then you can't stand it anymore and go off the diet, gain all the weight back, plus more, then you hate yourself and do it all over again. Up and down the scale, up and down—thus the term 'yo-yo.' Diets just don't work. That's what I've learned. I have to eat what my body is craving. My body knows what's healthy for it. And just for the record, I think you look great just the way you are." *Great? He looks perfect.*

For the first time it seemed that Argus could see an inkling of affection starting to grow deep down inside her. He stared at her for a few moments, and then a quirky smile spread slowly over his face. "Well, milady, I'll have to think on that for a while. I thought I had my whole life mapped out, depending on the outcome of this surgery. It'll be hard for me to give that up, you know."

"What would you say to a little help from your friends?"

He smiled. "I would like that very much." Then he chuckled and said, "You know, we have our own version of your 'diets' here. Doctors are always coming up with new ways for people to hearty up. But we call them 'plumping plans.' Let's see, there's the No Drinking With Meals plan, the Eat Dessert First plan, which became a national campaign to fight thinness— the If It Starts With C You Can Eat It plan—you know, corndogs, custard, creampuffs, cake, chocolate, and so on—the Low Blood Pressure plan, which involved a lot of creamy soups and milkshakes, and the most recent I tried was a liquid one called the Omnifat Plan."

He stopped to think for a moment, and then added, "Oh, and I tried one when I was in high school called the Berkley Hills plan. I had to eat one thing a day—like one day I'd eat nothing but pudding all day, the next day I'd eat nothing but lasagna—I couldn't take that one for more than two weeks. Then all the plumping powders. I've tried all the plans and all the powders, by the way, and as soon as I start eating regular again I lose whatever bits of weight I might've gained. It really is kinda crazy."

Trixie stuck her head in the door and interrupted Jenny and Argus, who were now sharing a good laugh. "I'm leaving now, Mack. Jimmy and I are meeting up at my folk's house, for—you know."

Jenny stood up. "Excuse me, Argus. I'll be right back." She walked with Trixie through the entryway and out the front door. "Good luck, Trix. I hope it all turns out like you're wanting it to." They hugged. Trixie's solemn expression made Jenny feel sad for her.

Trixie started to walk up the street. Jenny looked after her for a bit, knowing that all would soon be taken care of. When she went back into the boarding house Argus had gone into the kitchen, but he came right back out. "They just told me that there's not much to do in there."

Jenny had an idea. "Argus, do you know where to go to get money changed?" she asked.

"Sure. But you don't need to be spending your money."

"No. The whole time I was here last time, you all paid my way. If I'm going to be here for a while I want to pay for myself. Like a real vacation. Can you take me? Or do I need to find someone else?"

Just then Dotty came walking down the stairs carrying a small suitcase and holding a coat over her arm. "There's no need to go anywhere to get yer money changed," she said. "I'll change it fer ya."

"Oh, great. I'll go get it." As Jenny walked around Dotty and went up the stairs, Argus helped the old baker with her things and they went into the parlor to wait. Jenny riffled through one of her dresser drawers and finally found the envelope of money she had brought from home. As she was turning to leave the room something dark caught her eye. There, lying on her bed, was Driscol McBain's journal. She gently touched the cover, wishing she had time to read it. She was thankful that Dotty had entrusted it to her care.

She went back downstairs to the parlor with her envelope, but Dotty was sitting alone. Jenny looked for Argus.

"That boy is growin' on ya, isn't he?" Dotty asked.

Jenny blushed, "I—I—"

"I knew ya liked him when ya were here before." Dotty looked at Jenny over her spectacles. "I had a mind the two of ya would end up together all along."

"Well, we aren't—together."

"Give it time, child, give it time." Dotty held out several bills for Jenny to change.

Jenny quickly counted the bills. "Fifteen twenties and ten thirties equal three hundred," she mumbled.

"How much ya got there?" Dotty asked.

"A thousand dollars."

"Better make it five hundred, er—five hundred ten." Dotty held out a bunch of bills.

"Oh, okay." Jenny looked in her envelope again. "I think I might have a ten in here. Nope. Just take five hundred twenty," she said, handing her money to Dotty.

"Nope," Dotty protested, "I'm not takin' one cent that I haven't paid fer."

"Then I'll go up to my room and get a ten out of my wallet, and you can take five hundred seventy for your five hundred ten, since you gave me sixty that I never repaid you for when I was here last time."

Dotty eyed her seriously, and then reached out to swap her money for Jenny's. "Ya know that was a gift. Haven't ya heard ya shouldn't look a gift horse in the mouth?"

"You're the one making an issue of ten extra dollars. I can quibble right along with the rest of them," Jenny retorted.

"Land sakes, child, ya drive a hard bargain. Yer worse than Old Man Chiang—" Dotty stopped, looking flustered, as if she made a mistake. She cleared her throat and then added, "Uhh, the old man down at the grocery store."

"By the way," Jenny said, "thank you for letting me read your grandfather's journal. I'll take good care of it." She tucked her money back in the envelope and started back up to her room. She left the door slightly ajar and was sitting on the edge of her bed looking at the strange money when she heard a knock.

She stuffed the Fatropolitan currency into her wallet and went to the door expecting to see Dotty or Argus. But it was Leland who stood in the hallway, holding Dot. The little girl was dressed in her jumper and hat. Jenny was thoroughly surprised and didn't know what to say or do.

Leland didn't look good, either. "I just wanted to apologize again," he said in a soft voice. "And say goodbye. I'm sorry for the things I said. I hope everything works out for you and—"

"I'm sorry, too," she interrupted.

"Jenny," Dot called to her, holding out her arms and leaning toward her.

Jenny took Dot into her arms. "Jenny's going to miss you, sweetie. You have fun with Grandma."

"Have fun with Grandma," Dot repeated.

Jenny was fighting back tears as she told Leland, "If you ever need any help with her, you need only ask."

"Thank you." Leland had tears in his eyes as he took Dot back, said goodbye, and walked down the stairs.

Jenny closed the door, went into the bathroom, and cried for a bit. Then she got a grip on her emotions. *It's finally over.*

She decided to go back downstairs to see Dotty off. All the boarders except Trixie and Jimmy were gathered in the parlor.

"Dinner is almost ready, Aunt Dotty," Dixie was saying. "Are you sure you don't want to grab a bite before you go?"

Dotty shook her head. "No. I want to take my family out to dinner over there."

"Well, you can take me and Dot, but I'm paying," Leland protested.

Everyone was standing around them as if waiting for Dotty to make some sort of farewell speech. She looked around at everyone. "Well, I know I'm leavin' the bakery in capable hands," she said. "All of ya behave yerselves now." She turned and looked at Charlie and Hank. "And don't the two of ya forget that the order is comin' in Tuesday mornin'. Ya know how to pay fer it, and if any unexpected expenses come up, ya know where the checkbook is."

She turned back to the rest of the boarders and continued, "I don't have the slightest idea when I'll be back. All I know is I've been needin' a vacation fer a long time."

Hank patted her and Leland on the shoulders. "Don't worry. We'll keep the bakery running like clockwork." Everyone else nodded their heads, then followed them out the entryway to the front door, where they all stood and waved as Leland and Dotty walked down the street, carrying their bags, with Dot in tow.

But they were going the wrong way.

CHAPTER 16
MISSION ALMOST
IMPOSSIBLE

"**D**INNER'S READY," DIXIE SHOUTED. "CAN EV-eryone please help me get the food?"

The boarders filed through the kitchen, picked up the serving dishes, and carried dinner into the dining room. The food smelled delicious. They lined up at the buffet table and began serving themselves broiled chicken, twice-baked potatoes, brussels sprouts and fresh baked dinner rolls with butter. After filling her plate, Jenny sat down. Argus, who was behind her in line, sat right next to her, which made her feel a little uncomfortable. She knew how judgmental people could be about women who left one man for another, and didn't want the others to think she would jump right from Leland's arms into Argus's.

"Would you like some iced tea, Jenny?"

"It's okay, Argus. I can get it."

"No," he insisted, "let me get it for you. As he got up to get two glasses of tea, Lidia, who was sitting across from Jenny, looked up at her and smiled.

This made Jenny blush. *But I don't have anything to be embarrassed about,* she thought. *What's my problem?*

Argus delivered her glass of tea. She took a sip. It had plenty of ice and sugar. *He must have been paying attention to how I like my tea.* "Thanks, Argus," she said. "It's perfect."

Suddenly Trixie peeked in the door and waved for Jenny to come out. Jenny excused herself. Trixie and Jimmy were standing outside the dining room with smiles on their faces. Trixie was positively glowing. "We have news!" she squealed. "We're engaged!" She held her plump left hand out to show Jenny her engagement ring. "Jimmy officially proposed on the way to my parents'."

Jenny looked at it up close. "Oh, my gosh! That's gorgeous," she said. She was eager to hear the rest. "So what happened with your parents?"

"Oh, Mack, it was great. Daddy was so nice about it. He shook Jimmy's hand and gave me a big hug and a kiss. He actually *asked us* when we wanted to get married. Mom was just so excited to hear about her grandbaby."

"Well," Jenny looked from one to the other, "so when *are* you getting married?"

Trixie looked up at Jimmy. "I think it will be in a month or so. Daddy said he'd prefer that we get married right here, but then we're going to Europe for our honeymoon."

"Or Jamaica," Jimmy added with a smile.

Trixie rolled her eyes. "Apparently that's something we still have to talk about."

"So are you two going to announce anything?" Jenny asked.

"We're going to announce the engagement, but we'll wait until after the wedding to announce the baby," Trixie said.

Jenny held her hand out as if ushering them into the dining room. "You two hungry?" As they walked in, she added, "You just missed Dotty and Leland."

The newly engaged couple served themselves and sat down together and joined the conversation at the table. A few minutes later Jimmy tapped his water glass with a spoon to get everyone's attention. Then he stood up. "Well, everyone, Trixie and I have some news!"

It was taking a while for everyone to quiet down. "Calm down, everyone," he said. "Calm down." As the room got quiet, he cleared his throat. "Trixie and I—" he paused dramatically, "are getting married."

The room erupted with cheers and laughter and shouts of congratulations. The men stood up and started shaking his hand and patting him on the back. The women rushed over to look at Trixie's ring. After several minutes, however, they all sat back down and got back to eating their dinner.

Toward the end of the meal Dixie left so Dwyer, who was working in the bakery, could come in and eat. He served himself and ate quickly so he could get back, but when he heard the good news he also added his good wishes.

Lidia looked up from her plate to ask, "Have you set the date yet, Trixie?"

"We'll probably get married sometime next month," she answered.

After Dwyer finished eating he went back to the bakery and sent Dixie back in. She came over and hugged and kissed her sister. "Congratulations, sis," she said, and then she hugged Jimmy around the neck and squealed loudly, "and my new brother!" Everyone laughed. "So," Dixie asked, "are you two going to give me a bunch of nieces and nephews?"

Jenny looked over at Trixie, who didn't miss a beat. "Give us a chance to get married first. Jeez." As everyone laughed again, Trixie glanced back at Jenny.

A while later, when most of the boarders had finished their dinners and left the dining room, Jenny and Argus lagged behind, sitting with Trixie and Jimmy as they finished. Jenny was still working on her iced tea.

Jimmy finally finished his meal and leaned back in his chair, patting his big belly. "Ahh, that was good," he said, and looked at his bride-to-be. "Those twice-baked potatoes you made were delicious."

Trixie looked at Jenny and confided, "Before we got there today, I was afraid my dad was going to flip his lid."

Argus looked at her. "Why would your dad get mad about you telling him you want to get married?"

Jenny looked over at Trixie as if questioning why she had said it.

"Well, Argus, I don't want everyone to know this, but I'm pregnant."

Argus looked from Trixie to Jimmy and back again. All he said was, "Oh."

At the same time Jenny couldn't resist saying, "See? I told you I wouldn't tell anyone."

"So I'm just anyone, huh?" Argus said with a laugh, and Jenny smacked him playfully on the arm.

Then she remembered something she had meant to tell them. "Jimmy, speaking of someone flipping their lid, remember that nervous man you took through the portal with me?"

Jimmy smiled. "Yeah. What about him?"

"I saw him once when I first went back, but then I saw him again on the ten o'clock news a few days ago. He looked completely crazy. Dancing around in traffic, barking and growling. The reporter said it took four policemen ten minutes to get him into the back of the patrol car. They hauled him off for an evaluation."

Jenny was chuckling, but as she spoke she saw Jimmy's expression getting more serious. He was staring at her. "What's the matter, *Brickman?*" she asked sarcastically.

"You don't know what this means, do you?" Jimmy replied.

"Yeah," she said. "I thought he was kinda wimpy, but I didn't know he was wacko." She chuckled again nonchalantly and took another sip of her tea.

Jimmy and Trixie looked at each other, worried expressions on both of their faces.

"What?" Jenny asked.

"Jenny," Argus said, "you need to understand. Sometimes people from here have a bad reaction to going through the portal. They start to act strange over there. Sometimes it happens within just a few hours or days. After a few months, they'd probably look completely nuts. Insane!"

"Where did you say they took him?" Jimmy asked.

Jenny looked at her friends. Could something she'd been joking about be such a serious matter? "What? Well," she began, "the news person said they took him to— St. Joseph's? No—St. Jonathan's? No—St. Jacob's! They took him to St. Jacob's Hospital for an evaluation!"

"When was that?"

"That was—uhh—" she began counting on her fingers—"Wednesday night. This last week, five days ago."

Jimmy nodded. "Okay. So they would have taken him in and then probably put him on a seventy-two-hour hold. If he was still acting up, they would hold him for another—I think—fourteen days. So he's probably still there. That means I have to go get him and bring him back here. If I don't, he'll be crazy for the rest of his short life. He might even die from the reaction."

Trixie seemed excited. "I'll go with you," she said.

"No, Trix," he replied. "You can't go in your condition. It could be dangerous. I won't hear of it."

Then Jenny thought of something. "How can you get him and bring him back here? He's in a locked unit. You'll never get him out of there."

"I'll go and help you," Argus said. "I can take some time off."

Jimmy nodded, then thought of something. "Man, and they just promoted me to head chef, too. But I *have* to go. As soon as humanly possible. He's been there too long. He could go into a coma if we don't get to him in time."

Argus stood up and rushed into the hall to make a phone call.

"I'm going too," Jenny said.

"No," Jimmy told her. "I don't think that's a good idea. People know you over there."

"Not at St. Jacob's."

He gave this some thought. "Well," he conceded, "I guess it would be good to have some extra help on this mission."

"How long do you think it will take?" Trixie asked.

"Hopefully, no more than a day." Jimmy looked at Jenny again. "We leave first thing tomorrow morning."

Argus came back into the dining room. "I got the time off, Jimmy. I'm with you, man."

"We're good to go then. I told Jenny we leave first thing in the morning.

Wear comfortable clothing."

Argus looked pleased to hear that Jenny would be joining them.

Jenny grinned. "Should I bring my Batman utility belt?" she asked, but they all just stared at her blankly. "You guys have never heard of Batman?" They shook their heads. "How about *Mission Impossible?*" Silence. "No? Well, never mind."

Jimmy looked at Trixie. "I think we need to have *her* checked for the reaction. Can it work in reverse?" They got up from the table.

"Well," said Trixie, "there was that one weird hearty guy who tried to move here. Remember? After a while he started repeating everyone, like a parrot—I guess it was a delayed reaction. I heard he'd just signed a year lease when he had to go back. That must've been rough."

As they started to walk out Jimmy said, "Yeah, one of you all should've gotten a clue when he showed up in the bakery with that eye patch on—" They left the room still talking.

Jenny and Argus were alone again. She feigned a yawn. "Well, if we're leaving that early, I'm going to turn in."

"Hey," said Argus, "I'm sure glad you're staying for a while. I would have missed you—again." He smiled at her.

"Thanks, Argus. I'm glad to be staying, too. I'm nervous about tomorrow, though. I hope Jimmy knows what he's doing."

"I'm not worried. Jimmy's pretty smart."

She smiled back at him. "And thanks for the iced tea. Thanks for being so sweet to me."

"It's pretty easy for me when I'm around you."

Jenny blushed. "Well, good night. See you in the morning." She excused herself, went up the stairs, and locked herself in her room.

She knew she had to bathe, but for the first time ever while in Fatropolis her heart wasn't in it. She wanted to get into Driscol McBain's journal as quickly as she could. She'd never been so consumed with curiosity about anything in her life. So she took a quick shower, dried off, slipped into her robe, and hopped into bed.

She picked up the large leather-bound book. It had apparently been written with an old-fashioned fountain pen. Though there were splotches of ink here and there, Driscol's penmanship was impeccable. She skimmed the pages quickly, looking for parts about the little goddesses. She looked and looked but couldn't find any mention of the statuettes, so turned to a random page of the journal and began reading.

June 14th, 1941. *I was up drinking my coffee early this morning when I looked out the window and saw the lad who has been courting my Tressa climbing down the fire escape from her room. I was so mad I wanted to kill him. That scrawny coward of a boy, defiling my little girl instead of asking for her hand like a man. I have a mind to show him what for. I guess I will have to take matters into my own hands.*

June 17th, 1941. *I did not want to return through the same weir—it is too far away—so I took the wooden lady and the one to detect a weakness in the veil, and made another weir in the water closet of the department store not far from here. I took Tressa's cowardly beau and showed him the weir. I was acting like I was taking him into my confidence. I told him that no one should ever know, that it has to stay just in the family. Then I winked at him. I think he believed me, the dumb bunny. Ha ha. I will have the last laugh yet.*

June 21st, 1941. *I caught the boy climbing down the fire escape again this morning. I caught him and showed him my pistol—he was plenty shaken. He said he loves her, but I think he's just satisfying his animal urges with her. Tressa deserves better than that. I told him that if I ever see him again I will kill him dead. He ran off, but he yelled out like the yellow coward he is, "I'll get you, you hearty bastards! If it's the last thing I do!" I'm not telling Tressa what happened to him. I'm letting her think he's left her. I don't want her to know it was me.*

July 13th, 1941. *A lot has transpired since my last entry. It seems that coward of a boy got the last laugh on me. My precious Tressa is with child. We just came to know today. The girl is devastated, as he has not turned up since last month. I've asked around the neighborhood, and no one has seen him. I am starting to think maybe what I did was wrong. God forgive me for what I did. Bring him back so Tressa will not have a bastard child. Please, God!*

July 21st, 1941. *Now it's been a whole month and no one has seen hide nor hair of the lad. It looks like he's gone for good. God is punishing me for interfering in Tressa's love affair. But why would God punish me for their wrongdoings? I talked with Tressa and we agreed to tell folks that the lad forced her into the act. To save her the shame of everyone knowing what she did. Folks will be more understanding if they think she was forced.*

February 2nd, 1942. *It will not be long now before my grandchild is birthed. Tressa is heavy with child. I feel for her. She is so forlorn. I feel so bad for what I did, running the lad she loved off like I did. I would give my life to bring him back if I could. He has no idea what pain he's causing her.*

I went through the weir to the other side the other day. I suspect the coward went through to get away from me. He is nowhere to be found. His child will soon be born. I hope the child is not a boy that will turn out to be a coward like him. A real man would have fought for his love, even against a stubborn old fool like me.

Where did my life go wrong? What did I do to deserve this pain? I lost the only love of my life worth having, and now I've ruined my precious Tressa's life like mine is ruined. I would give anything to see a smile on her face again. She is so heartbroken. I fear that the birth of the child may do her in. I just want to go and meet up with my beloved Mona. Please, God, just take me to be with Mona.

Jenny was sobbing by the time she came to Driscol's plea for death and couldn't read any more of his sad confessions. She had finally learned what two of the statuettes were for, but hadn't found much of anything about the other little goddesses. She was getting tired, and knowing she was probably in for a long day tomorrow, she carefully tucked the journal in the drawer of her nightstand and turned off the light.

She was finally able to stop sobbing and catch her breath, though she kept thinking, *It happened right here. Right in the bakery. Right in this house—that's where they lived, that's where Dotty was conceived and maybe born.* She could still see it in her mind—Driscol running Dotty's father off with a pistol, Driscol later looking for him, Tressa pregnant, crying, wondering what had happened to her lover.

Jenny eventually drifted off to sleep, exhausted from crying.

IT WAS SIX-THIRTY the next morning when Argus knocked on Jenny's door and woke her up. She had slept through the night, but all her dreams had been about Dotty's mother and grandfather.

She stumbled over to the door and opened it. "Okay, Okay, I'm awake."

"Sorry to wake you up so early," he said, "but we have to get going."

Still half asleep, she walked into the bathroom, washed her face, brushed her teeth and hair, and got dressed in comfortable clothes and athletic shoes. She also tucked her little goddess in her pants pocket.

Her head still felt heavy as she entered the dining room. Jimmy and Argus were all ready to go, sipping on the last dregs of their coffee. Jimmy was wearing a long tan trench coat and looked like some sort of huge detective. Argus, in a gray hooded sweatshirt, looked more normal. Jenny poured herself a cup of much-needed coffee, grabbed a doughnut off the tray of pastries, and ate as fast as she could.

The bakery was packed full of customers. Boarders were going in and out of the kitchen and food was already being brought in. Jenny wished she could have a regular breakfast, but Jimmy had told her twice that they didn't have time to waste. Jenny considered this for a moment. "Is the department store even open this early?" she asked.

As Jimmy gave her a puzzled look, Argus said, "Good point. I guess we're staying for breakfast."

Jimmy shook his head. "But we aren't going through the department store," he protested. Then he said, "Okay. Wait. The other store won't be open this early, either. Carry on."

Jenny glared at him. "You mean I could have slept another hour? And I just inhaled a doughnut when I could've had *waffles?*"

Jimmy just shrugged his shoulders.

Breakfast was served and all the boarders except Clara, Dwyer and Theodore, who were working the early morning bakery shift, crowded into the dining room. Jenny was still hungry so she had eggs, sausages, and waffles, and Argus got her a glass of orange juice and sat down with her.

Jimmy didn't hesitate to have pancakes, eggs, and bacon. Halfway through his first plate he pointed at Jenny and Argus. "You two better eat up. Goodness knows when we'll get to eat again. And I don't want to hear any complaining about being hungry."

Trixie ate breakfast sitting next to her fiancé, then kissed him and wished them good luck, excusing herself to go to work.

Finally, a little after nine o'clock, Jimmy, Jenny, and Argus thanked the cooks and cleanup crew and said their goodbyes. They had to get going. Together the three rescuers set off in search of the nervous man, Emmett Newbury. Their mission was to bring him safely home.

Jenny had her bag with her. She had both kinds of currency and considered herself prepared for anything.

They left the bakery and went the opposite direction from the department store, just as Leland and Dotty had. Argus and Jenny walked together, with Jimmy in the lead. He was in a hurry, so he hailed a cab.

On their way across town Jenny asked, "Can I ask why we're not going through the department store?"

Although Jimmy seemed preoccupied, he said, "We're going through a different portal. It's closer to where we want to go."

"Leland told me there were a couple of other portals besides the ones in the department store," Jenny replied.

"Really?" Jimmy said. "I only know about the ones at Burley's and this one that we're going to at the furniture store."

"Yeah, those are the only portals I know about, too," Argus agreed.

Jenny just shrugged.

They rode for a while. When Jimmy told the cab driver to stop they got out on the street near a furniture store that sold huge furniture. Jimmy led his team past customers and through the displays, acting as if he were looking at the items for sale. The more inconspicuous Jimmy tried to be the more suspicious he looked, especially in his long trench coat. Jenny and Argus played along and practiced sitting on sofas and opening drawers and having a grand old time.

Finally, when the coast seemed to be clear, Jimmy motioned for them to follow him. They walked to the back of the store and into a tiled hallway where the elevators and restrooms were. Jimmy slipped into the men's room, then came back out using military hand signals to tell them to come along. Jenny had to smile. *He's enjoying this way too much,* she thought.

The men's room was empty. As with the other portals, one stall was marked *Out Of Order.* Jimmy quickly found the portal and stepped through. Argus told Jenny to follow, and he went last.

Jenny thought it was strange that this time they came out on the other side in a janitor's closet filled with the strong smell of wet mops and cleaning solution. They walked out one at a time, first Jimmy, then Argus, then Jenny. Before she stepped out, she reached into her pocket and pulled out the little goddess. It was glowing again.

Jimmy and Argus were waiting for her around a corner. As she approached them, she asked, "Why was the portal in a janitor's closet this time?"

There were some thin people nearby, so all he said was, "I'll tell you in a minute."

As they started across the store, Argus turned to her. "This building is sitting on the original site of Tammany Hall, which was demolished sometime in the 1920s. The notorious Boss Tweed moved the Hall to another building after that. I guess they made a portal in the bathroom of the original building, but when they demolished it and built this building, the portal didn't go away. It just stayed where it had originally been, which in this building happens to be the janitor's closet."

Jenny thought for a moment. "Why would they have needed a portal in Tammany Hall?"

"I don't know," Argus said. "I just researched this location on your Internet when I was here visiting my cousin."

They walked out onto the street and caught another cab. *I'm definitely home,* she thought as she squeezed into the back seat of the cab after Argus, who was in the middle crammed between his two tubby teammates.

Struggling with the lack of room, Jimmy said, "Somebody from here needs to get a clue and design cabs with some room."

"Tell me about it," Argus said in a strained voice.

They rode for what seemed an hour and finally arrived out in front of St. Jacob's Hospital, where they unfolded themselves out of the cab. After Jimmy paid, they walked up onto the sidewalk in front of the hospital.

"Okay," Jimmy said in a soft voice, "we're just going to go through the lobby and up to the psychiatric unit, and you—" he pointed at Jenny—"are going to go in and ask about Emmett, and say he's family and that you want to visit him."

"That sounds easy enough," she said.

They walked into the hospital and asked the security guard sitting at the information desk for directions. The guard was more than glad to explain how to find the unit. "You walk down this corridor to the elevators, go up to the third floor. When you get off the elevator, you'll be facing the opposite way. Turn to the left. Go down about three hallways, and you'll find another elevator. Take that elevator to the fifth floor. Walking off the elevator, you'll go to your right. You'll see signs for the psychiatric unit, and *voilà,* you're there."

Jimmy looked confused and looked up at Jenny and Argus.

"I think I got it, Jimmy," she said. She smiled at the guard. "Thank you, sir."

Following his instructions exactly, they came to the psychiatric unit, where they were stopped outside the locked doors by another guard at another desk. Jimmy and Argus stepped into the waiting room nearby, where Jimmy picked up a magazine. He was still trying to look inconspicuous.

Jenny approached the guard, who looked up at her as she approached. *This will never work.* "Yes," she said aloud, "I'm here to see my fa—cou—bro—brother. His name is Emmett Newbury, he was br—brought in last Wednesday for an evaluation."

The woman punched a few keys on her computer. "You said Emmett Newcastle?"

"No. Newbury, Emmett Newbury," Jenny repeated.

"You're his sister?"

"N—*Yes.*"

The guard read the screen and looked up at Jenny with a serious face. "It says here that he collapsed the other night and was taken to the emergency room. But when they took him, it says—he was in a coma."

"Oh—Okay, thank you," she said, taking her leave. Then she stopped and asked for directions to the emergency room. After another long explanation she headed back to the men in the waiting room. They had been listening, of course.

Jimmy remarked, "You know, that was really smooth. 'My fa—cou—

brother.' Is that a new relation or something?" Both men started to chuckle.

Jenny blushed and smacked Jimmy on the arm, "I can't help it if I'm nervous," she said.

"Well," Jimmy said. "Let's go down to the emergency room. Same routine."

After wandering around in the maze of identical corridors they finally found themselves in the emergency room lobby. Again Jimmy and Argus stopped in the waiting room while Jenny went to the reception area and asked about Emmett. The nurse searched her computer for some time, but was unable to locate him. Finally, asking Jenny again if she was family, she told her that Emmett Newbury had been moved to a step-down unit, as he was in a coma but had no other significant medical problems. She told Jenny the room number and how to get there.

After rides on two different elevators they reached the correct floor. They walked slowly down the corridor and passed another hospital security guard. *How in the world are we going to get out of this hospital with an unconscious man without anyone seeing us?* Jenny wondered. She smiled politely at the guard and nodded.

Once they had passed the guard she looked at Jimmy. "I don't mean to be a Negative Nelly," she said under her breath, "but this is never going to work." She looked back. The guard was nowhere in sight. "It's the next room," she said, and pointed.

Jimmy slipped into Emmett's room, but came right back out. "He's not in there. Jenny, go tell the nurse that you're Emmett's dau—cou—sister and that you're here to see him and ask where he is."

Jenny glared at Jimmy, then walked over to the nurses' station. Jimmy and Argus tried to stay out of the way and remain unseen.

The nurse at this station was less than enthusiastic to see Jenny.

"I'm here to see my brother, Emmett Newbury," Jenny said to the nurse. "But he's not in his room."

The nurse picked up Emmett's chart. "What do you mean, he's not in his room? He's in a coma." He got up quickly and walked into the room. Seeing that Emmett was indeed not there, the nurse quickly searched the room, then hurried back to his station to call security. As more nurses started to go into Emmett's room and look around, Jenny retreated to where Jimmy and Argus were waiting.

Jimmy sighed. "That's typical," he muttered. "Poor guy. He must be in the last stages. They can go in and out of a coma for days. We have to find him fast."

With that they rushed back down the corridor to the elevators, where Jimmy came to a sudden halt. "Wait! Maybe he's still here in the hospital."

"I'd think he'd get himself out as quick as he could," said Argus. "If he stays conscious long enough."

"Yeah," Jenny agreed. "I wouldn't think he'd hang around here and get caught again."

Jimmy leaned against the wall. "You two are acting like this dude is in his right mind. Well, he isn't. And he could be anywhere. He could be hiding in a closet somewhere. He could be disguised as a janitor mopping floors. He could be looking at newborn babies in the nursery. He could even be eating meatloaf and green gelatin in the cafeteria." Jimmy leaned on the railing and looked out the window as if hoping to see Emmett down on the street. "How the heck are we going to find him?"

Jenny looked around frantically. "God, what are we going to do?" She could feel herself starting to get emotional. *Please God,* she silently prayed, *help us find him before it's too late.*

Argus had an idea. He and Jenny left Jimmy standing by the window and walked down the corridor, peering into patients' rooms. No sign of Emmett. It seemed as though his trail had gone cold. Jenny and Argus continued to search the area, opening every closet they came to and peeking into every room. Finally they went back to Jimmy, who looked sad and defeated and was still gazing out the window.

All of a sudden Jimmy shouted, "Wait! There he is!" He pointed down. "On the street. Is that him? Come on, let's move!"

Jenny and Argus looked out. Sure enough, Emmett was scampering across the street from another entrance to the hospital. He was wearing a long, dirty-looking leather coat, most likely having swiped it from somewhere. The three would-be rescuers began scurrying around, bumping into each other, trying to figure out the fastest way to get down to the street.

They hurried down the corridor and waited in front of elevators, frustrated that hospital elevators move so slowly. They rode down, and when the doors finally opened they rushed out and around the corner. Argus ran smack into a housekeeper who was carrying a stack of folded towels. The towels went everywhere and the lady swore in Spanish under her breath. *"Menso,"* she said, *"voy a creer."* All three helped her pick up the towels, then rushed off again, but in the wrong direction.

They eventually found themselves at the back of the hospital and asked directions from another security guard. He told them how to get to the front of the hospital. Walking quickly, they finally found the door Emmett had used and exited the building.

It had taken so long to get out of the hospital maze that they knew Emmett could have gone anywhere, so they split up, searching for a glimpse of the escapee. It seemed that they had completely lost any trace of him when Argus shouted, "I think I saw him down there!"

Jenny and Jimmy hurried over to where Argus was standing, and he pointed down the street at a parked car. Emmett, laughing maniacally, was jumping and trying to do handstands on the hood of the car.

Argus ran as fast as he could, with Jimmy and Jenny hurrying close behind. They were closing in on Emmett when a nearby car alarm went off and a crowd of people started to form.

When Emmett saw the three drawing closer he climbed up on top of the car and began jumping up and down on the roof, still laughing like a mad man. Then he started growling and biting at his own arm.

A cab was approaching slowly on the street. The three surrounded Emmett and waited for their chance to grab him. Jimmy moved for his leg, but Emmett jumped from the roof of the car and landed on top of the moving cab. The startled cab driver sped up and Emmett was able to ride the cab a ways before tumbling down over the hood and onto the street, causing the angry driver to come to a screeching halt and jump out, cussing at him. Emmett pulled himself up and staggered away from the cab. Within a few moments he seemed to be more stable on his feet, as he started hobbling away.

Jimmy started running as best he could, shouting, "That fool's gonna kill himself!"

People were still standing around, watching and pointing. Argus ran as fast as he could past Jimmy, caught up with the nervous (now crazy) man, and tackled him. Jenny hurried over as well, and when they all finally had Emmett subdued he suddenly smacked Jimmy across the face and started laughing.

"Oh, no! You did not just hit me!" Jimmy grabbed Emmett's hands. Emmett opened his mouth to bite Jimmy's hand, but Argus held Emmett's head down.

Jenny looked up. Now the people around them were on their cell phones, calling for emergency services, and one bystander asked another, "What are they doing, trying to abduct that man?" Another person was taking a video with a cell phone, and for a moment all Jenny could do was just stare into the phone with her mouth open.

Jimmy stood up in the crowd that had gathered, pulled out his wallet and quickly flashed a badge. In his most official voice he shouted, "I'm Agent Brickman! Secret Special Forces. For your safety, I need to ask you to disperse. This man is a dangerous criminal. We're taking him in for questioning."

The crowd seemed to buy it, and began to move away.

When Jenny came to her senses, she still didn't know what to do. She was glad Jimmy was a good actor and could think on his feet. She turned away from the phone and started talking to Emmett. "We've missed you, Emmett," she said as soothingly as she could. "You're looking very handsome today!"

He stopped struggling and closed his mouth, looking straight ahead. His eyes had a dazed, glassy look, and the blood vessels on his temples were swollen. His overgrown hair was very greasy and his teeth were discolored. He started whimpering like an injured dog.

"Aww," Jenny said with a sigh.

At that he lashed out, growling and snarling again, startling her.

"This is the worst case I've ever seen," Jimmy said, standing over Emmett. "We need to get him through the portal, and quick."

Emmett stopped struggling. "Soon everyone in this world will know about the portals," he said all too loudly.

They heard a siren in the distance. More trouble was coming at them. "Go hail a cab, Jenny!" Jimmy shouted.

"Jenny!" a voice called from the crowd.

Who could that be?

It was Katy. "I thought you were on vacation," she said. "I took the day off today." She walked over casually, not realizing that Jenny was wrapped up in a serious situation. "Is there something wrong?" she asked. "You don't look so good." When Emmett snarled and lunged at Katy, she jumped back and screamed, "Oh my God! Who's that?" She walked very quickly back into the crowd.

"Nice to see you, too, Katy!" Jenny called as she held her arm up to hail a cab.

When a cab stopped Argus and Jimmy stuffed Emmett into the back seat and followed him in while Jenny jumped in the front seat, much to the consternation of the driver. As they pulled away a police car passed them, its lights flashing and siren blaring.

Suddenly having a lucid moment, Emmett blinked and looked around calmly. "What's going on?" he asked in a perfectly normal voice.

"Emmett," said Argus, "we came to take you back home, where you need to go."

"But I came here to save you all," Emmett said. Then his voice changed again. "My hair hurts!" He began scratching his neck and barking. Argus grabbed at his hands.

The cabby looked at them in the rearview mirror. "What in the world is wrong with *him?*" He looked like he was about to stop and order them out of his cab.

In reply, Jimmy pulled out his wallet again and flashed the badge. Taking his official tone, he said, "I'm Agent Brickman, Secret Special Forces." As

Jenny rolled her eyes, he continued. "We've detained this man. We're taking him back to the lab. He volunteered to be a subject for some special drug experiments, and he's having an adverse reaction. Turn right up here and take us back to Union Square."

"Yes, sir."

As the cab turned the corner and started up the way Jimmy had instructed, however, Emmett began to shake all over. He was now sweating profusely.

Jenny looked back and gasped. "Oh, my God, Jimmy! He doesn't look good."

"Don't panic," Jimmy said sternly.

Just then Emmett passed out. He fell against Argus, who tried to prop him up.

"Driver," Jimmy said, "on second thought, take us to the Upper West Side."

"Whatever you want, just as long as you take that *stiff* with you when you go," the cab driver said, still glancing at Emmett in his mirror. He waited for the light to change, then turned another corner.

They rode through the heavy Manhattan traffic for a long time, no one saying a word. It was mid-afternoon now and they were all hungry, but there was an air of satisfaction in the cab. They'd accomplished what they'd set out to do. They'd saved Emmett's life. They were also glad to be resting after all the running around they'd done.

Argus, still holding the limp Emmett, was the first to speak. "Man, I'm hungry."

Jenny's stomach was growling. "I'm glad we got to eat a decent breakfast."

"We can eat once we get home," Jimmy said. "We should be back in time for dinner."

Argus was looking out the window, "Hey, Jimmy, can we go by the American Museum of Natural History? I know we can't go in, but I just want to see it. I've seen pictures, but I've never been by it."

The driver looked back at Jimmy as if he was starting to doubt his story about the Secret Special Forces.

Jimmy looked at the driver and replied, "Uhh—we're not from around here—originally." He turned to Argus. "But that'll be too far out of our way."

"Actually, it's not that far out of the way," the cab driver said.

"Please, Jimmy. We're right here. It'll only take a few minutes."

Jimmy gave in. "Oh, man, I know I'm gonna regret this. Driver, take us by the museum."

The driver changed his course. Half an hour later they were approaching the museum. Argus looked out the window, enthralled, trying to see past

Emmett. As the driver slowed down, he said, "Wow, look at that!"

Just then Emmett, who had suddenly regained consciousness, sat up, grabbed the door handle, and jumped out of the cab. Argus followed, grabbing him by the back of the coat and wrestling with him, but Emmett broke free, turned and slammed his hands against Argus's chest, which knocked the wind out of him.

Jenny looked over her shoulder and gasped. "Argus! Are you okay?"

Laughing like a maniac again, Emmett ran up the steps and into the museum as Jimmy helped Argus to his feet. Argus slowly began to run after Emmett, coughing as he went, but composing himself quickly. He ran into the museum after Emmett, with Jimmy close behind.

As Jenny started to get out of the cab, she felt the cabbie's hand on her arm. "You owe me thirty-two bucks, lady."

"Can't you wait for us?" She tried to pull out of his grip. "We'll be right back."

"Lady, you pay me now or I call the police."

"Oh." Shaking her head, she reached into her bag, pulled out her wallet, and thrust a wad of bills at him. Then she jumped out of the cab and ran up the steps into the museum. It appeared that the men had already gone further in, but the security guard wouldn't let her by without paying admission, despite her explanations that she was with the party trying to catch the crazy man.

"You gotta buy a ticket, lady," he said as he blocked her way. "Same as everyone else."

Having no other choice, she went back to the ticket kiosk and slapped a thirty-dollar bill on the counter. The cashier looked at it, then looked at her. Realizing what she had done, she snatched it back and put down a twenty-dollar bill. She picked up her ticket, stuffed her change back in her wallet and threw it back in her bag. Slinging her bag over her shoulder, she pushed her hair out of her eyes, adjusted her bosom, and walked past the guard glaring at him the whole way.

She couldn't see any of them. She spotted a few astonished people standing nearby in the Theodore Roosevelt Memorial Hall and went up to them. "Did you just see a crazy man go by? And a thin handsome guy and a tall fat man in a Columbo trench coat?"

When one of the bystanders pointed toward the Hall of the Great Jungle, Jenny thanked her and rushed in that direction. She saw Jimmy crossing a corridor up ahead. The security guard was still eyeing her suspiciously.

It was late in the afternoon now. *This place closes at five forty-five,* Jenny thought. *I sure hope we can catch Emmett before that.* She walked quickly past people who were looking at a diorama of President Roosevelt's ranch. She smiled politely at them and rushed on to find her friends. As she came closer to the Hall of the Great Jungle she could hear Argus and Jimmy calling Emmett. She finally found them standing still just outside the huge jungle area, listening to the sounds of animals and birds emanating from within.

"Emmett," Argus called out into the jungle, "we're not going to hurt you. We just want to take you home where you can get better." Seeing Jenny coming near, he waved at her to come over.

Jimmy took his turn. "Emmett, get your crazy ass—"

Jenny glared at him.

"Come on out of there so we can help you!" When Emmett didn't answer, Jimmy turned to Argus. "'Jimmy,'" he said in a mocking voice, "'can we go by the museum, I just wanna look at it from the cab, I know we can't go in, but'—man, I'm a sucker! And I'm not just any sucker. I'm a starving sucker!" He rushed over to Jenny, pointing at her handbag. "You got anything in there I can eat?" He sounded desperate. "I'm so hungry I'm wasting away to darn near nothing!"

Jenny swatted him away. "Get a hold of yourself, mister!" she said sternly. "We're all in this together, and like you said, we can eat when we get back."

"But you don't understand," Jimmy whined. "I have a sensitive stomach, and if I don't eat regularly I get nauseated. And if it wasn't for your *boyfriend* here—" he pointed at Argus, who was smiling—"and his *dumb ideas,* I could be back at Dotty's bakery right now. Inside the case, eating doughnuts double-fisted!"

"Aww, does the wittle Bwickman get sick at him stomach if him doesn't eat?" she mocked, pursing her lips.

When Argus chuckled, Jimmy's head snapped around. Argus just whistled and looked around innocently.

So there they stood, in silence, at the entrance to the museum jungle.

"I vote we go in here and look," Argus finally said. "This would be a great place to hide."

An announcement sounded through the museum: "The museum closes in one half hour. We hope you've enjoyed your visit and that you'll come back soon."

"Come on," said Argus. "We have to hurry."

But Jimmy held back. "I don't like the jungle," he said.

Jenny looked exasperated. "How many times have you ever been to the jungle, Jimmy? This isn't a *real* jungle, you know."

Jimmy nodded. "All right, let's go. But let's stick together."

They entered the jungle by stepping on a path that reminded Jenny of the yellow brick road in *The Wizard of Oz*. The jungle was partially illuminated, but it still seemed daunting. Glowing eyes peered down at them from the huge trees. Vines hung down, obstructing their view. The sounds of the animals and birds were very realistic. The ceiling seemed to go on forever, just like the sky.

Jenny looked up through the canopy of trees and saw stars flickering in the ceiling. "This could be very romantic," she said.

"Could you just keep your mind on the task at hand?" Jimmy told her.

After they had walked for quite some time, Argus stopped and said, "Shhhh, listen!"

They all stopped. From off in the distance came a growling sound that seemed familiar. They started walking toward it and came to a fork on the path. "Let's go this way," Argus said.

They were so far in at this point that they couldn't see the light from the entrance. They started walking more cautiously now.

Jimmy looked up ahead. "I see somebody—it's him. Let's move!"

They started hurrying toward their quarry. When they caught up with him they easily surrounded him. Jimmy grabbed him from behind and lifted him off the ground. But suddenly an older woman let out a shrill scream and began hitting Jimmy with her little handbag. The older man Jimmy had his arms around was kicking and shouting, "Let me go!"

Jimmy set him back down. "I'm so sorry, sir. I thought you were someone else." Jimmy brushed at the man's clothes in an effort to make things right.

"Let's get out of here, Marge!" The man looked at his wife, then back at Jimmy. Straightening his clothes, he muttered a few choice words at Jimmy and then the couple hurried back toward the entrance.

Jenny tried not to laugh. She was careful to wait until the couple was out of sight before saying, "You should've seen the look on your face, Jimmy. That was priceless!"

"She's right, man," Argus joined in. "I don't mean to poke fun, but that was pretty funny."

Jimmy was thoroughly embarrassed.

Jenny repeated his orders in a mocking voice. "'I see somebody. It's him! Let's move!'" She and Argus started laughing again, and finally Jimmy even started to laugh a little.

"The museum is now closing. Please make your way to the entrance. We hope you've enjoyed your visit with us today."

Hearing the announcement, Jenny looked at her two companions. "What are we going to do now? The place is closing, and we still haven't found him."

As the museum began to close, the illumination in the jungle became dimmer and the animal sounds were turned off as well, making the jungle eerily quiet.

Jenny sized up the situation. "This is a nutcase wonderland right here," she said dramatically. "Three sitting ducks trapped in a jungle, looking for a madman, who's violent and could be armed by now."

The men stopped and looked at her. "Armed? What could he be armed with?" Argus asked.

"Well, for starters, those dirty fingernails of his that he hasn't worried about trimming for the last six months. If he scratched you, it could lead to a nasty infection."

Jimmy chuckled a little. "Yeah, those could be dangerous weapons." He paused and got serious. "So, if we get a hold of him again, just don't let go. If we stay in here too much longer they're going to call the cops on us and he'll get hauled back to the hospital. Then we'll have to start all over again. Or even worse, we could all end up in jail for trespassing."

All agreed that they had to try and get Emmett and escape from the museum without alerting security. Jimmy had placed himself in the middle, and they were arm in arm as they started walking forward deeper into the jungle, looking around slowly and hoping to spot Emmett.

Jenny's shoes squeaked with every step she took. "Why'd you have to wear those old creaky creepers, Jenny?" Jimmy whispered.

They kept walking, alert to any movements around them. Suddenly Emmett dropped out of a tree onto Argus's back and wrapped both of his arms around Argus's neck.

Jimmy grabbed Emmett, but the madman held on tight. So Jimmy had Emmett and Emmett had Argus, and Jenny didn't know what to do. She dropped her bag beside the path and started trying to loosen Emmett's stranglehold from around Argus's neck. Emmett started laughing again, and then he started trying to bite at Jimmy's and Jenny's hands.

Argus was desperately trying to grab at something, but couldn't seem to get a good grip on Emmett's hands to escape from his grasp. It was all he could do just to keep breathing.

"Oh my God!" Jenny screamed. "Argus is turning blue! Jimmy, *do something!*" Overcome with emotion, she started hitting Emmett with both fists.

Jimmy, growling himself now, kept yanking at Emmett, trying to jerk him loose. As Argus went limp Emmett finally let go and Argus fell to the floor. As Jimmy pulled Emmett into an unbreakable hold so they wouldn't lose him again, Jenny tried to remember what she had learned in her CPR class. She got down on her knees and tilted Argus's head back to open his airway.

Seeing that he was already breathing, she ripped off her jacket and stuffed it behind his head.

"Please be all right, *please be all right!*" she cried, leaning over him. She brushed his hair out of his eyes, still crying. "Please, God, let him be all right. Please, God!"

Now Emmett was growling, snarling, and thrashing about, but he couldn't get away from Jimmy.

Finally Argus started to cough. Jenny turned him on his side. He drew his knees up and kept coughing, and started rubbing his own neck. Jenny caressed his face. She was still on her knees looking intensely at him when he opened his eyes and looked back at her. He pushed himself up. Now they were both on their hands and knees, face to face. He smiled at her. They stayed that way for a long moment, almost nose to nose. They started moving slowly toward each other—

"Hey!" Jimmy interrupted their dramatic moment. "I don't believe what I'm seeing. I'm over here struggling with a madman—" he readjusted his grip on Emmett—"and you two are trying to have *your first kiss?* Well not on my watch, you don't."

All Argus could manage was an embarrassed laugh. He and Jenny both stood up and brushed each other off.

"Are you all right?" she asked him.

"Yeah. I'm sore, but I'll be fine," he said in a hoarse voice. "I heard what you said. You were crying and praying that I'd be all right." He smiled, as if he knew he had finally won her affections.

"Oh, stop it," she said, blushing. She smacked him gently on the arm, then got serious again. "I'm glad you're okay."

They saw a flash of light in the distance.

"Security," Argus said. "We have to hide."

Jimmy was still wrestling with Emmett, who was very wily, so Argus went over and helped subdue him. They moved toward a big boulder nearby, but suddenly Emmett began trembling and sweating again. They dragged him behind the boulder and got down to hide. Argus covered Emmett's mouth. The security guard came closer, his flashlight combing the area where he'd heard the commotion.

"If there's anyone in here," the guard called out, "you need to leave *immediately.* The museum is closed. I've called the police. They're on their way."

Emmett, unconscious again, sank back against Jimmy. The guard flashed his light over and around the boulder, apparently not seeing them, so he walked on and was soon out of sight.

Argus stood up and looked down at their captive. "It looks like he's out again."

When Jimmy nodded and pulled a switchblade from his pocket, Jenny gasped. "What are you going to do with that? He didn't mean it, Jimmy, he—"

Jimmy calmly reached down, cut the hospital bracelet off of Emmett's wrist, and tucked it in his pocket.

Jenny, now embarrassed, just said, "Oh." She had to laugh at herself.

With a grunt Jimmy picked Emmett up off the floor. His limbs and head flopped from side to side. Jimmy pulled one of Emmett's limp arms around the back of his neck and Argus shouldered the other. They both grasped the waistband of his pants and started to drag him toward the entrance. Jenny went in front so she could direct them.

After some time they arrived at the beginning of the path. Jenny peeked out. She could see what looked like police car lights flashing through the museum's front windows and into the corridor. Then she heard the main doors open.

"We need to hide again. Fast!"

The men pulled Emmett back into the jungle and tucked him down behind another boulder. Jenny ducked behind a large tree.

The security guard was leading two police officers into the jungle exhibit. "I think they're in here somewhere, but I didn't see them," he said.

"If they're still here, we'll find them," one of the police officers replied, and they started shining their flashlights through the trees and bushes. It seemed to take forever, but they finally passed by and disappeared from sight.

Jenny stepped out and whispered loudly, "Come on, you guys. Let's get moving. We may be able to get out the front door now."

Jimmy and Argus came around the boulder, dragging Emmett, and hustled as fast as they could back into the Theodore Roosevelt Memorial Hall, passing a forest diorama that Jenny hadn't even seen when she came in. They heard footsteps again.

It won't be long before they come out of the jungle. Jenny saw a hallway ahead to the left. "Let's go in there," she whispered. She opened the first door she came to and held it open.

"Hey," said Jimmy, "that's the ladies' bathroom. We can't go in there."

Jenny pushed the men through the door. "Just shut up and get in there." The bathroom was dark, and Jenny groped around on the wall trying to find the light switch. "The lights must be automatic or something," she muttered. She felt around in the dark, looking for some place they could hide.

"Emmett's awake again," Argus said.

The madman was struggling, but Jimmy held one hand over his mouth. Then Emmett began kicking against the bathroom stalls, making a lot of noise.

"The cops are coming," Jenny cried. "Make him stop!"

They could hear the faint footsteps of the police and the security guard running down the same corridor they had just come from.

"Jenny," Argus suddenly said, "look at your pants. Your pocket is glowing."

Jenny reached into her pocket, pulled out the little goddess and held it up, illuminating the whole bathroom. Jimmy and Argus looked stunned, but Emmett stopped struggling and looked up at the light with a smile on his face.

"There's a portal in here!" Holding the goddess out in front of her, she went straight to the back of the bathroom by the sinks and started feeling all around the wall. Within a few moments she came to the place where the wall gave way under her touch. It started to pull her in, but she resisted. "OVER HERE!"

The two men lugged Emmett to the wall, then Jimmy backed into the portal, pulling Emmett through. Argus turned to Jenny. "Get going!"

Just as he pushed her through the police burst through the door, flashlights blasting light everywhere. Argus stepped through the portal, confident he had not been seen.

CHAPTER 17
A KISS AND A CONFESSION

THEY WERE ALL IN ONE BATHROOM STALL, AND collapsed from exhaustion. They'd made it through the portal and brought Emmett back to Fatropolis. Jimmy was still holding on to him. He was awake, and no longer struggling.

This bathroom seemed to be unoccupied right now.

"Phew! That was close," Jenny said, trying to catch her breath.

Argus was on the floor next to her. "Are you all right?" he asked her.

"Yeah," she said. "Just a little worn out—and hungry."

"Sorry I pushed you like that," he said. "I just wanted to make sure you got through."

"No problem. I knew what you were doing." She looked at Jimmy. "Now what? Where do we take him?"

Jimmy was finally catching his breath. "I think we should take him back to Dotty's," he said after giving it some thought, "and just watch him until he's back to normal and wants to go home. Feed him, let him rest—you know, that kind of stuff."

"But shouldn't he go to a hospital or something?" she asked.

Argus shook his head. "No. This is something the medical community here doesn't know about. They wouldn't understand. Just being back here will start to bring him back to normal." He took a look at the now-listless Emmett, who was lying on the floor against the wall. "He was pretty far gone, though. It may take a few days for him to even start to recover."

"Why did he get like this?" she asked. "And why don't I? Not that I want

201

to, of course."

"It's rare," Argus explained. "If a person is sensitive to it, the change in dimension causes a chemical imbalance in the brain."

"But how do I know I'm not going to end up like him?"

Jimmy and Argus spoke in unison. "You'd already know." Then Jimmy added, "You would've been acting crazy by the time you went out to dinner with Trixie and them the first time you came to Fatropolis."

"Oh," she said, nodding. "Okay, I feel better now. God, I would hate to end up like that—it's so sad."

Jimmy started to stand up, but Emmett just sat there against the wall, looking around. He already looked a bit better—the blood vessels on his temples were not quite as swollen.

They all got up and were brushing themselves off when Jimmy opened the stall door. A large older lady was walking toward the stalls. When she saw Jimmy she gasped and, without a word, started walloping him with her purse.

"I'm sorry, ma'am!" Jimmy held his hands in front of his face in defense as he stepped out of the stall.

As Jenny and Argus started to chuckle, Argus pulled Emmett up off the floor, out of the stall, and led him to the bathroom door. Jenny followed. The old lady kept hitting Jimmy until he was all the way out the door, and then she stood in the door with a stern look on her face until Argus and Emmett were out as well. As Argus passed her she whacked him one time on the shoulder, apparently for good measure, which made him laugh.

Jenny smiled politely at her and said, *"Men*—in the women's bathroom."

They were all in the hall now, and once the door was closed Jenny started laughing.

Jimmy gave her a dirty look. "Genius here had to take us into the ladies' bathroom. Man, that old lady was violent. Just plain violent!" He began rubbing his arm, and Jenny and Argus just giggled.

As they started down the hall Jenny saw a sign on the wall that said *Fatropolitan Museum of Natural History and Evolution.* "Oh, God," she said, "let's get out of here before our inter-dimensional traveler gets ideas about wanting to visit the jungle again."

"I second the motion," said Argus.

Leading Emmett along, they made their way past the museum visitors to the exit and out onto the street. *It's a good thing this museum doesn't close so early.* Jenny felt as if she'd made it home. It was nice to be breathing the air of Fatropolis again.

Jimmy walked down the steps to the street and hailed a cab. One approached the curb and stopped. As they got in, Argus said, "Emmett in the middle this time."

"Lower East side, Dotty's Bakery," Jimmy said to the driver.

They were all starving, sore, and tired, though also relieved and satisfied that their mission had been successful. The cab ride seemed to take forever. As they rode, Jenny and Argus laughed and recounted highlights of their adventure to each other. Jimmy smiled a little and acted insulted as they ribbed him, but Jenny could tell he enjoyed being teased.

Their destination was finally in sight. It hadn't rained a drop in New York, but here the streets were wet. The sun had long since set, and the members of the rescue party had not eaten since breakfast.

"I sure hope they have some leftover food," Argus said. "I swear I could eat my own arm."

Jenny laughed. "I know what you mean."

As the cab pulled up in front of the bakery, they all got out and Jimmy reached into his pocket to pay.

"I got it, Jim," Argus said as he pulled some money out of his pocket.

"I have money, too," Jenny offered. "Jimmy, you need to start saving your money. I hear babies are expensive."

Emmett looked up at Jimmy and smiled weakly. Now his eyes were watering. "You havin' a baby, Jimmy?"

Jimmy looked at Emmett as if astonished that he was already coherent enough to follow a conversation. He smiled down at Emmett. "Yeah, man," he said. "Yeah." He patted Emmett on the back, took his arm to steady him, and walked him into the bakery.

Trixie was standing behind the counter. The minute she saw them walking through the door she let out a huge sigh of relief. "Oh, my gosh—look at all of you. You look like you've been through the mill." She came around the display case and gave Jimmy a big kiss.

"We have been, baby, you wouldn't believe the stuff we went through to get this character back here."

Dixie walked into the bakery. "I thought I heard voices," she said.

Emmett pulled free from Jimmy, stared at Trixie for a moment, then slowly walked over to her. "So you and Jimmy are having a baby?"

Trixie's eyes got big as she looked at Jimmy.

Dixie turned to her twin sister. "What? Is that true?"

As Jenny swallowed hard, Jimmy cleared his throat and rushed Emmett into the dining room. "Let's go in and see if we can find some food," he said. Argus also found an excuse to duck out of the bakery. The twins and Jenny were left alone.

"I'm sorry, Trixie," Jenny said in a quiet voice. "On the way from the cab to the bakery, I was teasing Jimmy about needing to save his money, that babies are expensive. We spent the whole day chasing Emmett. Over there he was crazy as a loon, and now, back here, suddenly he's Mister Coherent. I didn't mean for him to find out. I'm sorry."

Dixie looked at her sister. "You mean Jenny knew, and you didn't tell me?"

Trixie returned the look. "The only reason I told Mack was because I needed her opinion about what I should do. How to approach Dad. She gave me some good advice. Dix, please understand. And then Argus just happened to be sitting there—"

"Argus knows, too? How many other people know?" Dixie demanded.

"Well, there's Leland, and Clara, and Theodore—"

Dixie gasped.

"I'm just kidding," Trixie said. "Jenny and Argus are the only ones who know. I'm sorry, sweetie, but now you know how I felt when I was the last to know about you getting your appendix out. Dad told me that you went away to summer camp. I was so jealous I could've spit, and then you came home and I vowed never to speak to you again."

Dixie looked at her, obviously still hurt. "I can see how that story relates," she said sarcastically. "It is *so* the same kind of thing. I was twelve. I wasn't responsible for telling anyone at all. That was Dad's fault, not mine. You just wait until I get pregnant," she said, starting to cry, "I'm just going to wait and let the baby tell you when it gets big enough to talk."

Trixie burst into tears. "Dix, I'm so sorry. I didn't mean to *not* tell you. I was just so worried about how Dad would react. I didn't want anyone to know. Then after a while it was just awkward, and a lot of time went by. I thought you'd be mad if I told you then."

Jimmy came back into the bakery. "What's going on in here? Jenny, are you bothering my fiancée?"

Jenny looked at him. "Me? What?"

The twins were both bawling loudly, but now they turned to each other and hugged, still crying and sniffling.

Jimmy looked uncomfortable with all the crying, and it appeared he had no idea what to do. His hunger seemed to be the most important thing on his mind right now. It was obvious that he was grappling with himself over whether to bring up something like food at such a dramatic moment, knowing he had to get back to watching Emmett.

Jenny turned to him. "I guess this mess is my fault," she said, gesturing toward the twins, who were still hugging and sobbing together. "I'll go see if there's anything to eat in the kitchen."

When she walked into the kitchen, she found Hank and Charlie there, taking a break from baking.

"What's all the commotion out there?" Hank asked.

"Oh, you know, just the twins," Jenny muttered. "Is there anything left from dinner? Jimmy and Argus and I were gone all day. We haven't eaten since breakfast, and we're starving."

Charlie went over and opened one of the big refrigerators and looked in. "Looks like there's some burrito meat and cheese and some fixings. You want that?"

"That sounds great!"

Charlie helped her get out the bowls and the tortillas and warm them. Then they carried the bowls of food into the dining room where Argus and Jimmy were still keeping a close eye on Emmett.

"Here's some leftovers from dinner," Jenny said.

Jimmy came over to the buffet table. "Looks like Lidia knocked herself out making burritos again," he said. He got two plates and put together some burritos for himself and Emmett.

After Jenny made herself a plate Argus took his turn, and they sat down to eat.

Argus again made sure that Jenny had a glass of tea. Emmett ate slowly and carefully, but Jimmy ate fast and went back for seconds. As he was finishing Trixie came in and sat down by him, her eyes still swollen. A few minutes later Dixie came in carrying half a coconut cream pie and a pie server. "Here's some dessert if you all want any," she said. She set dessert plates and spoons on the table.

When Jimmy finally finished, he sat back and rubbed his belly. Then Dixie cut pie for everyone. Emmett stared at his pie, picked up a spoon, and raised a spoonful to his mouth. His hand was trembling slightly.

As she started in on her pie, Jenny chuckled. The men looked at her quizzically. "I was just picturing Leland and Dotty watching the news tonight in New York and seeing me staring into the camera. Boy, are they going to be shocked."

"There were news people there?" Jimmy asked. "Where?"

Jenny looked at him. "No, but there was someone making a video with a cell phone. If we're lucky, they got the part where Emmett slapped you across the face. That was priceless."

When Trixie looked at him with her mouth open, Jimmy showed her where his cheek had been slapped. She looked closely at it and then kissed it.

Argus took a bite of pie. "Too bad we couldn't get a replay of the look on Brickman's face when he realized he'd captured the wrong man in that jungle." They roared with laughter.

"You nabbed the wrong man?" Trixie asked. "How did that happen?"

"Well," he began, "you know maniacs. They all look alike."

"Tell her about that old lady beating you with her purse in the women's bathroom," Jenny said.

"What did you go into the women's bathroom for?" Trixie asked.

Jenny and Argus could not contain their laughter.

"Violent, violent—that old lady had a mean streak in her." He took a bite of pie. He chuckled a little, and then a serious look came over him. He paused, giving them time to stop laughing. "I realized when we were on the street and the Great Zambuki over here was on top of that car, jumping up and down, that there would've been no way I could've gotten him back here if it wasn't for you two. All joking aside, thanks for going with me and sticking your necks out like that." He looked over at Argus, "No pun intended, man. I appreciate it a lot."

Jenny and Argus smiled and thanked Jimmy back. "I think we made a good team," Jenny added.

"Was it really dangerous?" Trixie asked.

They nodded. "There were a couple of times I didn't know how we were going to make it back with him," Jenny said, shaking her head seriously.

Argus chimed in. "I started to have my doubts, too, especially when I passed out."

Trixie gasped, "You passed out? What happened?"

"Oh, Emmett was hiding in a tree and just got the drop on him and was expressing his love for ol' Argus here." Jimmy patted Emmett on the back. "Right, Emmett?"

Emmett gave them a blank look. "I don't know," he said, slowly chewing a bite of pie.

After finishing her pie Jenny gave Trixie a serious look. "Did you know that you're marrying an agent from the Secret Special Forces?" She took a drink of her tea, but couldn't hold the serious look any longer and started laughing and spewing tea. She tried to cover her mouth with her napkin.

Trixie looked at Jimmy. "What is she talking about?"

Jimmy just smiled, "Well, it made that crowd cease and desist, and it shut that cab driver up, didn't it? He didn't know what to say. When he said, 'yes, sir,' oh, that was funny."

"I thought I'd die when you flashed that badge," Jenny said. "Let me see that thing."

"No, now. Let's not get up close and personal. A man's badge is a serious thing. I'm not about to have my badge mocked and ridiculed by you two."

"Aww, come on, Agent Brickman," Argus said. "Let's have a look.

Still acting bent out of shape, Jimmy opened his wallet and plopped it open on the table. A hush fell over the room. Jenny reached over and picked it up, wanting to be the first to see. She took the badge out of its slot and felt how heavy it was. It was a real metal badge with an official looking emblem. Engraved on it were the words *Secret Special Forces.*

Jenny was astonished. She handed the badge to Argus, who smiled at the look on her face. With a satisfied smirk Jimmy took the badge back, put it back in its slot, closed his wallet, and put it back in his pocket.

Trixie looked at Jimmy. "You're really going to let her think that's a *real* badge?"

"Aww, why'd you want to go and spoil it, baby?"

Trixie looked at Jenny. "That's a badge that came out for a movie. You know, *Secret Special Forces?*"

Jenny smiled slightly and glared at Jimmy. "No, I'm not familiar with that movie."

"It was a movie that came out two years ago," Trixie said, "with Slade Barringer playing this Secret Special Forces agent. As part of their promotions they put out a limited number of those badges. Well, guess who had to have one?" Jimmy shook his head and waved his arms to protest her explanation, but Trixie just went on. "It cost him plenty, though. A hundred and twenty dollars, but it came with the Official Secret Special Forces wallet and everything."

"When do they come out with the sequel?" Jenny asked. "The *Super Secret Special Forces?*"

"Probably next summer," Jimmy muttered.

As everyone at the table started laughing again, Trixie and Dixie started to clean up. Emmett was now asleep in his chair. Jimmy and Argus moved him out to one of the sofas in the parlor, and Dixie brought a pillow and blanket for him. Jimmy put the pillow behind his head and covered him up. "I'll sleep on the other sofa tonight and make sure he's okay," he said.

Jenny walked up to the huge man and patted his shoulder. "Thanks, Jimmy. It was quite an adventure today. I'm going to go help the girls in the kitchen now."

"I'll help, too," said Argus.

After they'd done the dishes, Dixie went into the bakery to relieve Charlie. All the other boarders were already up in their rooms for the night. With nothing else to do, Jenny and Argus decided to sit out in the courtyard, where the soft outside lights were glowing.

Jenny sat down on a bench as Argus took a deep breath and stretched his back muscles.

"That was some adventure, huh?" she said.

"Yeah. I can't believe all we had to go through just to get him back here. You watch, though. Tomorrow he'll be fine."

"I sure hope so. That was sure awkward when he outed Trixie about the baby. Jeez, I had no idea he would repeat that."

After twisting and stretching a few more times, Argus finally sat down next to her. He looked at her and took a deep breath, as if he was trying to muster up some nerve to say something. He rubbed his palms on his pant legs.

Jenny just looked at him, not sure what was happening.

He finally spoke. "Look, I know you and Leland just broke up. But you know how I feel about you. Jenny, I'll just be honest with you." He stood up again. "I'm so in love with you I haven't been able to think about anyone else since you walked into the store that day." As Jenny stood up, too, facing him as if she wanted to hear more, he continued. "Would you go out with me?"

He was so close he could touch her. He looked down at her, gazing into her eyes. She looked up into his and stood there, mesmerized. As he slowly moved his hand up to caress her cheek, she closed her eyes. He moved in slowly and kissed her on the lips. Chills washed over her body. This was the moment she had been fantasizing about for months! She kissed him back— and then their innocent little kiss turned passionate. She wrapped her arms around his neck, he pulled her in close, and the two stood kissing under a tree in the soft lights of the courtyard. Jenny ran her hands up the side of his face and through his hair, and he caressed her and ran his hands down her back.

"My God, Jenny, you don't know how long I've been waiting to kiss you."

"Me, too."

He stopped kissing her. "You, too? What do you mean?"

Jenny was glad Argus had interrupted their heated moment. Another minute, she thought, and she would not have been responsible for what happened next. She sat back down on the bench to catch her breath and try to compose herself.

"I—I probably shouldn't tell you this," she said, "but when I was with Leland—well, I couldn't stop thinking about you."

Argus's smile was so wide his dimples were showing. He sat down next to her and took her hand. "So—you, uh, you—never answered me."

"What are you talking about?"

"Will you go out with me?"

"I'm out with you right now."

He cleared his throat. "What I mean is—is—will you be my girlfriend?"

"That kiss didn't just scream 'yes' to you?" she asked. "Yes, I'll be your girlfriend."

He smiled again, put his arm around her shoulder, and they sat back together, enjoying the cool air. Within minutes he moved in slowly again, and they sat kissing for a long time.

Jenny had loved Argus since the Annual Awards Event, maybe even before, although she hadn't realized it. Her time with Leland, as pleasant and painful as it was, had served to help her recognize her true feelings that much faster, and she was glad now that she had finally admitted it to herself and to him. Now she felt she could relax and enjoy her time in Fatropolis. She could also relax and enjoy her time with Argus.

When they finally came up for air, he looked at her and said, "You're tired. We should probably turn in. Can we do something tomorrow?"

"Don't you have to work?"

"No. I asked for the whole week off. To be with you." He paused and shrugged. "I was hoping."

Jenny smiled.

"I'd like to take you to see some of the sights here," he said.

"I'd like that," she replied. "Like what kind of sights?"

"It's a surprise."

"Well, I've gotta tell you, I'm not up for a bunch of walking and hurrying around. Not after all we did today."

"Me, neither. You'll have fun. Just trust me."

"Sounds like a plan," she said, standing up.

It was now approaching midnight. After another long goodnight kiss Jenny finally pulled herself away, and the couple walked quietly through the French doors into the parlor, where Emmett and Jimmy were both snoring. Holding hands, they walked quietly up the stairs. Argus stopped at Jenny's door, where they kissed again.

Trixie was just coming up the stairs. She stopped and looked at them until they both blushed. "Well, *finally,*" she said. "Everyone's been wondering when you two would finally get together." She went on to her room. "Thank God, now we can all relax."

Jenny and Argus just looked at each other, goofy smiles on their faces. He couldn't resist kissing her one more time, and then he finally bid her goodnight.

Jenny closed and locked her door, stripped down, and went in to draw her bath. *I have to soak tonight for sure, I'm so sore from all that running around.* She sank down into the hot water and groaned with pleasure. She couldn't stop thinking about kissing Argus. She loved the way he expressed himself to her, the way he looked into her eyes, the way he touched her, the way he was so loving and accepting of her. She felt so comfortable with him. She lay in the water, pondering the differences between Leland and Argus.

After her bath she put her robe on, but she wasn't sure if she wanted to look at Driscol's journal tonight, as upset as she'd gotten the night before. She decided she'd look carefully for more information about the goddess statuettes. She got into bed and picked up the book, then sat there for a moment with it on her lap.

She finally opened it and began skimming the pages. She didn't see any mention of goddesses. After several pages, she caught sight of the word "Tammany." This was a passage she felt she had to read.

March 12th 1930. I was thinking about my father today, it being the 16th anniversary of his passing. I was remembering him giving me the metal box with the bundle in it, a few weeks before he passed away. He told me to "mind the ladies closely" and not let them fall into the wrong hands. He told me that his father had accepted these little ladies from his friend who was trying to get rid of them, years ago. But now I know why my grandfather's friend wanted to rid himself of them. He found out that he should have never accepted them from that man who worked for the Boss Tweed. That man was unscrupulous, and he used one of the little ladies to make the weir to this world, thinking he could escape with money stolen from the city coffers. He was caught, though, and put in jail. The laugh was on him, too, as the currency is very different here.

I wanted to come to this side of the weir, thinking this to be a land of promise, but it turned out to be a world much like the one we came from, with a Depression of its own. One big difference, though, is that everyone here is healthy and hearty. I came here because the money dried up when the market crashed. Work got scarce. The owner of the bakery I was working for told me that he could no longer pay me, so I lost my job. Mona gave all her food to the little one—I worried that she was losing her reserves too rapidly.

I waited too long to come through the weir. I thought coming here would be a blessing and would save my Mona from passing on, but she was too far gone and died a few weeks after coming here several months ago, now. Tressa is still lost without her momma, and so am I. I wish I had found the weir that Pa told me about in the Tammany Hall sooner. I was wrong to wait so long to take my family through to the other side. When I finally searched out the weir, it was in desperation. I heard later that they demolished the building. I wonder if they tore it down on account of the weir.

I am binding the lady made of wood that made the weir, and hiding her, so she won't be used again. I wouldn't want folks in the other world to find out and all come here. Pa also told me that all the other ladies are made of stone and all have their own magick. One of them can divine a spot in the world with perfect conditions for making a weir, where the veil is thinnest between the worlds, and once a weir is made, another one of the ladies can detect where the weir is—he says it glows with a beautiful blue light when it's near the weir. My pa told me that he believed they were stolen from someone, and that they were imbued with a powerful magick, which is why his friend wanted to get rid of them. I think it curious that all the ladies in this world look like the little ladies. Hearty and substantial.

July 22nd, 1930. It's been a long time since I wrote any. I forgot to mention before that the folks are friendly here. I was able to get work straight away. Seems they have bakeries here, too—it looks like they have everything we have in the other world. It looks to be a complete world, just like ours. Except they are more advanced here. I owe my life to the old man that owns the bakery. He was plenty glad to know I had experience at baking. He's a nice old man and he seems to like me fine. A lady from the schoolhouse scolded me good for not having Tressa in school. So now she's going and learning to read and write. Tressa and I stay with the old man. He has a big house and rents rooms to different folks. We work for our room and board. The old man lost his wife years ago, too, and sometimes it seems he's not well.

Jenny was enthralled. "So Driscol was from my world," she said quietly. "And he didn't make the portal that was at Tammany Hall—it was made by someone else trying to steal from the city of New York. Interesting." She gave this some more thought. "So two portals have been explained. But I wonder why there's one in the museum."

Exhausted by her rigorous day, she fell asleep with Driscol McBain's journal lying across her chest.

CHAPTER 18
A DOCTOR'S VISIT
LIKE NO OTHER

IT WAS STILL DARK OUTSIDE WHEN JENNY STIRRED in her sleep and was poked by the corner of Driscol's journal. She closed the book and put it in the drawer of her nightstand, then settled back down under the covers. She slept until about six-thirty. She woke up thinking, *I'm sure looking forward to spending the day with my boyfriend. I like the sound of that.* She smiled to herself. *Argus is my boyfriend.*

She washed, dressed, and went downstairs. Breakfast preparations were well under way. When she went into the kitchen she found Emmett all cleaned up, wearing an apron, working with the other boarders and separating eggs. Hank and Charlie had taken over all of Dotty's supervisory duties. The bakery and meal preparations were running as smoothly as ever. As soon as she came through the door, Jenny was put on waffle iron detail. The banana waffle batter was already made—all she had to do was pour the batter in and bake the waffles. Dwyer was flipping pancakes, the twins were cooking bacon and link sausages, and Jimmy was peeling and cutting fresh fruit.

A few minutes later Argus came through the kitchen door. Jenny looked over at him. Everything happening in the kitchen came to a halt as he walked over to her and moved in for a kiss. Jenny blushed, knowing that this moment had to come sooner or later. Everyone was watching. As the kitchen crew dropped their utensils and began to clap, Jenny and Argus smiled at each other. The men patted Argus on the back and shook his hand. The women smiled and laughed.

Just then Clara came through the kitchen door. "What was the applause all about?" she asked. Her expression changed when she saw Argus standing with his arm around Jenny's waist. There was something about her face that made Jenny remember the dream she'd had some months ago.

Oh my gosh, she said to herself. *Trixie is pregnant. My dream came true. I wonder if Clara and Leland will end up together.*

"Argus and Jenny just kissed," Trixie said without hesitation. "Finally. They're officially an item now."

"Oh." Clara went back into the dining room.

Everyone else went back to their breakfast duties, and before long the food was ready to be hauled into the dining room. As the boarders stood in line at the buffet table, Jenny and Argus made their plates and sat down together. Everyone was in good spirits this morning and enjoying their breakfast.

After a little while Jenny overheard Clara ask Trixie, "So when is Dotty coming back?"

"She said she didn't have the slightest idea when she'd be back," Trixie replied, "so who knows?"

Emmett was quiet, and still a bit shaky on his feet, so Jimmy helped him get his food. Then both men sat down across from Jenny and Argus, who had already gotten a huge cup of coffee with cream and sugar. It still made her a little uncomfortable for him to serve her, but she decided it was something she'd just have to get used to. She took a sip of coffee. It tasted so good.

Argus's plate was piled high with buttered waffles and syrup, which Jenny enjoyed watching him eat. When she reached down and patted him on the leg, he smiled and leaned over for a kiss. She returned the kiss. The boarders who hadn't already seen their kitchen kiss were surprised.

"So, Argus, when did this happen?" Lidia asked.

"I asked Jenny to be my girlfriend last night—and she said yes." He was beaming.

Clara didn't even look at them. Lidia congratulated them and went back to her breakfast.

Jimmy had to join in. "Pretty soon they'll be announcing their engagement, too."

Argus nodded. "That's right, Brickman. If I have my way, that'll be happening soon enough."

Jenny looked up from her coffee. "Well, if you don't want to be picking me up off the floor, just don't spring it on me when I least expect it." As everyone started laughing, she leaned closer to Jimmy and asked in a quiet voice, "So what's going to happen with Emmett?"

Jimmy glanced at Emmett, who was eating enthusiastically. "I wanted to give him a little time to get more back to normal before I call his parents."

"Parents?" Jenny asked. "Isn't he like thirty-something?"

"Yeah. He still lives with his parents, though."

Another poor, unfortunate man who isn't fat enough to cut it in this fat-is-where-it's-at society, she thought, shaking her head. She leaned over to Argus and quietly said, "I'm eager to find out what you have planned for today."

Trixie said, "Mack, could I talk to you before you go anywhere?"

Jenny nodded and excused herself from the table. The two friends went out in the corridor, where Jenny asked, "What is it, Trix?"

"I'm sorry I didn't ask you until now, but would you go with Jimmy and me to my first prenatal appointment today? I thought this was something we should do as a couple, you know, but Jimmy's so nervous, it'll help him to have you joking and keeping him in line."

"Well," Jenny wasn't quite sure what to say, "I was going to spend the day with *my boyfriend.* He's got big plans for the whole week—"

"Surely he can share you for a couple of hours," Trixie responded adamantly. "Heck, if he wants to come, he can come, too. I mean, not into the room with us, but he can sit in the waiting room."

Jenny gave this some further thought, then said, "Wait a minute. You're not going to get me in trouble with Dixie again. No way, sister. Why don't you ask her to go?"

Trixie smiled. "I already cleared it with her. She doesn't like to go to the doctor. It makes her nervous, all that poking and prodding."

"Well, okay," Jenny said. "What time is the appointment? I'll talk to Argus. You know this is a *huge* sacrifice—we just got together, and we don't want to waste one minute that we can be together—"

Trixie held up one hand like a sock puppet talking as she said, "Blah, blah, blah!" She laughed at herself. "Tell him the appointment's at two o'clock this afternoon. We'll leave here at one."

Jenny laughed. She loved getting the best of Trixie, but even better, she loved getting one over on Jimmy. She'd never had such good friends until she'd come to Fatropolis. Back home, and before she met Jimmy, she'd never been able to joke with men.

The minute she went back into the dining room, Argus looked up at her. "There might be a little change of plans for today," she told him under her breath.

"What's up?" he asked.

"Oh, Trixie wants me to accompany her on a little errand."

"What time?"

"We have to leave from here at one. She said you can come, too, if you want."

He shook his head. "No, actually, this will work out fine. I have a little errand to do myself."

"Okay."

"How about we do something together right after breakfast? Then I'll take you to lunch and have you back here by one. Then this evening, I'll take you to dinner. How does that sound?"

"Lunch *and* dinner out? I'm going to go home so spoiled."

"Let's not talk about you going home yet, please."

Jenny smiled. Lidia had been listening to their conversation. She giggled and quickly looked down at her plate.

After they finished breakfast and put their dishes in the bin, they left the dining room.

"Let's go out to the courtyard," Argus said. "I have something to ask you." He led her back to the bench they had sat on the night before. "I know this is kind of sudden," he said, "but I was wondering—while you were here—if you wouldn't mind us having dinner with my folks this week. I'd love for you to meet them."

"Well—" Jenny hesitated, then said, "don't you think it's kind of soon? I mean, we just got together last night."

Argus looked disappointed. "Yeah, I guess you're right. It's just that I sort of already told them about you. They just want to meet you, that's all."

She looked into his eyes. "Argus, I hope you understand that I'm not going to be able to stand a lot of judgmental stares and stuff. About my weight—um, I mean, well—or about our age difference."

"Age difference?"

"Well, yeah, I'm old enough to be your—your older sister."

"I look young for my age," he said with a smile. "How old do you think I am?"

"Well, twenty-one? Twenty-two? I know I must have at least ten years on you."

His smile turned into laughter. "I just had my twenty-eighth birthday a couple months ago."

"Oh, my gosh! I thought you were just a youngster. I didn't want to scare you by introducing you to things you'd never seen before. That's one of the reasons I didn't consider you fair game when I first met you. Well, and then there was the fact that you already had a girlfriend. That was the main thing I couldn't get past."

"That's ancient history." He kissed her enthusiastically. "You are so beautiful!"

"You don't want to know how old I am?" she asked.

"It doesn't really matter. I love you, anyway."

"I'm forty-two."

"Really?" he asked, smiling.

She smiled back. "No. Well, I finally started admitting that I'm twenty-nine." She paused and then leaned over and whispered, "I'm really thirty-one."

"Well, I'm glad you're only a couple of years older than me. That means we'll have more years together.

That's so sweet, she thought. She looked at him and smiled. "I'd be glad to meet your parents."

He kissed her again. "They're just going to love you!"

"I hope so. I know what my parents will say when they meet you. They'll tell me, 'Don't you do anything to mess this up.' They would never in a million years think I could land a man as gorgeous as you."

He laughed out loud. "Then our families are more alike than you know. My parents will be telling me the same thing about you. They'll be so surprised I was able to reel in such a hearty babe." He paused. "I shouldn't say this, but you should have seen the looks on their faces when I brought Clara to the house. My mother practically ran her off with a meat fork." They both laughed again.

Jenny spoke before thinking. "But how are we going to deal with—you know, us living in different worlds?" She stopped. "Uh—I, uh—listen to me talking so seriously so soon." She blushed.

He patted her hand. "Do you think I haven't thought this through? I figured that once I buy the store, I can be gone for long periods of time, and just check in once in a while. But of course I'm hoping that you'll want to make your home here. We could get a little apartment here in Fathattan and just settle in. I'm sure you could find work here, but if you want to stay in your world, we could do that, too."

Jenny heaved a sigh of relief. "That makes me feel better. I was afraid you were going to insist on living here. I was afraid something like that might come between us."

"You don't ever have to be afraid," he said. "We can work things out."

In that moment she realized that she'd been worrying about having to give up her life in her world. She took another deep breath and felt more relaxed. "Okay. So what are we doing today?"

"Well, we have about four hours before you have to be back. There's a theater not far. We could take in a movie before lunch."

"I'd rather just sit here and talk until we go for lunch."

"That was my backup plan."

"What about helping out in the kitchen for lunch and dinner?" she asked.

"I told them not to count on us most of this week because we'll be in and out," he replied.

"Good."

They sat under the tree. There was a chill in the air, and so Jenny cuddled in close to Argus, which he didn't seem to mind a bit. Time seemed to stand still when they were together. She told him about the sad things she'd read in Driscol McBain's journal, about the little goddesses and where they probably came from, and about what she had read in the journal about the portals.

Finally she asked, "How did all of you boarders come to know so much about the portals?"

He sat up straighter. "You've got to understand that going through the portals is like a rite of passage to the kids here in Fatropolis. As soon as they reach high school, they're dared to go through and see what's over there. I think it all started back in the fifties. It's something kids do to defy their parents and the old folks. Then when kids get older, some go over there pretty regularly, but a lot of them settle into parenthood and then disapprove of their kids going over there. It's part of the generation gap here." Argus stopped, thought for a moment, and then continued, "Why, I would hazard to guess that a large percentage of the people here know about the portals. Or have been through them at least once. It's just common knowledge. But it's also a secret. Kids know not to go blabbing to their folks, and older people who have been through the portals just don't acknowledge it, and would never admit to it. And certainly no one talks about it. That's why it seems like a lot of people don't know. But you take folks who move here from other parts of the States or the world—now, they *really* don't know."

"Wow. And we thought it was sneaky to go out in the middle of the night and paint the old water tower."

Argus looked at her with a blank expression on his face.

"Where I grew up, that's what every senior class would do at some point in the year. They would sneak out one night with buckets of paint and defile the local water tower. I come from a small town. There wasn't much to do." She looked at him again and saw that his expression hadn't changed. "We had *a lot* of time on our hands."

"Yeah," he said. "I got that. I'm just trying to wrap my head around painting a water tower. Was it at least really high and dangerous?"

"Oh, very high, very dangerous. Extremely high and dangerous. In fact just the mention of the water tower in my home town was synonymous with 'danger.'"

"Okay, Jenny, I think I've got the picture." He hugged her. "I love your sense of humor."

They had a good laugh, and Jenny thought she understood things in Fatropolis a little better.

"Oh, by the way," Argus said after another minute, "Jimmy asked me if we could all go out this weekend. You know, dinner and dancing."

"Dancing? You dance?"

"Of course I dance." He started gyrating to nonexistent music. "Doesn't everyone?"

"I wouldn't miss that for the world," Jenny said with a laugh. "Basically, Argus, I'm just along for the ride here. Anything you want to plan, you just go right ahead. Just don't be springing any proposals of marriage on me."

"Okay. No surprise proposals. I get that, too. You don't want to faint again, and I don't ever want to be the cause of you fainting." He was joking, but Jenny could tell he was serious. "So I'll talk to Jimmy, and we'll make plans to go out for dinner and dancing." He looked at his watch. "It's getting late. Shall we head out for lunch?"

They took a cab uptown to a nice Cuban restaurant, where they had spicy grilled chicken, black beans and rice, and fried plantains for dessert. They sipped some sweet *tamarindo* water, which was like iced tea, but fruitier.

Jenny always liked to try new foods, so they had a wonderful time. Unlike her previous dates with Leland, she felt totally at ease eating around Argus. She was also starting to get used to the stares from people who assumed they were mismatched. The realization hit Jenny that she would probably get even worse stares in her world because Argus was so good looking (according to the standards there) that women would probably be jealous. But she didn't care. She enjoyed his company, and had already become aware that she was head over heels in love with him.

As promised, Argus had her back in time for her to go with Trixie and Jimmy. He greeted the couple, kissed Jenny goodbye, and left. Jimmy was visibly nervous, which seemed strange to Jenny, as he was normally calm, cool, and collected about most things.

Trixie seemed exasperated with Jimmy's bout of nerves. She looked at Jenny and said, "You'd think I was going in to have the baby today." She hailed a cab.

"I can't help it," the big man said. "I don't like going to the doctor's office. All those needles, and poking, and—oh, God, I've got to sit down."

Trixie rolled her eyes. "You can sit down in the cab. Or maybe you'd just prefer Jenny go with me and you stay here?"

Jimmy looked as if he were tempted to take her up on the offer, but then he reconsidered. "No, no, my sweet. I would never be able to live that one down if I didn't go."

Jenny patted Jimmy on the back. "Good answer, Butter Brickle."

Trixie gave them both a disgusted stare. "I would have preferred to hear, 'Oh, no, Trixie, I wouldn't hear of you going to our baby's first appointment without me.' But, no, I get Mr. Nerves over here." She looked at Jenny. "What's he going to be like when it's time for me to actually deliver?"

A cab stopped and they got in. As they were settling into their seats, Jenny looked at Jimmy and said, "Did you know that at the first appointment they like to get a sample of the father's blood as well? To make sure the baby's blood will be compatible and all—"

"Hold on! Hold up! Just one minute!" Jimmy protested. "There ain't no way I'm getting my blood drawn today."

Trixie and Jenny had a good laugh at Jimmy's expense. When they arrived in front of the building where the doctor's office was, Jenny paid the cab. Jimmy looked at her, astonished and half smiling. "That's nice of you," he said.

They walked into the building. Jimmy's legs seemed heavy and his movements were cumbersome. They took an elevator to the eleventh floor, then walked down a very long hallway, finally arriving at the offices of Dr. Marie Whittaker, OB/GYN.

Jenny and Jimmy sat down in the waiting room while Trixie checked in. Because she was a new patient she had to fill out a stack of paperwork. A diagram on the wall showed a cross section of a woman's body with a baby growing inside. The woman on the diagram was very fat. Even the baby growing inside her was fat. *This ought to be interesting,* Jenny thought, remembering a few grueling trips to the doctor in her world. Jimmy stood up and went over to look at the diagram more closely.

They looked at magazines, studied the art on the walls, asked the receptionist for water, and Jimmy even ventured out once to find the restroom. Nearly an hour after they arrived, the chubby nurse called Trixie into the inner offices. Jenny and Jimmy went with her. First the nurse asked Trixie to step into the volume scanner, which was their version of a scale. Jenny had never seen such a device. Trixie complied without any comments, complaints, or excuses, stepping into the huge glass box. The nurse hit some buttons and a scanning device shot lasers all around her body and scanned her from head to toe. The results came up on a screen in green numbers.

"You're green," the nurse said as she made notes on Trixie's new chart. Then she got out a blood pressure cuff that was long enough to go all the way around Trixie's large arm with cuff to spare.

As she watched, Jenny remembered the last time she'd gone in for a checkup. The thin nurse had tried to use the regular cuff on her, but it pinched her upper arm terribly. Then the nurse had searched the entire office suite to find a cuff that would fit. She couldn't find one, so she eventually took the reading on Jenny's lower arm, commenting that if her arm wasn't so big, they'd be able to get an accurate reading.

While Jenny was lost in her memories the nurse took Trixie's blood pressure and wrote it down, again not commenting. Trixie also had to urinate into a cup and bring the cup back to the nurse, who dipped a long paper strip into the urine. As the strip changed color, she wrote down the results, once more without comment. Then she slid the strip into a glass machine that did some calculations—results came up on the screen, showing all the vitamin, mineral, sugar, and protein levels in Trixie's urine.

"Does everything look okay?" she asked.

"Yes," the nurse said. "You seem to be in good health. How has your appetite been?"

Trixie told her about the bouts of nausea and vomiting and that her appetite was increasing at times. The nurse told her "that's all perfectly normal," and gave her some tips for dealing with the nausea and vomiting. "We don't want you losing any of your reserves."

Next the nurse led them into another room that had an examination table and some other complicated equipment. She handed Trixie a gown, instructed her to undress and put the gown on, and left the room. Jenny was filled with a sense of dread for Trixie. Her friend went behind a curtain and within a few minutes came out dressed in nothing but the gown and her socks. She asked Jenny if she would tie the ties. The gown actually went all the way around her, and even overlapped like it was supposed to.

"What's the matter?" Trixie asked.

"I just can't believe that the gown fits you," she said with a smile.

"Why would it not fit me?"

Jenny waved her hand and shook her head as if dismissing it. "It's just another one of the things in my world that shows me I'm too big and don't fit in," she said. "The gowns at doctors' offices and in hospitals never fit. Us fat ladies are forced to sit there, humiliated, wearing a skimpy little gown that only covers the front half of our body. Sometimes they have extra large gowns, but even *they* don't cover everything."

"Oh," Trixie said sadly. Even Jimmy looked at her with empathy in his eyes.

As is true of all medical appointments, even in other worlds, they had to wait a while for the doctor to come in. About the time Jimmy got bored and started looking through the cupboards in the room, the doctor came through the door. She was a large, mature black woman with streaks of silver in her hair, a warm smile, and a friendly demeanor. She shook everyone's hand as she introduced herself, then started asking Trixie some questions.

At no time was Trixie's weight (or volume) ever mentioned, nor any of the readings they had just taken, except for the doctor saying "everything looks good." Jenny was amazed. *This is how a fat person should be treated when they go to the doctor,* she thought. *Like a real person. Not an outcast.*

The doctor was very knowledgeable, and was even able to set Jimmy at ease. She asked Trixie to lie back on the table and poked around on her belly for a few moments, then asked Jenny and Jimmy to move to the head of the table. She dimmed the lights and turned on a glass laser emitter. After explaining to them what she was going to do, she passed a device over Trixie's belly that projected three-dimensional ultra-photonic images of their baby into the air above the emitter.

When she saw the fetus's legs moving Trixie began to cry with joy, and Jimmy got tears in his eyes. He started rubbing Trixie's shoulders as they watched the first glimpse of their baby.

Jenny felt privileged to be sharing such a private moment with her friends. When the doctor told them that everything looked normal and that there would be other tests as the pregnancy progressed, Jimmy kissed Trixie on the cheek. After the doctor finally left, Trixie went back behind the curtain and changed again. Jimmy seemed relieved that no one had asked him to submit to any tests or give any blood.

At a time when Trixie and Jimmy were feeling so elated, Jenny could not help but feel sad. First, she was taken aback by the difference in medical technologies here. Medical practice in Fatropolis seemed to be much more advanced than back home. Also, witnessing the difference in the way fat people were treated at the doctor's office made her angry. She remembered all the times she'd been completely humiliated in a doctor's office. One time she'd gone to the emergency room with a bout of bronchitis. They'd told her that her breathing would improve if she would only lose some weight. She'd been prescribed the necessary medications to thwart the illness, as was the thin woman next to her who had the same thing. But the thin woman was not lectured about her size. A woman in Jenny's support group back home had said she'd been told by her doctor that she was going to die if she didn't lose weight. *All of this in my world thanks to the actuarial tables.*

Back in the waiting room Trixie was given her next appointment and paid her insurance copay. Then the three of them left the office. Jenny was sullen and quiet.

Riding the elevator down to the ground floor, Jimmy finally spoke up.

"Jenny, why are you so sad all of a sudden?"

Jenny's eyes began to water. "You know, Jimmy, for once I'm speechless." She couldn't bring herself to talk about the humiliation she'd suffered at the hands of the doctors in her world—doctors who had supposedly vowed to harm none.

They caught a cab back to the boarding house. Everyone was nearly silent the whole ride. Jenny just stared out the window. Finally she spoke. "I'm sorry, you two. I didn't mean to rain on your parade. I'm so glad you got to see your baby. It looks just like you, Jimmy." At this, they all laughed.

When they arrived back at the boarding house, Jenny went straight to her room, where she locked herself in, peeled her clothes off, and ran a hot bath. Then she lay in the tub, sulking, shocked that fat people in this world were living the good life, whereas fat people in her world were the scorn of society. She couldn't get past the injustice of it all.

How unfair it all is, she thought angrily. Then her reasoning side spoke to her. *All those times at the doctor's office—you bought into their low opinion of you. You allowed them to treat you badly. You don't have to submit to being weighed if you don't want to, and you don't have to let them take your blood pressure with a cuff that you know will pinch you. You don't have to allow the doctor to talk to you that way, either. They are not gods. They have no way of knowing when a person will die. They are following protocols that were taught to them in medical school. You can refuse anything you want to refuse.*

"That's right!" Jenny said out loud. "I don't have to let anyone treat me badly any more. Not even doctors." Then she remembered a famous quote from Mahatma Gandhi: "No one can hurt me without my permission."

It was as if a light bulb went on. She stopped sulking and finished her bath. She was looking forward to dinner out with Argus.

As she was rushing around, dressing, she heard a knock. She opened the door and saw Argus standing there. He looked worried. "How are you doing?"

"I'm doing great! Come on in."

He looked so handsome, she thought, in a nice dark blue suit with a white shirt, the collar unbuttoned. She could tell he'd really fussed over his appearance. And his aftershave was almost intoxicating.

He came in and closed the door. Hugging her around the waist, he said, "Trixie told me you were upset."

"I was, but I'm okay now," she said, looking up into his blue eyes.

"Can I ask what the matter was?"

"It just upset me to see how well fat people are treated by the doctors here. It brought up a lot of unpleasant memories for me. But while I was bathing,

I realized that I allow them to treat me badly. That will just be another place in my world where I can practice my new attitude."

"Hearty people are treated badly at the doctor's office over there?" he asked.

"Yeah. Like everything that's wrong with us is because we're fat."

"Really?" His expression turned serious, and he went over and looked out the window. He looked shaken. "That's how *I'm* treated at the doctor. Because I'm not hearty."

"What?" Jenny asked as she walked over behind him.

"I got depressed after being with you at your Annual Awards Event, and I guess I wasn't eating right. I caught a nasty cold and went to the doctor because I was having fevers and felt terrible. That's when the doctor told me that he wanted to recommend me for weight gain surgery." He turned to look at her, and she saw his eyes were watering. "A *cold,* Jenny, I had a stinkin' cold. He told me I'd be a lot healthier if I'd put some meat on my bones. They make me wear those gowns that go around me three or four times. And they can never find a blood pressure cuff small enough for my arm, so they keep pumping and pumping and never can get a good reading on me. They measure my volume and the darned numbers always come up orange or even red, and then I get the lecture that I need to hearty up. I've been sent for optimal nutrition classes, conscious calorie classes, and living large lifestyle classes. It's so embarrassing." He paused for a moment, deep in thought. "One time when I was a kid, the red volume scanner lights were blinking. It's bad enough to have a red readout, but when it blinks, it means you're way too skinny. The doctor made my mom cry that day. He told her that I was extra susceptible to disease at my scant volume and would surely die if I didn't hearty up. Ever since then she's pushed food on me all the time. I could eat three plates and she'd still insist I eat more."

"Sounds like what I go through every time I go to the doctor. Only in reverse."

"And don't even get me started on all the skinny jokes. And the comments at my expense that I got while I was growing up."

"I know," she said sympathetically. "We have them, too—like, 'how do you make love to a fat woman?'"

Argus thought for a moment, and then smiled at her mischievously. "I know how to make love to a fat woman."

"No, silly. That's a cruel joke they have in my world," she said, blushing.

"Boy, I walked right into that one, didn't I?"

He grabbed her around the waist again. "Yep, and I know the punch line. It's not true, just like people saying I have to stand twice to make a shadow."

He kissed her. She was dressed, but her hair was still wet. He sniffed her hair, "Mmmm, your hair smells good."

Not wanting to hang around in her room for too long, she pulled herself away and went into the bathroom and put some lipstick on. Then she put on her shoes. "Okay. I'm ready to go."

"We'll need to dress up tomorrow," he informed her.

"Really? Why?"

"I'm taking you somewhere special, and it would be appropriate if we were dressed up nice."

"Oh, that sounds interesting. What time?"

"After breakfast. About nine or ten."

"Okay. I'll wear a dress." She picked up her bag. "Let's go."

"Hold on, hold on," he said. "Our reservation isn't for another hour. What's the hurry?"

"Frankly, Argus, I don't want to be alone with you," she said.

He looked offended. "What? Why not?"

"Well—I'm just afraid."

"Afraid of what?"

She didn't know what to say. Finally, "Going too far, too soon."

That made him laugh out loud. "I thought it was something really serious," he said. "Jenny, don't scare me like that. I know, I'm just so gorgeous that you can't trust yourself around me."

Jenny nodded. "That's about it."

"Come on," he said, as if he didn't believe her. "Look, I'm a gentleman, in every sense of the word. I'm not going to try *anything* that makes you uncomfortable. When it's supposed to happen, it will."

"I believe you, but let's go," she insisted. She took him by the hand and led him out of the room.

Jimmy and Trixie were in the kitchen, and Jenny had to talk to them. "I wanted to apologize for bringing your moment down today," she said as she hugged Trixie. "Congratulations, momma!" Then she hugged Jimmy. "Congratulations, papa!"

Argus shook Jimmy's hand.

"We got to see our baby for the first time today," Jimmy told him.

"That must have been an experience."

"It was wonderful! The doctor gave us this." Jimmy reached into his pocket and pulled out the ultra-photonic image of the baby. "Here's an arm. Here's the head."

Jenny and Trixie went off to the side together. "I'm really sorry, Trixie."

"Are you feeling better now? That's all that matters."

"Yeah, but Argus is making me uncomfortable," Jenny confessed.

"What?"

"No, no, no, not like that. It's just that I've never wanted a man so much in my life. I can't stand to be alone with him. *He drives me crazy.*"

Trixie had to laugh at that. "Oh, my gosh, you just need to go for it, girl!"

"I knew you'd say that. I get no help—no help at all."

"Well," Trixie laughed again, "you'll know when it's the right time. Just don't worry about it. And for crying out in the night, don't ruin your time with him just because of that. Life is too short, Jenny."

Argus walked over to Jenny. "You ready, baby?"

Jenny looked at Trixie and smiled as if to say, "See what I mean?" The two women giggled.

Argus looked at Jimmy and shrugged. "Hey, so are we on for Friday night? We're all going out dancing?"

Jimmy looked at Trixie. "Is that okay with you, Trix?"

"Yeah. That would be fun."

Argus and Jenny went out through the bakery. Clara, who was standing behind the counter, didn't look up as the two strolled through arm in arm.

Argus took Jenny to the Castle Tower, one of Fatropolis's most romantic restaurants. The décor was Central European. They were served fine Polish and German cuisine that included different meats and sausages, cabbage, potatoes, and hearty soups. The stocky waiter seemed enthralled with Jenny, staring at her every time he came to the table. He hardly made eye contact with Argus. He was quick to refill Jenny's sweet tea, but left Argus sitting for quite a while with an empty glass. Jenny finally caught him staring at her from across the room and waved him over. He rushed to her side.

"Could you please get my boyfriend more soda?" she asked. "Thank you."

He grabbed the empty glass and walked away.

Argus smiled at her. "I guess he doesn't care for good tips."

The waiter walked back with a full glass and set it in front of Argus, looking right at Jenny and said, "There you are, miss."

Argus cleared his throat. "Excuse me." The waiter turned to look at him. "I'll thank you to stop ogling my lady, and we're ready for the check now," he said. turning to Jenny. "Aren't we, baby? Or would you like some dessert?"

"No, I think we should go," Jenny said, feeling uncomfortable about the waiter, but elated that Argus had asked her if she wanted dessert. The waiter walked away in a huff and promptly brought the check. After their waiter collected Argus's credit card and left the table with an air of aloofness, Argus and Jenny had a good but quiet laugh.

After dinner Jenny wanted to look in the shops that surrounded the restaurant. Nearby, statues of fat people were displayed in the window. She had to go in. She bought some smaller sculptures of fat women for her apartment. Another shop had prints. She bought two—one of two little fat cherubs, the other of two fat women bathing in a lake. Argus also expressed his delight at the print of the fat women bathing, which caused Jenny to smack him again on the arm.

She was having a wonderful time. She stopped in other shops and bought other little trinkets and souvenirs. Argus tried to insist on paying for them, but she stopped him and showed him all the Fatropolitan currency she had.

She loved the freedom and sense of belonging she felt here. Most of the people looked just like her. She didn't care where she and Argus went, as long as she could spend time with him. She felt that if all they did all week was sit in Dotty's courtyard and talk, she'd be happy. She had never felt such unconditional love from a man in her life. He was always respectful and loving, and he always cared to hear what she had to say.

Every once in a while the thought about having to go back home and go back to work would creep into her mind, but she refused to entertain such thoughts. She knew that her relationship with Argus would not as be easy as love is for some couples. In addition to the difference in their sizes, there was also the fact that one of them would have to move to the other's world. This bothered her, but it was another thought she refused to entertain. *Stop worrying,* she told herself. *Just take things one step at a time.*

The two were content to sit in an open air café enjoying coffee and dessert. They laughed and talked until the wee hours of the morning, and finally took a cab back to the boarding house. Jenny's feet were sore from all the walking and looking in stores, and she was almost hoarse from talking so much and laughing at Argus' stories about his parents and his mother's constant pressure on him to give them some grandkids. He also had horror stories about past girlfriends running from the house trying to escape from his mother's grasp. The curious side of Jenny was now very much looking forward to meeting his parents, which made Argus happy. Because she laughed so much at his stories, she just had to see them for herself.

He walked her up to her room and they kissed good night. "Did I ever tell you how handsome you look tonight in that good-looking suit?" she asked. "It really makes the color of your eyes stand out." She was wondering how much longer she'd be able to resist his charms.

When Argus finally left, she closed the door and locked it. She wasn't in the mood to spend any time with Driscol McBain tonight. She just wanted to soak in her tub.

During her bath she thought about how much she had going on now compared to how she felt the first time she'd soaked in this tub. That first bath was really the only good thing Jenny had in her pathetic life when she had first come to Fatropolis. Although she had her job, her apartment, her cat, and her church, she hadn't had any real pleasures or happiness in her life back there. Now she lay there in the tub and prayed, expressing gratitude for all the richness in her life, for all the new relationships, especially the one with Argus.

She finished her bath, dressed in her robe, and turned on the television for the first time in days. She'd forgotten how much she enjoyed watching it, especially in Fatropolis. Knowing it was late, she turned the volume down.

A music video show was premiering one of Flint Mackelroy's new videos. It was sure to be a hit. She lay there in the dark, smiling and remembering the concert she'd seen at the Festival Fatropolis. Again she was filled with gratitude for the changes in her life since then.

It was now nearing two o'clock in the morning. Jenny was so tired, she fell asleep during the third video.

CHAPTER 19
A WISH COMES TRUE
AT THE COURTHOUSE

MORNING CAME ALL TOO SOON.

Argus knocked at Jenny's door at seven-thirty. "Wow, were you out late last night or something?" he asked, hugging her and trying to kiss her. "Good morning, milady."

She resisted the kiss. "Oh, God, Argus—my breath has to be horrible." Turning away, she went into the bathroom and brushed her teeth. "I'll be right down—let me get dressed."

"Are you sure you couldn't use some help?"

She leaned around the door of the bathroom to glare at him.

"Okay, okay. I'm going."

After fixing her hair and putting on her pretty dress and matching shoes, she went down to the dining room, where the other boarders were already enjoying breakfast. Lidia had prepared a Mexican breakfast with eggs and chorizo, refried beans, cheese, fresh salsa, sour cream, and tortillas. Jimmy was on his second helping of everything, and thoroughly enjoying himself.

Emmett was carrying on a conversation with Delia. *He looks so much better,* Jenny thought, *pretty much back to normal.* She took a plate and served herself, then gave Argus a quick kiss and sat down in the seat he'd saved for her. He already had her coffee waiting. He was wearing a tie. *Hmm, this must be some occasion he has planned for this morning. I hope he's not conspiring to propose to me. I don't want to faint again.* She smiled. *I crack myself up sometimes.*

As they ate breakfast, they made small talk. Jenny was a little curious about where they would be going, but she decided to just go with the flow. That was one thing she'd always had a problem with—she didn't like surprises. She trusted Argus, though, and knew he wouldn't do anything to make her uncomfortable.

They took their time eating and enjoying each other's company, but around nine-thirty Argus said they had to go. Jenny went upstairs to get her bag. When she came back downstairs, he was already out on the street hailing a cab. *He must be in a hurry,* she thought. The cab pulled up and he opened the door and they got in.

She couldn't stand the suspense any longer. "I wish you'd tell me where we're going."

He gave her a mysterious smile. "You'll see. I can tell you, though, that this will be a day we'll remember for the rest of our lives."

When Argus told the cab driver to pull up in front of the county courthouse, Jenny's heart sank. *Oh my God, he's not going to propose—he thinks we're going to get married today!* Her face went pale. She anticipated an ugly scene.

Then a new thought just popped into her head. *Wait! What am I worried about? It wouldn't be so bad to marry Argus. Get a hold of yourself, girl. Don't be ridiculous!* As he helped her out of the cab, she told herself to just wait and see what was about to happen. But her apprehension lingered. *What else could we possibly be doing at the courthouse?*

He took her hand and they walked up the steps to the entrance. She swallowed hard as he led her down a long tiled corridor. Nearly everything was made of the finest marble.

They sat on a bench outside the courtrooms. Argus was nervous. He was wringing his hands and then wiping them on his trousers. Jenny was wondering how much longer she'd have to wait to find out what the occasion was when a portly bailiff finally came through a courtroom door and called, "Argus Lippencott!"

Argus jumped up and motioned for Jenny to come with him. Inside the courtroom she saw only a court reporter, a secretary, and a pudgy little elderly man who was sitting in the first row. Argus and Jenny made their way to the front and the bailiff showed them where to sit. Argus looked over and nodded a silent greeting to the old man. *I wonder who that is,* Jenny thought. Her mind was racing, trying to put things into perspective, wondering what was going on.

"All rise, please!" the bailiff shouted. "The Honorable Stony Perkins presiding!"

A huge judge waddled out of his chambers and took his place behind the bench. The bald spot on top of his head shone in the lights of the courtroom. What hair he had was in thin curly locks that fell to his shoulders. She was surprised. She'd never seen a judge with long hair before.

She couldn't see much from where she was seated, but when she heard rustling through the microphone on the bench, she surmised that Judge Perkins was looking at some paperwork. Then he looked up and said, "Okay, folks, this shouldn't take too long. Mr. Trujillo, Mr. Lippencott, please rise and approach the bench."

The old man Argus had nodded to earlier struggled to stand up, then, leaning on his cane, hobbled to the front and looked up at the judge. Argus walked forward and stood beside him.

The judge addressed them. "Now I understand that you two have entered into a contract for the purchase of your store." He looked at the old man. "Is that correct, Mr. Trujillo?"

"Yes, your honor," the old man said.

"Have all the documents been signed and properly witnessed?"

"Yes, your honor. They have."

Again there was a rustling of papers as the bailiff handed a packet of documents from the secretary to the judge. Now the judge put on a pair of eyeglasses before he examined the paperwork. After a few minutes he said, "I see here that everything is in order." He picked up his gavel. "I hereby decree that as of this day, the store has officially changed hands and is now owned by Mr. Lippencott." He gave the gavel a loud bang. "Congratulations, Mr. Lippencott. This hearing is now adjourned."

Mr. Trujillo and Argus turned to one another and shook hands enthusiastically, then Argus lifted the old man off the floor as he hugged him. When he rushed over to hug Jenny, he also lifted her off the floor in his excitement.

"Congratulations, Argus!" *Well,* she thought, *I sure let my imagination run away with me today. That'll learn me.* She had to smile at herself.

The bailiff escorted them out of the courtroom, and once they were in the corridor Argus kissed Jenny and then turned to shake hands with Mr. Trujillo again.

"Jenny," he said, "this is my *former* boss, the *former* owner of Trujillo's Nutrition Supplement and Vitamin Store. Mr. Trujillo, this is Jenny, the love of my life."

Blushing and smiling, she shook the old man's hand.

"I was wondering when I'd have the pleasure of meeting you," Mr. Trujillo said. "The kid talks about you all the time." He turned to Argus. "Well, kid, you did it. The store is yours now. I want to thank you for all your years of hard work and dedication." He looked at Jenny again. "He's kept my store running like a well-oiled machine for the last seven years."

Argus shook his hand again. "Thanks so much for all you taught me about the business. And for giving me this opportunity."

"Well, Gus, I can't think of anyone who deserves it more than you." The old man turned to Jenny once more. "Take care of him," he said, winking at her. "You've got a real keeper there. He's a sweet kid. You might be able to find a heartier man, but never one as genuinely nice as him." He turned and started to walk down the long corridor, leaning on his cane. "You two stay out of trouble now," he called over his shoulder.

"Thank you, Mr. Trujillo," Jenny called after him. "I'll take good care of him."

Argus turned to Jenny and hugged her again. "I've been waiting for this day, it seems like forever."

"You've been working there for seven years?"

"Actually, more than ten years. When I was in high school I so desperately wanted to bulk up that I went in there just to talk to someone. Then when I saw the help-wanted sign I figured what better way to learn about all those nutritional supplements than to work there. Mr. Trujillo seemed to like me, so I started working there part-time. When I got out of high school I started working full-time. I started helping with the ordering and keeping the books. Over the years Mr. Trujillo started relying on me more and more, and eventually he made me the manager, then a partner. And now he's sold me his remaining share of the business. He and his wife want to travel now that he's retired. My store is *very* successful. I like the sound of that—*my store.*"

Jenny thought a minute. "Can I ask why you still live at the boarding house?"

"I started rooming there when I got out of high school. I was working long hours and just needed a place to sleep. Dotty and I and all the boarders became such good friends, it just got more comfortable for me stay. I'm sure you can imagine why."

"Of course. Don't think I haven't thought about staying there myself." She paused. "Okay, now for the next awkward question."

"Fire away, milady."

"If this is such an important day in your life, why didn't you invite your parents?"

It was his turn to pause before he replied. "Well, as you will see tonight, my mother is a little overzealous when it comes to my accomplishments." He smiled. "My mother would have shown up at the courthouse with balloons and made a fool of herself. I just didn't want anything to mess up one of the most important moments of my life. That's also why I didn't invite her to Dotty's the night I asked you to go out with me. I didn't want her to mess that up, either." They started to walk out of the building.

Jenny just smiled. "I understand. I think it's sad, but I understand."

"Just wait until tonight," he told her. "You won't be sad anymore, and I have every intention of telling them at dinner."

"I take it we're having dinner with your parents tonight?"

He laughed. "Did I fail to mention that? Oh, by the way, Jenny, the dinner with my parents is tonight."

"Thanks for letting me know ahead of time." She laughed. "So you had asking me out all planned ahead of time, did you?"

"Yes I did. Then when I heard you pleading with God for me to be all right, I thought, 'this girl just might like me.' So I had to put my plan into action before you changed your mind. And according to my plan, you would find me irresistible," he said with a fake cynical laugh.

"I guess it worked—here I am," she replied.

There was a black limousine waiting out in front of the courthouse. As soon as he saw it, Argus walked over and crouched down to look in the dark windows, as if trying to see who was inside. Jenny felt a little uneasy as the driver got out and quickly came around to Argus. When the driver stopped and opened the door, Argus motioned for Jenny to get in. She was so surprised she started laughing. Waiting in the back seat were a chilled bottle of champagne wrapped in a towel, and two glasses. As the driver pulled away from the curb Argus uncorked the bottle and poured Jenny, and then himself, a glass. They toasted to his success with his store, then to their future together.

Jenny laughed, thinking about how silly her thoughts had been when she first saw the courthouse compared to what really happened. When Argus looked at her she merely shook her head, not wanting to tell him what she'd been thinking. When she blushed, he frowned.

"Well, I might as well tell you," she finally said. "I had no idea what to think when we pulled up in front of the courthouse. People in my world get married at the courthouse all the time. I've never heard of a business changing hands through a court hearing."

"So you thought—" he burst out laughing. "You thought I had it all planned out and that I was going to try to pressure you to—" He was laughing so hard he couldn't speak. "Oh, Jenny, that's the funniest thing I've ever heard."

She looked embarrassed. "Well, I thought it was funny, but not *that* funny."

He continued to howl with laughter, looking at her and shaking his head and laughing some more. Every time he did this Jenny stared straight ahead, which made him laugh even harder. "Oh," he finally said, "wait until Jimmy gets a load of this. Is he going to have fun teasing you."

"Don't you dare tell him." She didn't even want to think about the teasing he would put her through.

"No," said Argus, still laughing. "The rule says that if you didn't want Jimmy to know, you would have said, 'Promise you won't tell Jimmy.' And then you would have told me. But you didn't say anything of the sort, so this is fair game."

"Rule? What rule?"

"The rule of 'all's fair in love and war'—that rule."

"Well," she finally consented, "I guess I deserve a good ribbing from Jimmy." She picked up the bottle of champagne and poured herself another glass. It was going to be a long day, especially once Jimmy got wind of her blunder. And then—dinner with Argus's parents. She really had a lot to look forward to. She had to admit, though, that she was having a good time so far on vacation in Fatropolis.

Jenny and Argus rode around the city for awhile, enjoying the luxury and comfort of the limousine. Jenny had never ridden in one and was thrilled at having people stare as if expecting to see a movie star. She never got tired of looking at Fatropolis, seeing all the fat people going about their business and living their lives. When she finally said she had a hankering for pizza, Argus had the driver take them to Papa Panson's Pizza Parlor.

They asked their waitress if Jimmy was available. After a few minutes Jimmy came over to their table and greeted them. He looked handsome in his chef hat. He was wearing a shiny nametag that identified him as head chef. "How's it going, you two?" he asked.

"We're fine," Argus told him. "And we have news."

"Let me guess. You're engaged."

"No." Trying to hold back a grin, Argus looked at Jenny. "Is it okay if I tell him?"

Jenny rolled her eyes. "I guess."

"Tell me what? Tell me what?"

"Wait until you hear, Brickman." Argus told Jimmy about the hearing to obtain the store and the erroneous thoughts that Jenny had had when she first saw the courthouse. The two men laughed and laughed.

"Oh, Jenny, you'll *never* live this one down," Jimmy said, wiping his eyes and starting to laugh all over again.

Jenny yawned. "Bring it on, Butter Brickle. I'm sure I can get some embarrassing stories about you out of Trixie." She turned and looked at Argus. "And you forget, my sweet, that I'm meeting your mother tonight. I'm sure she'll be more than glad to share some juicy, embarrassing tidbits about your childhood. So you two go right ahead and laugh at my expense."

Jimmy's expression changed as he tried really hard to look serious. "That sounds like a threat to me."

"Yeah," said Argus. "Maybe we should quit while we're ahead."

After asking Jimmy what pizza he recommended, they placed their order and enjoyed their lunch. Jimmy left them alone while they ate, but came back later to talk some more. Jenny still enjoyed joking with Jimmy, and especially enjoyed seeing Argus and Jimmy's friendship budding. It made Jenny feel good to know that she and Argus already had another couple they could do things with.

Argus signaled for the check, but it never came. Finally, the waitress came over. "It's been taken care of," she said. They got up to leave and thanked Jimmy for their lunch.

As they were getting back into the limousine, Argus said, "Jenny, is there any place else you'd like to go before I release the limo driver?"

"Well, I did spend a lot of money last night," she replied. "Do you know where I could get some of my money from back home exchanged?"

He took her hand in his. "You don't need to worry about that," he said. "I can handle anything you'd want to buy."

"I don't feel comfortable with you paying for things I want to buy for myself."

He considered this, then consented. "I'll take you to the currency exchange, but we have to go by the bakery first."

"Why would we have to go by the bakery?"

"I like to take the old man a gift when I go see him," was all he said. They crossed the city, and finally the limo pulled up in front of the bakery. Argus hopped out. "I'll be right back." Within a few minutes he came back to the car carrying a huge box of doughnuts. He showed Jenny the contents. "He loves the jelly filled ones."

Jenny couldn't imagine why they needed jelly doughnuts to exchange money, but this was not the first, and probably not the last, strange thing she would see in Fatropolis.

Riding downtown, they crossed through a commercial district and into Chinatown, with its little shops, boutiques, bookstores, and eateries. Argus told the driver where to stop, and they got out. Then he told the driver he'd be expecting the bill and handed him a wad of money. Looking pleased with his tip, the driver drove off.

It was late in the afternoon now. The setting sun and the neon lights lit the street with many colors. They walked for a while and then entered a little Chinese restaurant. The food smelled good, and Jenny saw plenty of fat folks sitting at tables and eating, some with chopsticks, some with standard flatware. One chubby patron stopped eating when he caught sight of Jenny and smiled at her. She was becoming accustomed to the extra attention men gave her here in Fatropolis.

The girl working behind the counter was wearing thick dark makeup, had tattoos down both arms, and was pierced in several places on her face and ears. *Man, I'd hate to tangle with her,* Jenny thought.

They stood in line. When they got up to the counter Argus said, "We'll have the New York Special."

Jenny looked at Argus. "But we just ate not two hours ago. I'm not hungry."

"Just wait," he whispered.

The girl glanced down at the box Argus was carrying, grabbed a stationary microphone, and spoke into it. "Two for the New York Special!" She then looked at Argus again. "Someone will be with you right away."

Argus and Jenny stepped aside and walked to the back of the restaurant, where an old Asian man came out of a door. "New York Special?" he asked. As they followed him into another room, the door closed behind them. The old man went over to a jade statue and twisted its head. A wall opened, revealing a second room that was opulently decorated and featured an old-fashioned cashier's cage against the far wall.

A fat customer who was trading his money at the cashier's cage seemed to be less than happy with the transaction. Judging by his accent, he was obviously from Jenny's New York. "You t'ink I was born yestaday? *T'irty percent? T'irty percent?* You t'ink I'm gonna pay t'irty percent for your money?"

The huge, rough looking man standing beside the cashier's cage was obviously the body guard. He took the New Yorker by his collar as the old, fat man in the cashier's cage said, "The more you make problem for me, the more money you pay me. You pay thirty percent and you go now, or you go with no money to Fatropolis and you figure out how to get along in the city with no money. You decide now. We have customer waiting." He looked at the bodyguard impatiently. "Give him a chance to change his mind, Phillip."

The bodyguard released his grip. The customer looked nervously around the room. "Awright," he said after giving the matter some thought, "go ahead and make the damn exchange." After the money had changed hands he grabbed up his stack of money, stuffed it into his wallet and stormed out.

"Argus!" the cashier said. "You look heartier since the last time I saw you."

"Thank you, Mr. Chiang. I think I may have gained a few." Argus walked up to the cage, motioning for Jenny to come along.

"Argus, you have something in that box for me?" Mr. Chiang licked his lips.

Argus held the box up as if it were filled with the finest jewels, and propped the lid open. "Mr. Chiang, only the finest jelly doughnuts money can buy."

Mr. Chiang eyed Argus suspiciously. "I'm afraid to ask what you want in return."

Argus waved Jenny in closer. "This is my girlfriend, Jenny. Jenny, this is Mr. Chiang. Jenny would like to make an exchange."

Jenny swallowed hard, but quickly produced the money she wanted to change.

"You give me doughnuts and I exchange for you for twenty-five percent."

Argus cleared his throat. "Now, Mr. Chiang, you know how far it is to Dotty's from here? Of course you do. I wouldn't want to have to take these doughnuts back with me. You know I'm a business man. We both know that twenty-five percent isn't a very good deal."

The old man chortled eerily and gave Argus and Jenny a piercing glare. "You drive a hard bargain, Mr. Lippencott. Suppose I have Phillip just take the doughnuts from you?"

Jenny acted as if she wanted to bolt from the room. Argus grabbed her gently but firmly by the arm. He looked the bodyguard up and down. Argus got a smug look on his face and said, "Well, sure. If you never want to see another doughnut from Dotty's again. Everyone knows the people you send to the bakery to buy doughnuts. We could easily *cut off your supply.*"

The old man didn't seem to like the sound of that. "Fifteen percent," he said after a long pause.

"Let's go, Jenny." Argus turned, and they started to walk out.

They had only taken a few steps when they heard the bodyguard protesting loudly to the old man. Then the two men started shouting back and forth in Mandarin.

"Stop right there, Mr. Lippencott!" Mr. Chiang shouted.

Argus and Jenny froze. Jenny could feel her knees trembling, and looked at Argus out of the corner of her eye. He was smiling.

"How much money does the girl want to change?"

"Three hundred," Argus said, not even turning around.

"Okay, you win. Argus, you hand over the box to Phillip, and I will change the money for her."

Keeping a straight face, Argus turned slowly around and relinquished the box of jelly doughnuts to the bodyguard, who growled as he took it. Jenny handed her money to the old man in the cage. It was then that Argus, the old man, and the body guard all started to laugh.

"That was good, Argus," Mr. Chiang said as he counted out Jenny's money. "I really believed you would take the doughnuts back."

Jenny looked at Argus. "That was all just an act?" she asked seriously, swatting Argus on the arm.

He laughed. "Yeah. It's a little game we play every time I come in here."

The old man handed her the Fatropolitan money. He hadn't charged her a cent for the exchange. "Looks like you got a feisty one there."

Argus nodded and grinned again. "It was nice to see you, Mr. Chiang." He turned to Phillip. "That was really believable, man. That whole growling thing, that was great."

"Thanks," Phillip said around a mouthful of doughnut. He licked his fingers and wiped a smear of jelly off the corner of his mouth.

"Give my regards to my nephew," Mr. Chiang said, "and tell Dotty I miss her. I haven't seen her in years. Leland came in the other day. He doesn't look so good—too thin. He didn't bring me any doughnuts, either. The cheapskate." He leaned forward and whispered, "So I charged him three percent."

They all shared a good laugh, then Argus and Jenny made their way to the exit. Out on the street, Jenny turned to him. "I was really scared in there," she said. "I can't believe you all were putting on."

Argus turned to her. "Don't think Mr. Chiang is a pushover," he said in a serious voice. "If he doesn't like you, he charges you plenty. And if he *really* doesn't like you, he won't even do business with you. I've heard he won't hesitate to have Phillip pummel people to within an inch of their life." He paused for a bit, then added, "And I'm just guessing, but I wouldn't be surprised if Mr. Chiang is mixed up in a bunch of stuff that you and I wouldn't want to know about."

"Wow," she said. "Then I guess it's good to have him as a friend." She thought for a moment, then asked, "What did he mean, he hasn't seen Dotty for years? Has it been a long time since he came to the bakery?"

"No. Mr. Chiang never goes out on mundane errands like that. He's a very influential man. He has staff to run his errands."

"Then why does he work in the cashier cage?"

"Rumor has it he doesn't trust anyone to handle his money." Argus thought for a moment, then added, "Maybe Dotty is, or has been, a customer of his."

"I thought she said she'd never been through the portals before," Jenny said. "So why would she need to exchange money?"

"Good question." They walked for a while, and then Argus saw something. "Hey, let's go into that Q cube store."

"Q cube store?" Jenny asked.

"You know. Quantum cube?"

"No. But okay, let's go in."

Inside the store there were posters of fat rock stars on every wall and loud music was playing. Fat teenagers were riffling through bins of quantum cubes. Jenny was once more amazed at this difference between the culture here in Fatropolis and what she was familiar with back home. The delivery system for music here seemed to be much more advanced. Just then a song by the Police started playing throughout the store. As she was listening to this familiar song, "De Do Do Do, De Da Da Da," Jenny continued to examine the posters. She finally spotted one of The Police, but every member of the band was fat. Jenny wondered if it could possibly be that there was actually a band in this world called The Police that played the same music as The Police back home, but were fat. She was confused.

"Argus," she tapped him on the shoulder. "We need to talk."

"Yeah?" he said absently as he looked through the cubes.

She pulled at his shirt and led him to the front of the store where no one could overhear them. "Okay," she said. "The Police are from my world, and they're not fat. What's with that?" She pointed at the poster.

"What do you think kids in high school do when they go over to your world?" Argus replied.

"What? I don't know. I don't understand."

"Well, what the kids have done over the decades is go to your music stores and buy your records and Compact Discs. They bring them back here and sell them to the people who have the technology to change them into quantum cubes and mass produce them. And now it's even easier, now that your music is going digital. The producers have to make the band look more palatable to the public here, so they *enhance* their photos. Only the kids who are lucky enough to go to a concert in your world ever really know if the bands are hearty or not." He cleared his throat and gave her a sad look. "And it's really disappointing to find out that someone you idolized is not the hefty heartthrob you thought she was," he said with a far off look in his eyes.

"Oh, my God, that is *so illegal,*" she said. "That violates every copyright law on the books."

"Do you think your copyright laws carry over to different worlds?"

"Well, I guess not. So you guys *steal* from our culture?"

"Just the stuff we want. Like your bulletproof glass, advancements in automobiles, little stuff like that," he said with a smile, but he could see she was upset, so he explained further. "You know what, Jenny? There's really no reason to get upset—you have a lot of things in your world that started here. Like the microwave oven, the food processor, instant pudding, stretch denim—*all* ideas that originated here. There are certain things we've absolutely mastered—food and comfortable clothing are just two of them. So it's been give and take between our worlds for a long time."

Jenny's mind was reeling. She was learning something new every day about Fatropolis.

They went back to looking through the music cubes, so she decided to see what other artists' music from her world was popular here. When she saw a music cube with a picture of a fat Madonna on it, she laughed out loud. Then she thought of something. "So you said kids have been going from here to my world since the fifties?"

"People from here have been into your music for decades. I even know several hearty people who attended Woodstock in 1969. We have some of our own music, but nothing like the richness of your culture. Because of the influence of your world's music, some of our artists have even crossed over to become popular in your world—"

"Like Flint Mackelroy?" Jenny interrupted.

"Exactly. See, baby? You're getting it." He hugged and kissed her.

"Who else started out here?"

"Let's see—The Mamas and the Papas started out here." He thought some more, "Mac Davis, Roy Clark—and Kenny Rogers, but if you ask me, all that facial hair was just an attempt on his part to look more hearty. And—Meatloaf."

"There's one thing I don't understand, though. When I saw Flint at the Festival, he was playing the banjo. His music doesn't have a banjo in it in my world. I thought that was odd."

"Most of the music in our culture was born out of farming and ranching, which permeated everything, so most of it has a country flavor. We had to come to your world to get any gutsy rock and roll."

She kept looking through the cubes and saw one of the Captain and Tennille, who were positively rotund. She put that one back and took another. Next was the Oak Ridge Boys. Seeing how fat they were, she automatically thought, *They look more like the Pork Ridge Boys.* Then the kinder side of her said, *You've got to stop bashing fat people. They look just like you.* In that moment Jenny realized how quick she always was to judge people based on their size, and that judgment was never more scathing than with herself. *That's why Dotty calls it brainwashing—it affects the very way a person thinks.*

She silently vowed to correct her judgmental thinking as it arose. She gazed at the enhanced photo of the band on the package. *I guess there's a kind of robust charm about them.* She shrugged and put it back in the bin.

Argus had found the cubes he wanted and checked out. He put the bag in his pocket as they left the store.

"What time do we have to be at your parents' house?" Jenny asked.

"Seven." He looked at his watch. We only have about an hour. I guess we'll just go from here?"

They caught a cab. As they started out to Argus's parents' house, Jenny laughed to herself.

"What's so funny, little lady?" he asked.

"Seeing all those fat rock stars reminded me of Elvis," she said.

"Well, I just wish he would've come out with some new music for his concerts before he died. I think people were getting tired of hearing him sing all his old stuff."

Jenny didn't quite understand his comment, "Well, I don't know much about that. I wasn't even born yet when he died."

"What do you mean?"

"My mom just about died herself when he died—" she said.

Argus had a serious look on his face.

"—back in 1977."

"Oh, that. Well, I have news for you. He's been alive and well here in Fatropolis. Well—at least until a couple of years ago. He passed away peacefully at Graceland. He was in his seventies."

Jenny just stared at him. "That's real funny, Argus. Okay, let's just stop with the serious face." She started giggling.

"I'm not joking. He faked his death in your world because by the early 70s his hearty genes started kicking in and the media over there was having a field day making fun of him. So he just came back home."

"You mean Elvis was from here, too?"

"He sure was. He wasn't very popular to start here, being so thin, and the fact that folks here weren't open to anything new. So his family moved him over there, where he made a much bigger splash. Then our teenagers got ahold of his rock 'n' roll records and brought them over here—after that he became very popular here. He used to come and do concerts. There's a Graceland here too, by the way."

"Oh, my God. I did a paper on Elvis in high school. No wonder his death was surrounded by so much controversy. Some people believed his coffin had a wax figure in it instead of his body—and then all the sightings." Jenny smiled, shaking her head.

"He must have gone back to your world even after he faked his death," Argus concluded.

"Oh, my God, I wish I could tell my mom. She would have a fit."

"You know John Candy was from here, too. A lot of people think his heart attack was brought on by criss-crossing too much."

"What about John Belushi and Chris Farley? Were they from here, too?"

Argus looked sad. "Yeah. They just couldn't take the pressure of living in your world."

Jenny was astounded.

It took a long time to get all the way to Argus's parents' neighborhood. They lived in an older home in a neighborhood that Jenny thought might be the Park Slope area in her world. Their two-story home was made of brick and had a roomy front porch that looked so inviting. Lace curtains hung in the windows, soft light shining through them.

As they approached the house, Jenny suddenly got the strong feeling that Argus was dreading the evening.

"Just try to keep an open mind," he muttered.

"I'm sure it won't be as bad as you're thinking," she said optimistically.

They slowly walked up the brick steps and stopped in front of the huge wooden door. Argus rang the doorbell and took a deep breath, but before the door opened they could hear a high-pitched squeal inside the house. The squeal got louder and louder and finally arrived at the door. Argus's mother, who was very fat, stylishly dressed, and had big hair, threw open the door and grabbed her son in an embrace. "Pumpkin! How are you?"

"Fine, Mother," he said, rolling his eyes.

Jenny smiled at him, trying not to laugh.

"Mom, this is Jenny."

Mrs. Lippencott looked at Jenny, opened her mouth, and squealed out a greeting that was almost deafening, "Oooooh, my gosh, look at you, you are so round and so beautiful!" She hugged Jenny and then grabbed her by the shoulders and held her at arms' length, looking up and down at every inch of her.

Unable to move, Jenny just stood there quietly letting her take it all in. When she glanced at Argus she saw the horrified look on his face. When Mrs. Lippencott finally let go, Jenny stuck out one hand to shake hands with the woman who might someday be her mother-in-law. "Nice to meet you."

Mrs. Lippencott shook her hand enthusiastically. "Come in, come in, you two," she said. They turned right at the foot of the oak staircase and went into the living room. Jenny positively startled as Mrs. Lippencott shouted at the top of her lungs, in a coarse voice, "Harold! They're here! Come and say hello!"

Munching on a stick of celery with some sort of cream cheese on it, Mr. Lippencott came sauntering out of the kitchen. He wiped his hands on his apron and shook hands with Argus. "Nice to see you, son," he said, then he looked at Jenny. "Now who might this be? Let's have a look at you." He reached out his hand and shook Jenny's, introduced himself, and then gave her a thorough once-over above his spectacles.

Jenny was surprised that both of Argus's parents were hearty. Argus was about the same height as his father, but much thinner. Mr. Lippencott was bald on top and had lighter hair and eyes. Mrs. Lippencott was about a head shorter than the two men.

Leaving Argus and Jenny in the living room, Mrs. Lippencott practically ran into the kitchen for the appetizers. She returned with a huge tray of vegetables for dipping, chips, mini-quiches, and something that was rolled tightly and sprinkled with cheese. "Dig in, you two," she ordered. "Argus, you don't look like you've been eating at all."

"Mother, please don't start. Let's just have a pleasant evening."

Mr. Lippencott turned to his son. "*Hey,* you know your mother means well."

"Dad, I eat plenty," Argus said. He turned to Jenny. "Don't I eat plenty?"

"He eats *a lot,*" she testified.

His mother disappeared again, and soon they heard noises coming from the kitchen. Then she called from the dining room, "Dinner will be on the table shortly. I hope you brought your appetites! Jenny, I sure hope you're a good eater. You all just get started on that tray now!"

"Oh, my God," Argus said under his breath. He picked up a little quiche and shoved it in his mouth.

Jenny also picked up an appetizer.

"So what do you do, Jenny?" Mr. Lippencott asked through his crunching.

Jenny chewed faster and then swallowed hard. "I'm a records room supervisor for a large financial corporation."

"Oh, really? Which financial corporation?"

"Oh, probably one you've never heard of. Dad, don't pry now," Argus said, apparently not wanting them to know she was not from their world.

Argus's mother shouted again, this time from the kitchen. "Harold, take them into the dining room!"

Argus and Jenny sat down, as did Mr. Lippencott. The table was immaculately set with fine china, matching glasses, and flatware. Mrs. Lippencott now came through the swinging doors, set the first dish on the table, and then swung back into the kitchen. She did this several times. On the third trip, as she was swinging back into the kitchen, she said to Argus, "Can I see you in the kitchen, pumpkin?"

As he stood up Argus leaned down to Jenny and said, "If I'm not back in fifteen minutes, *run.*" He reluctantly went into the kitchen. Shortly after the doors quit swinging, Jenny heard another squeal. She picked up her goblet and began to sip her water. At first she could barely make out what Mrs. Lippencott was saying, but soon she had no trouble hearing "Oh, my gosh, she's got child-bearing hips and everything!"

At this Jenny choked and coughed water on her place setting. She was busy wiping up when she heard Argus's voice. "Mother, don't start with the child-bearing hips thing again. I swear to God, if I go back out there and she's gone, like happened with Leslie, I'm never coming back here again!"

Jenny looked over at Harold, who was looking around the room and absently chewing on another appetizer. He looked over at her and gave her a cordial smile. There were a few more words from the kitchen and then one of the swinging doors swung open. Argus stood there for a moment, a large bottle of wine in one hand and a corkscrew in the other. He took a deep breath to compose himself, and then came in and sat down. His face was red and he looked angry. Within a minute he had the bottle uncorked and was filling a large water goblet with wine, which he gulped down without even taking a breath. Jenny just sat there and watched him.

He looked at her and raised the bottle. "Wine?"

"Just a little, thanks."

He poured her some in the proper glass, then turned the bottle upside down again to refill his goblet.

"Wow," was all she said.

His mother swung through the door again, her hands in oven mitts carrying a large casserole dish. As she stared at her guest she had the biggest smile plastered on her face that Jenny had ever seen.

Jenny looked up from her wine glass almost afraid. Argus rested his head on his hands and sighed, "Dear God, just let us get through this evening."

All the food had been brought to the table now, and Mrs. Lippencott finally sat down. A print of the famous painting of the Last Supper hung on the dining room wall. "I like that picture a lot," Jenny said, as she thought, *I wonder if they're Catholic.* When Argus's mother instructed them to hold hands as she crossed herself and said grace, Jenny nodded to herself. *Yep, they're Catholic.*

At that point they all dug into the food, which smelled delicious. There was a large chicken noodle casserole with broccoli and cheese, a three-pound meatloaf, fruit salad, green salad, steamed cauliflower, and rolls with butter.

Harold picked up the bowl of fruit salad and said, "Barbara, Jenny here was telling me that she's a supervisor at a big financial corporation uptown."

Barbara's eyes got big. "Oh, a supervisor."

"Only of the records department," Jenny corrected.

"Still—*a supervisor,*" Mrs. Lippencott repeated.

Jenny had taken a little of everything, and now she was getting the distinct impression that Barbara was watching every bite she took. All three

Lippencotts were drinking an excessive amount of wine, though it didn't seem to affect them. When Argus finished his second plate, his mother said, "Take a little more casserole, sweetie."

"Mom, I'm sorry, but I'm full," he told her. "Everything was delicious, but I'm *full.*"

"So, Jenny," she said, "what do you think of our little boy here?"

Argus sighed. "Mother, I'm twenty-eight years old."

"You'll *always* be my little boy," she said sweetly.

"Argus," Jenny said under her breath, "you shouldn't be so hard on her." She nudged him, and then turned to his mother. "I think he's wonderful, Mrs. Lippencott." She patted Argus on the leg.

"Just call me Barbara," the older woman said with a giggle. "Mrs. Lippencott is my mother-in-law."

Jenny nudged Argus again. He gave her a puzzled look. "Store," she whispered.

"Oh, yes." He raised his voice. "Mom, Dad, I have some news."

Just then Barbara gasped loudly and started to squeal again. "Harold, they're getting married! I knew it! Oh, my gosh, this is the day I've been waiting for forever. My little boy! Getting married!"

"No, Mom, wait!" Argus began waving his hands in the air as she continued raving. "No, Mom, wait! *MOM!*"

By this time his mother was crying for joy, her imagination obviously filled with the splendors of a glorious wedding. Harold just sat there calmly chewing, not saying a word, as his wife carried on.

Argus finally got her attention. "Mom, Jenny and I are not engaged." He stopped. "Well—not yet, anyway."

Mrs. Lippencott finally returned to her senses. She took a few deep breaths. "What?"

"If you would just listen to me for a second." Argus was obviously trying to control his frustration.

"Okay, pumpkin, what is it?"

"I took ownership of the store today. It's mine. I own it now."

Argus's parents looked at each other in silence for a moment, then his father stood up. Argus stood up as well and they shook hands. "Congratulations, son!" Harold said, and then he pulled his son in for a hug.

Barbara started squealing again. She jumped up, ran around the table, and hugged them both. "We have to celebrate!" She swung back into the kitchen for dessert. Moments later she burst through the doors again with a huge chocolate cake, a carton of ice cream and four large bowls, with a can of whipped cream tucked under her arm.

Argus and his parents finally sat back down at their places, and his mother started to cut the cake, scoop the ice cream, spray the whipped cream, and pass the bowls around.

When Barbara asked Jenny to tell them about herself, she explained that she had grown up in a small town and was one of three children. She talked about her parents and her siblings and her nieces and nephews. She shared quite a bit about herself.

As she talked, Argus just looked at her with a silly grin on his face. His mother seemed pleased by their adoration of each other, and asked Jenny questions about her job and her hobbies. They were deep in conversation when Argus excused himself to use the bathroom. The minute he was out of the room Barbara leaned forward and asked Jenny how she felt about having children. Jenny told her honestly that she would love to have children, but she wanted to settle down in marriage for a few years before starting a family. When Argus came back and heard the tail end of this conversation he gave his mother an angry look, but Jenny refused to get ruffled. She felt his mother had a right to know these things about her son's girlfriend. Barbara seemed completely taken with Jenny. Like her son, she looked at Jenny with adoring eyes.

Dinner was over, and most of the food had been eaten. As they adjourned to the living room the two women sat together and began talking about church while Argus and his dad talked about local politics. Finally Argus yawned and looked at his watch. "Gosh," he said, "it's almost ten already. We better be heading back."

"Aww, *shucks!*" Barbara said, her eyes watering. "Do you have to go so soon? Jenny and I were just going to sit down with the photo albums."

"Mom, do you have to drag those darned things out?"

Jenny gave him a stern look. She did not approve of his tone with his mother.

Shrugging his shoulders, he walked into the kitchen to phone for a cab. When he came back, he added, "You two will have plenty of other occasions to look at my baby pictures."

Barbara started bawling. "I've missed you so much. Why don't you ever come to visit anymore?"

When Jenny patted her on the back consolingly (and gave Argus a pitiful look), Barbara leaned in and started sobbing into Jenny's shoulder. At that Jenny also started to cry. They stood there together, crying, embracing one another, each patting the other's back.

Argus looked at his dad, who just shrugged. "Get used to it, son. Welcome to my hell," he said with a smirk on his face.

Argus threw up his hands. "I give up!" He went over and hugged his mother, and she started sobbing into his chest. He took her by the shoulders. "Stop crying, Mom. I promise we'll come back soon." He kissed her on the cheek. She straightened up and wiped her eyes.

Jenny was wiping her eyes, too, when a car honked in front of the house.

"Come on, Jenny. That's our cab. Let's get going." Argus grabbed Jenny's hand and led her out the door.

Barbara and Harold followed them all the way out to the sidewalk. Argus and Jenny got into the back of the cab in the seats facing each other. Jenny still looked sad. When they were finally out of sight of his parents' house, he snapped his fingers loudly in her face. "Snap out of it!"

She jumped. "What?"

"I can't believe she sucked you in like that."

"Sucked me in? Your mother is a sweet lady."

"She's a barracuda in polyester pants!" he nearly shouted. "Didn't our little visit give you a glimpse of what it was like to grow up with her? It's a wonder I'm sane."

"Well, she may have been a little overbearing, but—"

"A *little? A little overbearing?* That's like saying a werewolf is a little moody."

"Well, maybe if you visited her more often, maybe then she wouldn't be so needy when you finally do show up."

"Seeing her more often only makes it worse. Then she starts criticizing everything she hears. She thinks I actually want her advice about stuff. You watch. The next time we visit it will be, 'So you two aren't engaged yet? You know I'm not getting any younger, and I'd sure like to have some grandkids before I die.' If she visits the store, she asks why I don't have this product or that product. It's never, 'Oh, this is nice.' She only sees how she thinks things could be improved. Like tonight. Was it 'Thanks for coming to dinner and bringing your girlfriend, son'? No! It was, 'Why don't you visit more often?' Jenny, please don't let her suck you in."

Jenny wasn't sure what to say to all that. "I would think you'd be glad I could get along with your family," she finally replied.

"Well, I *am* glad you can get along with them, but I don't want you taking their side against me."

"You really think your mom is against you?"

He took a deep breath. "Well, that's what it seems like sometimes. Especially while I was growing up. She couldn't have any more children after me, and she wanted a hearty kid so bad that she was *constantly* after me about my size. She couldn't just love me for me." He paused. "I'm actually scared to give her a grandkid. I'm scared she'll put the poor kid through the same stuff she put me through. I swear, Jenny. I know it's too soon to talk about this, but if we ever have children, I don't want them ever pressured to eat. Or not eat. *Not ever.* I just want to let them be who they are."

Jenny thought about this for a moment. "I want that, too," she said in a quiet voice. "Argus, when and if that time comes, we can make sure we set rules for your mom." She touched his cheek. "I'm sorry this upsets you so much."

"I'm sorry, too. I didn't mean to get so irate. She just presses all my buttons."

She gave him a gentle smile. "I understand. My parents do the same thing to me."

He took her hand and held it against his cheek. "I was afraid that after you met my folks you wouldn't want to be with me anymore."

Now Jenny had to laugh. "It would take a lot more than a barracuda in polyester pants to turn me against you." They both started to laugh. "I have to say, though, I think it's pretty funny the way your mom squeals when she gets excited."

The cab ride home was relaxing but long, and by now Jenny was looking forward to a good soak in her wonderful tub. She also wanted to read further in Driscol's journal and see if there was any evidence that Dotty might have gone through the portals at some point.

When they finally arrived at the boarding house, Argus walked her to her room and kissed her goodnight, and then Jenny commenced with her usual routine. While soaking in the tub she thought about Argus's mother and giggled as she saw her holding the casserole with her oven mitts and her big smile. Mrs. Lippencott had obviously wanted very badly to impress Jenny.

After her bath Jenny settled into bed and picked up the journal. She skimmed through it again, looking specifically for the years when Dotty was a teenager.

December 12, 1957. Nevan came calling on Dotty again last night. The boy seems quite taken with her. Tressa is concerned that their romance is progressing too fast, as the girl is not quite sixteen. I refuse to get involved, as I don't want anything to happen to Dotty like it did to Tressa. The boy seems quite upstanding and comes from a good family. Mr. O'Flannigan approves of their union and is quite pleasant to me and Tressa when we see him and the missus at church.

December 25th, 1957. We had a nice Christmas. I bought Tressa a new television with higher resolutions. It's nice to have such a big screen, too. The colors look so good, it's like we are there. I can't wait to see the Rose Parade on the new set this year. Tressa bought me a microwave oven and a vegetable chopper. We gave Dotty a portable optical chip player. She was thrilled. The other day I saw some strange little black platters in her room. They had big holes in the middle. One of them had a label that said Fats Domino "Blueberry Hill" on it. I asked her what they were—she said it was music. I have never seen the likes of these black platters before, except for my father's Victrola. I wonder where she got them.

Jenny thumbed forward in the journal. She soon found what she was looking for.

May 2nd, 1960. The boy has asked for Dotty's hand. She should be happy with him. She's going to graduate from high school very soon. They will marry in the fall. Her mother and I will be glad when she marries. She's been up to some questionable activities. Her and Nevan go places together and are gone for whole days. I hope she doesn't turn out to be with child before they marry. I will be so relieved once she's married. Her mother showed me more of those black platters from her room. Then I saw my metal box had been tampered with. I opened it. The little ladies were gone. I called the girl on the carpet about it and she said she just wanted to see them. She gave them back to me, though I have no way of knowing how long she had them, I hope she was not up to no good with them.

That was all Jenny needed to see. She knew Dotty had been going through the portal, probably for years, and buying records. *That little dickens.* Jenny turned off the light and snuggled down under the covers.

CHAPTER 20
JENNY LEARNS
THE BEST OF THE REST

BECAUSE IT HAD BEEN SUCH A BUSY WEEK, JENNY and Argus rested most of the day after their dinner with his parents. It was Thursday by now, and Jenny just wanted to hang out around the boarding house. They were looking forward to their night out with Jimmy and Trixie tomorrow.

Emmett seemed to be on his way to a complete recovery from his painful reaction to the other world, but he didn't seem to want to leave the boarding house. Jimmy had decided to let him stay until Dotty returned. She could decide what to do with him. Hank and Charlie were still keeping the bakery running and seemed to enjoy being in charge. All the boarders were cooperating nicely with schedules, meal preparations, and cleanup.

As the cleanup crew was clearing away the dinner dishes that night they heard a commotion in the bakery. Dotty, Leland, and Dot had returned. Everyone gathered around them, waiting to hear Dotty's stories.

The old baker was smiling and looked rested. "We had a wonderful time," she said. "We ate out every day and I got to spend more time with my grandbaby. Leland took me to their festival grounds—I mean, Central Park. And we saw a Broadway show. It was wonderful."

As they listened, Argus was standing with his arm around Jenny. When Leland glanced over and saw them, his jaw muscles tightened. But she didn't care how he felt about her relationship with Argus. She was proud to finally be with a man who appreciated her for who she was, not who she could be after a diet and exercise.

After a few minutes Clara walked over to Leland and asked if she could hold Dot. Dot went willingly into her arms. As Clara carried her around, she and the other girls began fussing over the toddler. When Leland began talking with Jimmy, Argus seemed uncomfortable. After all, Jimmy and Leland had a history.

Soon everyone walked through the kitchen and the office and into the parlor, where Dotty plopped down on one of the sofas and heaved a huge sigh.

"Can we get you and Leland anything, Aunt Dotty?" Dixie asked. "We had spaghetti and meatballs. There's a lot left over."

Dotty kicked her shoes off. "We just ate right before we came back, so I'm full, but thanks, dearie."

Clara went over to Leland again and asked, "Would it be okay if Lidia, Delia, and I take Dot out to the courtyard? We'll take good care of her."

He smiled at Clara. "Sure." It was obvious that he was attracted to her.

After the girls took Dot outside, Leland sat down with Jimmy and visited some more. Trixie sat down by Dotty and called Jenny to join them. She brought Argus with her. As they sat down, Jimmy started to tell Leland about their adventure getting Emmett back, and looked over at Argus. "Hey, come on over here, man! What are you doing sitting over there with all the women?"

Even though Leland looked a little uncomfortable, Argus went over and sat down by Jimmy and they all continued talking.

Dotty asked, "So what were ya up to in the city on Monday? We saw ya on the news broadcast." When Trixie looked surprised, Dotty explained. "They got a good shot of Jenny starin' into the camera. Leland and I were watchin' the news. They were reportin' on some sort of commotion downtown. I said, 'Hey, there's Jenny,' and we could hardly believe our eyes."

This was the cue for Jimmy, Argus, and Jenny to launch into the story of their hair-raising adventure and tell how they had risked life and limb to go to New York City and bring Emmett back before it was too late. However, when Jenny recounted how they'd narrowly escaped from the museum security guards and the New York police, Dotty began to look uncomfortable, especially when she mentioned the portal in the museum bathroom.

Jenny particularly enjoyed telling about the old lady in the women's bathroom beating Jimmy with her purse. This part of the story made Dotty and Leland laugh. "Oh, I wish I could've seen that," Dotty chuckled.

Having read Driscol's journal, Jenny understood almost everything now. All she needed to do was confirm a few details and she would know the whole story.

After the storytelling ended, Jenny took it upon herself to announce that

Argus had taken ownership of Trujillo's nutrition supplement and vitamin store. Everyone cheered and congratulated him. Only Leland looked at him—and then back at Jenny—with a sober look on his face.

"Argus, I'm proud of you," Dotty said as she leaned forward and put her shoes back on.

Then Trixie announced her engagement again.

Dotty seemed surprised. "So much has happened," she said as she looked at Leland. "How many days were we gone, son?" Everyone started to laugh. They congratulated the couple and Dotty looked at Trixie's ring and glanced over at Jimmy approvingly. "Now I need to go upstairs and unpack."

Leland also stood up and went across the room to call to the girls and Dot. "I need to take her upstairs," he said. "She's had a long day."

Clara handed the toddler to her father. "She sure is an adorable little girl, Leland," she said. Dot reached out for her father and started to whine.

As Leland and Dotty picked up their bags and went up to their rooms, Trixie and Jimmy went back to their kitchen duties. Argus and Jenny followed to see if they could help. Once all the dishes were in the dishwasher, Jimmy said he needed to go down to the restaurant to check on something and invited Argus to go with him. Trixie and Jenny went back into the parlor to relax and have some girl talk. "So how are you and Argus getting along?" Trixie asked.

"We're doing fine, thank you, but we've sure had a busy week. He took me to his folks' house for dinner last night."

Trixie apparently knew the Lippencotts. She gasped. "And how did that go?"

"Well, his mom is a little—overbearing at times. But she's very sweet. She seems to like me real well."

Trixie wasn't surprised. "Well, you're the heartiest girl he's ever dated. I'm sure she's pleased about that."

"I hope that's not the only reason she likes me."

"No. I'm sure that's not the only reason."

Jenny had a few questions of her own. "So how are you and Jimmy doing with your wedding plans?"

"We've got a little over a month to plan this thing," Trixie said with a smile. "Daddy said he'll pay for everything, so I'd like to have a big wedding. I think there'll be nearly two hundred guests. I finally went down and engaged the services of a wedding planner. I also have to secure a place for us to live and buy some furniture."

"When is the wedding?"

"Mid-November. The invitations are going out as soon as they're printed.

I'm excited, but I'm nervous, too. So many changes all at once." She paused and looked as if she were dreading what she had to say next. "Mack, I have something I wanted to talk to you about."

"Yeah?"

"I'm afraid you might not be too happy about this."

"Oh, for the love of Pete, what now?"

"I'd like you to be my maid of honor," Trixie said.

Jenny smiled and excitedly hugged Trixie. "Why wouldn't I be happy about that? I'm honored! I'm an honored maid of honor." She giggled with delight over her play on words.

"Well—brace yourself, Mack. Here's the part that you might not be too pleased about—guess who Jimmy wants as his best man?" Trixie looked at Jenny and cringed.

"Oh, God, don't tell me—Leland? Come on, Trixie. You can't expect me to walk with him and dance with him—*please*. Jimmy doesn't have any other friends? I'll walk with *anyone* else. *Please.*" Jenny stopped to think for a moment. "Oh, here's an idea. Have Dixie walk with Leland. It's perfect. They're cousins, then later he can sit and dance with Clara—*hey, Clara!* She can be your maid of honor."

"What?" Trixie sounded insulted. "If I'd wanted Dixie or Clara, I would've asked them! I'm sorry for the way things are working out, but you two are just going to have to live with it." She stood up and stormed out of the parlor.

Jenny sat alone, thinking about how awkward the whole thing would be, having to walk down the aisle arm in arm with Leland while Argus stood by— and then she'd have to dance with Leland at the reception. She thought and thought, but there was no way to get out of it without ruining her friendship with Trixie. *Well,* she reasoned with herself, *it'll just be a day in my life, it'll make Trixie happy, and I will live through it.* Having persuaded herself, she went into the kitchen to tell Trixie. She found her talking to Hank, who was kneading a huge mound of dough. "Trixie?"

Trixie turned to look at her, obviously still upset.

"I have a bad feeling about this," Jenny told her, "but I'll do it for you."

Trixie smiled and hugged Jenny.

"Is Argus going to be in the wedding party?" Jenny asked.

"We were thinking about asking him," Trixie said.

"Well," Jenny said slowly, "if you're going to put him in, please don't pair him with Clara. That would just be too weird for him. And everyone. Let him walk with Dixie or someone else."

Trixie nodded. "Okay, we'll do that."

"You promise?"

"Yes, I promise."

Jimmy and Argus had just come in.

"Promise what?" Jimmy asked.

"We'll talk about it later," Trixie told him.

Jenny shook her head. "I think we should talk about it now."

Trixie sighed. "Okay."

"Argus," Jenny began, "Trixie has asked me to be her maid of honor at her wedding."

"That's great!" He smiled and gave her a peck on the cheek. Trixie, Jimmy, and Jenny were all looking at him with serious looks on their faces. At first he looked from one to the other curiously. When the light came on, he turned to Jimmy. "Oh, and Leland will be your best man?"

"Yeah," Jimmy replied. "You know we've been friends forever."

"Well, I don't know what you all are so serious about," Argus said. "It's just a ceremony and a dance. Then I get to have her for the rest of the festivities. Can I at least sit by her at dinner?" he asked with a nervous chuckle. "Well, I guess I'm assuming I'll be invited, too."

Trixie flashed Jenny a triumphant look. "I'm glad you're being so adult about this, but the bridesmaids sit on the bride's side and the groomsmen sit with the groom. You can dance with her, though—I mean after Leland dances with her."

Argus's expression became serious. "But if he says one thing out of the way to her, I'll beat the crap out of him, right there in front of everyone."

Trixie acted flustered and Jimmy got serious, imagining the scene that would cause.

Argus burst out laughing. "Hey, you guys. I'm just kidding. I'll behave myself."

Jimmy sighed with relief. "You had me goin' there, man." He reached out to shake his friend's hand. "Will you walk with us, too?"

"Sure!" Argus said. "I'd be honored to."

Jimmy gave him a man hug. "You'll have to be right next to Leland, you know. Is that cool, man?"

"And he'll be walking with Dixie. Right?" Jenny insisted.

"Well—" Now Jimmy looked uncertain. He glanced at Trixie. "I—I don't know."

"Honey," Trixie said, "that was the thing I promised—that if Argus was in the wedding party, I would have him walk with Dixie instead of Clara."

They hadn't noticed, but now Dixie had walked into the kitchen. "Who am I walking with?" she asked.

Horrified that Dixie had overheard, Trixie just stammered, "Uh, uh, we just—" Then she straightened up as if realizing she didn't need to explain anything and said matter-of-factly, "I've just asked Jenny to be my maid of honor."

Dixie burst into tears. "I can't believe that! After sharing a womb, and our lives and—"

Hank stopped kneading so he could watch the spectacle.

"And," Trixie said in a desperate voice, "I want you to be my second maid."

"Really?" Dixie sniffled again and wiped her eyes.

"Of course!" Trixie said, putting her arm around Dixie. Then, apparently thinking she was consoling her sister, she added, "You'll see when you get married—you won't necessarily want me to be your maid of honor."

Dixie burst out bawling again. "First the baby, now this?"

Unnoticed, Clara had come into the kitchen to investigate the hubbub. "Baby?" she inquired. "What baby? Who's having a baby?"

Trixie's eyelid started to twitch. Everyone was talking over everyone else, and the conversation was getting louder and louder. Clara just looked from one person to the next, pressing for her question to be answered. Argus was teasing Jenny and Dixie was still bawling because her feelings were crushed. Jimmy stood back, flabbergasted at the sudden free-for-all.

"That's it!" Trixie shouted. "I can't take it anymore! Everyone be quiet!"

There was sudden silence in the kitchen.

She glared at them all with tears in her eyes. "Okay, I didn't mean for the end of the world to happen just because I asked Mack to be my maid of honor. I want Dixie to be my second maid. Jimmy is going to ask Leland to be his best man, and Argus is going to walk with Dixie. It's *my* wedding, and that's the way *I want it*. Any questions?"

Looking disgusted, Clara folded her arms across her chest.

At that point Leland walked in. "Did I hear someone mention my name?"

Jimmy laughed. "Come on in, man," he called to Leland above the crowd around him. "Is there anyone else out there in the whole house who wants to join us? We were just having an *intimate conversation* about the wedding and who's going to walk with whom. By the way, Stringbean, would you be my best?"

Everyone, including Hank, stood silently, waiting for Leland's response.

"Why sure, Brickman!" Leland walked over and shook Jimmy's hand.

"There's only one catch to it," Jimmy said quickly. "Jenny is the maid of honor. Hit it, Trixie—" he pointed at her as if turning the program over to his fiancée.

Trixie turned to Leland. "So—you'll be walking with Jenny, Dixie will be walking with Argus, and we haven't gotten any further." Then she turned to

Clara. "And, yes, Clara, we're having a baby. And if you tell anyone I'll never speak to you again."

Clara stormed out in a huff.

"Thank you for that, Dixie," Trixie said, pointing at the door, which had slammed closed behind Clara.

Jimmy seemed pleased. "Well, I'm sure glad we've gotten all that straightened out."

As Dixie grabbed some napkins and wiped her eyes, Jimmy and Trixie walked out of the kitchen. Leland was right behind them, asking about the baby. Hank returned to his kneading, and Jenny and Argus were left to console Dixie.

Jenny didn't know what to say. Once again she felt she'd been put in an awkward position. As she reached out to hug her friend Dixie broke down and started sobbing into her shoulder.

Jenny patted her on the back. "You know, Dixie, this isn't about who's more popular with Trixie. It's about her having her day the way she wants it. Come on, it'll be fun. We get to dress up and dance. As far as I'm concerned, we're *both* the maids of honor. Okay, sweetie?"

Dixie looked up and managed a reluctant smile. As Jenny wiped her face and brushed her hair out of her eyes, Dixie sniffed a few more times. "Okay," she finally said. "I feel better now. That sounds good."

I'm sure glad that's over, Jenny said to herself as Dixie left the kitchen still wiping her eyes. Feeling exhausted, she turned to Argus, who took her into his arms and led her out to the courtyard. Jimmy and Trixie were there, and it looked like Trixie was sulking. Jimmy was sitting next to her, a worried look on his face. Jenny knew it would be better not to disturb them.

It was getting on toward nine o'clock, so Argus walked Jenny to her room. While they were standing in the hall saying their good nights Dotty opened her door and looked out, then closed it again without saying a word.

After Argus walked down the hall to his own room, Jenny went into her room and picked up Driscol's journal. She couldn't wait to talk to Dotty about her visits through the portals. Although she understood that the older folks didn't like talking about the portals, she was wondering why Dotty felt it necessary to lie to her and say she had never been through. Carrying the big book down the hall, she knocked lightly at Dotty's door. Dotty opened it and looked at her.

"Are you up for a gab session about the journal?" Jenny asked.

"Child, I'm a little tired, but I suppose we can chat awhile." She invited Jenny in and turned off her television. They both sat down.

"Well," Jenny began, gesturing at the journal on her lap, "you'll be surprised at some of the things I've read in here."

"Really? Like what?"

"Well—" Jenny was glad to be finally talking with her about it—"it seems your grandfather caught your father climbing down the fire escape from your mother's room and wanted to kill him. Instead, he showed him the portal. Then the next time he caught him, he showed him his pistol and threatened him, just like you told me. So you've read the journal?"

"No. Well, I may have glanced at it a time or two when I was young."

It seemed to Jenny that Dotty was not surprised. Jenny thumbed through the journal. "I'll show you the part that says that." She found the entry and handed the book to Dotty.

The baker read for a few moments, and her chin started to quiver. "Yep," she said, "that old codger was the one responsible for me not havin' a father." Dotty's demeanor seemed to stiffen.

"I'm sorry, Dotty," Jenny said.

Dotty pulled a hanky out of her pocket and wiped her eyes. She sat thinking for a moment. "What else did ya find out?" she asked cautiously.

"Well, Dotty—"

"Come on, girl. Ya know ya can tell me. It's my family."

Jenny wasn't quite sure how to broach the subject. "Well, Argus told me that the kids from this world always go over to my world for the music. And that the tradition started in the fifties."

"Yes, I've heard about that," Dotty said flatly.

"And I read in the journal that Driscol found some black platters in your room. A few times." She paused, trying to gauge Dotty's reaction.

"Black platters? What's that?"

"I assume they were records. Vinyl records from my world. What we call forty-fives. Is that true, Dotty?"

Looking defensive, Dotty stood up, walked across the room, and looked out her window. "No, child. It's not true."

"Are you sure? He mentioned one in particular, Fats Domino's 'Blueberry Hill.'" That was a popular song in the fifties in my world—"

"Why, that old buzzard!" Dotty turned to face Jenny. "I never thought all this would come back to haunt me. Not this many years later. I thought those days were over and done with."

Jenny persisted. "Did you go and buy records in my world?"

Dotty sighed and fiddled with her hanky, then finally nodded her head. "I guess you've got the goods on me," she confessed. Her voice quivered as she continued. "I used to love to sneak into my grandfather's room and rummage through his things while he was at his lodge meetin's. He was so secretive about everythin.' One day I found his journal and started to read it. I knew I shouldn't have, but I couldn't resist. Then I found his metal box with the little goddesses in it. Nevan and I had been dating, and we thought it would be real keen to go through the portal and see what was over there. My grandfather had made a portal in the men's bathroom at Burley's, so I made one in the women's dressin' room. So I could go, too, and no one would see me." She smiled at the memory. "Ya know, I waited for over an hour for that dressin' room to clear out, and then I made the portal, in the fittin' room closest to the drinkin' fountain. The hardest part was findin' the weak place in the veil. The weak spots always seemed to be near water. Then, because the portals only go one way, once I got over there, when I wanted to come back, I had to make another one in the dressin' room over there."

Dotty went over to her closet and dug out an old box with a handle on it. She blew some dust off the box, unlatched it, and took the cover off. It was an old portable phonograph that played forty-five rpm records. After plugging it in she brought another box out of her closet and opened it. It was full of forty-fives, still in their paper sleeves. She looked through them, found the one she wanted, and put it on. As "Blueberry Hill" started to play, the old woman started singing along, tears rolling down her face.

Jenny couldn't stop the tears from streaming down her own face as she watched. Then Dotty walked over and picked up the photograph of her and Nevan on their wedding day and sat back down.

"This was our favorite song," she said. "All us kids thought Fats Domino was just the livin' end. We were all so darn tired of country music. Folk music, too. Once I read my grandfather's journal and found out what he had done to my mother and father, I lost all respect for the old coot. Ya might say I became a little rebellious.

"I'd overheard my grandfather tell my mother that the money is different between the worlds. I had a girlfriend in high school whose father was involved in a lot of *questionable activities,* and she told me about a business man in Chinatown who frequently traveled between the worlds. So, me and Nevan went to Chinatown to see him and get some of yer money before we criss-crossed."

She paused and smiled. "He was one tough customer, and he charged us plenty, too. When we went to yer world for the first time, we were mighty scared, *believe you me.* There weren't hardly any hearty kids there, and the kids in yer world stared at us like maybe we weren't even human."

Having been stared at herself, Jenny could only nod.

"The first thing we did," Dotty continued, "was duck into a soda fountain and get milkshakes. They had a huge beautiful jukebox that was playin,' and that's when we heard this song for the first time. Over the years, that wonderful jukebox was where I got my first earful of Elvis Presley, the Big Bopper, Chubby Checker and all the rest of them. We just fell in love with yer music. Time and time again, we went over and bought records and brought them back. We went to our own music stores and asked them if they could convert the records, but pretty soon they started wonderin' where we had gotten them from. I said they came from another country. After a while Nevan went through and bought me this here phonograph so I could at least play my records at home."

"So you were the first teenager to go through the portal and bring back the music?" Jenny couldn't keep the excitement out of her voice.

Dotty smiled. "I guess that's right," she said. "I certainly didn't mean for it to become a tradition or a rite of passage." She put another record on, this one by Buddy Holly. "I'm glad we have all the good music, though. Well, except for some of the music the kids listen to nowadays. Land sakes, it makes my head hurt."

"So I'm assuming someone figured out how to convert the music?"

"Yes. It took about a year, then someone in the music business came out with yer music on our optical chips. About two decades later they came out with the quantum cubes we have now. It became a big business. They started to pay the teens who brought the music over here. There were so many different artists and genres, it was wonderful. Yer music has opened the door to our youth to experiment with all different types of music."

Jenny nodded. "Argus told me our world has a lot of things that were originally thought of here, too. Like microwave ovens, food processors, instant pudding. Stuff like that."

"Don't forget frostin' in a can, child. And pre-grated cheese. Those are important ones, too," Dotty said with a laugh.

Jenny started to laugh, too, then looked seriously at her friend. "Did you make the portal in the museum, too?"

Dotty looked down at the floor. "Yes, child, I'm afraid I did. Nevan and I were at the museum in yer world and we lost track of time. I didn't want to be late fer my curfew 'cause my grandfather was really knucklin' down on me then. I didn't have time to go across town to Bountiful Britches to the portal there, so I took Nevan into the bathroom after the museum closed and made the portal. But because we were so young and daft, it wasn't until after it was made that we realized—we still had to cross town. I felt real bad for doin' it. I've often wondered if the portals can be undone."

"I didn't see anything in the journal about that, but I didn't read the whole thing, either. For what it's worth, I'm glad there's a portal there. It sure saved our necks." Jenny paused to think for a moment. "So there isn't a portal in the men's bathroom in the museum?"

"No. We didn't have time. Nor is there a portal that goes into the museum."

"Oh—well, thank you for taking the time to explain all this to me." She thought for a few moments again, then decided to broach another subject with Dotty. "There's something else I'd like to discuss with you."

"What else is there?" Dotty chuckled, but then she saw the worried look on Jenny's face.

"Right before Leland and I came back here with Dot, we saw a program about an archaeological dig in my world. Dotty, archaeologists are looking for those goddess statuettes."

"Well, as far as I'm concerned, they can just keep lookin.' I'm certainly not goin' to give them over and take a chance that a bunch of greedy thinfolk will come to our world makin' portals on every block so they can come and spread their prejudice in our world like they've done to yers. And I'm trustin' ya that the little goddess that I let ya take won't fall into the wrong hands."

"You can trust me, Dotty."

"Well, how did ya find the portal in the museum?" she asked, looking at Jenny over her spectacles.

"The little goddess was glowing," Jenny admitted.

"So now Jimmy and Argus and Emmett all know that the little goddess has the power to detect the portals. Am I right?"

"And Leland—he saw it for himself. Yes, they all know because of me. But we would all be in jail right now if it weren't for that little goddess." Now it was Jenny who was defensive. "She enabled us to escape."

"I understand. It was a noble gesture for all of ya to go and rescue Emmett, and saints be praised that all of ya are safe. All I'm sayin,' child, is that ya have to be more careful. Hopefully ya won't have another occasion to use it. Do ya want the hearty folk in this world sufferin' the prejudices of yer world?"

"Of course not. Would you like me to give her back?"

"Heavens, no. I didn't mean to be scoldin' ya. It's just important that folks in yer world don't get wind of the portals, that's all.

Jenny nodded solemnly. "I'll be more careful. Don't worry." She started to get up, but there was one more question that still begged an answer. "Dotty, why didn't you go look for Leland when he first went through the portal? If you don't mind me asking."

The old woman shook her head. "I thought it would drive him further away. After all, he was already grown up. I just hoped that someday he'd come back. And he did!" She smiled. "Sometimes all ya can do about a problem is pray and wait. Instead of tryin' to force things to come out like ya want."

Jenny understood this perfectly, remembering her own prayer. She got up from her chair and hugged Dotty. "Thanks again for sharing all that," she said. "I feel so much better knowing the whole story." She looked at the clock beside Dotty's bed. "I'll get out of your hair now, so you can rest."

"Okay, dearie." But as Jenny started to walk toward the door, the baker had a question of her own. "Are the two of ya havin' a good time together?"

Jenny turned around to look at her. "Yes, Argus and I really care a lot about each other. And I'm really sorry about the way things ended with Leland."

"Don't worry about it, child. The important thing is that ya got him to come back. And besides, Leland told me he already has his eye on Clara. I've always liked Clara. Not as much as I like *you,* but we won't tell either of them that." Dotty gave her a wink.

Jenny turned toward the door with a mischievous grin on her face and started to walk out. "Oh, by the way," she said, pausing, "Old Man Chiang said he misses you."

Dotty just sat there, her mouth open. For the first time since Jenny met the old baker, Dotty had been rendered speechless.

CHAPTER 21
A NIGHT OUT
WITH THE EXES

SOMETIME AFTER LUNCH THE NEXT DAY, JENNY WAS summoned outside by Trixie, who asked, "Would it be okay with you and Argus if Leland and Clara joined us when we go out tonight?"

Jenny just stared at her friend. "You know, Leland and Clara seem to be horning in on everything lately."

"Yeah," Trixie said. "I'm hoping you'll understand. It's just really difficult when Leland and Jimmy are such good friends."

"You two just go with them."

"Well, if you and Argus don't go, then I'm not going, either. Jimmy and Leland and Clara can just go together."

This made Jenny feel annoyed. "You know," she began, "I'm noticing a pattern here. I keep getting put in the most precarious positions by you."

"But the baby thing was *your fault!*" Trixie said defensively.

"Well, yes, that's true. I did open my big mouth in front of Emmett," Jenny conceded. "I just feel like you kinda knew that your sister was going to react badly to finally hearing about the baby. And the maid of honor thing, too."

"She's always been so darned sensitive. I just hate it sometimes. I guess you're right, though. I have been putting you into awkward positions. I'm sorry, Mack. This has been the most stressful time of my life. You know, it's hard to make everyone happy."

"I know. It's really hard." Jenny thought for a moment, then finally said,

"I have to tell you, I'd really rather not go tonight. I haven't felt comfortable around Clara since Argus dumped her—well, since meeting her, actually. She's always seemed jealous and like she doesn't like me."

"Leland is just so nervous about their first date," Trixie said. "He just wanted a little support and asked me and Jimmy to go with them."

"So instead of taking Clara out and being nervous, he'd rather go with his ex and her ex? That seems like dating *suicide* to me. Why don't we save our little club excursion for tomorrow night and you and Jimmy go out with them tonight? *Please,* Trixie, *I'm begging you."*

"Do you think I hadn't thought of that? But, no, Jimmy has to work tomorrow night."

"Then you and me and Argus will go out dancing tomorrow night." Jenny was desperately grasping at some sort of a solution that would prevent the impending doom of their evening.

"Let's get Argus out here and see if he can come up with a viable solution," Trixie suggested.

They went into the office, where Argus was helping Dotty with her profit and loss statements, and invited him outside. As he helped her with one last calculation Jenny saw that the tile had been replaced and was now level with the rest. *Wow,* she thought, *what a professional job they did.*

As soon as they were out in the courtyard Trixie explained the situation to him, plus the alternative solutions. His expression changed several times. He seemed a little annoyed that the plans were changing, but he was gracious about it.

Trixie finally got to the part where Jimmy had to work tomorrow. "So what do you think we should do?" she asked.

He looked at Jenny first. She was just staring off in another direction. "Well," he said, "I agree with Jenny. I don't relish the idea of spending the evening trying to make small talk with our exes. We'll just bow out gracefully and catch you two another time."

Jenny looked up at him. *What a relief,* she said to herself.

But now Trixie started to cry. "You two have spent the whole week together. You can't spend a few hours out with the rest of us?"

Jenny looked at Argus and rolled her eyes. "Oh, for cryin' out loud. We might as well just go along with it. We'll never hear the end of it!"

"If you're okay with it," he replied slowly, "then I am, too."

Jenny turned to Trixie. "I guess we'll go," she told her, "but we're going *under duress."*

"I'm sorry I started crying. It's hard to control my emotions right now." She started bawling again. "It seems like I'm making everyone mad lately. I'm *so tired* of all the conflicts."

"Stop crying, Trixie. We'll go," Jenny said, and Argus nodded.

"Really?" She smiled, though her eyes were still watery. "You won't regret this. Jimmy and I will try and make it as painless as possible."

Argus patted Trixie on the back. "We appreciate that."

With another big sniffle, Trixie walked back into the house, leaving Jenny and Argus alone.

"Well," said Jenny, "this ought to be a *fun* evening."

"Cheer up, sweetie. If worse comes to worst, we just strike out by ourselves and get our own table and take our own cab home."

Jenny looked at him as if that idea had not occurred to her. "I guess you're right. Once we're at the club, we could just go off by ourselves."

Jenny and Argus were still grinning at each other when Trixie came back out and said the seamstress was there to take Jenny's measurements for her maid of honor dress. The two women went inside. Jenny's measurements were taken, and then she got to see a picture of the style of dress she'd be wearing. When she saw that the dress was sleeveless she protested vehemently, but then was shown a picture of the lacy long-sleeved jacket that would go over the dress and felt better. The fabric for the dress was a lovely shade of pale orange.

Late afternoon rolled around and there was a fall chill in the air. As Jenny soaked in the tub in preparation for the triple date, she thought about home and realized she was starting to miss her apartment and her cat. *Maybe,* she thought, *I should return home and start back to work on Monday.* She knew she'd want to take some time off for Trixie's wedding in a few weeks, but she couldn't afford three weeks of vacation. She half decided to go back on Sunday, but had to strategize when to tell Argus.

She dressed, curled her hair, and put her makeup on. She was dreading the evening, so she gave herself a pep talk. *Come on, it might be fun to see Leland and Clara squirm.* But her very next thought was, *That's not a very nice thing to think.* She didn't care.

She shouldered her bag and walked down the stairs. It was just getting dark, and she heard the loud *beep* again. She went into the parlor, where Trixie and Clara were waiting for the men. "What is that beep that sounds every night?" she asked them.

Clara and Trixie looked at each other and then back at Jenny. "It's the indicator on the solar cells," Clara said.

"What is it indicating?"

"That the cells are switching over to the battery."

Jenny still looked puzzled.

Trixie decided to explain further. "The solar cells on the roof store power in a battery during the day, and when the sun goes down, the battery takes over. You got it now?"

"Oh, okay. Thanks."

Argus came bounding down the stairs, and soon Jimmy and Leland followed. The three couples walked through the office and into the kitchen, where Dotty, holding Dot on her hip, was talking with Hank.

Leland stopped and kissed his mother and daughter. "You be good for grandma now," he told Dot.

"She'll be fine," Dotty said. "You kids have fun, and don't be gettin' into any trouble."

After Leland reassured her that they would all behave properly, they walked out to the street and Jimmy hailed a taxi. As they piled into the cab, the men sat facing their respective ladies, with Jimmy and Trixie in the middle. The men seemed to get along fine, but the women were rather tense. *I must be crazy to have agreed to such a ridiculous venture,* Jenny thought. The ride was long and very quiet, with intermittent bouts of forced pleasantries.

They finally arrived at the club where they were to dine and dance. Leland and Clara got out, then Jimmy and Argus.

As Jenny and Trixie were climbing out of the cab, Jimmy whispered loudly, "Argus, you got the ring, man? Shh—shh—here she comes," and then glanced at Jenny. The two of them smiled and looked at her. Judging by the silly look on Jimmy's face, she guessed they were teasing her about her mistake at the courthouse. Judging by her deadpan expression, the men could have easily guessed she was not amused. But that didn't stop them from chuckling none the less. Jenny swatted Jimmy on the arm as they all entered the club. "You know Jenny, violence never solves anything," he told her with a serious look, but then cracked a smile.

Because they had reservations, they were promptly led to their booth. Like every other restaurant in Fatropolis, the tables in the booths here were hanging from lines so they could be pulled away from the seats until everyone was seated. There was a candle burning in the middle of the table. Jimmy and Trixie sat in the middle of the booth, but after that, the seating plan seemed to backfire, as Jenny was straight across from Clara and Argus was straight across from Leland. But the table was large, so there was adequate distance between them. Loud music was already playing.

As the waitress came and introduced herself, Jenny quickly looked at the drinks menu, but recognized only a few. Due to the strange circumstances of the evening everyone was quick to order alcohol, and lots of it, except for Trixie. Ten minutes later the waitress came back with huge fruity, delicious-looking beverages of many colors, plus a strawberry shake for Trixie. After taking their food orders, the waitress left the table.

Jenny looked at the huge thick drink with its straw standing straight up in it and looked over at Argus in surprise. "I've never seen a drink this big before!" she said loud enough to be heard over the thumping music.

"Well, we're experts with alcohol," Argus said. "It's one of our things."

Jenny didn't understand what that meant, but the music was too loud to ask any more questions. She took a taste. *God, that's strong,* she thought. *If I drink that whole thing I'll be positively snockered!*

She recognized many of the songs as music from her world, and occasionally they played a hit from this side of the portal. Because the music was so loud each couple had to snuggle in close to hear one another. Soon they were all talking, and when the lights dimmed, the atmosphere became very romantic. With only candlelight illuminating the table, she could hardly see Leland and Clara. They heard some of Jenny's favorite songs, and Argus said they were some of his favorite songs as well.

It was about half an hour later when the waitress delivered their food on a huge serving tray. Jenny had ordered fish and chips with coleslaw. Clara and Jimmy had cheeseburgers with fries, Trixie had clam chowder in a sourdough bowl, Leland had a turkey sandwich, and Argus had a chicken pot pie. All of the plates and portions were very generous. They ate and enjoyed each other's company.

"Is it hot in here?" Jenny asked, fanning herself. Argus just smiled.

Pretty soon a plump man climbed up into a booth above the monstrous dance floor and started to coax the patrons to come and dance.

"I just love this cube jockey," Argus told Jenny. "He plays the best music."

The B52s' "Love Shack" came on, and a crowd of nearly all fat people jumped up and danced out to the dance floor. Jenny and Argus also got up and went out to dance. She was surprised at what a good dancer he was. Jimmy and Trixie were dancing as well, though Leland and Clara were still talking at the table.

Jenny loved to dance, but she'd always felt self conscious dancing in clubs in her world. She'd dance in her apartment, but it was no fun having to keep the music low because of her neighbor's sensitive ears. But here the music was loud and all the bodies around her were bouncing to the music, just like hers. She felt completely comfortable and was soon enjoying herself.

Once "Love Shack" ended the cube jockey said they were going to play a favorite song of Fatropolitans. When "Fat Bottomed Girls" by Queen began, everyone lined up. Even Leland took Clara's hand to lead her out onto the dance floor. Jenny had no idea what was happening.

"Watch this," Argus told her. "It's so much fun!"

They sat down together at one of the smaller tables surrounding the dance floor to watch. As the song played the dancers moved in sync with the music and each other, creating a line dance that everyone knew. It was curiously elaborate, and Jenny giggled as the crowd turned, twirled, and stomped in unison. When the song ended the cube jockey played Jean Knight's "Mr. Big Stuff," and Argus and Jenny got up again to dance. For this song the men and women separated into two sides, the women strutting and singing to the men, "Mr. Big Stuff, who do you think you are?" The men danced on their side, watching the women.

A popular song by Notorious B.I.G. was next, followed by one from Heavy D, and the whole crowd sang along with the choruses of both songs.

By the time those songs had ended, Jenny told Argus she had to take a break. The cube jockey played a slower song to give the crowd a rest: "Big Legged Mommas Are Back In Style" by blues singer Taj Mahal.

Jenny enjoyed all the good music they were playing, mostly by fat people or about fat people. The three couples, sweating and tired, went back to their table, where they took big swigs of their drinks and started talking and laughing. Argus sang along with the Taj Mahal song, "You ain't had no real good lovin' 'til you been loved by one o' them."

They were just about breathing normally when the cube jockey started "She's A Bad Mama Jama" by Carl Carlton. Jenny thought Jimmy was going to have a conniption before he could get back to the dance floor. Trixie made it plain she didn't want to dance again yet, so when Jenny said she wanted to dance, Argus suggested that she go with Jimmy.

As Jenny had put on her weight she hadn't thought the words to this song applied to her, but hearing it in Fatropolis surrounded by other fat women, she now felt like it described her perfectly.

Jimmy was dancing with every ounce of strength he could muster. "She's A Bad Mama Jama" led into "This Is How We Do It" by Montell Jordan, and they just kept dancing. When Jenny glanced at their table, she saw Trixie and Argus laughing at them. Jenny was having a wonderful time. Huge fans circulated the air around the dance floor. By now, however, Jimmy was sweating and ready for a break.

Clara and Leland seemed to be enjoying themselves. Leland, already on his fourth drink, and already tipsy, was laughing and joking. The music stopped while the cube jockey took a break, which made it possible for people to hear each other talk. Leland was obviously trying his best to impress Clara, who seemed completely taken with him. This didn't bother Jenny at all. In fact, because they had each other it made her feel less guilty about Argus breaking up with Clara and her having broken up with Leland.

I never realized that before, she thought. *I'm glad we came out together so I could see it.* She started to relax and turned to Argus. "You said you're masters of alcohol here, and it's one of your things," she said. "What does that mean?"

"Well, since our history is rich in agriculture, food and alcohol are two things we do best. In fact, the original ideas for all those fruity, creamy, and chocolaty alcoholic beverages you all have in your world came from here. But our alcohol is much stronger than yours."

Jenny looked at him as if she didn't believe it.

Leland was listening. "Maybe I can help explain."

Argus looked over at him as if he didn't appreciate the interruption, but then he nodded, and Leland continued.

"We industrialized around agriculture, and you all industrialized around the military and transportation."

"That's why our music centers so much on farming and ranching," Argus added. "It's nearly all country-western, bluegrass, and folk music. So we had to get good music from somewhere." Everyone at the table laughed.

So that's why everyone here is hearty, Jenny thought. She was glad to be learning more. She looked at Leland and smiled. "Thanks, that's interesting."

"No problem," he said with a smile.

They continued drinking and dancing for what seemed like hours. Trixie danced a few times with Leland, Clara danced with Jimmy, and Trixie and Argus even danced a few songs while Jenny was temporarily too tired.

At one point Trixie leaned over to Jenny and said, "See? We can all get along. This makes me feel better, knowing that my wedding reception won't be a complete fiasco."

Finally the cube jockey announced the final dances. As "Always And Forever" by Heatwave began to play, Argus led Jenny back to the dance floor. Embracing and slow dancing, they sang to each other along with the music. Leland and Clara were holding each other and dancing, as were Jimmy and Trixie.

The final song was one of Jenny's favorite songs by Flint Mackelroy, "My Darling, My Sweet." There, in Argus's arms, she was overcome with emotion. He sang the whole song to her. She had listened to this song at home so many times and cried so often, hoping that someday she would find the man of her dreams. Hearing it now, dancing to it with the man she loved, was the perfect culmination to a wonderful evening. When the song ended, he kissed her sweetly on the lips and they walked back to the table.

It was nearly two in the morning now, and the club was starting to close. Jenny was tired, her alcohol buzz had worn off long ago, and now she just wanted to fall into bed and sleep.

They all walked out to the street and after Jimmy hailed a cab, all climbed in, this time not being careful to sit in pairs. Jenny ended up between Argus and Jimmy. She put her head on Argus's shoulder. Clara, who was facing her between Trixie and Leland, took Leland's hand, and soon Trixie and Jimmy were also holding hands.

Besides having a great time, Jenny had learned more about this strange and wonderful world that included the great city of Fatropolis.

Back at the boarding house, all six of them wearily climbed the stairs. Jimmy saw Trixie to her room and went into his own, and Leland walked Clara to her room. Argus stopped at Jenny's door. They talked for a few minutes, then he kissed her tenderly just as Leland came walking up to his door, which was still straight across the hall from hers. "Get a room," he said with a chuckle.

They giggled a little and once Leland closed his door, Jenny pulled Argus into her room and quietly closed the door. He looked surprised as Jenny grabbed him and started kissing him.

"Are you drunk?" he asked, around her lips.

"No, my buzz wore off hours ago," she reassured him. "I just can't take it anymore—you're driving me *crazy!*" She forced his jacket off his shoulders and frantically began unbuttoning his shirt. His unbuttoning of her dress was interrupted by her hiking it up over her head and continuing to kiss him as she flung it across the room. They stood there kissing—her in her slip and bra, him in his unbuttoned shirt. He fiddled with her bra, trying and trying to unhook it. She reached around back with both hands and helped him.

"Thanks," he said, "we might've been stalled right there all night." He slipped his hands up under her loosened bra and sighed as he touched her soft breasts for the first time. She struggled with the fly of his pants, all the while never missing a kiss. He wrapped his arms around her and kissed her neck. As his pants dropped to the floor, she pushed him over to the bed. They flopped down loudly and both began to laugh.

He pulled off her slip and panties and buried his face in her belly. "Oh, my God, *I love your body!*" They both groaned as he kissed her all over.

Jenny had never felt so comfortable with a man. She didn't tense up when he touched her belly, her thighs, or her behind. She savored every breath, every touch, every growl and groan that came from him.

Eventually they fell asleep in each other's arms, exhausted and completely spent.

THE NEXT DAY Jenny had a serious talk with Argus, explaining about her vacation situation. "I need to get back to work," she told him, "so I can come back for the wedding and spend some time here." He was sad, but understood and even admitted that he had to get back to minding the store.

After lunch on Sunday, Jenny went to Burley's Department Store and found the portal in the women's dressing room, went through, and was home by mid-afternoon. After relieving Mrs. Grabowski from cat duty, she straightened up the apartment and took all her souvenirs she had bought out of her suitcase. She loved the validation she felt when she looked at the fat women in the prints. Next she put the little goddess statue back in its place on the table in her room. She went to bed early and as she said her prayers, expressed gratitude for the way things had worked out. She prayed for blessings on Leland and Clara's union, and that Dotty and Dot would be happy, too. The most important thing she gave thanks for was Argus.

WHEN THE NEXT WEEKEND rolled around, Jenny seriously thought about going back to Fatropolis to surprise Argus, but then she thought better of it. It would be harder to say goodbye after just a couple of days, and besides, she was feeling confused again. She was sure about her feelings for Argus, but she couldn't decide whether it would be better to move to Fatropolis or stay here in her New York. She had worked hard to get a good job here, and she'd been promoted and felt a sense of accomplishment. She also loved her little apartment. As she petted her cat, she wondered if Patches would have an adverse reaction to going through the portal. Her whole family lived in this world, and she didn't think she should have to give up contact with her family just to be with the man she loved.

All of this she pondered deeply. Her indecision and doubts led to inaction. It was easier to just do nothing than to cause herself more confusion.

ABOUT A WEEK LATER, Jenny received an invitation in the mail with a note attached:

Mr. & Mrs. Roland and Murielle Kavanagh
of Fatropolis
Request the honour of your presence
as their daughter
Trixie Louise Kavanagh
is united in holy matrimony to
James Heratio Littleton, III
son of
Mr. James Littleton II & Mrs. Helen Littleton

FATROPOLIS

also of Fatropolis
on the 2nd Saturday in November
at two o'clock in the afternoon
at Our Lady of Fatima Church
in Fathattan

Jenny was thrilled to receive such a fancy invitation engraved in golden letters and decorated with fall leaves and colors. She carefully opened the note from Trixie and read it:

Hey Mack,

I got your address from Leland—I hope you don't mind.

Argus has been moping around here terrible since you left. Too bad you two can't communicate somehow. We've had your dress made and just need a final fitting on Friday night before the wedding, so please try to be here by six o'clock.

Leland and Clara are quite the item now. They actually look kinda cute together, and Dot has really taken to her. We found a lovely two bedroom apartment in Fathattan. I picked out furniture and it's being delivered next Tuesday.

Lots to do. Can't wait to see you again!

Love and Hugs,
Trixie

As Jenny put the note down, she began to wonder if there might be a way to send mail from Fatropolis, though after more thought she decided they had probably just come through a portal and stuck the invitation in the mail. She felt bad to hear that Argus was lonely for her, but, still confused and still actively ignoring the choices that lay before her, she decided to wait until the wedding to go back.

One thing that Jenny didn't like about herself was the fact that she could easily be paralyzed by confusion. The more confused she felt, the less desire she had to go back through the portal before the wedding.

CHAPTER 22
A RUN-IN WITH
A POLICE OFFICER

FALL HAD LONG SINCE FALLEN ON NEW YORK AND winter was approaching fast. Jenny had returned from Fatropolis just in time for the peak season of autumn foliage in Central Park. She loved to see the spectacle the trees in the park presented at this time of year.

As soon as she could, she put in for another week of vacation to cover the time needed for the wedding. It was approved. She didn't have much to do to prepare except just be there on time. For her wedding present she bought Trixie and Jimmy a set of matching plush robes to lounge around in. She guessed their sizes, but was pretty confident the robes would fit. She was hardly surprised that the matching robes were not easy to come by. She had to order them online because no stores (that she knew of) anywhere in New York had anything of the sort for two such *robust* people.

The day of the wedding was fast approaching, and she longed to be with Argus again. She missed him worse than anyone else, ever, with an ache in her heart and butterflies in her stomach. Even though it had only been a little over a month, she was miserable without him. She kept remembering what her mother used to tell her, that "absence makes the heart grow fonder." Now she believed it was true.

On the Friday before the wedding, she had her suitcase all packed. She went home from work, finalized the arrangements with Mrs. Grabowski for cat care, and set off toward Bountiful Britches with her suitcase and her huge wedding gift.

Emerging from the portal, she couldn't wait to get to Argus's store. She walked all the way through the department store, but her gift was getting heavy, so she sat down for a little while on a bench at the front of the store. When she had her breath back she readjusted her load and went out to the sidewalk. It was thrilling to see all the fat people walking along the sidewalks again. By now she had an inkling that she might want to make Fatropolis her home, but she still wanted to wait for a while to decide for sure.

Hoping to surprise Argus, she snuck up on the nutrition supplement and vitamin store, the biting wind here making her walk a little faster. She walked up to the window from the side where he could not readily see her, set her package and suitcase down, and peered in. He was busy helping a customer. He was wearing a pullover sweater that showed the muscles in his arms and shoulders, and looked more handsome than she remembered. She just stood there, gazing at him, until he finished with his customer and the lady left the store.

He was busy behind the register when Jenny stepped out in plain sight. He was writing, glanced up, and returned to the task at hand. But when he suddenly realized who was standing in his window he whipped around and his mouth flew open. He tossed the papers into the air and ran out to greet her, hugging and kissing her passionately. People walked by and stared, and some even giggled, but Jenny and Argus paid no attention to the onlookers, who may have thought they were trying to devour each other right there in front of the store.

Argus finally came up for air. "Oh, my God, I missed you so much."

"I've been so miserable not being able to see you or talk to you, too."

"Why didn't you come to see me?" he asked.

"Because I knew it would be that much harder to leave. I knew I was coming for the wedding, so I just waited, but there towards the end I was absolutely miserable."

He smiled and took her hand. "Well, I don't know what the answer is, but I don't want to be away from you anymore."

"I know." She paused and saw that the clock inside the store, said it was almost five-thirty. "I have to be at Dotty's by six," she said. "The seamstress is coming for my last fitting before the wedding. I have to go."

"Okay. I'll see you there a little later." He kissed her again, and she set out for the bakery.

A girl in her twenties that Jenny had never seen before was working in the bakery. Jenny explained who she was and went on through the kitchen, already feeling the excitement in the air. She found Dotty in the office. After greeting Jenny warmly, Dotty told her to put her things in the same room as always.

Jenny walked through the parlor to the stairs, around a stack of huge folding chairs. There was a fire crackling in the fireplace and the parlor was festively decorated with an elaborate garland, candles, and wreaths, all in fall colors. The garland and wreaths were made of dried leaves, wheat stalks, acorns, nuts, lentils, seeds of all sorts, and sunflowers. *How lovely they are,* she thought as she went up and put her things away. When she came back down, she visited with Dotty for a while.

Soon Trixie and Dixie came walking in through the kitchen. Trixie squealed as soon as she saw Jenny. "It seems like *forever* since I've seen you. And you look—*great,*" Trixie said awkwardly. She leaned in close to Jenny and whispered, "How was that? Still insulting?"

"It still needs a little work, but thanks," Jenny laughed.

"Ohhh—what? I didn't do it right? Oh yeah, I'm supposed to ask you if you've lost weight, right? By the way, I don't mean this as an insult, but you do look like you're losing some of your reserves."

Jenny was surprised at this.

Trixie seemed to notice the confusion on Jenny's face and said, "So I still insulted you? I'll never get the hang of your greeting customs."

"It's okay, Trixie. I know you meant well. Anyway, it does seem like forever since I've been here. I don't know what to do," Jenny confessed. "I miss this place so much when I'm not here."

"Well, child, ya could always move here," Dotty said. "With yer experience, I'm sure ya could get work. And with Trixie and Jimmy leavin'—well, my door is always open if ya want a room here—" she paused—"fer a price." She reared back and cackled.

"I'll have to think about that," Jenny said.

The seamstress arrived promptly at six o'clock and fitted Jenny's dress. After some pinning and readjustments, she stood in front of the full-length mirror on her closet door and stared at how stunning the pale orange floor-length dress looked on her, even though it was sleeveless. Then she put the lace jacket on, which made the dress even more elegant, and slipped into the modest heels that had been dyed to match. She took the jacket off again and looked more closely at her reflection. She had never dared to go out in public wearing anything sleeveless. Now she turned from side to side, looking at her bulging upper arms. She finally had her fill of gazing at herself in the dress and relinquished it to the patient seamstress.

Being in her room again always made Jenny realize just how much she missed Fatropolis when she was home in the regular New York. She stood in the middle of the room, looking around and remembering all the good times she'd had in Fatropolis, all the ways she'd changed and learned to love herself. She didn't know what would happen in the future, but for now she had the old familiar feeling that her life was about to change drastically.

There was a knock at the door. She opened it, and Argus was standing there. She invited him in. They stood and kissed for a few moments, and then Jenny turned and looked out the window into the courtyard.

"Is there something wrong?" he asked.

"Well," she began, "I just don't know what to do . . . I feel like I'm at a crossroads here." She continued to stare out the window. "I have a good job in the city, but I'm completely miserable without you."

"I was afraid you didn't want to be with me anymore," he said.

"Why? What do you mean?"

"Well—Leland comes to see Clara every weekend."

She stood without speaking for a few moments, then said, "His life is here. His mother, his roots, his history. But everything I've worked for in the last eleven years is back in New York. My parents, my brother and sister and her kids all live in my world. To be with you, I'd have to give up everything I have."

Argus's eyes started to water. "Are you saying you don't want to be with me?"

"No!" she practically shouted. She turned to him. "What I'm saying is that I'm confused."

He took a deep breath. "I would be willing to go to your world."

"I don't want you to have to sacrifice your store."

"What sacrifice? People commute all the time. I can live in your New York and come here to run the store on the days I work. It wouldn't be that complicated. I can have the money exchanged by Old Man Chiang for practically nothing."

"You would do that for me?" she asked. She went over and hugged him, elated that she might not have to sacrifice everything in her life to have love.

"I would do *anything* for you," he said.

They stood for a while kissing. Jenny started to unbutton his shirt. Argus stopped her and said, "As much as I'd love to tear your clothes off and have my way with you again, Leland is throwing Jimmy a bachelor party tonight. I kinda have to participate in that, you know. So let's go back downstairs and join the others."

"Well, you better not get drunk and be ogling some strange hearty stripper," she warned him.

He gave her a puzzled look. "What do you think we do at our bachelor parties?"

She looked at him. She knew about bachelor parties back home, but maybe they had different customs here.

Argus let her ponder this for a few moments, then grinned and said, "I'm just teasing you. Yeah, strippers and liquor. That's about it for us, too. Lots of liquor."

She smacked him on the arm and they both started to laugh. "I guess some things are so important, they transcend different worlds," she said.

"But," he said, "don't underestimate the good time *you* might have tonight. Because you weren't here, Dotty took it upon herself to plan a party for Trixie tonight. I saw *a whole crate* of champagne being brought in yesterday. And Dotty has nothing to do with planning the reception."

"Ooooh, goody!"

He gave her a stern look. "So don't *you* get drunk and be ogling some hearty hunk cowboy stripper that Dotty's got lined up for the party."

Jenny laughed at the thought of a fat male stripper. She laughed even more at the thought of Dotty engaging the services of a stripper.

When they came through the kitchen door they found Jimmy, Leland, and the rest of the male boarders, including Hank, Charlie, and even Emmett, all standing around waiting for Argus. They were all nicely dressed.

Man, Jenny said to herself, *the aftershave is so thick in here you can practically see it.*

"Come on, man!" Jimmy hollered. "We've been waiting for you."

"Sorry," Argus said. "We were talking about some *really* important stuff."

Trixie turned to Leland after getting a tender kiss from Jimmy, and said, "I swear, there better not be any strippers at this party."

"Gosh," the best man replied, "I guess I'll have to call them all and cancel them. There was going to be a dozen or more."

As everybody laughed, Leland grabbed Clara around the waist and kissed her goodbye, which wasn't easy with Dot hanging on her hip. Then he leaned over and kissed the little girl and told her he'd be back soon. After Argus kissed Jenny again, the men left for Jimmy's bachelor party.

Jenny got another glimpse of the new girl working the bakery. "Who is she?"

"She's one of the crew that Dotty hires for special occasions," Dixie said. "You know, the same crew that comes in for the Festival every year. The other two will be here at two in the morning to start the baking. She wanted everyone to be able to attend the wedding."

"That's nice of her," Jenny said.

All the women, including all the female boarders, adjourned to the parlor, where there was already a heap of exquisitely wrapped gifts on a table. Minutes later a group of women of all ages, including Murielle, the twins' mother, came under the archway and into the parlor. Murielle was carrying a large gift wrapped in foil of different shades of blue. This caused quite a commotion with Trixie and Dixie. There were more women coming in all the time—there had to be at least thirty.

Toward the last an older, sophisticated, hefty black woman walked in with her twenty-something-year-old daughter. They immediately walked over and hugged Trixie, who introduced them to the room as Jimmy's mother, Helen, and his sister, Tia. Dotty already knew them and hugged them both enthusiastically; Jenny remembered that Leland and Jimmy had been school chums way back when. Mrs. Littleton had a small gift wrapped in sea-foam-green paper with a little white bow.

As the women stood talking, a crew of fat caterers came in through the office. "Where do you want us to set up, ma'am?" the head caterer asked. They were carrying not only pans and trays of food, but a portable stereo.

Dotty, who was now in charge of little Dot, waved the caterers into the dining room, where they set up a bountiful spread and a huge cake. Pretty soon the head caterer came back out and said they were finished, and Dotty led all the guests into the dining room. They filed through and picked up plates, served themselves, and sat down to eat.

Dinner took at least an hour. The food was delicious: slices of roast turkey, mashed potatoes and gravy, cornbread stuffing, green beans with mushrooms, dinner rolls with butter, fruit salad, and the huge cake. After eating, Dot fell asleep on her grandmother's shoulder, so Dotty laid her down in the sitting room.

As the cake was being cut and served, one of the plump caterers began uncorking the champagne. All the ladies took glasses and Dotty looked at Jenny, inviting her to say something. Trixie had a glass as well, but it had very little champagne in it.

Jenny stood up and cleared her throat. A hush fell over the room. "I want to offer a toast to the bride on the night before her wedding," she said, raising her glass. "Trixie, I'm sure I speak for everyone here when I wish you and Jimmy all the happiness in the world. I wish you love, good health, and prosperity."

Jenny raised her glass, thinking the toast was finished, but Dotty stood up, too. She raised her glass and said loudly, "And a house full of hearty children!"

All the ladies shouted, "Here, here!" and stood up. The clinking of glasses lasted for several moments. Jenny had never seen a room full of demure ladies down so much champagne, but no one seemed to be getting intoxicated. Everyone seemed to be full and happy. As they finished dessert they started to file back into the parlor.

All of a sudden music started to play, and the caterer who had just poured the champagne snapped the towel he had over his arm and began to dance. *That's a novel idea,* Jenny thought. *To have one of the caterers be a stripper, too.*

The women sat around the room and watched the man dancing. They began whooping and hollering, and pretty soon his shirt came off and he was dancing with his hairy chest and belly hanging out. Another fat caterer joined in and the two men started dancing in unison, just wearing Speedos, bumping and grinding with their hands behind their heads. The women shrieked at the raunchy exhibition. One shouted, "Shake those rolls, mister!" Another, "Looks like there's a lot stashed in that meat locker!"

Even Dotty was giggling, which astonished Jenny. She refused to believe that Dotty would hire strippers, much less enjoy such a spectacle. She gave the old baker a joking look of disapproval. Jenny had not drunk their alcohol, or any alcohol for that matter, since her night out with Argus, so the strong champagne went straight to her head. After just one glass, she was positively woozy.

The caterers had been bumping and grinding through at least three songs— with one and three dollar bills stuffed in their Speedos—when suddenly a Fatropolitan policeman came through the office and into the parlor.

Jenny burst out laughing. "Hey, Trixie," she called out, her voice slurry from the champagne, "he's here to arrest you! Go on, officer, frisk her! She's the one getting married tomorrow!"

Trixie looked at the officer. She looked back at Dotty and Jenny. She shook her head.

The music stopped. The men stopped dancing. The whole party came to a screeching halt and the room fell silent.

"Cuff her!" Jenny shouted, still laughing. She looked at the officer again and took another sip of her champagne. "Take it off, take it off—off—officer! Hmm," she muttered into her glass, "he's a cute one."

Dotty grabbed her by the arm and took the glass out of her hand. "Jenny! Stop actin' a fool. He's not here to strip. Someone here is in trouble."

The mistake was just too hilarious. Jenny got so tickled she started laughing in snorts and wheezes. After a few awkward moments some of the other guests started to laugh, too, and even the pudgy policeman cracked a smile. Dixie had to take her, still snorting and wheezing, to the sitting room so the officer could tell the rest of the party what he was there for.

"Boy, you are some wild woman, aren't you?" Dixie said, pushing Jenny into a chair. "Don't move. Stay here." She went out and came back again with a cup of strong coffee. "Here, drink this."

Dixie stayed with Jenny until she was starting to feel less tipsy. She told Dixie to go back in and enjoy what was left of the party. She could hear lots of *oohs* and *ahhs* coming from the parlor. *Trixie must be opening her gifts now.* As Dixie went back, sure enough, Jenny got a glimpse of Trixie holding up a lacy black lace negligee. All the ladies were ogling it and teasing her.

When Jenny finally felt a little more like herself she quietly got up, not wanting to wake Dot, and returned to the parlor. Everyone looked at her and snickered under their breath as she ducked into the back row of seats and sat down to watch Trixie open the rest of her gifts.

The next gift was the one from Trixie's mother for the wedding night. It was a full-length white lace nightgown with a matching robe and high-heeled slippers. After showing the nightgown around, Trixie picked up the little box from Jimmy's mother and opened it. All the women gasped as she unwrapped a matching necklace, earrings, and bracelet made of delicate blue and white diamonds, set in white gold.

As there were more *oohs* and *aahs* Dotty came over and sat down beside Jenny. As the next gift was opened, she leaned over and said under her breath, "Cuff her!" Then she laughed quietly.

Jenny stared straight ahead and sipped her black coffee. "What did that cop want, anyway?" she asked after a long minute.

Dotty straightened up and smoothed out her apron. "Oh, he had the wrong house."

"You're kidding me," Jenny said. Her voice was too loud. All the women paused in their festive conversation and stared at her. She just smiled politely and nodded, then took another sip of her coffee. The guests turned back to the opening of the gifts.

When the last gift had been opened, Trixie had received exotic soaps, lots of lingerie, robes, slippers, bath oils and beads, jewelry, and candles. If it was soft and feminine and smelled nice, she had it. The caterers had long since left, leaving a half-eaten cake and only a few unopened bottles of champagne behind.

As the party came to an end, Trixie spoke with her mother and Jimmy's about their plans to meet at the beauty salon in the morning. The guests began leaving, hugging Trixie and wishing her well. As the maid of honor Jenny stood beside Trixie, thanking all the guests. She figured that was the least she could do, since Dotty had thrown such a lovely party.

As Murielle and Mrs. Littleton hugged Trixie one last time, they laughed at Jenny about her drunken display. "You can't hold your liquor very well, can you, sweetie?" Murielle asked, giggling.

"I'm sorry I made such a scene."

"No need to apologize, dear. We thought it just added to the entertainment."
She looked at Mrs. Littleton and her daughter, who both smiled and nodded
in agreement.

When all the guests had finally left, Dotty and the boarders sat cozily
around the parlor, still laughing and talking about their evening. There was
no end to the ribbing Jenny received about her *faux pas.*

"All I have to say in my own defense," she replied, able to laugh about
it by now, "is that it's a well known fact in my world that any policemen,
firemen, or construction workers arriving at a bachelorette party are ninety-
five percent sure to be strippers in disguise. How was I to know that you all
have stripping caterers?"

At this the women positively howled with laughter. Trixie said, "We do the
same thing, except we have stripping farmers, cowboys, bakers, and chefs."

Jenny didn't know what to say. She thought it was a funny difference in
the two cultures. Their ultimate idea of manliness was men who produced
food, not men who protected, fought fires, and built things.

Finally, it was cleanup time. As Jenny was helping she asked Trixie, "So
what's the procedure for getting my dress tomorrow? And where should I be
at what time?"

"All the women in the wedding party will meet at the salon, Chez
Rubenesque, at eight in the morning for our hair appointments. We'll all
be having our hair done up fancy. Your dress and shoes will be at the church
waiting for you. You should be dressed and ready to go by twelve-thirty for
pictures of the wedding party. All the men will be ready and at the church by
the same time."

"I thought we would be having a rehearsal tonight. How am I going to
know what to do?"

"We aren't working under a normal timetable," Trixie replied. "We just
couldn't fit one more thing into our schedule, so we had a quick rehearsal a
few days ago. All you have to do is follow the wedding planner's instructions
tomorrow. Don't worry, you'll be fine."

After congratulating Trixie one more time Jenny went up to her room,
where she immediately went back to her usual routine. After locking herself in
she stripped down and went to draw a nice bath. *I wonder what embarrassing
shenanigans Argus is going through right now.* Thinking again about her blunder
with the surprised Fatropolitan police officer, she smiled again. *Sometimes I
just crack myself up.* She realized for the first time that she was a lot easier on
herself now when she made mistakes than she used to be.

She lay there in the warm water, remembering an incident years ago
when a man who worked at Kronkin International had overheard Jenny tell

a female coworker that he was a hunk. The hunk took it in stride with only a bashful smile, but Jenny couldn't let it go. For months she avoided the cafeteria where the incident had taken place, and every time she thought about it, she cringed. It had been a long time before she could forgive herself. *Yes,* she thought, enjoying the warm water, *I've always been overly critical of myself.* She admired people who could make an overt misstep and just laugh it off. *How much I've grown since I first stumbled into this world.*

Her mind wandered to the bride-to-be, and she began wondering if Trixie felt nervous about her big day tomorrow. Thinking about Trixie's pregnancy, she caressed the soft curve of her own round belly and wondered what it would be like to have a child growing in there.

After her bath she got ready for bed and lay there with the curtain open, looking out at the sky. She had a feeling deep down in her soul that all of this growth she had experienced was preparing her for the rest of her life, and that her *real life* was about to begin. Sometime after thinking about the soft touch of Argus's lips, she fell asleep.

CHAPTER 23
A NOVEMBER WEDDING

TRIXIE'S WEDDING DAY DIDN'T START OFF LIKE a normal Saturday. Jenny quickly found out that Dotty had decreed some days earlier that due to the parties on Friday and the wedding on Saturday, there would be no breakfast prepared in the boarding house this morning. Knowing that she would be putting on her maid of honor dress at the church in just a few hours, Jenny threw on some old jeans and a comfortable shirt when she got up, and went down stairs. She was feeling a little surprised that she hadn't heard a peep from Argus. She went into the dining room, got coffee and a doughnut, and sat down. A few minutes later Trixie came in, looking pale and haggard.

"What happened to you?" Jenny asked her.

"Oh, gosh, Mack, I had the worst night ever. I was so sick all night. The men didn't get in until three in the morning, and Jimmy was stinking drunk. I was up, throwing up again, and I heard them laughing and singing when they came in. All three of them were falling down drunk. That darned Leland!"

"Well, what did you expect? It was a bachelor party. Did you expect them to get together and exchange recipes? Or maybe knit?"

Trixie smiled. Jenny always had a way of cutting right to the issue. "I guess you're right," she said, grabbing some packages of saltines from a bowl on the buffet table. "I just thought he'd want to get back at a decent hour so we would have a good wedding day and a fun reception and be able to leave tonight on our honeymoon."

"You two can still do all that," Jenny assured her. "He just needs some sleep right now. As long as he gets his tux and makes it to the church on time, everything will be all right. Right?"

Trixie opened the wrapper, stuck a cracker in her mouth, and nodded. Jenny looked at her friend more closely. "You look a little green around the gills. Are you going to be okay?"

Trixie's eyes started watering. "Of all times, why does this nausea have to kick back up now? I was doing so much better."

"It's probably because you're stressed. Try to relax. Just let everyone tend to themselves. Everyone knows what they're supposed to do, right?"

"Well, yeah. I guess so."

"And Jimmy and Leland and Argus? They all know what time they're supposed to be at the church, right?"

"Well, yeah."

"Okay. So let them all be responsible for themselves." Jenny took a sip of her coffee. "They're big boys," she added. "They'll be there on time, and the extra sleep will ensure that Jimmy's rested and ready to go." She set her cup down, went over to Trixie, and began massaging her shoulders, trying to get her to relax. "Why don't you go up and take a bath or a shower? It's time to get ready. We need to go to the salon pretty soon."

Jenny walked Trixie up to her room, speaking consolingly the whole way. When they arrived at Trixie's door she went in and Jenny stood at the door listening. When Jenny heard the water start, she hurried into her own room and took her little money purse out of her bag. She went back down and straight to the kitchen, where Charlie was holding a wedding gift and talking with the interim bakers, telling them how to proceed for the day. Jenny rushed up to Charlie and said, "I need to speak with you."

Charlie followed her to the office. "What's wrong, Jenny?"

"Is it true that Jimmy, Leland, and Argus all got tanked last night?"

Charlie grinned. "They sure did. They weren't feeling any pain, but it wasn't *that* bad."

"Were there strippers?" Jenny asked for her own edification.

"No, just an exotic dancer—she wasn't hardly hearty at all. And she didn't take *anything* off."

Jenny heard the disappointment in Charlie's voice, but couldn't hide her slight smile. She looked at the gift he was holding. "What's with the gift?" she asked.

"Oh, I'm taking all the wedding gifts from Dotty and the boarders down to the ballroom where the reception is going to be. That way we don't have to lug them around all day."

"Good idea. Say, do you mind taking mine, too?"

"Sure, but I'm leaving in a few minutes."

"I'll go get it right away. But first—" she reached into her little purse and pulled out a thirty—"can you make sure that all of the guys get up on time to get their tuxes and make it to the church? Trixie is worried sick."

"Sure I can. But I'm not gonna take your money."

"Come on, Charlie, I know how busy you are with the temporary crew, and it's not fair to ask you to do one more thing on top of everything else. I'd wake them up myself, but I have to go to the hairdresser with Trixie and the other women."

"It's a noble gesture," he said, "but put your money away. What time should I get them up?"

"They have to be at the church with their tuxes, dressed, and ready for pictures, by twelve-thirty. So I guess by ten or ten-thirty."

"Okay. Consider it done."

"Thanks, Charlie. You sure I can't tempt you with this money? You could buy yourself something real nice." She grinned and waved the bill under his nose.

"Get outta here." He chuckled at her and walked back into the kitchen.

She put her little money purse in her pocket, rushed back up the stairs to get her gift and brought it back down to Charlie. Then she went back upstairs and stopped outside Trixie's door to listen. The sound of her friend vomiting made her cringe.

Dixie came up the stairs and saw Jenny listening at her sister's door. "What's wrong?" she asked.

Jenny shushed her and, not wanting anyone to hear, whispered, "Trixie is really sick. She's having a rough morning."

"You don't have to worry about the others hearing about the baby," Dixie said. "She told all the boarders a couple of weeks ago. Hank slipped and told someone, so she just gave up and told everyone at breakfast one morning."

"Oh, that's good." Jenny was still whispering. "But I'm worried about her, and I don't want her to know I'm spying to see if she's okay."

Dixie moved in closer. "Did she eat some crackers? I've heard that eating crackers helps."

"Yes, she ate at least one that I saw."

"You're supposed to eat them before you raise your head off the pillow."

"Really?" Jenny had a sarcastic tone to her voice, and stared at her. "I think she's been up most of the night throwing up."

Dixie started back down the hall to the stairs. "I'm going to get more crackers," she said in a normal voice.

Clara opened her door and asked Jenny what was wrong. Jenny explained about Trixie. Clara came to Trixie's door and said, "I've heard that ginger cookies made with real ginger will take nausea away."

"I don't know if there are any downstairs."

"I'll check," said Clara. "And if not, I'll run and get some."

"Hurry," Jenny said quietly. "We have to get to our hair appointments."

At this point Lidia and Delia heard their voices and came out of their rooms. Upon hearing what the problem was, they made suggestions of their own. Lidia's grandmother on her father's side had always said that peppermint tea would help, and Delia said that Trixie should sniff a lemon peel. They both went to fetch their remedies.

Well, Jenny said to herself, *at least everyone is keeping busy.* She heard the water in Trixie's bathroom turn off and put her ear to the door again. When she didn't hear anything, she knocked lightly.

Trixie came to the door, looking very pale with just a hint of green in her cheeks and red rings around her eyes. "I feel terrible, Mack," she said, motioning for Jenny to come in. "What am I gonna do? I can't walk down the aisle hanging onto a barf bag." She sat down on the foot of her bed.

"Sure you can," Jenny said. "We'll get a nice, fancy white lace bag and line it with plastic, and voilà—there you go. A barf bag fit for the bride."

Dixie came in and tried to hand her twin a handful of saltines. "Here's some crackers, sweetie."

Trixie moaned. "I'm all crackered out."

"Crackers are supposed to help," Dixie said, desperately wanting to help.

Trixie motioned for her to set them on the table beside her bed. Next Lidia and Delia appeared in the doorway, Lidia with a cup of peppermint tea and Delia with a cut-up lemon. When they offered Trixie their remedies she just asked them to put them down on the same table.

When Clara arrived in the doorway with a package of gingersnaps— "These are the only gingersnaps the corner market had," she said, tilting her head to read the label, "but it says they have real ginger in them—" Trixie merely pointed to the table. Clara added the gingersnaps to the collection of remedies. Now all five women stood towering over Trixie with worried looks on their faces.

Trixie looked up at them. "Oh, God—who's got the perfume on?" She moaned and held her stomach, then started to gag and ran to the bathroom.

Jenny went in with her to hold her forehead, followed closely behind by Dixie, Lidia, Delia and Clara and their remedies. So there they all stood, crowded into the bathroom, holding their remedies and watching Trixie retch. When Trixie finished and went to the sink to wash her face and brush her teeth, the crowd parted so she could go back to her bed to lie down.

The women followed and put their remedies back on the table.

"I've heard you're supposed to lie perfectly still—" Lidia started.

"—with your eyes completely closed," Dixie interrupted.

"Here," Delia said, holding the lemon close to Trixie's nose, "sniff this lemon."

Clara picked up her package of gingersnaps. "And these cookies have real ginger in them, which is supposed to alleviate nausea."

"And I brought you some *té de hierbabuena,*" Lidia said. "That means peppermint tea."

Trixie didn't even open her eyes. "Girls, I appreciate all your help and suggestions, but seriously, the person who has the perfume on, you need to go shower. Now. I can't take one more whiff of it. And don't even think about coming to my wedding with it on. Please. Go now."

Dixie sighed and stamped her foot. "This is really expensive perfume!"

Trixie opened her eyes and looked up at her sister. The rest of the women stared at her, too.

Dixie looked from one woman to the other. "Fine!" she said, and stormed out.

Trixie closed her eyes again. "You all go and get your hair done. I'll be down there as quick as I can. They can just get all of you started and do mine at the last minute. Or I'll just throw a hairnet on over this mess and go like this. Jenny, you go with them. I'll meet you down there."

Jenny herded all the women out of the room, leaving Trixie to rest. Jenny closed the door and they set off to Chez Rubenesque.

Clara knew how to get there, so Jenny paid for a taxi. None of them wanted to ride public transportation on such a stressful morning. She felt bad that they didn't wait for Dixie, who was still in the shower, but they had to get there and get started with the shampooing, rolling, hair drying, manicures, pedicures, and makeup.

A team of hefty cosmetologists were waiting for them. Each woman was taken to a dressing room and given a robe to wear, then all were taken to shampoo bowls with privacy dividers between them. Jenny had never been to such a swanky salon. The stylist scrubbed and massaged her scalp. The products used on her hair smelled heavenly, making her feel completely relaxed. Next she was ushered to a huge salon chair with plenty of room to spread out. The chair's arms didn't even touch her thighs, much less dig into them like the chair at the salon she frequented in New York. She was draped and the stylist consulted with her about a cut that would complement her features.

First she got her hair cut and shaped, then it was rolled onto rollers covering her entire head. She was led to the hair dryers. She sat down and the stylist put the dryer hood down over the top of her head. The warm air felt nice and made her shiver. She was handed a short menu of beverages, sandwiches, and pastries, but there were no prices. *I'm sure I have enough Fatropolitan money to cover whatever I want,* she thought.

A waiter wearing a tie and vest, with a white towel over his arm, approached her and asked her in a French accent, "What can I get for you while you are waiting, mademoiselle?" Not wanting to look like she didn't know what she was doing, even though she didn't, Jenny ordered a *café au lait* and a chocolate croissant. A little table was brought to her side before her order came. As she took her first bite she saw Trixie and Dixie walk through the door, accompanied by their mother.

Trixie looked better. The team was ready for them. Some of the stylists, who knew the twins, squealed with excitement for Trixie's big day. It was obvious to Jenny that they were regular customers at this posh salon. Helen and Tia came in a few minutes later. Even though Jenny was still under the dryer everyone greeted her, then the newcomers were taken to the dressing rooms.

Before Trixie allowed them to lead her away, she crouched down so Jenny could see and hear her. "You won't believe it," she said, "but all those remedies the girls brought me worked. I ate some gingersnaps and crackers while sipping the tea and sniffing the lemon. I feel a lot better."

"You better feel better," Jenny retorted, smiling up at her. "You have a wedding to go to! I sure hope the makeup artist can cover up those red raccoon eyes of yours."

Trixie laughed and walked back to the dressing rooms.

Jenny sat there sipping her coffee, eating her croissant, and feeling like a lady of high society. Once she had finished a whole station was wheeled over to start her pedicure and manicure. She didn't even have to move.

First the pedicure. Her feet were soaked, massaged, scrubbed, and scraped. Her toenails were clipped, shaped, filed, and painted. Her toes were put into little machines that blew air to dry the polish faster.

Next came the manicure. Once her fingers had soaked for several minutes, the manicurist took Jenny's hands and massaged them clear up to her elbows. Her hands were washed again and her nails polished, then her fingertips were put into the little dryers. By the time her nails were dry so was her hair, and she was led back to the chair, where her rollers were removed. Her hair was brushed and teased up into a beehive. The stylist went to the rear of the salon and came back with a package that had Jenny's name on it—fall-colored feathers, which were stuck into her hair for decoration. The stylist next consulted with her about how she liked her makeup, and before long Jenny looked like she'd just walked out of a magazine. She looked perfect.

Finally released from the chair, Jenny went to find Trixie. It was nearly ten thirty, and Jenny wanted to go back to the boarding house to make sure the men were going to be up, ready, and at the church on time. Even though she trusted Charlie, she wanted to see they were up for herself.

She found Trixie lying on a curved chaise lounge, her hair in rollers and her head under a portable dryer. Her face was covered with a special cream, and there were cucumber slices over her eyes. She also had separators between her recently polished toes, and she was lying with her hands on her chest, fingers separated, as her nails had just been polished. Trixie's mother, under a dryer with her feet soaking in a foot bath, was reading a magazine and munching on an éclair. Jimmy's mother and sister were having their hair styled into very fancy up-dos. Jenny walked over to Trixie. "Wow."

Trixie didn't move, and because the face cream had hardened, couldn't smile. "Don't make me smile," she said, trying not to move her lips. "My face will break." Saying that made her start to laugh anyway, and she moaned. "Leave me alone, Jenny!" she joked.

"I have a couple of things I need to do," Jenny told her. *I could just call the boarding house. No, I want to see for myself if Charlie made sure the men are up.* "I'll be back before they finish with you." She leaned down and whispered into Trixie's ear. "How does this work? Do I pay? Or just tip? What do I do?"

Still trying not to move her lips, Trixie whispered, "Mother is paying for everything, and don't worry about tipping. It's all included."

"What about the stuff I ate?" Jenny whispered back.

"You really don't get out much, do you? Food and beverages are complementary with the salon services."

Jenny stood up, feeling kind of foolish. "Oh," she said, making sure no one had heard. "Well, good luck with that facial. I'm going now."

Trixie waved a stiff hand, and then carefully laid it back on her chest.

After Jenny left the salon people on the street were staring at her, as her hair and makeup didn't match the casual clothes she was wearing. When the cab dropped her off at the bakery, the temporary crew was already working. No one was in the kitchen or the parlor, which made her feel relieved, as it was well past eleven now. There was no one upstairs either. When she asked the bakery crew, they told her everyone had left about an hour before. Satisfied, Jenny took a cab back to the salon to wait with the other girls.

Trixie was now in the chair, having her hair teased and shaped into a lovely cascade of curls. Her fat feet had been pedicured and looked soft and smooth. Her nails were lovely and her engagement ring glistened.

It didn't bother Jenny to see Trixie's engagement ring. That, too, made her realize how different she felt about things now.

Dixie was also getting the finishing touches put on her hairdo. The other girls were looking at magazines, talking and giggling excitedly in the waiting area, which was as nicely decorated as the parlor at Dotty's house, with luxurious antique sofas and elegant lamps. Jenny sat down with them and picked up a magazine, expecting to be barraged with images of how society insisted she *could* look if she would just put forth some effort.

The salon carried the most cutting edge cosmetology magazines as well as the best in high fashion. She was pleasantly surprised when she saw that *Fatropolitan's Finest* magazine had a hefty fashion model on the cover. She leafed through it quickly. *Not a skinny person in the whole magazine,* she thought. *How refreshing!* Jenny glanced at the other magazines, too, all of which featured the latest fashions in fat wear. Even the sexy perfume ads had scantily clad fat couples kissing or looking longingly at each other.

The magazines were one more thing that validated Jenny as a large woman. The women both in the magazines and around her were beautiful, had nice hair and makeup, and were of varying sizes of fat. Jenny asked the receptionist if she could take one of the magazines. "Certainly."

It was now after eleven thirty, and Jenny was getting a little nervous. Trixie and Dixie were finally done. All the bridesmaids looked lovely with the fall-colored feathers in their hair. Two women Jenny didn't know came from the depths of the salon with similar hairdos and feathers. Lidia introduced them as friends of the twins. *Wow,* Jenny thought, *there are going to be seven bridesmaids!* Just then she saw Tia was being adorned as a bridesmaid, too. *Eight bridesmaids.*

A few minutes later a stretch limousine pulled up in front of the salon and a burly driver wearing a smart black suit and chauffeur's cap stepped out. Every one of the women piled into the limo, and they headed for the church. On the way the limo stopped outside a high-rise building. The driver got out and went inside past the doorman. Minutes later Mr. Kavanagh came out and joined them. He was wearing a handsome wine-colored tuxedo with salmon vest and ascot tie.

The ride to the church took about half an hour. Although Murielle had gotten out a chilled bottle of wine and poured a glass, Trixie complained about the smell, so no one was able to imbibe. Everyone went into the church, where a few people were still decorating the sanctuary and the organist was practicing the wedding music. A huge basket was near the front doors with little bundles of dried corn, oats, and rice to throw at the couple. Murielle kissed her husband, and he walked off to join the men.

All the women filed out a side door, walked down a sidewalk sheltered by hedges, and went into a huge room near the rectory that was obviously used for dressing and preparations for weddings. A team of robust seamstresses and attendants were waiting to help the bridal party get into their elaborate dresses.

Each of the bridesmaids had her own attendant to help her get dressed. They had brought a rack of undergarments of every size and style and chose one based on each woman's figure. As Jenny undressed, she asked what would happen with her street clothes and magazine, and was told by her attendant that her clothes would be taken back to the boarding house. Jenny was fitted with an undergarment with crinolines to give her dress the fullness it deserved. Her dress was the lightest shade of orange, and each bridesmaid's dress was a shade darker. She had expected to have to wear pantyhose, but there wasn't a stocking or a pair of pantyhose in sight. After Jenny was zipped into the sleeveless dress and jacket her attendant put little nylon socklets on her feet before she stepped into her shoes. She stood in front of the full-length mirror. *I look gorgeous!* She turned and looked at herself from every angle.

A photographer had come in by now and was taking tasteful shots of the bridal party getting ready. Each time a photo was taken, a laser image was projected above the camera.

Having nothing else to do, she watched Clara being tucked into her dress. Clara looked like she had gained about fifty pounds. Jenny couldn't figure out how this sudden weight gain had happened, and then remembered the undergarments she'd seen in the department store when she first arrived in Fatropolis. The attendants had dressed Clara in similar undergarments to pad her figure. Clara had a sweet smile on her face, she was blushing and her eyes were watering. She finally looked big like the other girls, which seemed to make her very happy.

Next Jenny turned to watch the exhibition as Trixie was dressed. First the bride stepped into a huge hoop skirt, then two seamstresses unfurled Trixie's white Victorian dress from its zippered bag and lifted it over her head. Jenny had never seen such an elaborate wedding dress. They adjusted and straightened the satin bodice of the dress and then began buttoning the numerous crystal buttons up the back, one by one. The train was at least ten feet long, and there was a wide border of delicately beaded lace around the entire skirt. Due to the chill of the fall air the dress also had a little coat that covered the bride's shoulders and fat upper arms. The coat was made of fluffy feathers that looked soft around her bosom and neck. Her headdress was just as elaborate, with yards and yards of netting and lace. Jenny stood with her mouth gaping open at the frills and frocking on the dress.

She had expected to see tight undergarments and corsets with straps and bindings to tame and smooth Trixie's rolls and curves, but there were none of those. The seamstresses wanted all of the women, especially Trixie, to look as big as possible.

Trixie's mother stood watching and smiling, occasionally wiping her eyes with a lace hanky. Once the bride and her maids were all dressed, the florist came in and gave them their bouquets. Trixie's bouquet was a stunning arrangement of pale peach, burgundy, and white roses with burnt orange mini-calla lilies, green leaves, and a few brown seed pods. Everyone else in the wedding party had rose bouquets that matched the color of their dresses.

Finally, just as the photographer was announcing that it was time for the formal photographs, Dotty came through the door with Dot, who was dressed up like a little Victorian doll in a burnt-orange dress that was the darkest of all the dresses. Dot's hair, too, was curled and decorated with feathers. Dotty was dressed immaculately in a lovely tan evening gown, her hair done up in a bun.

All the women immediately began fussing over the little flower girl. The florist gave Dot her little basket of rust-colored flowers. The photographer got their attention again, and the women and Dot stood around Trixie in several different poses. The photographer snapped picture after picture.

Jenny couldn't help but look at the laser image instead of the camera lens, which made the photographer lose his patience. "Stop looking up every time I snap a picture," he shouted at her. "You're not a baby anymore! You're ruining all the photographs."

"I'm sorry, I can't help it." Jenny forced herself to look at the lens, but then would catch herself looking up again.

The photographer took Trixie and her mother aside. He was obviously angry. Trixie's voice got loud. "I don't care how many times you have to try, we're not asking her to stand out of the photos!"

Then Trixie pulled Jenny aside. "I'm sorry, Jenny, but he's really getting upset." Seeing the puzzled look on Jenny's face, she explained. "Okay, here's the deal. Everyone who's born here gets their picture taken with these cameras. I take it your cameras don't project images?"

"No. It's very distracting—it's like I can't control my eyes." Jenny was starting to get upset herself.

"Well, every kid here gets the hang of it by the time they're five or so. We all have baby pictures where we're looking up instead of into the camera." Trixie lowered her voice. "Actually, I got the hang of it before Dixie did. My folks have tons of pictures where I'm looking into the camera and she's staring up at the laser. What can I say? I guess I was just a little more photogenic." She giggled. "Don't tell anyone I said that. So, anyway, this is kid's stuff. Dot will probably come out in all the photos looking up, and everyone expects that from a three-year-old. But you, you're an adult. You can get the hang of it. I'm going to have him take some pictures of you by yourself so you can get used to it."

"Okay," Jenny replied, and the photographer led her outside to a garden that was part of the church grounds. He posed her near some roses bushes and started coaching her and snapping photo after photo. Jenny concentrated on not looking at the image above the camera. It was hard, but she was starting to understand. On what felt like the fiftieth shot the photographer told her to look over his shoulder and into the distance. That's when she caught sight of Argus, who was dressed in his lovely cocoa brown tuxedo with a peach vest, shirt, and matching tie. He was standing there with his arms crossed, smiling and watching Jenny's private photo shoot. She blushed and smiled.

"What a beautiful smile," the photographer said. "There you go! That's perfect, Jenny." He took another shot. "I think you've finally mastered it. I'm going back in. Please come back in so we can redo the bridal party photos."

After the photographer went back inside Jenny walked toward Argus instead. His smile got bigger and bigger as she approached. "Wow! Just look at you. You look stunning!"

They hugged and kissed. "You're not so shabby yourself," she said, thinking he was the most gorgeous hunk she had ever seen. She told him about the photographer.

He smiled and said, "I'm sorry you had a rough time, but you better get back in there. You don't want to upset him again."

She started back inside. "I'll see you later, mister."

The photographer was just finishing up a series of photos of Trixie with her mother and sister, with Dotty, Dot, and with Jimmy's mother and sister. The entire bridal party lined up again for more photographs. He didn't complain about Jenny anymore. She'd mastered having her picture taken in Fatropolis.

Just when Jenny thought she couldn't stand to have her picture taken one more time, the photographer said he was going to go photograph the groom and his groomsmen. Finally the women had a few moments to rest before the wedding. According to a clock on the wall, it was already one-thirty. When Dotty told them that the church was already packed, Trixie began looking worried. Jenny went over to her. "What's the matter, Trixie?"

"How am I supposed to go pee?"

One of the attendants approached her and said, "This way, miss," and two more attendants accompanied her into the bathroom. Fifteen minutes later Trixie and the three attendants came out. Trixie was smiling, "You should have seen it in there. I've never seen peeing be a team effort before. It was kind of funny."

Jenny just shook her head. "I'm glad you got taken care of and were amused at the same time."

The head seamstress talked to Trixie, then called Jenny over. Two seamstresses showed Jenny how to bustle Trixie's dress for the reception. That, she learned, was one of her duties as maid of honor. "I don't have to help her pee, do I?" she joked.

"No. Jimmy can help me after the wedding." They all had a good laugh.

Jenny remembered some of the wedding traditions from her world and asked, "Do you have something old, something new, something borrowed, and something blue?"

"Yes. And I even have a sixpence for my shoe," Trixie boasted.

A fat, handsome thirty-something year old man with big hair and glossed lips, wearing a brown suit with a soft peach lace ascot, walked in the door. Jenny decided he must be the wedding planner. He clapped his hands briskly and shouted, "Places, ladies. It's almost time."

He walked over to Trixie, kissed her hand, and squealed over her beauty. He put his hand over his heart as if he were floored, sighed deeply, and said, "May I just say, you look absolutely exquisite. James is going to go gaga over you." Then he shepherded all the women and Dot to their places and went over the directions one more time. They stood around until two o'clock finally arrived, at which time he led them out to the walkway and into the lobby of the church.

The wedding planner cued each member of the wedding party when to walk down the extra-wide aisle. The grandparents of the bride and groom were directed to walk first, then Jimmy's parents. When they got up to the front of the church and took their seats, Murielle's entrance on the arm of a man Jenny had never met marked the official start of the wedding procession. Mr. Kavanagh had gone to the back to be with Trixie. Dotty and Dot were right in back of Jenny. The organist played lovely music as all the bridesmaids began to walk down the aisle.

Jenny was inching closer and closer to her entrance. Pretty soon she was next in line. All the little bundles of corn, oats, and rice were gone already. Just before she stepped into the aisle, the wedding planner handed the groom's ring to her. It was her turn.

She had never seen so many people attending a wedding, and nearly everyone was hearty. She walked up the center of the aisle, smiling and walking slowly. People all around her were snapping pictures. She tried not to look at the cameras.

Jimmy, Leland, Argus, and the rest of the groomsmen were all in their places. Jimmy, she decided, looked pretty good for having gotten smashed the night before. He had a pleasant smile on his face and was eagerly waiting for his bride. Jenny was surprised to see Hank and Charlie in the wedding party, but as with the bridesmaids, there were also a few men she didn't recognize.

The men's tuxedos were all different shades of brown, with their shirts, vests, ties, and boutonnières corresponding to the shade of their bridesmaids' dresses. Jimmy's tuxedo was the lightest, a creamy coffee brown with a white shirt, tie, and vest.

Leland seemed to be in awe of how pretty Jenny looked, but she only had eyes for Argus. Everyone in the church smiled as Dot toddled down the aisle carrying her flowers, Dotty holding her hand.

When the entire wedding party was in place the music stopped and then a few chords sounded, announcing the arrival of the bride. Murielle stood up, followed by everyone else, as Trixie entered, her hand on her proud father's arm. She looked like a huge white float in a parade. She seemed to be quite a ways into the church before the end of her train could be seen, and it took a while before they reached the front of the church.

As the bride arrived Mr. and Mrs. Littleton rose and stood next to Jimmy. Then Trixie and her father were joined by Murielle. All six of them stood there as attendees took photos from every angle. Finally Mr. Kavanagh gently took hold of Trixie's veil and raised it back over her head. He kissed her and turned her toward her groom. At the same time Jimmy's parents hugged and kissed him and turned him toward his bride. All four parents took their seats, and Trixie and Jimmy joined hands and approached the priest.

Trixie had confided to Jenny that Jimmy and his parents were not Catholic, but they'd realized how important this was to Trixie's family and consented to participate in the traditional Catholic ceremony. Jimmy had taken classes so he could marry at the altar and partake of communion during the ceremony.

The first time the couple had to genuflect, all the guests began to chuckle. *What's everyone laughing at?* Jenny wondered. She glanced back and saw people pointing at Jimmy and craning their necks to see what was happening. The same laughter broke out every time the couple had to kneel. Finally Jenny looked back at Murielle, who was giggling. Murielle whispered, "Someone painted 'lucky duck' on the bottoms of Jimmy's shoes."

What a dirty, but clever, trick, she thought. *Who did that?*

After the candle-lighting ceremony it was time for communion, which was much more elaborate in this world. A lot more wine, and she thought the Hosts had to be multigrain, as they were thicker, actually soft and chewy, and had little seeds in them.

Within another half hour the vows and rings had been exchanged and

Trixie and Jimmy were married. The smiling newlyweds turned to face their guests as the priest announced, "Ladies and gentlemen, may I present to you Mr. and Mrs. James Heratio Littleton."

The entire congregation burst into applause as laser images shot up all over the church. The parents went forward to kiss the newlyweds, then Jimmy and Trixie started back down the aisle.

The rest of the wedding party had to wait a long time before Trixie's train cleared the front of the church. After Dotty and Dot followed them out, Jenny stepped forward and took Leland's arm, thinking how weird it felt being that close to him again. They walked together to the lobby of the church, and then Jenny let go of his arm to go and hug the bride and groom.

At the direction of the wedding planner, the entire wedding party—several of the bridesmaids carrying the bride's train—walked out the side door from the lobby and around to a door that led back to the front of the church. They waited outside until the church had emptied out, then went in to pose for more photos. Trixie was posed with her train spread out in front of her, nearly covering the steps to the altar. The entire bridal party, including Dot, crowded in around the couple. Then came photos with parents. Again, the photos seemed to take forever. Finally the photographer was satisfied with the countless pictures he had taken, and the doors were opened. The bridesmaids and groomsmen were instructed to go outside first.

The crowd of guests was waiting outside for the bridal party to leave for the reception. Jenny and Leland were the first to step out, followed by the rest of the bridal party. Several limousines were parked in front of the church. The bridal party walked down the steps and waited for Trixie and Jimmy to appear. Finally the crowd clamored with excitement as the newlyweds walked out of the church.

Someone had laid an old-fashioned broom on the ground right outside the door. The broom was elaborately decorated with wheat stalks, fall leaves, seed pods, harvest fruits, and ears of corn. When Trixie and Jimmy, holding hands, stepped over the broom at the same time, the wedding guests went wild, and then the corn, oats, and rice began flying through the air, raining down on the couple as they hurried out to the first limousine. Soon it pulled away from the curb.

The parents of the couple rode in the second limo with Dixie and Tia. Leland and Jenny were directed to get into the next. Dotty and Dot got in as well, as did Argus, Clara, and Charlie. Finally Jenny was able to sit with her boyfriend. Leland and Clara were also sitting together. Dot crawled from Dotty's lap over to Clara. She was still holding her little basket.

"Can I have kisses?" Clara asked her. The little girl kissed Clara on the cheek. "Thank you," she said as she buckled the little girl in her seat.

It warmed Jenny's heart to see that Clara and Dot had bonded so well and were looking so happy. Clara's padded dress seemed to bolster her self-esteem, and she looked confident and sure of herself. Leland looked down at Clara's padded belly as if he didn't approve. *I'm sure glad I don't have to deal with that anymore,* Jenny thought.

When they arrived at the fancy hotel where the reception was to be held, Argus accompanied her into a small banquet room. Eventually the entire bridal party arrived, including the newlyweds and their parents, and it was here that Jenny bustled Trixie's dress and hooked her veil over one arm.

The mood was lighter now. Argus kissed Jenny as the women gathered on one side of the room and the men were talking on the other side of the room. The men laughed as Jimmy finally took his shoes off and looked at the soles. No one would confess as to who had done the deed, but Jenny suspected it was Leland.

A while later Leland and Clara were standing away from everyone else. They seemed to be having a little tiff. She overheard Clara saying, "I'm not taking it off! I like the way it makes me look. I'm going to buy one, and I'm going to wear it whenever I feel like it!" Leland looked shocked as Clara stormed off to rejoin the women. *You go, girl!* Jenny thought.

It seemed as if no one was in a hurry to get to the reception. Jenny didn't know what was going on, so she sidled up to Trixie and asked, "Why are we all in this holding room?"

"Haven't you ever been to a wedding reception?"

"Well, not as big as this—and not *here.*"

"This is the cocktail hour. We're letting the guests get their first cocktails of the evening and have some *hors d'oeuvres.* We'll make our grand entrance in about fifteen minutes."

A minute later the wedding planner came in. He seemed very pleased with how the wedding had gone. "Oh, heavens!" he exclaimed, "that was the most beautiful wedding I've ever seen. Everyone did such a wonderful job." He was embraced by Murielle, and the two began talking quietly.

Jenny was very hungry, as her *café au lait* and croissant were long gone.

The wedding planner spoke up over the crowd and gave directions as to how the entrance would go. The couple's grandparents and parents went first, then the bridal party, with Jenny and Leland at the rear. Then Dotty and Dot, then Jimmy and Trixie. They all paired up and waited for the planner's signal, and at long last all made their way to the grandly decorated ballroom.

A master of ceremonies announced each couple as they entered to the applause of the guests. A fifteen-piece band started to play soft music as the newlyweds passed under a huge arch of flowers and walked onto the dance floor. The guests crowded around to witness Trixie and Jimmy's first dance as man and wife. After they had begun the dance the parents and bridal party were summoned to join in. Jenny danced with Leland. It was awkward, but not as bad as she had imagined it might be.

"You look nice," he said.

"Thanks," she replied. "You do, too."

They danced without looking at each other, and then he spoke again. "Congratulations—about you and Argus, I mean. He's a good guy."

"You and Clara sure make a handsome couple," Jenny added, all too quickly. "And Dot sure seems to like her."

"Yeah, she's quite a woman. I really think she might be the one."

"I'm really happy for you and Dot, Leland—really happy."

He smiled. Finally the song ended and the emcee announced that dinner would be served.

There were tables as far as her eye could see, each one adorned with a different fall-colored tablecloth, ten place settings, and a autumn bouquet in the center. Each place setting had twelve pieces of gorgeous gold flatware surrounding a huge charger with a cloth napkin folded in the shape of a crown, two small plates, and three goblets of different sizes. The bridal table was even more elaborate.

When Jenny found her place and laid her bouquet on the table, she was very tired and badly in need of food. Looking down at her place setting, she felt intimidated by the four forks, four knives, and four spoons of different shapes and sizes. She had no idea what courses they were all for. Then the thought occurred to her: *Just watch everyone else and do what they do. It's not brain surgery.*

First they were served a charcuterie plate of sliced meats including prosciutto, spicy *nostrano* and *coppa* salami, served with freshly toasted crostinis lightly drizzled with olive oil and an assortment of dijon and wholegrain mustards. Then came the first course: buttermilk lettuce, dried cranberries, sliced apples and a creamy red-wine-and-herb vinaigrette. The second course consisted of braised short ribs, three-cheese garlic- and herb-mashed potatoes and sautéed asparagus in a creamy orange sauce, served with herbed parmesan oregano lightly toasted on a baguette. The first dessert was a puff pastry ravioli stuffed with a thick raspberry mint *coulis* topped with shaved milk chocolate. Then came the cheese plate: twelve-year-aged cheddar cheese, blue cheese from Milan, triple-cream *boursault* served with strawberry preserves, oven-roasted grapes, and lightly toasted crostinis.

Trixie and Jimmy finished their plates quickly, stood up and made the rounds, talking to their guests as they ate. Somewhere between first dessert and the cheese plate the speeches began. The newlyweds were across the ballroom at the time, visiting different tables and talking with guests. Leland was handed a microphone. He stood up and called out for everyone's attention. A hush fell over the ballroom, and the couple came back to their seats at the bridal table.

"Good evening, everyone," Leland began. "As the best man, it is my distinct pleasure to congratulate Mr. and Mrs. Littleton." The guests started to applaud. "You know, I guess I can take full credit for Jimmy and Trixie even knowing each other. You see, Trixie is my cousin—well, more like my little sister." Trixie smiled at him, but Jimmy looked at him as if pleading for mercy. "And Jimmy and I met in kindergarten and have been friends ever since. But when Jimmy and I met, Trixie actually hadn't been born yet." The guests weren't sure if they should laugh or not. "Actually we're eight years older than Trixie." Trixie glared at Leland. "Now I see you glaring at me, Trixie, but I haven't told the best part yet."

Trixie had to speak up. "This isn't a roast, Leland. It's a toast."

Leland continued. "When Jimmy and I were about eleven, we used to hang out a lot at my house, where there are a lot of places to hide. Well, Trixie used to hide and sneak around. She'd follow us, and then go tattle to my mom about what we were doing. In fact, when we were thirteen, Trixie was instrumental in Jimmy being banned from the house for a month because he brought a frog in and put it down her back. I have never since heard anyone scream as loud or long as she did that day. So I was quite surprised when they walked in together one day and Trixie told me that they were dating. She didn't even remember who he was."

"Okay, Leland," Trixie said. "You can wrap it up any time now. Other people want to say a few things." The guests laughed again.

But Leland wasn't about to give up the microphone yet. "When I saw them together for the first time, though, I really got a feeling they were meant to be together. So I want to offer a toast." He raised his glass of champagne. "To a match made in heaven. My cousin Trixie and my best friend James." Everyone raised their glasses, and Leland finally sat down.

It was Jenny's turn. She had been feeling a little nervous before the champagne, but now that her belly was full and she had imbibed a little, she was fine. She stood up and received the microphone.

"Good evening," she said. "I'm Jenny, the maid of honor. I haven't known Trixie and Jimmy for very long—only about eight months—but it seems like I've known them forever. I have to say that I've never felt so close to two people in my life. They are great together." She turned to them and raised her glass. "I wish you all the happiness that marriage can bring—health, wealth, prosperity, and a house full of hearty children."

After the guests applauded, it was the turn of each grandparent and then parent to make a speech. Dixie and Tia were given a chance to say a few words as well. Most of the speeches were short and sweet. Murielle cried a bit, but her speech was tasteful yet sentimental.

The emcee announced that the cake was about to be cut and invited the guests to gather around the cake table. Jenny had never seen a bigger cake. The black forest cake was topped by figures of a fat bride kissing her fat groom, something Jenny had never seen before in her world. There were no fat bride and groom figurines available back home.

The cake was cut and Trixie and Jimmy fed each other the first piece. Jenny hoped they wouldn't shove cake in each other's face, and sure enough, they were respectful and loving and even used forks. Coffee was served as the cake was sliced by the caterers and distributed to the guests.

About half an hour later, as the music and champagne started again, Jenny finally had a chance to dance with Argus. She felt like she hadn't seen him all evening. It felt nice to be in his arms again.

Emmett danced by with Maddison Colby, taking Jenny by surprise. "Look at Emmett dancing! He made a full recovery, didn't he?" she commented.

Argus smiled and said, "Yep, it took him a while, but he's fine now. Jimmy got him a job making pizzas, and now he's rooming at the boarding house. He and Maddison have sure been spending a lot of time together recently."

Jenny was delighted to see Emmett looking so well and enjoying the company of a young lady. She was pleased he'd overcome whatever issues he might have had and had started a life for himself. She was also pleased for herself, for the same reasons.

Even though it was Trixie's day, it was an important day for Jenny as well. With the help of all of her friends in Fatropolis and their friendly inclusion of her in their lives, she'd learned that she didn't have to march to the beat of a society that condemned her for being different and taking up too much space.

She was no longer ashamed of her size. Finally able to allow herself to laugh, have fun, and to love, she was enjoying everything that life had to offer. On this important day she felt that her transformation into a hearty woman was complete.

As they danced she looked at Argus with new eyes. She had found the man she wanted to be with, and she was determined their two worlds would not keep them apart.

They had danced a few songs when the emcee made another announcement.

"The anniversary dance and money dance are coming up soon, so make sure you all have your money ready. But first," he continued, "Mrs. Littleton would like to invite all the single ladies in attendance this evening to come out to the dance floor for the throwing of the bouquet."

Jenny watched as all the giggling single women found their way to the dance floor. Trixie was standing near the bandstand and talking with the emcee. Twenty-eight women crowded around her and stood waiting for her to toss the bouquet.

"Okay," the emcee announced, "are all the single ladies out on the dance floor?"

Clara, Dixie, and all the other female boarders were out there waiting. It didn't even occur to Jenny to go out and join them.

The emcee said, "Jenny—Jenny Crandell. We're waiting for you."

Jenny looked at the bandstand, where Trixie was standing with one hand on her hip. She summoned Jenny to the dance floor with her index finger.

"Go on," Argus said.

She reluctantly walked out onto the dance floor and stood beside Dixie, toward the back of the crowd. Clara was about twenty feet away from her.

Trixie turned her back to the crowd. The MC shouted, "One—two—*three!*" The bride tossed her bouquet backward over her head.

Trixie evidently had a good arm, as the bouquet sailed above the heads of the crowd. Jenny saw Clara running toward her and looked up. The bouquet was coming right for her. She reached up automatically, almost in self-defense, and the bouquet dropped into her hands.

Dixie had also reached for the bouquet, and both she and Clara walked away disappointed—especially Clara—as they realized Jenny had caught the prize.

Holding the bridal bouquet in one hand, Jenny turned to the applauding crowd and curtsied. As she stood there enjoying her moment in the spotlight, she thought, *To hell with you actuarial tables. I'm going to live my life knowing that my large voluptuous body is nothing to be ashamed of.*

She looked over at Argus, who was clapping along with everyone else in the crowd. He had the cutest little grin on his face. Jenny smiled back at him.

ACKNOWLEDGEMENTS

I WOULD LIKE TO THANK THE COUNTLESS LITERARY agents who passed on my manuscript so I could look harder and find Dr. Peggy Elam, founder and owner of Pearlsong Press. I am honored that *Fatropolis* has been added to such a magnificent collection of fat/size-friendly literature. An extra special thanks to Dr. Elam for this opportunity of a lifetime. Thank you also for the creative insights which have helped *Fatropolis* become the story it was meant to be. Peggy, you truly are Healing the World One Book at a Time.

A great big thank you to my editor Barbara Ardinger, Ph.D (http://www.barbaraardinger.com): Without your command of English and your editorial talents *Fatropolis* would have been merely a bunch of good ideas (even if I do say so myself) floating around in a vortex of bad grammar and rampant points of ellipses.

I'd like to thank one of the literary agents, Sandy Lu in particular, who suggested I change the setting of the place where Jenny falls into Fatropolis and then would not acknowledge any of my further queries—proving to me that sometimes people come into our lives for a short time, for a specific reason, and then are gone just as quickly.

I also give thanks to Susan Koppelman (http://www.susankoppelman.com), Frannie Zellman (http://fatfrannie.wordpress.com), and Lynne Murray (http://www.lmurray.com), for taking the time to read and critique my manuscript. Thank you, Susan, for helping me to become a better writer. The changes that were made to the manuscript due to your wonderful critiques have improved the story immensely. Frannie, thank you for pointing out the problems with Dotty's accent. The resulting changes helped define Dotty's character even more.

I would like to acknowledge my family for their loving support of me all the time, but especially during the time I was researching, writing, editing, researching some more, writing, cursing, and editing. When I say "my family," I mean my husband Guy Thompson, who, with his extensive love and knowledge of science fiction, inter-dimensional travel, and alternate worlds, helped me in defining the world of *Fatropolis*. I also want to thank him for being my best friend, my rock, and the voice of reason in my life. To my five children, Levert Olmedo, Loy Olmedo, Jose Olmedo, Emma Olmedo, and Hayden Thompson, who constantly amaze me with their love of life and their healthy sense of self-esteem: Thank you all for loving me, for being so excited for me, and for talking to others about my book being birthed and published. I love you all. I also want to say "I love you so much!" to my granddaughters, Ryleigh & Cecilya Olmedo. Thank you, also, to everyone who loves my children and grandchildren. To my son Loy, who made all the gourmet meals in the book come to life: Without your knowledge of food and catering, the characters in my book would not have had such rich dining experiences. To my daughter Emma: Thank you for your suggestion about the end of the story—it works quite well. And thank you for coming to Virginia—it's nice to have family close by. To my brother William "Ed" Savage: Thank you for your loving support of me through this process, and thanks for your help through our two household moves. To my mother, Nancy May Savage: Thank you for loving me and raising me with a sense of right and wrong, and for knowing me so well. I miss your visits and our talks. To my father, William Lee Savage: Thank you for your love and support, and for giving me my sense of humor. I love you and miss you both.

I'd also like to acknowledge the members of the Rainbow's End Women's Teaching Lodge in Southern California: Thank you all for your love and wonderful undying support, and a special thanks to all of you who volunteered to take a trip to Fatropolis and give feedback on the manuscript. And to my magical spiritual teachers, Valerie Eagle

Heart Meyer and Carrie Laughing Heart Bissmeyer: Mere words cannot express the depths of gratitude and love that I feel for you, but thank you for teaching me the meaning of unconditional love, honor, respect, non-traditional tradition, work, worship, and how to sit the drum in an honorable way. Thank you for teaching me what it is to be a Woman, a Daughter, a Sister, a Granddaughter, a Wife, a Mother and a Grandmother. Thank you for allowing me to be part of the "we," and thank you for taking care of me during the most important Quest of my life.

I'd like to acknowledge and give thanks to the ladies of the Circle of the Beloved Moon in northern Virginia, who have given their loving support through the past year of editing and anticipation of publication, but especially to Rev. Karen B. Paris, who willingly opens her heart and home so we can grow spiritually and make this world a better place.

A special thanks to four ladies who answered my (sometimes) incessant questions about life in New York: Antoinette Hoffer, Yuliya Fisher-Nayyer, Addie Jones, and Brenda Cooper. Early on, when I was first researching New York, I had a long conversation with my good friend Antoinette Hoffer. She told me that the walls are sometimes thin in New York apartments, which gave way to an idea that in turn gave birth to Mrs. Grabowski. So, thanks, Toni. A special thanks also to Rev. Uki MacIssac for speaking up about an important aspect of the story.

To my wonderful friends and family who have always been encouraging of me and respected my drive to write a novel and see it through to publication: Virginia "Ginger" Emmons, Doris Usher, Mark Jueschke, my daughter Emma Olmedo, and my sons Loy & Jose Olmedo. And to all other co-workers, friends, family and acquaintances (and anyone I may have inadvertently left out) who have asked me when the book is coming out, and been excited for me: Thank you all! Your interest and excitement means the world to me.

And—a grateful and humble thanks to whoever it was in the Universe (my Creator, the Angels, the Ancestors or Clan Mothers) who trusted me with the vision I received into the world of the hearty-folk.

ABOUT THE AUTHOR

TRACEY L. THOMPSON WAS BORN AND RAISED IN southern California and now resides in northern Virginia with her husband Guy, son Hayden, dog Violet, and two cats, Blessing and Boon. She is a wife and the mother of five children.

After overcoming domestic violence, divorce, single motherhood and low self-esteem, she went on to earn a master's degree in psychology with a specialization in marriage and family therapy from Chapman University, and now has written a novel that sheds light on the issue of weight discrimination in a fun and fanciful way.

In the last twelve years she has made a living at social work for hospice, working with at-risk youth and their families, training military families about aspects of resiliency, and now social work at the community level assisting needy families and the homeless. Her interests include spending time with her family, spiritual pursuits, drumming, playing Dungeons & Dragons, reading, writing, knitting, scrapbooking, movies, and music.

ABOUT PEARLSONG PRESS

PEARLSONG PRESS IS AN INDEPENDENT PUBLISHING COMpany dedicated to providing books and resources that entertain while expanding perspectives on the self and the world. The company was founded by Peggy Elam, Ph.D., a psychologist and journalist, in 2003.

We encourage you to enjoy other Pearlsong Press books, which you can purchase at www.pearlsong.com or your favorite bookstore. Keep up with us through our blog at www.pearlsongpress.com.

FICTION:

The Falstaff Vampire Files—paranormal adventure by Lynne Murray
Larger Than Death—a Josephine Fuller mystery by Lynne Murray
Large Target—a Josephine Fuller mystery by Lynne Murray
The Season of Lost Children—a novel by Karen Blomain
Fallen Embers & Blowing Embers—Books 1 & 2 of The Embers Series,
paranormal romance by Lauri J Owen
The Fat Lady Sings—a young adult novel by Charlie Lovett
Syd Arthur—a novel by Ellen Frankel
Bride of the Living Dead—romantic comedy by Lynne Murray
Measure By Measure—a romantic romp with the fabulously fat by
Rebecca Fox & William Sherman
FatLand—a visionary novel by Frannie Zellman
The Program—a suspense novel by Charlie Lovett
The Singing of Swans—a novel about the Divine Feminine
by Mary Saracino

Romance novels & Short Stories Featuring Big Beautiful Heroines:

by Pat Ballard, the Queen of Rubenesque Romances:
Dangerous Love | *The Best Man* | *Abigail's Revenge*
Dangerous Curves Ahead: Short Stories | *Wanted: One Groom*
Nobody's Perfect | *His Brother's Child* | *A Worthy Heir*
by Rebecca Brock—*The Giving Season*
& by Judy Bagshaw—*At Long Last, Love: A Collection*

Nonfiction:

A Life Interrupted: Living With Brain Injury—poetry by Louise Mathewson
Talking Fat: Health vs. Persuasion in the War on Our Bodies—
nonfiction by Lonie McMichael, Ph.D.
ExtraOrdinary: An End of Life Story Without End—
memoir by Michele Tamaren & Michael Wittner
Love is the Thread: A Knitting Friendship by Leslie Moïse, Ph.D.
Fat Poets Speak: Voices of the Fat Poets' Society—Frannie Zellman, Ed.
Ten Steps to Loving Your Body (No Matter What Size You Are)
by Pat Ballard
Beyond Measure: A Memoir About Short Stature & Inner Growth
by Ellen Frankel
Taking Up Space: How Eating Well & Exercising Regularly Changed My Life
by Pattie Thomas, Ph.D. with Carl Wilkerson, M.B.A. (foreword by
Paul Campos, author of *The Obesity Myth*)
*Off Kilter: A Woman's Journey to Peace with Scoliosis, Her Mother
& Her Polish Heritage*—a memoir by Linda C. Wisniewski
Unconventional Means: The Dream Down Under—
a spiritual travelogue by Anne Richardson Williams
Splendid Seniors: Great Lives, Great Deeds—inspirational biographies
by Jack Adler

Healing the World One Book at a Time